Not so New in Town

MICHELE SUMMERS

sourcebooks
casablanca

V

Published by Sourcebooks Casablanca, an imprint of Sourcebooks, Inc.
P.O. Box 4410, Naperville, Illinois 60567-4410
(630) 961-3900
Fax: (630) 961-2168
www.sourcebooks.com

Printed and bound in Canada.
MBP 10 9 8 7 6 5 4 3 2 1

Chapter 1

LUCY DOOLAN WATCHED STEAM CURL FROM BENEATH the hood of her seven-year-old Honda. She had always hated being called "Loco Lucy," but right about now, she thought she might be a little nuts. Unaware of how long the red temperature light had been sending a distress signal, she had pulled her overheated car onto the shoulder of the empty two-lane highway and killed the engine, thinking she might've killed her car too.

"Moose muffin balls. This is not good." Her forehead hit the steering wheel as she groaned. She'd been too busy stressing over her sudden move.

Home.

To Harmony, NC, where everyone knew your business, and where everyone remembered her as Loco Lucy.

Lucy rubbed her temples. "This is not how I pictured the end of my day…week…life." She glared at the dead cell phone sitting next to her. So uncool for someone who made her living by phone. Dead backup cell phone in the trunk. How had she gotten to this place?

She had so many regrets, from tuning out her mechanic when he'd recommended a trade, to putting all her faith, time, and hard-earned money into a business venture that had blown up in her face. So what did Lucy do? She panicked. Cried. Freaked. Cursed. Consumed large quantities of junk food. And then she pulled on her big-girl britches and started the ball rolling for her next plan of attack.

Overloaded with supergluing fragments of her broken heart (and life) back together, Lucy had subleased her apartment and quickly patched up what was left of her business affairs, and agreed to come home.

After seventeen long years.

And now she was stuck ten miles outside of Harmony.

Gut clenching, heart racing, and palms sweating, she stepped out of the car and onto the gravel shoulder. "Come on, Luce, everything's gonna be fine. So you're going home. No big deal. Home is just a word. Means nothing."

Except it meant everything.

Breathing deep, she exhaled slowly, squinting behind her large, white, speckled sunglasses. No cars had been by since she'd veered her sizzling car onto the shoulder. Wavering in the heavy July heat, she spied a crumbling, abandoned barn, sitting at the back of the grassy field off the right shoulder. It had to be ninety-nine freakin' degrees, at least. Lucy plucked at the yellow silk tank top sticking to her chest and belly. She lifted her hair to fan her hot neck.

"Looks like I'm gonna have to hoof it." Her white cotton skirt stuck to her thighs, and she attempted to smooth the wrinkles. She'd dressed casual but not sloppy, wanting to appear pulled together for her unexpected homecoming. Not wilted, frazzled, and covered in road dust—not her idea of a banner homecoming. Entering Main Street on foot would only give everyone more reasons to call her Loco.

Reaching back inside the sweltering car, she grabbed

her purple snakeskin handbag and her emergency bag of Cheetos off the passenger seat. She might need sustenance. Ten miles was a long hike.

———

"What the hell?" Brogan Reese rounded the curve in his convertible. Even in the ninety-degree heat, he'd been riding with the top down. He squinted against the late-afternoon sun. Up the road a ways, a woman was digging inside her broken-down car on the side of the road and exposing a lot of leg as her short, white skirt crept up the backs of her thighs. Nice. Brogan pushed his aviator sunglasses back up the bridge of his nose as he slowed his car.

Snap out of it, dumbass.

He eased off the road onto the shoulder, coming to a complete stop. His new XK Jaguar purred low and quiet. He sat for a moment as the woman shoved a purple bag over her shoulder and started down the highway in the direction of Harmony. As much as he enjoyed the sway of her hips marching toward town, he couldn't let her go without offering a ride or, at the very least, to check under the hood. Besides, he needed the distraction. Coming home to settle his mother's estate had morphed into a much bigger commitment than he'd planned, and it looked as if he'd be staying for a while. He pushed open his door and stepped out.

"Hey, there. Need some help?" he called to her retreating back.

Swaying hips stopped as she swung around on silver strappy sandals. Huge white sunglasses swallowed the upper half of her face. She didn't speak, but clutched the funky bag closer to her body.

"With your car?" He motioned to the dinged-up bucket of bolts posing as a car on the side of the road.

Gravel crunched beneath her sandals as she inched closer. He still couldn't see her eyes, but he detected wariness as lines of tension bracketed her full mouth.

"I'm no mechanic, but I can certainly take a look under the hood." He gave an apologetic shrug. She continued to stare at him, biting into a perfect, plump bottom lip as if contemplating what to do next. "Look, I'd offer you a ride into town, but since you don't know me, I figured you wouldn't accept. How about I call for roadside assistance?" Brogan pulled his cell from his jeans pocket. "You can wait in your car, and I'll wait in mine until they come. Would that help?"

Straight, layered blond hair flopped on her shoulders. The tilt of her head rang familiar, but he couldn't quite place her.

"Better yet…you can call, if that would make you more comfortable." Brogan extended the cell. She stepped back suddenly. "Whoa." He raised both hands to show he meant no harm. "Okay then. Maybe not," he said slowly. Her head moved side to side as if hunting for a place to hide. "Look, lady, only trying to help. I'm from Harmony, which is right up the road. I'm—"

"I know who you are," she said in a flat voice, catching him off guard.

"You do?" He stared at her highlighted hair glinting in the sun and hunched shoulders as she crossed her arms. Who was this chick? Thick Southern accent meant she didn't hail from the North, where he'd lived the last ten years. He racked his brain.

"Yeah," she said to the gravel mashed beneath her

sandals "Brogan Reese. Harmony High's football star, homecoming king, and heartbreaker."

Shit. Here we go again.

Chapter 2

NOT HIM! LUCY SEARCHED FOR A PLACE TO HURL herself, like a ditch or some kind of hole. She'd rather be bleeding out in shark-infested waters than standing on the side of the road talking to *him*. Brogan Reese. The guy she'd always dreamed about. Her high school crush. The stud of Harmony High. The guy who'd always been a friend until…

Lucy couldn't think about that now. She needed to figure a way out of this embarrassing mess. Damn, Julia. If she weren't already seven months pregnant and bedridden, Lucy would come up with more painful ways to punish her.

Julia. The bane of Lucy's existence. Childhood nemesis. Boyfriend snatcher.

Stepsister.

"How do I know you?" Brogan interrupted her mental rant. Lucy's head snapped up. He didn't recognize her. At. All. She would've laughed, except her thudding heart, causing chest pains, prevented it. It had been a long time. She and Brogan hadn't spoken or even seen each other since the day she'd left. She couldn't blame him for not recognizing her; she'd changed…a lot. And to be fair, he'd had eyes for only one person in high school, and it wasn't the gawky freshman who'd skulked the halls, hoping for a glimpse of her crush. Maybe, just maybe he wouldn't recall the way she'd ruined his homecoming date with Julia, the homecoming queen. His girlfriend. The love of his life.

Or the night she'd practically begged for his kiss in an awkward attempt at seduction. Yack. Don't go there…please.

At one time or other, every girl fantasized about running into an ex-boyfriend or crush. She would look marvelous, with flawless skin, coiffed hair, and major cleavage perfectly displayed. The fantasy always included flaunting great success, such as being hugely successful in some philanthropic career. Watching him grovel at her feet, begging for crumbs from her table. Lucy had millions of those fantasies tucked away—all starring Brogan Reese. But none of them featured her broken-down car steaming on the side of the road, or Lucy in her wrinkled skirt and sweaty tank top.

With furrowed brow and tilted head, he studied her, trying to place her. He'd find out sooner or later. In a small town like Harmony, everyone knew your business, from birthdays to bunion surgery. No need to prolong the suspense.

"Lucy. Lucy Doolan," she supplied for him.

"L—"

"Don't say it! Don't you dare say *loco*." She pushed her sunglasses to the top of her head and narrowed her eyes.

Brogan had the good sense to appear confused as he blinked. "I was going to say *little*…Little Lucy."

"Oh, well. That's not so bad. But I'm not little anymore." She cocked one hip. "As you can see."

A grin cracked wide-open, lighting his entire face. "Uh, yeah, you are. In a short way."

Not him. He was bigger than she remembered. Broader shoulders. Thicker arms. More gorgeous than even in her fantasies. Gone was the smooth, baby-skinned face. Replaced by dark stubble covering a strong jaw. Why couldn't he be balding, with a dough-nut expanding his middle?

His gaze moved across her face to her now sleek, straight hair, and his look of surprise changed to appre-ciation. "Wow. It's really great to see you. You look amazing. Different." He motioned toward her head. "I don't remember your hair being so…straight?"

Or so blond. Lucy twirled a hank of hair around her finger before flipping it over her shoulder. "Thanks. I got tired of all those curls."

"Curls. That's it." He snapped his fingers. "You had huge curls that bounced when you walked." He chuck-led and flashed his heart-stopping smile. Insides melt-ing on cue. Not from the heat of the sun, but from the friendly, familiar smile she'd committed to memory and had always loved.

"What brings you to Harmony after all these years?" he asked.

Stupidity. Guilt. Loneliness. "Change of scenery. I'll be here for a few months," she said.

"Everything okay?" His voice sobered as he studied her face. Brogan had this way of seeing inside her brain. Lucy could remember the feeling of flushed excitement on those rare occasions when he'd given her his undi-vided attention back in high school, listening to her as if he truly cared.

Right now, Lucy wished she didn't have to answer his question, but again, it would take about five minutes before the rest of Harmony heard she was back and why. And then it hit her like a wrecking ball to the head… Brogan was probably here for the same reason.

Julia.

~~~

Little Lucy Doolan. Brogan couldn't remember the last time he had seen her. It had to have been back in high school. Being back in Harmony had conjured up different feelings and memories, but he'd almost forgotten Julia's younger sister. She'd always been an odd duck, but in a cute, shy way. Not in a Goth, pierced, walking dead, scary way. He was two years older, but he remembered her hanging around when he'd come by to visit Julia or spotting her in the halls at school. She'd been hard to miss. She'd had great, riotous curls. Even when she sat behind the players' bench at the football games with her Harmony High baseball cap drawn low over her brow, you couldn't miss the curly tail that hung out the back.

He'd known she'd harbored a crush on him back then. High school girls loved to gossip and pretend they had crushes on upperclassmen, especially the star quarterback. Brogan had been flattered, but it hadn't meant anything. And yet, Lucy had been different. He recalled how staunchly she'd defended his stats to anyone who would listen, and how she'd blushed crimson when he'd handed her a jumbo bag of M&M's to cheer her up after she'd lost the Clean Up Harmony High competition her freshman year. Brogan had known she'd kept a secret stash in her locker. He'd liked her, even though she was Julia's little sister, and Julia had made things difficult.

Lucy had been spunky and kind, not cruel like Julia could be on occasion.

He had liked her in a little-sister way...until that one night.

Suddenly Brogan felt even hotter, and it had nothing to do with the ninety-degree heat. A cool swim in the lake would be good right about now. Lucy shifted uncomfortably. Brogan remembered whenever he'd come by their house, she'd always seemed happy to see him. Not today. She looked like she'd rather be crunching cockroaches between her teeth than talking to him. Funny. He also recalled her being kind of shy, wearing baggy shirts, as if afraid of drawing attention. Not now. With clingy tank top, jumbo sunglasses, and short skirt, she looked like a woman who commanded attention. Male attention.

"Would you like me to check under the hood? Looks like you're overheated. Could be low coolant or, worse, a clogged radiator. If you're over fifty thousand miles, the radiator can get gummed up," he said, pointing to the curls of steam still whistling from beneath her hood.

"You think that's what the red temperature light was trying to tell me?"

"That *you're* overheated? Absolutely." He chuckled at the surprise lighting the backs of her exotic gray eyes. And that familiar flush creeping up her neck and onto her baby-doll cheeks. She'd always been fun to tease, but seeing the grown-up Lucy brought teasing to an entirely different level.

She cleared her throat. "Uh, yes, overheated. Aren't we all in this wretched heat? But how bad is the real question."

Real bad if the unwanted heaviness in his groin was any indication. Brogan gave his head a quick shake. He didn't need to be thinking heated, sweaty thoughts of Little Lucy Doolan. Not now. Not ever. They'd been high school friends—barely. Because Julia had made darn sure she occupied most of Brogan's time and thoughts. But not anymore. Everyone had grown up and moved on. Especially him. And that was how it should be.

He glanced at her car dying of heatstroke on the shoulder of the road. "Hard to say without checking under the hood. We should wait until it cools down before trying to start the engine." She nodded, twirling a blond lock around her finger. He remembered that too. Whenever she got nervous, she'd twirl a curl around her finger. Something or someone was making Lucy mighty nervous.

"So, Little Lucy, how can I help you?" He smiled, because Lucy Doolan inspired smiles. He'd always liked that about her.

She stopped mid-twirl and gave him a steady look. "Pop your trunk. I need a ride into town, and I might as well do it in style."

"By riding in my trunk?" he asked, trying not to laugh.

Pert nose lifted, as if she found his humor juvenile, she brushed past him. After trying unsuccessfully to open her trunk with the key remote, she whacked it several times with the palm of her hand until it popped up.

"This key thingy never did work," she mumbled under her breath.

Brogan shook his head and chuckled. Cautiously, he leaned forward. Bags and more bags filled his vision.

Not suitcases, but totes with various logos. Lucy shoved a bulging one in his arms.

"All this stuff yours?" he asked, slinging a clear vinyl bag imprinted with bright-yellow lemons over his shoulder. Lucy continued to rummage through mounds of crap in her trunk.

"It's a mess, but I didn't have time to get organized," she said in a muffled voice, head deep inside another large bag.

"You give new meaning to 'junk in your trunk,'" he said, chuckling louder.

"Yay! Found it." She popped up with a jumbo box of strawberry Pop-Tarts in her hand.

Brogan's lip curled. "You're kidding, right? That's the most important thing you needed to find?"

She blinked. "No point in buying more when I have some right—" She stopped talking. His expression of complete disgust must've registered. He couldn't imagine anyone with a brain eating that nasty shit. Nothing but empty calories and sugar. No nutrient in sight.

"What?" She shook the oversized box. "Breakfast of champions. Pop-Tarts are awesome. Don't tell me you've never had one. On super busy days, I've been known to eat these for lunch and dinner."

"I can't believe you're still into junk food. I thought you only ate that crap when you got nervous." He peered at her stash of boxes and bags of garbage food. Judging by the contents of her trunk, Lucy must be close to a meltdown. "What's going on, Luce? Either you're having a nervous breakdown, or you're some kind of hoarder." He silently counted six boxes of instant mac and cheese. How could she eat all that crap and stay thin? Her clogged arteries probably resembled a corn dog.

She shot him an uneasy glance. "Look, it's nothing. I had to move out of my apartment kinda fast. And cooking has never been a priority for me. Besides, what I eat is none of your business." She shoved a yellow-and-green tote over her shoulder and smashed a few bags farther down into the bowels of the dark trunk. "That oughta do it until I can get my poor baby towed in." She slammed the trunk closed. "All set."

Poor baby his ass. More like a bucket of rattling bolts. Broken-down car. Trunk full of junk food. Nervous hair twirling. Brogan remembered Lucy's nervous habits with perfect clarity. Something big must've gone down for Lucy to be here, and he planned to find out what.

Lucy's bag slipped, and he reached for it, his hand trapped for an instant between the padded strap and the smooth silk of the tank top covering her shoulder. She felt warm, and he took a moment to enjoy the sensation, wondering what it would be like to kiss her. She had a very kissable mouth. Lush, full, plump lips. The flush shading her cheeks told him she felt the same attraction…or she was dying of heatstroke. But the set to her chin and furrowed brows told him she had no intention of acting upon it. Brogan gave a mental shrug as he hefted her bag over his other shoulder. Not a good idea to start something. He had enough trouble in Harmony, trying to live down his past relationship with Julia. No need to arm the town with any more ammunition.

"Come on, pack rat. Let's get you settled."

—⁓—

Lucy followed Brogan to his sleek dark-blue convertible. Picturing him in this expensive car only enhanced her colorful fantasies. Brogan came from a lot less than she, but he'd always been hardworking and smart. Must've paid off. She worked hard too, but she didn't have a flashy new convertible to show for it. Instead, she had a useless business contract, broken-down old car, and depleted savings account. Brogan's remote popped his trunk open seamlessly. Lucy gave a silent sigh. Okay, so she had to reinvent herself…again. Not the end of the world. But to be coming home to Harmony not in the healthiest financial situation—that was a bitter pill to swallow. And for Brogan to be her first eyewitness… well, make that a bitter *horse* pill.

Brogan placed her jam-packed bags inside his pristine trunk. "Nice car. Aren't you a little young to be having a midlife crisis? Or are you trying to overcompensate for something?" she asked.

Clear green eyes twinkled as he smiled at her. "For someone who used to be shy, you sure are mouthy." He opened the passenger-side door. "Your carriage awaits, my lady," he said with a mock bow.

She slid into the smooth leather seat, breathing in the new-car smell, and reached to buckle her seat belt. Brogan tossed a broken-in UNC baseball cap in her lap.

"Don't want your hair getting tangled. What happened to your curls?"

Lucy fed her sleek hair through the hole in back of the cap as Brogan pulled onto the road. She patted her ponytail, still loving the way straight hair felt to her fingers. "Not that it's any of your business, but my boyfriend thought straightening my hair presented a more professional image, and I happen to agree."

He gave her an odd look. "Boyfriend?" he said, as if the mere thought of her having a boyfriend defied credibility. "Why would your boyfriend care about your professional image?"

Lucy screwed up her mouth. How could she explain? Not that she owed him or anyone an explanation, but it'd be better he heard it from her than from Dottie Duncan, or worse, Miss Sue Percy, who could spread gossip faster than a bullet train. High-speed Internet had nothing on the ladies of Harmony.

"Ex. Anthony is my ex-boyfriend. He had certain standards for taking his business to the next level." And she'd been the perfect tool, buying into his total BS. The Jag cruised down the road at a nice clip, and Lucy tilted her face toward the sky, catching the breeze caressing her heated skin, when suddenly the car slowed to a crawl, and Lucy caught Brogan staring at her.

"And your hair factored into taking his business to the next level? What am I missing here?" He appeared baffled.

More than she cared to reveal. Thinking about her ex-boyfriend made all the hurt and anger bubble to the surface. And talking about him with Brogan, who was one of the good guys, made her feel foolish and stupid. Lucy would curl up and die if Brogan laughed, or worse, pitied her. She didn't lay the blame on others for her own mess. But that didn't mean she wanted everyone bantering about it. Talking about Anthony only infuriated her. *The temp pimp rodent.*

Lucy motioned toward the road. "Are we going to crawl to town? Because I can walk faster than you're driving." Brogan gave her a questioning look as he accelerated and resumed his normal speed.

Lucy almost bit her tongue at her unnecessary rudeness. "Thank you. I'm sorry for sounding testy."

"You didn't sound testy. You sounded mad."

Not good. Not good at all. The whole reason for her coming home was to help Julia and to show everyone she'd changed. Riding into town with steam pouring from her ears and acting like a mad Doberman would not be putting her best foot forward.

"Not that I blame you. Tell me about the temp pimp rodent." *What?* Brogan answered her shocked expression. "You said temp pimp rodent out loud."

Holy crud. She was worse off than she imagined, leaking her thoughts with loose lips had to be a sign of loconess. Crossing her arms, she said in a tight voice, "Well, if you must know, Anthony and I worked together before we started dating. He runs his own temp agency, and I did a lot of work for him." Before he reneged and cheated her out of a partnership deal. The conniving, lying, heartless jerk.

Brogan nodded. "Temp pimp rodent. Got it. Makes perfect sense."

Clearly it didn't, but Lucy ignored his sarcasm. "You don't know the half of it," she mumbled under her breath.

Brogan could only imagine. Lucy had *catastrophe* written all over her. But in a funny, fascinating, weird way. He liked that about her. "I can feel a story there. Lay it on me. Scale of one to ten, ten being the highest, I'll score it for hilarity content." Brogan glanced at her profile. Soft pink highlighted her cheeks. From wind or embarrassment, he had no clue, but he admired the flush.

Lucy pursed her lips. "What makes you think it's funny?"

"Hunch. Sixth sense. ESP." The sound of snorting came from her general direction as she rummaged through the jumbo handbag resting on her lap.

"Cheetos?" The smell of fake, factory-produced cheese assailed his nostrils as Lucy waved a bag in his direction.

"God no," he snarled. "And neither will you." He snatched the bag from her hand.

"Hey!"

Brogan shook his head, shoving the Cheetos beneath his seat. "Little Lucy Doolan, I think it was destiny that we met again today."

She swigged some water from a bottle she'd pulled from the bottom of her bag. God only knew what else lurked in there. "How do you figure? So you can monitor my diet?"

A curl of pleasure bloomed from the bottom of his gut to the top of his wind-blown hair. Lucy would be his test market. If he could get her on board, an obvious junk-food-aholic, then maybe his business would survive in Harmony after all. "Hunch, sixth—"

"Yeah, yeah. ESP. Whatever." She gripped the dashboard, leaning toward the windshield as he turned off the service road and down Main Street, the heart and soul of Harmony, where most of the local businesses resided.

"When was the last time you were home?" he asked.

Lucy's shoulders tensed. "Couple of years ago. For Bertie Anderson's wedding. You know she married Keith Morgan, that famous ex–tennis player, right?"

Brogan knew him real well. Keith had managed to strong-arm him into opening his store in Harmony with statistical projections, data, and a hefty investment. After opening the Keith Morgan Tennis Academy a couple of years ago, traffic in Harmony had increased. And Keith had taken a special interest in sprucing up Main Street and attracting new businesses. His proposal had included BetterBites providing concessions at the academy. Healthy food choices for tennis players of all ages. Endless possibilities. And Brogan had had enough smarts to jump on board at the ground level. Feeding athletes was his specialty.

"Yeah. Keith's cool. Bertie seems real happy. Her baby boy is going to be as big as Keith one day, and her stepdaughter is a sweetie too." Lucy nodded, but Brogan wondered if she heard him. He slowed as someone pulled onto Main from the parking lot at the Daily Grind, the local coffee shop. Lucy adjusted the baseball cap over her eyes. People bustled over the brick paver sidewalks, browsing and window-shopping. He straightened in his seat as he tracked a family of four he didn't recognize entering his store.

"What are you doing in Harmony?" she asked. "Hey, what's that place?" She inched up from her slouched position as they crawled past BetterBites.

"That's what I'm doing…for now." He wished he could pull over and follow the family inside, but he needed to get Lucy settled first.

"Huh?" She glanced at him.

Brogan nodded at BetterBites. "That's my newest location." Whipping her head around, surprise lit her eyes as she lowered her sunglasses for a better look. "My fourth store. I have three more up North." And his fifth and largest location would open in New York City, if he could get this one running smoothly. Brogan thrived on challenges, but the heavy breathing down his neck from his investors made his adrenaline speed up, and not in a healthy way. By September sixteenth, his butt needed to be the hell out of Harmony and in NYC. Simple. Better marketing and better customers. The reoccurring tension churned his stomach.

"Wow. What is it?"

He laughed as his anxiety eased. "Something you're gonna learn to love." Along with everyone else in this offbeat Southern town.

Chapter 3

LUCY WISHED THEY'D MOVE IT ALONG. CRUISING DOWN Main Street in a flashy convertible with Brogan Reese made her stick out worse than the last time she sat atop the Oscar Mayer Wienermobile during the Fourth of July parade dressed as a bottle of mustard. Although rushing to Julia's side to play nursemaid didn't inspire warm and snugglies, spending time with her nephew did.

Lucy slid lower in the cushioned leather seat as Brogan waved to a group of women walking with covered casseroles. Must be potluck camp-song night at the Harmony Community Center. Once a month, Harmony Huggers got together and sang along to an old player piano while sampling new recipes and drinking spiked punch. Drunk dialing usually followed, and husbands or significant others would be called to the rescue. Coco's Cab had gotten smart and now waited out front to cart the tipsy women home.

Lucy really wanted to know if Brogan had moved back home for good, or if Harmony was only a bump in the road. She prayed he had more exciting places to be. She didn't need any more Brogan encounters. The past fifteen minutes in his car had been enough to last a lifetime. Being with Brogan brought back a myriad of flashbacks. Not all pleasant, as she remembered how he smiled and hung on Julia's every word while Lucy worried if Julia was spreading more lies about her.

Lucy glanced from beneath her lashes and watched as the wind whipped his sun-streaked tawny hair, which kind of ticked her off, since she knew he didn't spend hours in a salon chair with foils sticking from his head like some sort of new-age cactus. Just looking at all that natural male hotness made her crabby. His big shoulders, tanned arms, and muscled thighs left her with a queasy stomach. Sparkly green eyes, cute smile revealing white teeth, and nice strong hands used for lifting boxes and opening stubborn peanut butter jars. Brogan Reese had been living in Lucy's dreams for years, and he needed to remain there. She couldn't afford getting all starry-eyed and moondoggie over him. Not this time around. One crumbled heart needing major repair was more than she could handle right now.

Heat from embarrassment infused her neck and cheeks as she recalled that night after the football game when she'd waited for Brogan like she always had. After a huge win against Harmony's biggest rival, he hadn't seemed himself. Lucy had only wanted to make sure he was okay. She'd had no intentions of sitting on the bleachers with him or talking to him…or almost kissing him. Lucy bit the inside of her cheek and started cataloging the urgent things needing attention, like opening a new bank account, replacing the chargers for her phones, and buying more Hershey's chocolate. Anything to keep her mind off the past and Hottie Hotcakes burning the seat next to her.

The sleek Jag cruised through one of the older residential neighborhoods. A canopy created by huge oaks lowered the heat level by at least ten degrees. Despite the welcome shade, Lucy's body temperature shot to boiling as she spied the redbrick, two-story Georgian-style house on Daffodil Lane that used to be her home. But it hadn't felt like home in a very long time. Not since the day Julia had moved in… twenty-some years ago.

"You okay?" he asked.

Okay? She'd rather be cleaning gas station toilets with her bare hands than coming home to nurse her nemesis. And what did she know about babysitting her fifteen-year-old nephew? Lucy's insides shriveled. She loved her nephew Parker and had enjoyed playing with him, but it had been a while. A long while. And now Parker was all grown up. He probably didn't even remember her. Shaking off the shroud of doubt, Lucy straightened her spine.

Brogan pulled into the circular driveway lined with clusters of pink and purple daylilies, and stopped the car. "You don't look so good. When was the last time you ate? Real food, not garbage?"

"Breakfast. Don't worry. I'll be fine." She hefted her handbag over her shoulder. "Thanks for the lift. If you'll just pop the trunk, I'll unload my stuff and be on my way."

"If I didn't know better, I'd think you were trying to get rid of me."

"What gave it away?" He narrowed his gorgeous green eyes. "I'm kidding. Clearly you've gone beyond the call of duty, but I can take it from here." She hopped from his car and moved to the rear. *Hang tough, Luce.* She couldn't allow herself to fall in the lust-filled Brogan trap. Not this time.

Brogan stretched his tanned arm across the back

of the seat and peered over his shoulder. "You never answered my question. What brings you home?"

Lucy removed the UNC baseball cap and tossed it on the backseat, shaking her hair loose. "Your girlfriend and her baby, for starters. Or should I be saying *your* baby?" Loose lips struck again. Ugly words suspended in the air between them. She could've smacked herself.

A knot appeared on Brogan's jaw; his expression darkened. "Aren't you too sophisticated for small-town gossip?" He met her by the trunk.

Lucy shrugged, trying to feign disinterest even though her heart raced and her palms sweated. "I've heard the same thing everyone else has heard."

"And you believe it?" His brows drew together in a fierce frown, and murky green eyes shot sparks of anger. "Shame on you. Of all people, you should know how rumors spread, hurting those involved."

Heat prickled her cheeks. Boy, did she ever. And she hated being reminded of it from the Golden Boy of Harmony. She'd been the brunt of many convoluted stories over the years, hence the nickname Loco Lucy. A part of her didn't believe the wild stories about Brogan and Julia. But on some level, natural curiosity had taken root, making her wonder what had really gone down.

"Parker's not my kid." His voice deepened along with his intensity. "And neither is this one."

All righty then. Hope sparked to life inside Lucy only to be doused by a big bucket of doubt. To be fair, she needed to hear Julia's side of the story.

Pop went the trunk, and Brogan started yanking bags out with unnecessary force. "I'll get thos—" She tried reaching past him, but his broad back blocked her access. A whiff of clean soap, layered with exotic coffee and expensive leather, made her pause. Wonderful smell…all Brogan. She could take a long bubble bath in his smell. Unable to resist, Lucy leaned toward his white polo shirt and sniffed just as he turned toward her. His odd look confirmed she'd been busted. Lucy stumbled back, face aflame.

Brogan chose to ignore it. "After you," he ordered, jerking his head toward the front door.

Two things: she hated that she'd upset him, *and* she dreaded entering the house. Lucy couldn't decide which one disturbed her more.

"Look, Brogan, I'm sorry—"

"Save it." The jumbo box of Pop-Tarts nudged her hip. Dragging her feet up the front steps, she gave a sharp knock on the solid, mauve-painted door. Yes, mauve, thanks to Babs, her ex-stepmother-turned-NASCAR-lover groupie. Lucy turned the brass knob and pushed the door open. Unlike Atlanta, where she'd been living, residents of Harmony left front doors open and cars unlocked. Crazy. But Harmony had never been a hotbed of crime.

Her feet tangled with a pair of dirty, size eleven football cleats as she stepped inside the foyer. Brogan followed close behind, dropping her bags on the dark, rose-painted Chippendale bench serving as a catchall. Familiar smells bombarded her, from the lemon-scented, polished wood floors to the floral potpourri favored by Babs. Afraid of looking past the foyer, Lucy stood frozen to the spot.

"You gonna be okay?" Brogan's gentle voice brought her back to the present, making her feel worse, because he was being nice. A wave of nostalgia rushed over her. She could remember waiting by the front window for Brogan to pull up in his used red Ford Ranger. She'd always wanted to be the first to open the door and secretly savor the exclusive smile he gave her before Julia entered the room and hogged all his attention.

Lucy shook the past from her head. "S-sure. Just going to take a little getting used to, that's all." She willed her voice to sound convincing.

He chuckled softly. "You'll knock 'em dead. I guarantee it." His crooked smile warmed her insides, making little ladybugs dance in her stomach.

She was thrilled to see him smiling and not frowning. "Thanks. And listen, I didn't mean what I said…you know, out there when I was being a Twinkie-sponged jerk. You came to my rescue, and I acted…um, like an ingrate. Will you accept my apology?"

"Nope."

Lucy looked up into laughing green eyes. "Why not?"

"Because it's going to take more than a lame apology. You owe me, little Lu-Lu." He reached for a hank of her hair, twirling it around his finger. "Payback's a bitch." Lucy's jaw dropped, and Brogan's endearing, lovely, crooked smile, irresistible only moments ago, suddenly lost all its appeal.

"Don't look so appalled." He fiddled with her hair, rubbing it between his fingers. Appalled? She was terrified. Terrified of falling for him all over again.

Then he pulled her forward. "Ow." She narrowed her eyes, reclaiming her hair with her hand. "Look, I'm about to dive into a very stressful situation with Julia. I'm not interested in hooking up with some high school crush…er, classmate." *Jelly bellies*. She hoped he didn't notice the slip. No such luck.

"That's not what I had in mind, but now that you mentioned it…might not be a bad idea."

No freakin' way.

"Look, Bro. Wrong sister," she snapped.

Another odd look came over him, and he paused. Lucy held her breath, hoping… Her mind went blank.

After what felt like ten years, he said in a low voice, "I don't think so." He reached for the door. "Glad you're home, Little Lucy."

She blinked, and he was gone.

Chapter 4

BROGAN CHUCKLED AS HE CRUISED BACK TOWARD Main Street. Lucy Doolan could pretend all she wanted not to be flustered. But standing close to her, fingering her soft hair, he'd caught a whiff of citrus that smelled a whole lot like desire. "Little" Lucy was no longer shy or unassuming. Lucy Doolan knew how to leave her mark. Man, did she ever.

He smiled, thinking about the drama that Lucy had caused the night of the homecoming parade. Hacking off half Julia's hair had caused quite the scandal.

Brogan eased his car into the owner parking space located in the alley behind BetterBites. He wished the entire back alley were filled with food trucks, unloading new merchandise due to stock flying off shelves, but that was not the case. Not even close.

He pushed his way through the metal service door in the back and stopped. Margo Ray was standing next to the supply shelf, wearing a green BetterBites apron tied around her waist, blue bandana around her short, spiky gray hair, and whole wheat flour on her face, glaring at the shelves as if they'd been having an argument.

"What's going on?" he asked.

"Where's the damn granola? I know I put it here just the other day. I need to make another batch of those banana nut muffins."

"Really? You mean we sold out?" Brogan couldn't keep the excitement from his voice.

"No. Had to throw the old ones out. Passed their expiration. But you got a customer in front of the house asking for muffins." Margo pushed aside containers of oats and spices as she hunted. Brogan crossed the doorway and entered the kitchen. Margo had been busy baking bread from the looks of the loaves cooling on the racks and the smell of warm yeast filling the kitchen.

"Found it." Margo bustled past him and plopped the sealed container of granola on the stainless steel mobile island. "You better get to work. After this batch of muffins, I'm gonna be low on granola."

"Sure. I'll be thrilled to make more. Just wish we'd sell more." Brogan's recipe for healthy, tasty granola was not necessarily a corporate secret, like the original Coke recipe, but he'd made a living off that granola and took pride in the natural ingredients and the making of it. Each of his stores had one person who knew the recipe, but since Harmony was his newest location, he hadn't handed off that particular baton yet.

Margo stopped measuring cups of granola and gave him a steady stare. "I do too. What's going on that everyone in Pleasantville gives you such a wide berth?"

Brogan shook a handful of granola into his palm, avoiding her penetrating gaze. Margo continued to talk. "I can't figure it out. Aren't you the Golden Boy around here? Most straight women would have heatstroke over someone who looks like you. All buffed with more product gunking up your hair than Vidal Sassoon."

"Thanks, I think," he said dryly. No product gunked up his hair except shampoo and conditioner. But

Margo's spikes didn't stand on their own without the aid of some gel. He'd hired Margo away from Whole Foods in Raleigh, the next largest city, about twenty minutes east of Harmony, so she didn't know the history or the mysterious workings of this small town. Where everyone knew everybody, and old stories never died. In fact, they only got embellished…and not in a flattering way. He may have been the Golden Boy in the past, but today he was the subject of some erroneous gossip.

"So, what is it? You post creepy pictures on Facebook?"

"No."

"Worked for the IRS and audited everyone in town?"

"Nope."

"Sell Ronco vacuum cleaners door-to-door?"

"Nah."

If only. Any of those scenarios would be easier to explain and even rectify than the one he presently dealt with.

"Who's out front?" he said, changing the subject as he entered the front of the store.

He immediately spied the guy Margo had referred to, because he was the only customer in the store and because he did indeed know him.

He smiled. "Javier, glad you're here."

"Bro!" Javier pulled Brogan in for a man hug, pounding him on the back. "This is awesome."

Brogan shook his hand and watched as Javier Coloma, his business partner, sized up the new location for the first time.

"So, this is the latest?" He took in the shelves lined with packaged organic products, baked goods piled on round tabletops, and bins filled with dried beans and grains.

Javier nodded with approval. "I like it. Much smaller, but has a nice homey feel. How are the numbers?"

Not good, but Brogan would catch Javier up to speed later, poring over the books. "Plenty of time for that later." Brogan opened one of the coolers on the far wall and grabbed two organic beers. And the last of the freshly made oatmeal-and-raisin cookies from the bamboo mobile display rack. Javier followed him to a cozy seating area near the front picture window. "Sit." Brogan twisted the caps off the beers. "Help yourself to some cookies."

They folded themselves into comfortable, armless lounge chairs covered in teal blue chenille, and Brogan slid the container of cookies to the center of the glass coffee table.

"Business is slow. Haven't met my projections yet, but we'll get there. We've only been open for six weeks. There's still time." Brogan tilted the beer bottle toward his mouth, hoping he didn't choke from the lies spilling from his lips. Half lies. True, he'd only been open six weeks and hadn't met his projections. Ten weeks remained in this quarter, but business still sucked, despite all the money he'd poured into this location and the quality product he sold.

"You need to wake this sleepy town up. Don't they know that greatness has returned to live among them?" Javier was referring to Brogan's football glory days in Harmony and at Georgetown. Even though Brogan had loved playing football in high school and college, he'd never entertained thoughts of going pro.

"That would be Keith Morgan, the famous tennis player. Not me," Brogan grunted.

"I remember reading about that. Didn't the Prince move here a few years ago to raise his daughter? Gave up his wild party days in Miami," Javier said, shaking his head as if he couldn't comprehend such strange behavior from a fellow man.

"Got married, too. Some local *chiquita*, right?" Javier added.

Brogan leaned back and crossed his ankle over his knee, fiddling with the beer bottle in his hand. Keith Morgan's first wife had died and left him with a baby girl at the height of his tennis career. He retired from the professional tour and moved to Harmony to raise his daughter. And after meeting Bertie, the interior designer who renovated and decorated his old Victorian house, he'd finally found love and a place he could call home.

"He married Bertie Anderson, and she's gorgeous, with a heart of gold. They don't come much sweeter. And they were married *before* she got pregnant," Brogan explained, smiling.

Javier's brown Gucci loafer nudged Brogan's foot. "Any more choice gals left in town, or did Keith snag the last one?"

Lucy Doolan's silky straight hair popped into his head, along with her clingy tank top that molded to her curves. And her gray eyes, with their exotic tilt at the corners, snapping as she slung her barbs. He doubted she'd be categorized as blazing, but only because Javier didn't know her like he did. All right, maybe knowing her was a stretch. He remembered her, but didn't really

know her now. He planned to change that. Sooner rather
than later.

The bell over the glass front door tinkled, and
Brogan glanced up to see a metal walker push through
the entrance with Ethel Cornwaddle shuffling behind it.
He jumped up to assist her before the heavy glass door
knocked her down.

"Hey, Miz Cornwaddle. How you doing?" he asked
as he gripped a bony elbow beneath her lavender cotton
housecoat covered in yellow daisies.

"I'm breathing. That makes it a banner day!" His
sixth-grade teacher smiled, revealing loose dentures.

"You're looking mighty pretty all covered in daisies
and"—his gaze traveled down to orthopedic knee-highs
and beat-up combat boots—"and those…comfort-
able boots."

"Don't waste those sweet words on this old geezer.
You always were a charmer." She stared at him through
watery blue eyes. "How come you're not married? A
good-looking boy like you. Is it true you came home
to do right by Julia? I never did understand why y'all
couldn't iron out your differences." Ethel's frizzy gray
hair moved like dandelions in the wind as she shook her
head. She shuffled toward the stainless steel racks holding organic chips. "You got any pork rinds? I've been to
the Piggly Wiggly and Toot-N-Tell, and they're all out."

Pork rinds? Brogan's stomach lurched as he almost
stumbled over the yellow tennis balls covering the front
feet of her walker. Growing up, he remembered how that
had been a favorite snack among the older locals, but
he and his mom had never developed a taste for them.
Even Lucy had turned up her nose at pork rinds in the

lunchroom vending machine. A smile curled his lips as interesting ways of reforming Lucy crossed his mind. And they didn't all include food.

"No, ma'am. They're not exactly organic…uh, why don't you try these popped chips? They come in lots of different flavors." He reached for a smoky-bacon-flavored bag.

"Hmmm, I don't know. I don't like to buy something I've never tried before. What if I don't like them? Can I bring them back?"

Brogan repressed a groan. "Absolutely. You give them a try, and if you don't like them as much as pork rinds, you can bring them back, and I'll give you"—he wanted to say store credit, until he felt that teacher's eagle-eyed stare leveled at him—"a refund. Will that be okay?"

"That'd be fine."

Brogan helped her to the register where his part-time high school clerk stood texting on her iPhone. "Bailey, please ring Miz Cornwaddle up."

Pop went her pink bubble gum. "Sure," Bailey said as she scanned the bar code.

"And what about that boy?" Ethel asked. "I know he's not yours, because I can count. I didn't teach sixth-grade math for forty years for nothing."

Ethel was referring to Julia's fifteen-year-old son, Parker. At least Ethel could add and knew the kid wasn't his. Julia had gotten pregnant eight months *after* he'd already left town.

"Your mama, God rest her soul, was so heartbroken when you skipped town." Skipped town? Hardly. He'd left for college like any normal high school graduate.

Ethel stuffed her coins inside her orange plastic change purse and snapped it shut. "Poor Charlotte. She never got over your leaving. She missed you something fierce."

Brogan's jaw locked. He missed his mom, too. But she hadn't died of a broken heart like everyone yammered on about. She'd had a major stroke and hadn't lingered very long. Charlotte Reese had been a strong woman, always encouraging Brogan to expand his horizons, and he'd done that by attending and working his way through Georgetown before he'd started his own business.

"And I miss her, but my mom encouraged me to leave, and I appreciated her advice," he said, trying to keep the irritation from his voice. Truth be told, he couldn't wait to leave. He'd had no intentions of settling in Harmony, and even though he never spoke the words, his mother had known.

Ethel nodded. "You were always a good boy when it came to your mama."

Brogan wanted to bang his head against the brick column. She'd just told him he'd broken his mother's heart. He couldn't win this battle.

She patted his arm with her gnarled hand. "Not sure about all the shenanigans going on with the young ladies in town, but I know you loved your mama," she said, thin lips forming a smile. "I'll let you know about these popped things"—she jiggled the bag of chips—"but I'd sure like to find some pork rinds. You let me know if you get any in, ya hear."

"Will do. Good to see you." Brogan held the door as she shuffled out with her walker.

Javier had finished his beer and was loading up on cheese, crackers, and specialty olives as he browsed the aisles. But Brogan knew Javier had heard every last word, and he needed to prepare for the next inquisition.

Before the door had fully closed, it swung back open, and Dottie Duncan barreled in along with another blast of hot July air.

"Hey, Miz Duncan. What can I do for you?"

Dottie crossed her arms beneath her massive chest and cocked one hip as she tapped her red, white, and blue cowboy boot on his repurposed wood floor. "You selling ciggies?"

"No, ma'am."

"Chew tobaccie?"

"Nope."

"RC Colas and MoonPies?"

"No."

"Cheerwine and four-cornered Nabs?"

"Wouldn't dream of it."

"Good. Then I don't see any problems." She lowered her arms and straightened the form-fitting red top with sequined blue stars that matched the blue eye shadow from the bottom of her penciled-in eyebrows to the end of her eyelids. Not to be outdone by the black eyeliner and ruby-red lipstick. But for all of Dottie's wacky taste in fashion, she was probably the richest woman in town. She owned sixteen Toot-N-Tells across the state. Drive-through convenience stores, selling all kinds of garbage, including Lucy's favorite, Cheetos, by the truckloads.

"No, ma'am. We shouldn't have a problem. I sell mostly organic items not sold anywhere nearby. The closest competitor is Whole Foods in Raleigh."

Dottie reached with bedazzling long red nails for a cellophane bag of his special granola. "People actually eat this…stuff?" She held it between two fingers, away from her body, as if she were holding a bag of fresh dog shit.

"Yes. I've managed to open four stores based on that granola alone," Brogan said, not bothering to rein in his pride.

"Umph. Looks suspicious. Any funny stuff in there?"

"Funny stuff?"

"You know, like pot?" Laughter erupted down aisle five. Javier would have a field day with this. "Mind-altering things. You're not making this stuff"—she gave the granola a vicious shake—"with any of those druggy herbs, are you?"

"Miz Duncan—"

"Call me Dottie. Miz Duncan reminds me of my mother-in-law, that meddling, cantankerous hag."

"Er, Dottie, there's nothing but healthy caramelized oats, nuts, and dried fruit in my granola. Tastes great. Try some."

She turned the bag over. "Seven ninety-five! Hell, you can buy two bags of groceries for that at the Toot-N-Tell."

Define groceries.

"Hmmm, I don't know," she added. "You ever run a fifty-percent-off sale?"

A sharp, hammer-like pounding started behind his forehead. He hadn't worked this hard to sell something since junior year, when he tried to convince Julia to go to second base down by the lake. "Nope. No current sales, but from one businessperson to another"—he took the granola from her hand and plopped it inside a BetterBites eco-friendly shopping bag—"it's on

the house. I want you to try it and let me know what
you think."

"Alrighty. I'll do that." She spun on her cowboy
boots, and her swinging hips headed for the front door.
"You been by to visit Julia and that son of…er, her son?"

This time he pressed his fingers into his aching forehead. Weird reality TV like *Wild Bachelorettes Over
70* didn't hold a candle to his life these days. "No, but I
spoke with her over the phone last week about putting
my house on the market. Lucy's back in town to help
Julia. She got here today."

Dottie turned, holding open the front door. "Loco
Lucy? Aw, well, isn't that sweet? I hope those two can
make up and act like real sisters." If they didn't kill each
other first. Brogan worried about the sisters' reunion.

"Good to see you." Brogan gave a short wave as the
heavy door closed, taking Dottie and the hot air with her.

A hard hand clapped him on the shoulder. "This is
one screwy town," Javier said, shaking his head.

"Shee-it. Don't I know it."

Chapter 5

LUCY HAD WRESTLED HER BAGS UPSTAIRS TO HER OLD bedroom and dumped them on the oval braided rug covering the wood floor. Even after all these years, the hint of Charlie perfume, Lucy's favorite as a teenager, still lingered in the air. Lucy remembered the excitement of feeling all grown-up on her thirteenth birthday, when her dad had given her a bottle of it. She'd worn that scent for years. Her old wrought iron double bed remained, with her butterfly quilt and matching shams. Valences in the same fabric crowned the two windows, and baby-blue chintz panels framed the sides. Gone were the painted butterflies, bees, and small white daisies that had dotted her walls. The rock-band posters of Bon Jovi and Counting Crows had been removed, holes had been patched, and fresh, pale-yellow paint covered the walls. Familiàr and yet different. The same way Lucy felt being back home.

Happiness and sadness collided and turned Lucy's insides into a tidal wave. Part of her was excited to be spending time with Parker and getting to know him. But melancholy hit her over the lost time she'd never get back. Her own stubbornness had played a major role, as well as the feud between her and Julia. Rolling her knotted neck to relieve tension, she exhaled. Time to hunt down her disjointed family. She peeled off her sweaty travel clothes and pulled on a soft, aqua knit top over a pair of clean white jeans. After washing up, she applied fresh makeup, pulled her hair back in a sleek ponytail, checked her jewelry, and squared her shoulders.

"Now or never. Operation Lucy to the Rescue is about to commence." She barreled down two flights of stairs to the bonus room where Harper Doolan's navy-blue Naugahyde recliner sat with its worn head and armrests. The upholstery emitted a faint smell of her dad's favorite cigars. Swamped with memories, she pictured herself sitting in her dad's lap, reading while he surfed the sports channels. Her heart clenched, and she wished he were home where he belonged…not living in some Oceanside condo in Naples, Florida, with his latest bride, Constance La Rue, a trade-show model. They'd met at the Miami Beach Convention Center's boat show, where Harper had been hunting for a new fishing boat. Instead of coming home with a boat, he'd come home with the *Princess Yacht*'s hood ornament: Constance, his thirty-four-year-old wife. Only two years older than Lucy. How was that for crazy and colorful?

Her sweet nephew, eyes glued to the flat-screen TV mounted on the wall, sat on the overstuffed sofa with his size-eleven sneakers propped on the pine coffee table. Above his head, her dad's pride and joy hung mounted on the wall, a large blue marlin, flanked by numerous photos and brass fishing plaques. For a moment, she stood quietly and drank in the sight of Parker, wishing she knew him better. He'd shot up at least two feet since the last time she'd seen him.

"Hey, Parks," Lucy called out in a cheery voice. His head jerked up from whatever gaming thingy was keeping him entranced. Dark blue eyes peered at her from under a lock of wavy brown hair that fell over his fore-head. No more soft, baby-fat cheeks she remembered kissing. Instead, patches of new beard grew in spots on his half-man, half-boy face.

"Remember me? Aunt Lucy?" She bent to retrieve a plastic plate and burger wrapper that littered the pat-terned mauve-and-navy carpet. "I know it's been a few years, but—"

"I know who you are," he said as if Moron was her middle name.

"Sure, sure. It's just that it's been like two years and…you've gotten so big. Wow. What do you eat these days? Brontosauruses? Along with a side of beef?" A nervous laugh bubbled forth.

Parker's fathomless blue gaze drilled her. Lucy's heart tumbled. One day he'd be a real lady-killer. Not today. Lucy could've sworn his lip curled in disdain. *Look, kid…cut me some slack. At least I'm trying.* She lifted her chin. "Anyway, I'm here now. You know, to help take care of you and your mom." Another bored look. "I mean, I know you can take care of yourself. You're practically a grown man, but your mom thought it'd be helpful if I could run car pool. That kind of stuff." Parker had refocused on his game and didn't appear to be listening. His hands gripping the black plastic control as if it might crack told a different story. "Uh, I'm get-ting ready to check on your mom. Anything you want to tell me? We're going to review your schedule and—"

"Whatever. I don't need you managing my sched-ule." Parker tossed the game control on the table and blew past her. Before Lucy could react, the sound of the slamming back door rang in her ears.

"Lovely." She planted a fist on her cocked hip. She'd known this wasn't going to be easy, but the attitude hitting her in the face from her sullen nephew would be tough to smack down. Not the welcome home she'd been expecting. Lucy sighed, gathering bowls covered in dried-up ice cream, and candy wrappers. "Well, looks like we at least have our diets in common…that's something."

"Lucy! Is that you?"

At the sound of Julia's whiny voice, Lucy's insides lurched. "Coming," she answered as she detoured to the kitchen to dump the garbage and dishes. Muffled by the thick navy-and-hot-pink Oriental runner, Lucy's steps hesitated as she walked down the hallway toward the master bedroom. As she stood outside the door in the darkened hallway, the urge to flee almost overcame her. She squeezed the brass doorknob. She and Julia had so much dirty water under the bridge, it had become an ocean. Could she put the past behind her and extend the olive branch? Would Julia graciously accept or throw it back in her face? Taking deep breaths to calm her nerves, Lucy almost convinced herself that everything would work out. Almost. She tapped at the partially closed paneled door to the master bedroom before pushing it open.

"Hey. How you feeling?" she asked, poking her head inside.

Julia, surrounded by white fluffy pillows, sat in the middle of the four-poster, king-size bed that used to be Lucy's dad's. A pink chenille throw covered the lower half of her body. Soft light from the lace-covered windows lit her shiny, dark hair. If not for the slight baby bump under the covers, Lucy would've never guessed

Julia was pregnant, much less seven months along. Papers and folders littered the bed as Julia tapped on her laptop. When she and Julia had spoken over the phone, she'd known Julia's doctor was taking every precaution to keep her from going into early labor.

"You're here, finally." Julia barely glanced up from the computer screen in her lap. "I really appreciate you coming to help." *Tap, tap, tap* went the keys. "I have so much work to do, and my assistant is out with the stomach flu. So now I'm relying on Jake the Snake to show my properties. That scheming jerk," she growled at the screen. "I've been working on this client for over three months and—" Julia's head popped up, and perfect plump lips opened on a gasp. Her beautiful oval face and dark blue eyes hadn't changed. The same eyes her son had. "Your hair. What in the world have you done with it?" She clutched her silky pink camisole, as if somehow Lucy's hairstyle was contagious. Julia's expression reflected all the horror associated with anything hair related. The night before Julia's big debut as Homecoming Queen had to be flashing through both their minds. The night Lucy had pulled the scandalous "hair emergency" prank that had gotten the whole town talking.

"I straighten it with a hot iron. And a few blond highlights are nothing to get worked up over." Lucy brushed her silky ponytail. "I decided to try something new…you know, fresh." Actually, Anthony, the lowlife locust-eater, had insisted she tame her unruly, curly mass, but she had no intention of mentioning that. "Uh, you look great. You feeling okay? How's the baby?" Lucy rearranged a couple of pillows near Julia's back, scurrying to change the subject before they started down the unwanted path called memory lane.

"Wonderful. As long as I don't move or lift anything heavier than a tissue, the baby will be fine." A huge exaggerated sigh escaped her lips. "I'm the miserable one. Sitting in this bed, watching my baby grow is great, but I'm about to go *loco*."

Lucy flinched at her least favorite word, *loco*. With narrowed eyes, she studied her sister, who appeared innocent, but appearances could be deceiving.

"I can't believe I'm stuck here for two months. It might as well be two years!"

Lucy could only imagine. Not one to sit around much herself, she knew this confinement would be hard for Julia, with her type A personality. As one of the top-selling agents in her brokerage firm, Julia stayed very busy with her real estate business, running from one appointment to the next.

"I know, but I'm here to help. You need to rest and not stress yourself out, like the doctor ordered."

"I'm trying. Knowing you're here eases my mind. Even though it took some serious convincing on my part."

Lucy's smile tightened. "You explained your situa-tion, and I agreed to help." Okay, so Julia laid on the guilt, and Lucy crumbled like a saltine cracker…it was still the right thing to do. "But we need to talk about Parker. I don't think he's too happy to see me."

Julia waved her hand dismissively. "He'll get over it. Parker is…I can't explain—"

Alarmed, Lucy asked, "Is he okay?"

"Oh yeah, he's fine. He's just having a hard time

adjusting…to the baby, that's all. Thank goodness football practice is starting up, because he needs a purpose
and some place to go to hang out with guys. He doesn't
get much of that here."

Living inside this bubble-gum-pink house probably
didn't help either. "I'm sure. I'll do my best—"

"Ugh! I'm dying here." Julia flopped back against the
mahogany headboard. "Sorry, but I need more flavored
water. Only two cubes of ice, a dash of lemon, and three
mint leaves. Use the fresh mint growing in the red pot on
the windowsill. Not the ones stored in the fridge. They
make my water bitter. Oh, and while you're at it, please
make me an egg-white omelet with Gruyere cheese and
a few chives. Use two eggs and the chives in the green
pot next to the mint. Just a dash of salt…not too much.
It makes me swell up like a hot-air balloon."

Julia eased forward, holding her stomach, refocusing
her attention on her laptop as she extended one hand
with a large plastic tumbler to Lucy. *And* that was the
extent of their reunion. Not that Lucy minded. Her
system could only handle one shock per day. Being
home and back in Harmony was heart-attack inducing
enough; add in Brogan Reese, the crush who kept on
crushing, and Lucy might need medical assistance.

"Sure," Lucy mumbled as she took the cup from
Julia's manicured fingers. "Julia, we really need to talk
about Parker and his schedule."

"Yes, I know. I've already emailed it to you."
Tapping from the keyboard filled the room. "Annnd,
send." She clicked the Send button with flourish. "Feed
me, and we can have a good long chat. Now that you're
finally home." Julia settled back against the pillows,

appearing relaxed. "Oh, and Luce, I have a wonderful hairdresser, in case you're interested." The syrupy pageant smile that had won Julia the crown at homecoming, along with queen of Harmony's Pickle Parade, appeared on her face. The smile that always meant trouble when directed at Lucy. Lucy might as well get it over with and shave her head bald, because she wasn't going anywhere near Julia's hairdresser. *Note to self: buy dead bolt for bedroom door.*

Lucy slipped from the room, escaping into the kitchen. *Holy crud balls!* How was she ever going to last two months? Dante's *Inferno* had nothing on Lucy's current purgatory. She twirled a lock of hair, first pulling straight down and then rolling it around her index finger. Round and round the soft strand went until she practically cut off her circulation.

"Don't be such a ninny. You're thirty-two. Not fifteen. She's just messing with you. So you pulled a nasty prank. You were an immature teenager with hurt feelings. Nobody cares anymore." She continued to lecture herself as she refilled Julia's water and pulled eggs and cheese from the refrigerator. "It's not like the whole town will still be going on about how you whacked Julia's hair off with gardening shears while she slept." But after all these years, Lucy got the sneaky feeling Julia still wanted to extract her pound of flesh.

She fumbled while trying to separate egg whites from the yolks. Beating with a fork, she hoped Julia wouldn't notice the slight yellow color. She chopped a few chives and grated some cheese. And who was she kidding? Of course all eleven thousand Harmony residents remembered that ill-fated night. And of course they'd still be talking about it. Talk, talk, gossip, gossip, chirp, chirp, cheep, cheep all over the place like a bunch of pecking Henny Pennys. Hell's bells, Harmony held an Olympic gold medal for the sport of gossiping.

Lucy struggled to fold the thin layer of egg whites with lots of yolk in the bottom of the Teflon-coated frying pan. After several futile attempts, she dumped the mangled mess onto a plate, attempting camouflage by sprinkling chives on top and hoping Julia wouldn't notice her lack of culinary skills or the fact that the eggs were scrambled. With plate and glass in hand, she trudged down the hallway to the shark tank where her stepsister bent on revenge swam.

"Here you go. Just as you ordered." Julia had cleared her lap of papers and reached for the plate.

"Thanks. You're a lifesave—" Julia blinked at the mauled mess of eggs hiding under the chopped chives.

"Sorry. Must've missed the class on omelet making, but I'm sure they taste fine. The baby won't know the difference." Lucy plumped a few lacy pillows behind Julia and smoothed the pink blanket. "Eat those yummy eggs while you give me the lowdown on Parker. When I spoke to him earlier, he seemed to be in a hurry to leave. Clearly, he's not thrilled with the present situation…or me."

Lucy scooted the pink armchair close and sat. Julia proceeded to pick at the eggs with her fork, as if Lucy had scrambled slugs, chasing each bite with huge gulps of water, trying not to gag.

After swallowing half her water, she said, "Parker is just being Parker. Moody. Sullen. A pain in my butt. Basically, a fifteen-year-old kid." She placed the barely eaten eggs on the nightstand.

"Football practice starts next week, and he's going out for quarterback. You'll need to make sure he gets to practice, has clean workout clothes, eats three healthy meals per day, drinks plenty of water…you know the drill."

Uh…not really. Lucy didn't have much experience in taking care of fifteen-year-old boys…especially one with a bad attitude. "About that meal thing…er, when you say *healthy*, what exactly do you mean? Like Lean Cuisines? Or low cal on the Taco Bell menu?" *Twip, twip,* she wrapped a strand of hair around her finger.

Julia stopped reaching for her laptop, slamming Lucy with an incredulous look. "I mean healthy. Like steamed veggies, grilled chicken, homemade pasta. You need to make him protein shakes and make sure he packs granola bars and fresh fruit for snacks. I don't want him eating crap from Taco Hell or any other fast-food joint."

Funny. Parker didn't share this love of healthy eating, if all those candy and burger wrappers Lucy had thrown in the garbage were any indication. "Uh, Julia, you must've missed the email, but I'm no chef." Lucy crossed her arms to stop from twirling her hair. "I can barely boil water, and from those uneaten eggs and gagging noises you were making…I think you know what I'm talking about."

"I realize you're not a chef, but surely you can sauté—"

"That would be a big NO. I can't sauté, flambé, or soufflé. But I do run a mean microwave. I can heat all kinds of food up in less than three minutes."

Julia's lovely blue eyes narrowed in what Lucy remembered as her bitchy glare-down. Anybody within striking distance of that glare felt fried, sizzled, or toasted. How appropriate, since they were discussing food.

"You can't be serious, Lucy. How can you be thirty-five and not know how to cook?"

"Thirty-two. You're the one pushing thirty-five," Lucy snapped. Immediately regretting her tone, she said, "Look, learning to cook was never a priority for me. I always preferred working to cooking. But—"

"Whatever. Listen, you've got to figure something out. I can't be stressed wondering if Parker is eating healthy." She clutched her rounded baby bump. "I'm starting to feel sick already," she moaned.

Lucy jumped up and placed her palm on Julia's forehead. Cool as a mountain brook. "Just calm down. Don't curdle that baby's milk. I'll figure out something."

Julia's eyes drifted closed as she groaned. "Okay. Stop poking me." She nestled her head against the pillows. "For tonight, order takeout from the Dog. They have delivery service now. There's an envelope of money on the kitchen counter. Make sure he doesn't eat only French fries and milk shakes."

The Dogwood Bar and Grill was known to all the locals as the Dog. One of Lucy's best friends, Bertie, owned it with her brother, Cal. The same Bertie who'd married Keith Morgan, the drop-dead fabulous, finest piece of man-flesh this side of the Atlantic Harmony had ever seen.

"Oh, and order me a spinach salad with a side of balsamic vinaigrette dressing. Tell them to hold the chopped egg and onion, but add croutons and a little Parmesan cheese."

"Let me get my pad so I can take all this down."

Sarcasm laced Lucy's voice, but Julia didn't seem to notice…or care.

Her eyes remained closed, and she added, "And a baked potato with a tiny dollop of sour cream…not too much. And caffeine-free iced green tea. Unsweetened."

Next to the cut crystal lamp on the nightstand lay a notepad with Julia's name printed across the top in hot pink. Lucy grabbed it. "My name is Lucy, and I'll be your server…anything else, ma'am?" she drawled as she scribbled Julia's complicated order.

One eye peeked open. "Make sure Parker gets to bed on time. He needs his rest."

"He's fifteen. What exactly is bedtime? I can assure you, he's not gonna want me tucking him in."

"He's fifteen, thinks he's twenty-eight, and acts like he's six. So, yes, you need to make sure he washes his face, brushes his teeth, and is tucked in with lights *out* by ten thirty. No later." Julia rolled her head toward Lucy. "And take his phone. He's not allowed to charge his phone in his room at night. Charge it on the kitchen counter. Also, no videos, TV, or computer."

Oh, goody. She could add drill sergeant to her résumé. "Dang. You're tough. I'm assuming all these rules are spelled out and he knows the drill."

"Don't assume anything when you're dealing with a teenage boy," Julia mumbled before her eyes closed. "Oh, and Lucy"—her voice barely above a whisper—"don't even think about leaving town. I need you."

Julia's breathing evened out, indicating she'd dropped dead asleep. Massive amounts of guilt coupled with a little sadness seared Lucy's pinched heart. She adjusted Julia's blanket and gave her hand a gentle pat. She had no clue why Julia had never married and had kept the fathers of her babies a mystery, allowing Harmony to speculate and gossip, instead of setting the record straight. They'd never been close or shared those kinds of confidences, and Lucy had never gotten up the nerve to ask. But Julia must've had her reasons. She took motherhood seriously and wanted to do right by her kids. Why else would she be having another baby out of wedlock? Lucy had to admire that. Any single, working mother deserved that little bit of respect.

Lucy turned off the bedside lamp and removed the computer from Julia's lap. She picked up the plate of uneaten eggs and tiptoed from the room. Time to hunt down her darling nephew and have a little come to Jesus talk.

Chapter 6

BROGAN GLANCED AROUND THE CROWDED BAR AS HE nursed his second beer at the infamous Dog. For newcomers, the Dog took some getting used to, with its green-and-yellow Dalmatian-spotted vinyl booths, zebra-striped barstools, and chicken-wire pendant lights. Not your typical small-town diner. But it always drew a crowd, and this Friday night was no exception.

Javier had left a few minutes ago to check into his room at Hazel's Boarding House, the only place to rent a room near Main Street. Hazel and Frank Conway, both pushing eighty, had converted their three-story Victorian into a quaint bed and breakfast. Brogan would've invited Javier to stay with him, but he'd hired Bertie Anderson Morgan as his interior designer, and she'd already started renovations on his mother's house, making it uninhabitable for guests.

"Hey there, Brogan!" Bertie wove her way around the colorful tables to reach him at the bar. "Got some flooring samples to show you, and I need your approval."

Brogan stood, scooting his barstool down to make room. "Hey. Where's Keith?"

"Sent him home with Maddie and the baby. He says all the pros at the academy really love BetterBites. I've been meaning to check it out."

Brogan squeezed her shoulder. "No worries. I'd rather you finish the house so I can get it sold." He motioned the bartender over as he offered her a stool. "Can I buy you a drink?"

"Oh, no. Heading home. Can't work these shifts anymore. My feet are killing me."

He glanced at the feet in question and raised his brows. "Woman, they should be, in those ridiculously high contraptions of torture."

Bertie shimmied her curvaceous hips onto the barstool and turned her small foot as she admired her strappy silver shoes. The bartender slid another icy mug of beer in his direction. "They're my favorite wedges."

Brogan shook his head but remained quiet. He'd learned from Kathryn, his ex-wife, not to question females about their love affairs with shoes. *Zap*. Yep, it still hurt.

"You decide to list your house with Julia?" Bertie gave him a pointed look. "She's the best…even stuck in bed."

"Probably." Did he have a choice? To not use Julia as his realtor would seem petty, and he didn't need any more negative gossip. Then again, to start working with Julia would fuel the rampant speculation over whether they'd get back together.

Even though Keith Morgan had presented a solid business plan with growth potential, opening BetterBites was only one reason why he hadn't hit the trail yet. Unresolved issues from his past was another reason why he was sticking around.

"Heard you picked Lucy up today on the side of the road. I give her credit for coming home to help Julia and take care of Parker, but she's gonna go bonkers if she doesn't find something else to keep her occupied."

Brogan shoved his unwanted thoughts from his mind. "She seemed a little nervous about being home."

"She and Julia aren't very close. They still have unresolved differences." Bertie snapped her fingers. "Hey, you should talk to Lucy about marketing. She could really help if you need someone for BetterBites."

Now that was good news worth sinking his teeth into. Brogan set his beer down slowly. "Really?"

"She's amazing. She helped me on a couple of projects, and Keith plans to talk to her about promoting one of his tournaments."

"If she's so awesome, why is she here? I got the impression she didn't have a choice."

Bertie shrugged. "She got burned bad in a business deal. I don't know all the particulars, and it's not my story to tell, but being home and reconnecting with some of her old friends will be good for her." Bertie straightened the condiment rack on top of the bar. "Hate to leave you alone. Is your friend coming back?"

"Nah. Javier is settling in at Hazel's."

"Ooo, sorry to hear that. You know Hazel has Bible study on Wednesday nights, and attendance is mandatory for her boarders."

He grinned into his beer. "I know that. But Javie doesn't."

Bertie laughed. "You trying to run him off?"

"Javie's a charmer. He'll have them eating out of his hand and probably converting to Catholicism before he leaves."

"Conways are die-hard Methodists. They will welcome the challenge." She chuckled and patted his arm. "I'll be by first thing tomorrow with those samples."

"Thanks."

Bertie eased off the barstool. "See you then—oh, it's Lucy. Luce. Over here!" She waved as he peered over his shoulder toward the entrance. Lucy maneuvered around the colorful tables, wearing a tight knit top that did nothing to disguise her curves, over snug jeans, a grimace marring her face. She clutched the funky handbag over her shoulder, ducking her head as she worked her way across the bar.

"Loco Lucy! Is that you?"

"Hey, Lucy, glad you're home."

"Look, it's Lucy. We've missed you, girl."

Lucy hadn't gotten two feet before everyone at the Dog seemed to perk up and give a shout out. Brogan watched in wonder as the imaginary welcome wagon practically barreled her over in its eagerness to greet her. Looking embarrassed, Lucy kept her head tucked as she waved and smiled. Shit. He'd give his right arm to receive a welcome like that. He'd encountered only polite nods and condolences about his sainted mother on top of nosy inquiries about his relationship with Julia. Lucy had been the one who'd left town like the prodigal son. And like the Gospel story, returned home to welcoming arms and fatted calf.

As she approached the bar, her feet, clad in soft-pink Keds, hesitated when she spied him next to Bertie. With a resigned shrug, she continued across the colorful terrazzo floor.

"Where's Parker? You lose him already?" Bertie asked, and then ordered a margarita on the rocks, no salt.

"Don't even joke about that," Lucy said, horror registering on her face. "He's home. I had dinner delivered from here for him and Julia. I'm thankful for any help I can get."

Brogan stood and pulled a barstool out for Lucy on his left, while Bertie hovered on his right. Another hesitation. Brogan waited, locking gazes with Lucy. Stepping closer, his heartbeat turned erratic. Gray eyes widening, Lucy appeared to suffer from the same malady. Finally, she sighed and hopped up on the stool.

"Are all fifteen-year-old boys sarcastic, nasty, and rude? I don't remember our friends from high school being—" Lucy stopped, as if mentioning high school was taboo in his presence.

"Drink. You look like you need it." Bertie slid the icy margarita in a blue Mason jar Lucy's way. "Most of the teenage guys we knew were really nice. Unless you're thinking about Buck Evans, that stupid pothead. Remember when he set the boys' locker room on fire?"

Good ole Buck, the dumb fuck. Brogan had forgotten all about him. "He did more than set the locker room on fire. Remember, he flew his boxer shorts up the flagpole and got caught by Deputy Dog, the security guard?"

"I'd forgotten about that," Bertie said, grinning.

No longer able to contain her laughter, Lucy choked as margarita went down the wrong pipe. Brogan patted her on the back. "You okay? Need some water?"

She wheezed and laughed simultaneously, clutching her throat. Hank the bartender filled a glass of water, and Lucy reached for it, gulping half of it down. "Th-thanks. I'm good." Brogan pressed his palm into her warm back and felt the catch of breath. A slight blush highlighted her cheeks, and she shot him a sideways glance as he reluctantly removed his hand. Yep. Funny Lucy was no more immune to him than he was to her. And didn't that complicate matters?

"Try not to choke to death." Bertie chuckled. "Hank, bring Lucy another 'rita on the house and whatever Brogan's drinking. I'm shoving off." Bertie gave Lucy a brief hug. "I'm here for you if you need anything," she said close to her ear but loud enough for Brogan to hear. "Don't kill your nephew. And remember, not all the guys we knew were jerk-wads. Some were adorable and sweet in their obvious, cocky way." Direct hit. Bertie gave Brogan a wink and then said to Lucy, "Don't forget…Keith wants to talk to you about some marketing ideas."

Lucy nodded. "Tell Keith I'll call him this week."

"Bye, y'all." Bertie waved as she left, and Lucy stared after her as she exited the bar.

A good minute passed, then he said to the back of Lucy's head, "You going to keep ignoring me?" Her shoulders stiffened, and he pulled a strand of silky hair to gain her attention.

"Stop that! You keep yanking on my hair." Stormy gray eyes met his.

Lucy wanted to erect big stone walls with thick mortar, and Brogan couldn't blame her. On this, he kinda had to agree. Too much weird history and too many years had passed. They both had lives away from Harmony. But an alluring warmth that emanated from Lucy snagged his attention, a warmth with the power to penetrate his dormant heart and make him feel alive again.

He let the strand of hair slip through his fingers. "It's irresistible. I always liked pulling it, especially back in high school when you had all those curls."

Brogan smiled at her skeptical face. "Still don't understand how you get it so straight."

Lucy gathered her blond hair up in both hands and deftly knotted it on top her head. She snorted, and her heavy hair knot listed to one side. "The only thing you ever liked doing in high school was Julia."

"True. Doesn't mean I didn't notice your hair."

"Hey, Loco Lucy! We heard you were back. How does it feel?"

"Not planning to lop off any more of Julia's hair, are you?"

Julia's best buds from high school, Amanda Hobbs and Marcia Williams, slipped onto barstools next to Lucy.

At the sound of her nickname, Lucy cringed, flashing her discomfort before her features veiled in indifference. The town meant no disrespect. It just had a weird, in-your-face way of showing its affection. Everyone loved Lucy, except maybe Julia's two high school besties. Brogan resisted the desire to tuck Lucy into his side for safekeeping and tell her she had nothing to worry about.

"Hey, Brogan. Have you seen Julia?" Amanda picked up a menu from the bar. "It's so cool you're back, and Julia's, you know…available." She winked at Brogan.

Pain pricked behind his eyes. *Note to everyone: not going to happen.*

Lucy chugged her margarita and slammed the glass back down on the bar. As she reached for her handbag, Brogan grabbed her arm.

"Wait," he whispered. Against his better judgment, he rubbed her wrist with his thumb, amazed at the softness of her skin. Lucy tugged her arm away as if she'd been burned.

Brogan countered by resting a heavy hand on her shoulder to keep her from bolting as he addressed Amanda and Marcia. "I plan to see Julia this week." Low growling came from Lucy's direction. Repressing a laugh, he squeezed her soft shoulder. When had Little Lucy become so prickly? Brogan liked that he made her nervous. "Been busy with the opening of BetterBites. When are you coming to the store?"

"You sell prepared foods?" Amanda asked.

"Yes. Healthy organic foods you can't easily find around here. Come on by, and tell all your friends."

"Sounds perfect. I'll stop by the store tomorrow. Will you be there?"

"Absolutely."

Lucy made a production of coughing, which gained Amanda and Marcia's attention. "You okay, Luce? You haven't said two words. How are you and Julia getting along?" Marcia asked, broadcasting with her smirk what she thought of the sisters' reunion.

A strained smile appeared on Lucy's face. "Like straw and berries, poly and ester, stud and bolt. Speaking of Julia"—she pulled her cell from her jeans pocket and read the screen—"better get home before she develops calluses on those fingers. She's giving that keyboard a real workout."

Digging for her wallet in her handbag, she slapped a ten on the bar. "Great to see you guys. Be sure to let me know when you want to visit Julia." Her unspoken message rang loud and clear: *I'll be sure not to be there.*

Brogan ducked as she slung her heavy hobo bag over

her shoulder, narrowly missing his head. God only knew what she carried inside. Skirting around him, she aimed for the front door. He wasn't ready to let her go. For the first time in weeks, he'd been enjoying himself. He fished for his wallet, threw some bills on the bar, and snatched up Lucy's ten.

Chapter 7

EIGHT HOURS. LUCY HAD BEEN IN TOWN EIGHT LONG hours, and she wanted to run screaming for the hills. Preferably Blowing Rock, North Carolina, where her dad owned a small house with a glorious vista of majestic Grandfather Mountain.

"Lucy, wait up."

No. Not three times in one day. She didn't have this many Brogan sightings when she used to stalk him back in high school. All these years later, she still felt gawky, and the familiar butterflies marauding her stomach had worsened and not receded at all.

"Where you rushing off to?" Brogan caught up with her.

Lucy spoke without stopping or looking his way. "Need to check on Julia and Parker." Parker had ignored Lucy all through dinner. Trying to gain his trust, Lucy had said he could stay up a little longer if he promised to be in bed by eleven. The ice in his gaze seemed to thaw a little after that, and Lucy had left him entranced in video-game heaven as she scooted out, needing to escape the confines of the house for a few minutes. She'd walked around the neighborhood, waving to some of her old neighbors sitting out on their front porches, until she found herself standing in front of the Dog. Deciding a drink would go a long way in calming her frayed nerves, she'd ventured inside.

Brogan shortened his long, easy stride to match hers. "I'm sure they appreciate all you're doing." Lucy wasn't sure of anything these days.

Her phone vibrated for the millionth time, and she read the text. "Sheesh, I'm coming. Don't have a wedgie," she mumbled as she tapped back a message.

Brogan touched her elbow, sending tingles down her arm as he guided her toward the alley next to BetterBites.

"Hey! What are you doing? You're not taking me inside BetterBites and forcing alfalfa sprouts down my throat, are you?" Lucy squirmed, trying to free her arm from his now firm grasp.

"Don't have a wedgie," he mimicked, pulling her along, exerting no effort. "Besides, I have better things to force down your throat than alfalfa sprouts."

Oh my. Lucy gulped, willing her mind not to think of what *better* things he had in mind and failing miserably. She hoped hers was the only dirty mind between them, picturing naughty, *better* things. *Back off, baby sister.*

In the alley behind his store, his convertible sat with the top up, and Brogan held the car door open. "Hop in."

"Ooo, two rides in one day in this slick car. I feel special. What more could a girl ask for?" He slid behind the wheel and opened his mouth. "Don't answer that. It was rhetorical."

Crooked white smile and crystal green eyes glowed in her direction from the dashboard lights. Hint of coffee and expensive leather tickled Lucy's nose. Good smells. Yummy, rich smells. He flicked something at her. A crumpled ten-dollar bill landed in her lap.

"Your tip from the bar. Thought you might want it back."

"Why? I left it for Hank."

"I took care of Hank. Just thought you might need it. Maybe put it toward a new radiator or something." Like a new car? Lucy hated she'd let things get so bad. It reminded her of how she'd been ignoring her life and not taking care of her needs.

"Thanks. But I'm afraid even Grady's rates have gone up. And Grady's gone fishing. I'm gonna have to drive her into Raleigh for service." Grady's Gas & Bait repaired cars and had serviced Harmony for as long as Lucy could remember.

"I'll take care of it for you." Startled, Lucy jumped as he reached across her, brushing her chest with his forearm. "Buckle up," he said, pulling on her seat belt. Stunned both by his actions and his offer, she allowed him to fasten the clasp into the buckle. Goose bumps broke out on her skin. She rubbed her bare arms, hoping he didn't notice.

"Thanks, but I can handle it. Probably only needs coolant." And maybe new brake pads and, uh, a new engine.

Brogan flashed his wonderful smile again. "You know where to put the coolant?" Her look of confusion must've tipped him off. "Didn't think so. We'll take care of it tomorrow." Lucy appreciated his offer. But she didn't want to spend another day with Brogan Reese, who still carried a torch for Julia. And she didn't relish Brogan witnessing the shambles her life had become these last few months.

"Where would you like to go?" Again, that melting caramel voice, making her resolution to avoid him darn near impossible.

Vegas. Key West. San Francisco. Top down. Hair

blowing. And Brogan Reese behind the wheel. Her heart leaped and then plummeted. "Home. Julia is having another pillow crisis, or there's one too many ice cubes in her water. Something earth-shattering."

"Home it is," he said, shifting into reverse and backing out. "If I remember correctly, Julia thrives on crisis. Lots of drama. It's the way she deals. Don't let it get to you. Once she figures out you're not available 24-7, she'll stop demanding your attention."

She speared him with a sharp look. Spoken like a true expert. "That's just it. I *am* available 24-7. I don't have any other job at the moment, and she knows it." More like a failing career needing a steroid shot to wake it up.

"Maybe we can fix that."

"Huh? Here you go again with 'we.' What does that mean?"

"You. Me. We. As in you and me together." His lips twitched with an effort not to smile.

Fried frog legs! Lucy's eyes widened. She didn't have the strength to play games with him. He'd see straight through to her soul in less time than it took to consume a bag of Lay's potato chips. She leaned forward, pointing a finger at him. "No *we*. You and I don't do we. Got it? Besides, I'm on a break. Eight months of Anthony Tiger is enough to turn any woman off."

"Anthony Tiger? What are you talking about?"

"Anthony, my ex-boyfriend."

Brogan came to a stop at the intersection of Main and Carver. The street and sidewalk were empty of cars and pedestrians. The late summer air hung heavy, thick as peanut butter, but the air-conditioning inside Brogan's car blasted arctic temperatures.

Despite the cold AC, heat prickled her neck and attacked her cheeks at Brogan's surprised stare.

"You dated Tony Tiger? As in, 'They're grrreat!'"

"That's original." She didn't hold back the exaggerated eye roll. "Yes, I dated Tony the dipweed Tiger."

"Did he eat Frosted Flakes?" Brogan grinned, enjoying himself a bit too much at her expense.

"Ha-ha. You're a real comedian. Look, in my defense, my work schedule was beyond chaotic, taking temp jobs when we were short staffed while trying to keep up with all the marketing. I took the safe way out on relationships. I wanted easy and predictable." Lucy stopped. What had possessed her to babble about her personal life in front of Brogan Reese? Like he was her shrink…not the crush-gush that got away.

The car idled at the four-way stop. "Uh, maybe we should go or something." She motioned toward the windshield. Brogan crossed the intersection instead of turning left onto Carver, which led to her house. He kept driving down the winding road until he pulled into the side parking lot at the high school. Easing to a stop between two light posts, he shifted in his seat and faced her. The three-story stone school building loomed to her right, and the car faced the two-story detached gymnasium. Strategic spotlights on the sides of the buildings lit part of the school grounds for security, but it was still too dark and intimate for Lucy's liking, conjuring up memories best left buried. Like how Lucy used to wait for Brogan behind the pillars. Invisible. After every home game, win or lose, just to make sure he was okay.

"What are you doing?" Panic worked its way from

the pit of her stomach as she wondered if he remembered too.

"Parking."

Lucy gulped. "Er, in case you've forgotten…this isn't where kids go to make out. That would be down by the lake. Remember?" Not that she'd ever made out by the lake. She'd spent her junior and senior year in Chattanooga with her grandparents. A self-imposed ban from her home. Away from Julia.

But a few times, sophomore year, she'd snuck down to the lake with her best friend Wanda Pattershaw…to spy. On Brogan and Julia. She squirmed in her seat at the memory. From what she could see hiding in the brush, Brogan took kissing to a whole new level. Deep, slow, lazy kisses. Not awkward and jerky like the other boys. Yuck.

Humor lit his clear green eyes as if he'd read her mind. He made a slow top-to-bottom survey of her person, grinning like a naughty boy finding his dad's secret stash of porn.

"Don't get any ideas!"

"Awww, you're no fun." He patted the top of her leg in a buddy way, but her thigh prickled in a not-so-buddy way. "Finish the story. I want to hear about Tony Tiger."

She groaned. Why had she opened her big mouth? "If I tell you the embarrassing story of my life, will you take me home?"

"If that's where you really want to go." He made it sound like she had choices. She had a worthless business contract, a depleted savings account, her poor baby broken down on the side of the highway, and her commitment to Julia and Parker. Kind of limited in those choices.

"We dated for eight months. Three weeks ago, during one of our business meetings to discuss the new partnership we'd be forming…with me, Anthony makes a huge announcement. The usual suspects were there: Anthony; his accountant; his new assistant, Shannon; and me. Anthony and I had made big plans to partner and expand the business. I had invested time, energy, and funds toward our new goal. The money wasn't huge, but for me it was a lot."

Lucy took comfort in the concern etched on Brogan's face. He didn't like the direction this story was heading any more than she did. "I won't bore you with the humdrum details, but Anthony cut me out of the deal. He announced his wonderful news like I was supposed to be thrilled or something."

Brogan gave a sympathy nod, but his eyes had narrowed, and his jaw hardened as she continued the story detailing her complete humiliation. "He joined forces with another agency…and Shannon. And yes, they're sleeping together." Brogan had the decency to flinch. Lucy loved him for that. Okay, not love like *in love*.

She fiddled with the braided leather strap on her handbag. "Yep. I'm a cliché."

"What do you mean?" His voice was low and soothing.

"What's the saying? The wife or girlfriend is always the last to know." She snorted in disgust. "I think I'm more ticked at losing out on the partnership than being jilted. Dumb, right?"

"Not at all. This whole thing sucks…big time. You have every right to feel mad and angry. For the record, Tony the Tiger is a class-A jerk, and you're better off without him. Wish I'd been there. I would've kicked his sorry ass."

Lucy would've paid good money to see that. With a wry smile, she said, "I should've known."

Brogan shook his head. "He hid it well to keep you off track. He played you, Luce."

"I know that now. I meant while we were dating. I should've known. All those months, I kept wondering why he wasn't interested in…er, well, you know"—she fluttered her hand between them—"we never actually…"

"*What?* Come on now, you're joking."

She chuckled at his flabbergasted expression. "Nope."

"Stop. You mean to tell me you dated a guy for eight months and you never had sex?" The horror on Brogan's face was almost comical.

She shrugged in her defense. "I stayed busy marketing and increasing the agency's numbers, because I was working toward a partnership. At least I thought," she mumbled. "The more jobs we filled successfully, the more referrals we got, and the higher our rankings shot up on all the job sites. By the end of the day, I was so pooped I had no energy or desire to work on the relationship. Exhausted. Fried. Unexciting. No wonder he ditched me." Lucy slumped against the seat.

"Come on, Lucy. You're not allowing that creep to mess with your head, are you? Consider yourself lucky." She glanced in his direction. Brogan's brows had hiked up and hid under the tawny wave of hair that fell across his forehead. "You did nothing wrong except believe in someone you thought had your back. Face it, Lucy, Tony the Tiger is a dick."

Amen to that, brother. Relief washed over Lucy, making her feel lighter than she'd felt in weeks. Knowing Brogan staunchly defended her side brightened her world. Even if only for a few moments, it was something to Lucy.

Brogan's smile turned friendly. "Look, you may feel exhausted or fried. But there's no way you could ever be unexciting. Not a chance."

Lucy sighed. What a nice guy. She remembered that about him. He'd always spoken to adults in a polite manner, and he'd never made her feel insignificant those rare moments he'd happened to notice her. Brogan was as steady as the Rock of Gibraltar. Why hadn't she met someone like him over the years?

"Nice of you to say, but I'm afraid I was terribly uninteresting and dull. I stayed busy, helping the bottom line, marketing day and night, and sometimes filling in when we were short temps." *Not* working on her own career plan, like she should've been.

"Were any of the jobs interesting?" Brogan fiddled with the nautical rope bracelet he wore on his right wrist.

Some of the more off-the-wall jobs came to mind and made her chuckle. "You could say that."

"Like Stanley Cup Keeper? Paper Towel Sniffer?"

"No, but I handed out jocks and socks at the gym one semester at Georgia Tech."

"The guys must've loved that." He laughed. "What about golf-ball diver?" he asked "You ever done that?"

"No, but I clipped coupons for my old neighbor, Mrs. Bunkins. She's really loaded, but you'd never know it. Made me go through everyone's recycle bins, hunting for coupons. She never spends more than forty-seven cents on groceries each week."

Brogan shook his head in disbelief. "Just my kind of customer. Hey, ever been a pet-food taster?"

"No. But golf-ball diver sounds kind of fun. Don't know if I could stomach pet-food taster. Has to be disgusting."

"Not any more disgusting than what you put in your system," he said under his breath.

"As opposed to garbanzo beans and nasty tofu?"

"I'm with you on the tofu. Can't handle the texture. But BetterBites has some great-tasting food. You should give us a try."

Lucy would like to give Brogan a *try*, but she was pretty sure he meant his food and not his tasty beefcake self.

He tilted his head and gave her a long, unwavering stare. "You studied marketing in college?"

"Yes. Marketing and PR. I had several jobs before I succumbed to the underbelly of Anthony's obsessed rise-to-temp-stardom."

A sudden calculated look flashed across his face, or maybe she imagined it, because when she blinked, he appeared as relaxed and affable as usual. "Word around town is you're pretty good."

She straightened in her seat. "Pretty good? Who's been talking about me?" She hated being the topic around town.

"Calm down, tiny dancer." Brogan laughed. "At marketing. Bertie told me you did a great job for her, and Keith wants your help."

Lucy had helped Bertie market her interior design business, which had led to bigger clients for Bertie in other cities. If Lucy could sign more small businesses with little or no in-house marketing, she could put her own marketing plan in motion. She nodded. "I like working with small companies that need marketing. That's really my focus."

"And Keith's a shrewd businessman. If he's asking for your help, then he must think you're qualified." He shifted toward her, taking up more space, along with all the oxygen inside the car. "I also might have a job to keep you busy."

Her mouth gaped open. Did his voice drop an octave in a sexy, suggestive way? Why this sudden interest in her? She forced her gaze past Brogan's five o'clock shadow, firm lips, and white teeth. The teasing laugh lines at the corners of his eyes fueled her suspicious nature. "What kind of job? It better not require a French maid's outfit, fur-lined handcuffs, or sneaking off to some Motel 6."

Surprise lit his face. "That thought never occurred to me, but now that you mention it—"

"Let me warn you…I'm packing and have a black belt in karate." She crossed her arms and tried for Julia's bitchy glare-down. He appeared innocent, but she could never be too sure.

"Little Lucy, we need to channel all this aggression you carry around into something more productive." His tone playful, Brogan tilted her chin up with his finger and slayed her with his most endearing smile, designed to break hearts and cause all rational thought to flee from heads. "I've got the perfect solution."

Mesmerized by sparkling green eyes and his unique blend of scents filling her head, Lucy swayed toward his firm, wide mouth…

"What the—!" She pushed on his rock-hard chest as she leaned toward the driver's window, practically crawling in his lap.

"Uh, okay. This works too," a surprised Brogan said, wrapping his hands around her waist.

"Pay attention." Lucy turned his head from the magnified view of her chest region toward the window. "That's my nephew. What is he doing out at this hour?" She jabbed her finger at the side of the school gymnasium, where Parker stood with two other boys, holding a football and a canned drink.

"That better not be beer, or he has drawn his last teenage breath. Julia is going to kill him." Her breath came out in short bursts. Holy hush puppies. She smacked her palms to her cheeks. "First me and then him." She scrambled from his lap and reached for her door. "I haven't been home for twenty-four hours, and I'm already dealing with a runaway teen. He's dead meat."

Chapter 8

"HOLD ON THERE, SUPER NANNY." BROGAN REACHED for her upper arm.

This whole night had taken a sharp turn. Lucy Doolan's sweet, luscious form had been in his lap, and her lips within inches of his mouth. Lucy. The same girl who'd hidden behind columns, sneaking peeks at him back in high school. The girl who'd handed out socks and jocks or clipped coupons, all for the bottom line. Julia's younger sister. He had zero feelings for Julia these days, but he couldn't be too sure about Julia's feelings for him, and he didn't want to complicate Lucy's life any more than it was.

And kissing Lucy would be a complication. But damn…he'd been tempted.

"Let go!" She wriggled like a fish on a hook. "I need to karate kick his lying little butt back into bed before Julia finds out."

"Calm down. You're not going to gain anything by going all dingo-dog wild in front of his friends."

Lucy stopped squirming. "Okay. What do you suggest?"

Hell if he knew. He looked through his windshield at Parker and his friends leaning against the brick gym wall, drinking their beers. Shit. He'd participated in some underage drinking, trying to be cool. Peer pressure could be a real son of a bitch.

"Sit back." Brogan released his hold. Silky hair spilled past her shoulders, tantalizing his fingers. The oddest urge to scoop it up and bury his face in the glossy strands came over him.

"What are you going to do?" she whispered, as if they were conducting top-secret surveillance. Her concern dragged him back to the problem at hand.

"Just pay a little visit." He put the car in gear and slowly rolled forward toward the group of boys.

The boys jumped to attention as soon as they spied his car. Parker stood frozen to the spot. His friends tossed their beer cans and hauled ass around the building and across the football field. Parker unfroze and started to chase after his friends.

Brogan slammed to a stop, jumped out, and yelled, "Parker! I wouldn't if I were you."

Parker skidded to a halt. Shoulders slumped, head hanging, he slowly turned.

"Parker! What in holy peanut brittle are you doing?" Lucy stood next to her door as she banged it shut. "You told me you were going to bed. I…what…how…?"

Parker narrowed a disgusted look at Lucy. "I'm not a baby. Quit treating me like one. It's only eleven thirty. What the fuh—"

"That's enough." Brogan used his most commanding voice. "Pick up those beer cans and throw them in the garbage and get in the car." Parker stayed put, aiming a rebellious glare at Brogan. "Now!" Brogan roared. Parker moved as if crossing hot coals in bare feet. After he tossed the cans in the garbage, Brogan held the back door open and ordered, "Get in." Parker slid onto the seat. "Stay there and don't move."

Brogan closed the door and glanced over the car top at Lucy.

"What are you doing?" Lucy asked in a loud whisper, surprise written all over her flushed face.

"I'm not sure. But I wasn't about to let him start blaming you. And if he ever cusses at you, I will tear him apart."

"But…he's just a kid. He doesn't even know me. I don't think—"

"No excuses. You can't let him talk to you like that, Luce. It's disrespectful. You need to show him you're in charge." They held their whispered conversation over the convertible's top.

She pressed fingers into her forehead. "Remind me never to have kids." She massaged her temples and then reached for the door handle.

Brogan couldn't agree more. He remembered how hard his mom had struggled to rein him in while working a full-time job.

He slid behind the wheel into a tension-filled car. Lucy twirled her hair and gnawed her bottom lip, and Parker sat in stony silence in the back. The urge to smack his own forehead against the steering wheel overwhelmed Brogan as he wondered what he'd gotten himself into.

Brogan backed up and pulled out of the parking lot, and Parker broke the uncomfortable silence. "Who are you anyway?"

Lucy swiveled in her seat. "Parker, this is Brogan Reese, a good friend of your mom's and…er, mine."

"Yeah, I've heard of him. So what's he, like my dad? Decided to come home and play daddy all of a sudden?"

Lucy gasped. "Parker, that is rude—"

"This is bullshit!" Parker exploded. "I don't need some long-lost daddy. I'm doing just fine."

Yeah? The kid's attitude said differently. Brogan wasn't Parker's dad, but it was obvious the kid needed one, or someone to keep him in line. He'd heard enough. He hit the brakes in front of the school and stopped. Alarm widened Parker's blue eyes as he caught Brogan's expression in the rearview mirror. Brogan turned and blasted the little snot with his fiercest scowl.

"Let's get something straight. I'm *not* your daddy. I'm sure you've heard a lot of gossip in this town, but none of it is true about me being your daddy. And if you don't believe me, I'll be happy to take a paternity test." Parker crossed his arms over his skinny chest. "But I'm gonna be your worst nightmare if I ever hear you speak to your aunt Lucy or your mom like I've heard just now. Do you understand?" he growled.

Parker stared out the window. "Yeah, whatever."

"Nope. Not good enough. Apologize to—"

Lucy's small hand gripped his wrist, pressing his nautical rope bracelet into his skin. "Brogan, it's all right. He didn't mean anything—"

He didn't give Lucy a chance to finish. "Apologize to your aunt…*now*."

Parker cut his sullen gaze to him and held it for a few beats, but when he looked at Lucy, he swallowed hard and lowered his lids. "Sorry, Aunt Lucy."

"Sure, Parks."

Brogan eased Lucy's death grip on his wrist. "How many beers did you drink?" he asked Parker in a calm voice.

"I didn't—"

"How many?"

Parker shifted in his seat, turning his cell phone over in his hands. "One. Not even. I only had a few sips. Give me a Breathalyzer test if you don't believe me."

Brogan waited. Parker lifted his stubborn chin. "I don't even like the stuff. It's kinda gross."

Brogan remembered that too. "Okay. I believe you." He settled back in his seat, more than ready for this night to be over.

Parker leaned forward, grabbing Lucy's headrest. "Aunt Lucy, you gonna tell my mom?"

"Um, well, I don't know. She's going to ask, and…"

Pure panic replaced the tension as Parker spoke. "Don't! I swear not to do it again. She doesn't have to know. I'll be real quiet when we get home and go straight to bed. Please, Aunt Lucy. It might upset her… and something might happen to…you know…her." Parker's voice trailed off as he struggled to tamp down his emotions. The impulse to shake his fist at the skies and howl at the moon came over Brogan. One more screwed-up boy trying to wrestle the world without the guidance of a father.

Lucy glanced at Brogan, searching for answers. What the hell did he know? Maybe tonight was a wake-up call, and Parker really would behave from now on. And then again, maybe not. Brogan gave Lucy a pathetic shrug.

Lucy blinked. "Okay, Parks. Just this once. But don't test me again, understood?"

Parker nodded. "Thanks, Aunt Lucy."

They drove the next five miles in silence, until

Brogan pulled into their driveway, and before he'd put the car in park, Parker bolted.

"Thanks again, Aunt Lucy," he called as he raced toward the front door.

"*Shhh*, you'll wake your mom," Lucy hissed.

Parker disappeared inside without making a sound.

"You think I'm doing the right thing?" A tiny frown creased her brow. Witnessing Lucy's anxiety did something weird to his insides. Made him want to step up and take charge…set things right.

"We'll see. I think this isn't the first time he's slipped out."

"Yeah, me too."

Brogan opened her door and tugged on her hand. "Come on." Pulling her behind him, he said, "I've got an idea that might work."

Lucy skipped in her Keds to keep up. "Good. Does it involve metal bars and one meal a day of stale bread and tepid water?"

He stopped under the covered entrance and released her hand. "He's going out for football, right?"

Light from the outdoor sconces made her blond highlights shimmer. "Yeah," she said slowly. "Practice starts Monday, why?"

"Have him up and ready to leave tomorrow at six a.m."

"Like in tomorrow morning?"

"I'm afraid so."

Her shoulders sagged. "I hate early-morning assignments. I'd rather be dragged around town by my tongue."

Brogan smiled and wondered how she'd look first thing in the morning, with sleepy eyes and mussed-up hair. Dangerous thoughts. He shook his head and refocused on the problem at hand.

"This will be different. Make sure he's dressed in workout clothes and running shoes. I'm taking him to the track at the school."

"No one should rise before six. It's inhumane." A small pout formed on her lips.

Lips Brogan wanted to kiss. But kissing Lucy was still a bad idea…for tonight.

"I'll make it worth your while. I promise." He smiled down at her flushed face and suspicious gray eyes.

He watched as she seemed to wrestle with wanting to argue but instead weighed her next words. "Why are you doing this?" His brow lifted. "Why are you helping me?"

Why indeed. He'd spent half the day wrestling his own demons about the dad he'd never known. He didn't need to take on Lucy's and Parker's problems too. But something about Lucy felt like unfinished business. He couldn't put a finger on it, but he sensed it. She intrigued him with her courage and honesty. Her willingness to open up. Rage had drummed through him, vibrating every cell, when she'd told him how Tony the dick Tiger had screwed her. He hated like hell that she'd been hurt. But he didn't put voice to any of those thoughts. Instead, he simply said, "Because that's what friends do. Help each other."

"If you say so." The doubt written all over her face said she didn't believe him. Tough. She didn't have a choice.

"You promise to have him ready? At six?" he asked as she reached for the doorknob.

"Yeah, yeah, yeah. And when I open this door, there better be a box of hot Krispy Kreme doughnuts in your hands."

"Even better than that. A hot, homemade banana nut muffin."

"Hmmm. Krispy Kremes are hard to beat." She paused. "Add a large latte."

"Deal." He grinned, thrusting his hand out. She wavered before slipping hers into his. He squeezed with a gentle shake, savoring the feel of her small palm pressed against his.

Reaching up, she gave his right shoulder an offhanded pat. "You look like a nice guy, but I know you're up to no good." She opened the front door. "That banana nut muffin better be worth it," she said before slipping inside.

Brogan moved through his dark, empty house, dodging construction debris left over from the crews, until he settled in his bedroom, the only room still intact. Propped up in his queen bed, wearing only boxers and a goofy smile on his face, he cruised through sports channels on the ancient bulky TV still sitting on top of his dresser.

Something about Lucy ate at him, making him want to help her. The huge chip on Parker's shoulder would be hard to knock off, but he'd placed his money on Lucy. He didn't doubt that she'd win Parker over, but there'd be some severe bruising and battering in the process. Taming a stubborn teenager with attitude had to be one tough job. He didn't know anything about raising teenagers, but he remembered the hell his mother went through when he'd started to give her trouble.

With the remote in one hand, he stretched his other arm behind his head. That had to be the reason he'd volunteered to train Parker at the crack of dawn. Atoning for his own sins against his mom. Brogan rolled his shoulders. Nothing like an early morning workout to knock the 'tude right out of a guy. It would be good preparation for Parker.

Exercise had become an addiction to Brogan and had eased a lot of pain over the years. Like whenever he thought about his dad, who'd abandoned him when he was two. Or why his mom never spoke about it. Or the night he'd pulled the stupidest stunt of his life by having celebratory sex without protection. Didn't get much dumber than that.

Yep, he was a healthy guy, and so were his swimmers. After one night of not suiting up and what he thought had been no-strings-attached sex, he found himself two months later standing inside a small chapel along the Chesapeake Bay, pledging his love to Kathryn St. Johns, his biggest investor's *pregnant* daughter. Brogan still winced, picturing his mom sitting in the first row, wearing a pale-yellow silk suit and a strained, worried look on her face. He hated that he'd been the one to put that look there. But that paled in comparison to what he really hated—the panic he'd felt at being trapped and how often he'd thought about running…just like his dad.

Brogan pressed the Off button, plunging the room into darkness, and tossed the remote on his nightstand. He rolled to his side, punching his pillow beneath his head. The fear and anxiety he'd felt the day he'd married

Kathryn made his chest constrict in terror, but the knife-stabbing pain to his heart twisted whenever he thought of the miscarriage two months after the wedding. He and Kathryn had stuck it out five long months after losing the baby before separating. And for three excruciating years, he'd swallowed the overwhelming urge to flee and struggled to work things out. The sharp edge of failing sliced his insides to ribbons. But in the end, the broken marriage won the fight. Too many holes in the bottom of the boat. He couldn't save the sinking vessel. It never got easier. He still felt the pinching inside his skull, even after all this time.

You didn't build a marriage on one bottle of Jack Daniel's and a night of drunken sex. There had been no real love—not even much lust. Just responsibility topped with a heavy dose of guilt. He'd paid for his mistake with a high-priced divorce, a very expensive buyout, and a lifelong distaste for whiskey. Now, permanent relationships remained crossed off his list, and he never traveled without a healthy supply of condoms.

Tossing on his bed, he kicked his blue cotton quilt to the side. The irony in all this had to be, no matter how careful he'd become, he was still being accused of fathering someone's child. His swimmers hadn't been anywhere near Julia...*ever*. Sure, he and Julia had made out...a lot. And a few times they'd come pretty darn close, but for some unspoken reason, they'd always stopped.

He flopped on his back, staring at the shadowed ceiling. A face-to-face talk with Julia was long overdue. By telling the truth, she could put a stop to all the nonsense and gossip Harmony thrived on. Not for one second did he believe Julia went around saying Parker was his kid, but it was what she *didn't* say that fueled the rumor mills. Shutting that mill down and encouraging the town to support their golden boy was on top of his to-do list. An idea had been percolating since running into Lucy. She didn't know it yet, but her temp days might be a thing of the past.

Chapter 9

LUCY STUMBLED DOWNSTAIRS, NOT BECAUSE SHE wanted to be awake at 5:45 on a Saturday morning, but because her nose smelled coffee, and she always followed her nose when it picked up a delectable scent. Sitting at the round oak table in the kitchen was the reason for the bags under her eyes and her foggy head.

Brogan.

Again.

Looking gorgeous and well rested. Not dog tired, wearing an oversized Georgia Tech T-shirt, one fuzzy green sock, and a pillow-creased face. Lucy had lain awake half the night, reprimanding her heart for pitter-pattering over Brogan. She'd certainly lost her fair share of sleepless nights over the heartbreaker of Harmony High. She didn't want to spend her early thirties in a repeat performance. But every time he appeared interested or showed any sign of caring, Lucy's heart went whirligig crazy, and she'd start to hope…again. And didn't that add to her crankiness at this god-awful hour?

"Why am I living in the nightmare on Daffodil Lane? And what is that green slime you're drinking?" Lucy pointed to the large BetterBites tumbler in his hand. He jumped up with way too much energy and pulled out her chair.

"Good morning, Little Lucy. As per your request"—he

slid an extra-large cup from the Daily Grind toward her—"a piping-hot latte and the best banana nut muffins you'll ever put in your mouth." Lucy peeked inside a brown-and-green BetterBites bag and spied two jumbo, delicious-looking muffins. "Still warm. Just came out of the oven," he said, using his rich voice designed to soothe cranky, non-morning persons.

Lucy sipped her coffee, hoping to jostle her brain awake as she dug in the bag and pulled out a sticky muffin that smelled of bananas, nuts, and total delicious-ness. "Do I have to share?" She broke a piece off and popped it in her mouth. Coconut, vanilla, and banana danced on her tongue. "Mmm, these are good." Lucy sipped more coffee and broke off another piece.

"Better than Krispy Kremes?" Brogan asked, his moss-green eyes twinkling as he dropped back into his chair and reached for his cup of slime.

"Nothing is better than hot Krispy Kremes, but these aren't bad." She pointed with her coffee cup. "What is that green stuff? It looks vile."

"Energy smoothie. Made with kale, cucumber, honey dew, and protein powder."

She recoiled at the listed ingredients.

"I made one for Parker too. Where is he?"

At the mention of the runaway-teen-aunt-hater, Parker stumbled into the kitchen, wearing long Nike basketball shorts, running shoes, and a case of bedhead worse than Lucy's.

"Here's my sweet, adorable, sneaky nephew. Good morning, Parker."

Through sleepy eyes, Parker still managed a pretty effec-tive glare-down. Brogan jumped up again, making Lucy dizzy with all his morning energy. "Have a seat, Parker. Your smoothie is in the fridge." He opened the refrigerator and pulled out another cup of slime, handing it to Parker. "Drink up. You're going to need the boost of energy."

"Why do I have to do this? Why am I being punished? I said I was sorry." Parker eyed the drink with trepidation. Lucy didn't quite blame him. "This looks like sheee…gross. I'm not drinking it." On this, Lucy agreed with the kid. She gulped more coffee, hiding behind her cup.

"Drink it. Or you'll be sorry when you lose steam halfway through our run." Brogan shot Parker a stern look. "Football takes a lot of hard physical work, and if you want to be any good, you have to be dedicated to getting in shape, eating right, and getting plenty of sleep." Brogan leaned his forearms on the table. "Sneaking out at night and drinking beer isn't going to help you make the team. It will catch up with you. I know."

Lucy didn't know anything about working out or trying out for football, but she knew Brogan had been an incredible athlete. And from the way his muscles bulged in his arms and the looks of his strong legs, she had no doubts he still knew what he was talking about. Slumped lower in his seat, Parker took a tentative sip of the nasty sludge. Lucy barely suppressed a shudder.

"You almost done there, Lucy?" Brogan asked in an easy tone that didn't match the calculated look behind his eyes.

"Not exactly. Why?" she answered slowly.

"You need to change. Unless you want to go in your"—he motioned at her ratty T-shirt—"tarp, or whatever you're wearing."

"Go? I'm not going anywhere." Alarm colored her voice. Parker perked up, sitting straighter as he continued to drink his smoothie.

"We won't make you run sprints, but you can walk the track while we exercise. Right, Parker?"

"Yeah, sure. Why not? If I have to, then you should too. Don't you want to set a good example?" What Lucy really wanted was to wash all that sarcasm out of her nephew's beautiful mouth, starting with the green gunk.

Brogan checked his electric-blue techno sports watch. "Parker, finish up. Go get changed, Lucy. We're leaving in five."

Panic started to set in. "But I have to be here for Julia. She's going to need—"

"Mom won't wake up before nine. We *will* be done before that." Parker challenged Brogan with his look.

"We'll be back in plenty of time." Brogan grabbed the bag with the remaining muffin and closed it up. "Take your coffee. I have water in the car."

This went beyond her job description. "What did I ever do to deserve this? I'd rather be clipping Mrs. Bunkins's toenails than exercising at six in the freakin' morning." She headed for the stairs to the sound of Brogan's laughter.

At the school track, Brogan and Parker warmed up their muscles by stretching. Brogan moved with the ease of a finely tuned athlete, and skinny, lanky Parker followed his examples. A spark of interest showed in how Parker listened at Brogan's instructions, given in a low tone.

Lucy sat on one of the metal bleachers, sipping her

coffee in the muggy morning air. The temperature hadn't reached stifling, but by midmorning, it would be a scorcher. Bugs swarmed in circles over the grassy field, and the air smelled damp with morning dew. When she'd left the kitchen earlier, she'd splashed cold water on her face to help the wake-up process, thrown on a pair of yellow nylon Nike shorts, an orange-and-white T-shirt with "Eat a Peach" on the back, and sneakers. She'd knotted her hair on top of her head and wore a skinny rubber headband to keep the flyaways off her face. Not that she had any intention of taking off down the track like Brogan and Parker, whose long legs made running look effortless. Not in this lifetime. She was content to sit and watch the glorious display of well-toned muscles rippling under bronzed skin—Brogan's, of course. Not her nephew's. That would be creepy.

When Brogan approached her, he had Parker doing short sprints between orange cones on the red-surfaced track. "Time to get your legs moving." He reached for her hand.

"Not gonna happen. I'm not running with you guys." She tried pulling back, with no success, as he propelled her off the bleachers. "And *why* am I being tortured? I wasn't the one who snuck out after curfew."

"Come on. You don't have to run, but you can walk a few laps, right?" Brogan placed her coffee cup on the bleacher. "Do a few jumping jacks to get your heart and legs moving." He cocked his head. "Please. Don't you want to set a good example for Parker?"

No. She really wanted to crawl back into bed and sleep for a month. Preferably with Brogan. Except with him, she'd be doing more than sleeping. *What?* Lucy's naughty thoughts shocked her into jumping like no Jack had ever seen.

Brogan chuckled. "Slow it down there, Richard Simmons. You'll give yourself a heart attack." He trotted toward Parker as she slowed her flapping arms and legs to a more normal speed, enjoying the view. Straining muscles and glistening sweat on Brogan Reese was a mighty fine sight. Maybe she'd learn to run or jog or jump rope or whatever if it meant ogling his chiseled form. Inspiration didn't come any finer. Sigh. Lucy sucked in huge breaths as Brogan and Parker headed down the track in a fast jog.

Just when she thought she'd dodged the exercise bullet, Brogan turned and jogged backward. "Come on, Lucy! Start walking. Give me two laps." She'd like to give him a kick to his shin in her pointed Jimmy Choo pumps.

"Don't make me come get you," he yelled, laughing.

"Go on. Be healthy. I'm walking, but that doesn't mean I have to like it," she yelled back as she started around the track at a brisk pace.

—⁓—

Brogan couldn't keep the smile from his face as he drove a pooped Parker and perky Lucy back to their house. Parker had risen to the challenge and shown real potential. After Brogan had shared stories about his playing days, Parker had warmed up to him and started listening, asking smart questions about running plays and leading as quarterback. Even Little Lucy showed promise as she power walked three laps around the track. Bright pink glowed on her cheeks, and light shone

in her gray eyes. Exercise looked good on Lucy…real
good. He tried not to stare at the trickle of perspira-
tion that snaked down her neck, across her chest, and
into her rock-star cleavage. Her V-neck T-shirt clung
to her form, and he didn't dare contemplate what "Eat
a Peach" meant, because it conjured up images of juicy,
sweet peaches, along with other fantasies. All starring
Lucy in various stages of undress. *Slam that door
closed, man.* Not now. Not here. And not with Little
Lucy Doolan.

"Well, this has been an interesting morning. Can't
say I've ever spent one like it before," Lucy said as she
pressed the icy water bottle to her flushed cheeks and
then to her heated chest. Brogan tore his gaze away
and concentrated on the curve in the road approaching
Daffodil Lane.

"How do you feel, Parker?" she asked.

"Fine."

"You did real well out there. I was impressed.
Looking forward to starting practice on Monday?"

"I guess. Maybe if I had more…" Stubborn pride
stopped Parker as he shifted in the backseat, crossing
his arms over his sweaty T-shirt.

What was one more day with the kid? He was going
to exercise anyway, so if the kid wanted to join him,
then he didn't have a problem. "I'll be by tomorrow.
Same time. We can run a few different drills. Okay?"

"Yeah, sure. I can do that." Eagerness lit Parker's
usually sullen face.

"Gah! Does this mean what I think it means?"
Lucy said.

Brogan pulled the car in the driveway and killed

the engine. "Drink plenty of liquids today and eat some protein," he said to Parker's image in the rearview mirror.

"Got it. See ya tomorrow, Brogan." Parker bounded from the backseat.

"And no more sneaking out," Brogan called before Parker slammed the car door and vaulted over the blooming daylilies, heading for the front door.

He turned to Lucy's flushed, suspicious face.

"Please tell me I'm not getting up again at the godforsaken hour of six."

"No can do." Her gray eyes narrowed under thick lashes. "I'll bring more coffee and another treat." He grinned. "Admit it. You had fun." She gave a snort. "You were even singing while you walked…I guess it was singing. Sounded more like a dying bullfrog. Hard to tell."

Lucy rubbed her damp hands down the front of her shorts. "Everyone sounds like a dying bullfrog when they try to imitate Adele. If you don't want me to offend your ears, you better add earbuds to your list of goodies. I can't find mine."

"How's that going to help? You'll sing even louder because you can't hear yourself."

"Not me. I only improve when I hear the music." Lucy snapped her fingers and started swaying in her seat as she belted a verse from "Rumour Has It."

"Christ. Stop that croaking. I'll bring buds and earplugs for Parker and me."

Lucy snapped her mouth shut and grinned. "Thanks. You're a real prince. Now, I need to check on the bedridden princess inside and eat a box of Pop-Tarts. Want some?"

She had the diet of a river rat. "Hell no. Eat something healthy."

She reached for the door handle. "Okay. I'll eat a Snickers bar. It's chock-full of peanuts." He glared at her. "What?"

"Look, give me an hour, and I'll be back to pick you up. I'll bring some food when I come."

"Why are you coming back? I don't need a food Nazi calculating my intake."

"To help you get your car. Remember? The steaming bucket of bolts you left on the side of the road? If we don't hurry, someone's gonna cart it off and park it next to their double-wide and use it as a dog house."

"Pickled pops on a stick." She gave a huge sigh that drew his attention to her plump breasts. He tried leveling his gaze on her stubborn chin. "Okay. But you better not bring any quinoa or flaxseed. I hate that stuff." She hopped from the car and slammed the door. As she trotted toward the house, he couldn't help but admire the cute sway of her butt. She looked good in workout clothes. She probably looked even better out of them. Nope. Not gonna happen. He shook his head, willing away the image of Lucy wearing only him and a satisfied smile. Nothing a pile of unpaid bills and crunching lagging sales numbers with Javier wouldn't cure. That and maybe three or thirty cold showers and having his eyes surgically removed from his head.

"Candy corn niblets." Lucy rushed around the kitchen, trying to make Julia's eggs as specified. Her success rate didn't seem any better than the day before. The good news: Parker actually spoke in a civil tone when she asked him to pour his mom's cranberry juice and fix her special mint-flavored water.

She slid the mangled eggs on the Lenox china plate rimmed with pink roses. "They don't look so bad, do they?"

Parker leaned over her shoulder and grunted. "I wouldn't eat 'em."

Neither would she.

"Parker, run outside and pick some of those black-eyed Susans for your mom. Let's make her tray pretty, and maybe she won't notice the burnt toast and green eggs and ham."

"Yeah, like that's gonna help," he mumbled. "She's pregnant, not blind."

"Lucy! What's taking so long?" Julia's bellow carried down the hall.

"Parker, hurry." He dragged his feet to the back door as she opened upper cabinets, searching for a bud vase. "Coming, Julia! Be there in a sec."

Parker returned moments later, holding three black-eyed Susan's with their perfect black velvet middles. "Nice. See that vase up there?" She pointed to the top shelf. "Pull it down for me, please."

He reached up without standing on his toes or having to drag a stepladder over. So unfair. "Thanks." She filled the vase with water and shoved the flowers in. Picking up the tray, she asked, "You coming?"

Parker opened the fridge and peered inside. "In a minute."

"Oh…okay. Well, I'm off. You know…to feed your mom and—"

"Aunt Lucy, quit stalling. She gets bitch…er, crabby when she doesn't eat."

Bitchy. He had it right the first time. "Right. Okay, wish me luck."

Parker gave her the you're-so-weird-I-can't-believe-we're-related look. Lucy straightened her shoulders and marched down the hall to the ominous tune of *Jaws* playing inside her head.

Chapter 10

"Mom...Aunt Lucy. Brogan's here," Parker announced forty-five minutes later as he rapped his knuckles on his mom's bedroom door. Lucy had been taking extensive notes on all that needed to be done that day, while trying to keep from bludgeoning herself with the brass andirons framing the fireplace. Lucy didn't envy her stepsister. Sitting around all day had to be as boring as watching hair grow. But this to-do list as long as her arm made Lucy's temp job as the U-Store-Em manager, where she sat in a trailer and babysat empty self-storage units, seem like a day on South Beach.

"Brogan? Really?" Julia perked up at the mention of her old boyfriend. "Parks, tell him to come in." Parker nodded and turned to go. "Wait! Give me five minutes." Julia smoothed the front of her light-pink cotton tank top that did nothing to hide the tops of her voluptuous, milk-filled breasts. "Luce, grab my hairbrush, mirror, and makeup bag on the bathroom counter."

Great. Helping her beautiful sister primp for Brogan made her stomach queasy.

"And don't forget my eyelash curler," Julia said as Lucy rummaged through her sister's designer cosmetics in the master bathroom.

Five minutes and a glamorized Julia later, Brogan strolled through the bedroom door, holding a beautiful bouquet of light-pink peonies and a green shopper filled with food from BetterBites. "Hey there, Julia. How you feeling?" he asked in a soft, concerned voice intended to soothe the crabbiest of hearts.

"Brogan." His name rolled off her tongue in a sigh. "For me?" Perfectly manicured hands reached for the bouquet. "They're lovely." She brought the flowers to her nose, inhaling while slanting him a provocative glance. "Lucy, be a love and put these in some water." Julia used her saccharine-sweet voice, which grated on Lucy's last remaining nerve. Thrusting the bouquet at her with one hand, Julia indicated the pink chair with her other. "Brogan, please sit."

Brogan paused before dropping into the chair. A whiff of clean soap and expensive leather reached Lucy's nose as he filled the feminine room, giving it a much-needed boost of testosterone. Leaning on his forearms, he fiddled with the straps of the shopper. Brogan wore a green polo shirt with a yellow BetterBites logo over his left breast, and a tight expression on his face. Maybe sitting in a room the color of Pepto-Bismol, with a seven-month pregnant ex-girlfriend, made him uncomfortable. Lucy couldn't imagine why.

"I'll put these in water," she said, watching Julia preen like a pink flamingo, slicking her tongue over rosy-glossed lips. Brogan cleared his throat and shifted in his seat. Awkward.

"Lucy, bring Brogan a drink, please," Julia ordered.

"No! Thank you. No drink for me." The frantic sound of his tone made Lucy pause.

"Are you sure? Lucy doesn't mind. That's what she's here for." Big blue eyes batted in Brogan's direction.

To fetch and wait on Julia and her entourage. Funny, Lucy thought she was here to help take care of Parker and to keep Julia from going into early labor.

Brogan nodded. "Positive."

"Oh. Well, Lucy, please brew a pot of fresh coffee. Amanda and Marcia are stopping by for a visit," she said in a clipped voice.

"Yes, ma'am!" Lucy saluted and bowed out of the room but not before she caught Julia's bitchy glare-down and Brogan's attempt to hide a chuckle with a forced cough.

Lucy dropped the bouquet of peonies on the creamy tile countertop and started the pot of coffee. The nosy part of her wished she'd stayed in the room to hear the reuniting couple's every word. The freaked-out part wanted to run to the nearest bar and get snockered. Staying away all these years had done nothing to her stupid, weak heart. Talk about a dumb muscle. It did nothing but race, causing high blood pressure, and then broke into millions of pieces every time she allowed it to surge, searching for love.

Opening upper cabinets, she hunted for a vase. Parker, having mastered "evade and hide," had bolted downstairs to play his computer games. She hated to call him back up to help her hunt. She spied a crystal vase tucked in the corner on the highest shelf. She went in search of a stepladder but came up empty. She improvised by pushing an old ladder-back kitchen chair with a rush seat next to the counter. Jiggling it to test for sturdiness, she started to climb.

"What are you doing?"

Lucy wobbled at the sound of Brogan's voice, and

the rush seat beneath her feet gave a moaning creak. "Whoa." She grabbed hold of the cabinet door for stability at the same time Brogan encircled her waist in a tight grip. The seat creaked again under her weight. "I don't like the sounds of that."

"Me either." He lifted her by the waist and placed her feet back on the sturdy tile floor. "Allow me." He pointed with his finger. "Which one?"

Brain freeze. Brogan's other hand still rested on her waist as if it belonged there, causing temporary amnesia. "Uh, the crystal one in the right corner," she said, shaking her head clear.

Lucy stepped away from Brogan's heat. "Where's Parker? He could've gotten it for you."

With trembling hands, Lucy placed the vase under the kitchen faucet. "He already played Green Giant earlier, and I hated to ask again." She arranged the peonies. "There. Perfect." She extended the flowers to Brogan, maintaining a proper distance.

He picked up the BetterBites shopper and turned his back as he started unloading containers of prepared food in the refrigerator.

"Don't you want to take the flowers to Julia?"

"Not really," he said with his head halfway inside the fridge.

"Oh. All done reminiscing? That didn't take long." And didn't that make Lucy happy?

"I'll be back. We have more catching up to do. Today, we discussed business." He finished emptying the bag. "Tell Parker to take the flowers to his mother. You ready to go?"

Yes. No. Not with you. Again. Sheesh.

"Okay, give me a sec." She placed the peonies on the kitchen table and went to the opened basement door. "Parker? Come here, please." To Brogan, waiting patiently in the kitchen, she said, "Be right back."

In her bedroom she retrieved her handbag. She caught her reflection in the white oval mirror over her dresser. Biting her bottom lip, she hesitated for less than a second before rushing into the bathroom and pulling a comb through her hair, securing it with a ponytail holder, swiping mascara on her eyelashes and blush on her cheeks. She reached for her favorite bottle of Viva la Juicy and spritzed behind her ears and down her cleavage. Smoothing her hair one last time, she left the room and reentered the kitchen. Parker slouched against the countertop, waiting.

"Parker, please deliver these flowers to your mom. Fresh coffee has been brewed. Amanda and Marcia can serve themselves." She motioned to the coffeepot and mugs on the counter. "I'm going to pick up my poor car and then run your mom's errands. Anything you need while I'm out?"

Parker shoved his hands in the back of his bright-blue Nike shorts and gave Lucy his classic bored look. "What's for lunch? I'm starved."

"Oh. Lunch. Didn't you just eat breakfast?"

"I've stocked the fridge with some healthy meals you can microwave. There's fresh fruit too. Keep drinking water to stay hydrated," Brogan said, digging for his keys in his pocket.

Parker gave a jerky nod. "Sure."

"Wow, Parker. Looks like you've got your own personal trainer," Lucy said.

"Not officially, but I have trained enough over the years and know from experience." Brogan pointed a finger at Parker. "Do not follow your aunt's lead in the food department." He gestured at the package of Double Stuf Oreos on the countertop.

"Studies have shown that chocolate is good for you." Lifting her nose, she shoved the cookies in an upper cabinet and closed the door.

"*Dark* chocolate, and only in small quantities."

"Whatever." Lucy ruffled Parker's soft, dark hair. "Call if you need me." She leaned close to tuck down the tag at his collar and whispered, "I'll bring you a milk shake from the Dog." Surprised, Parker's face brightened, and Lucy winked.

Lucy's citrusy scent filled the interior of his car and Brogan's head as he drove down Main Street back toward the highway.

Being back in the Doolan/Brooks house, where he'd spent a huge portion of his high school days, brought back a rush of memories. Most good, but not all. Since Brogan had grown up an only child, he'd always enjoyed spending time with other kids and their families. Even if it meant witnessing Julia and Lucy bicker or Mr. Doolan fawn over his second wife, Babs. Maybe not the perfect all-American family, but it had come close enough. He'd have given his throwing arm to have a sibling to boss or fight with. Since his mom had worked full time, he'd come home from school to Tulip, the housekeeper. Once in a while, Tulip's son, Deshawn, would be there, and he'd toss the football with him, but mostly Brogan would be alone.

Today, sitting in Mr. Doolan's master bedroom, talking to a flirty, pregnant Julia had felt strange. He should've stayed and forced Julia to talk about Parker's real dad, but he'd chickened out. Harsh memories had washed over him at Julia's decision to keep Parker in the dark. He'd experienced that same black history. Remembering the embarrassment and shame he'd felt when other kids would ask why he didn't have a dad and never having an answer...made it worse. At those uncomfortable times, Brogan had resented his mom and her stubborn pride.

Instead, with Julia, he'd provided specifics about his mom's house and how much he wanted to net. The mention of a potential sale lit Julia's eyes. Her business mask replaced her flirtatious face. Whenever Julia wanted something, she got that scary, calculated look, and nothing or no one could sway her otherwise.

Brogan harbored no illusions that Julia had pined over him all these years. Parker and the baby on the way proved she hadn't joined a nunnery. No, Julia had set her course in life and showed little signs of suffering. The real mystery was Lucy. Somewhere beneath the straight hair, suspicious eyes, and feisty mouth was a story. A unique story with a pinch of sadness peppered with humor, piquing his curiosity.

"Looks busy today. You get a lot of traffic in your store?" she remarked at the shoppers crowding the sidewalk on Main.

Not nearly enough. "Some. Still need to get our name out. Keith Morgan's tennis academy has helped, because the players training want healthy food."

"Some guys in tennis clothes just went inside,"

she said, swiveling her head and peering out the back window.

Good. "How many?" He tried to keep the desperate edge at bay. The business needed picking up fast, or he'd be missing his NYC deadline in September. The fighter inside him wouldn't abandon Harmony's BetterBites. Determination and pure stubbornness drove him. Harmony's location would thrive with the help of the new hometown attraction: Lucy.

He glanced at his ticket to success sitting uncomfortably stiff next to him. Getting her to agree was the rub.

"Ran into Amanda and Marcia this morning. Did they warn you about stopping by?"

"Yeah, they texted me. I'll run Julia's errands while the Witches of Harmony hold their broomstick convention. Give them time to plot their revenge without my presence."

"Revenge? What are you talking about?"

Lucy shot him a wary look. "You know. Since I chopped off her hair, Julia has never really gotten me back. She's either planning to shave my head and tattoo a scary, fire-breathing dragon across my chest or boss me into an early grave with her incessant demands and endless lists."

"But you were banished from your home the last two years of high school. Personally, I thought the punishment didn't fit the crime."

Lucy straightened in her seat. "Not exactly banished. I chose to leave, since Julia and I never got along. At the time, it felt right." Brogan's knuckles tightened around the steering wheel at the crack in her voice. "I was young and foolish, leaving all my friends my junior and senior year to live with my grandparents in Chattanooga. Starting over was tough." *Twip* went a lock of hair around her finger. "I still came home…for vacations and holidays. Unless they weren't going to be here. Babs would arrange these silly trips to Dollywood or Graceland and whisk my dad away."

Lucy crossed her arms and tucked her chin. "As a kid, all I could see was some woman and her daughter taking away my dad. Whacking Julia's hair and gluing her butt in biology was wrong, but as a threatened fifteen-year-old, it was my only weapon."

Brogan had stopped on the shoulder of the narrow two-lane highway behind Lucy's broken-down car. "I remember when you left. I was angry and thought you didn't get a fair deal. So you pulled a few pranks." He shrugged. "I knew what Julia used to do to you."

Lucy blinked in shock. "How did you know?"

"Because Julia had a mean-girl streak and loved to spread baseless rumors. I wasn't as blinded by love as you think." Lucy shifted uncomfortably, and Brogan spied light-pink lace hugging the tops of her breasts beneath her pink tank top. He bit hard on the inside of his cheek.

Lucy fluttered her hand. "Water under the bridge. High school is so dumb. Why do we give it such power over our lives?"

"Because it's a powerful transition from childhood into adulthood. Breaking away from total parental dependency and forging long-term friendships. It becomes a part of you. Even if you don't want it to."

Sheesh, you could say that again. This time Lucy zipped her loose lips. Old hurts and embarrassed feelings rushed to the surface, causing shortness of breath. These were the very reasons she hadn't wanted to be back in Harmony, reliving her awkward high school days, invoking old memories. They had caused endless nights of soaking her favorite Spice Girls pillow with hot tears.

Outside the car, Brogan reached for the jug of coolant from his trunk. "What did you do after graduating from college?"

"Worked in marketing in Atlanta for the convention center downtown, but when the economy tanked…all the new hires lost their jobs."

Brogan gave an understanding nod as he popped the hood to Lucy's car. "So you took up temp work?"

"Not exactly. I worked for a couple of small companies before getting into temp work. Temp work wasn't all bad. It allowed me the time to consult with small businesses and boost their sales." Lucy shook her head. Somewhere along the line, she had started chasing a paycheck, losing sight of her goals and ending up helping Anthony for almost three years achieve his ambitions…instead of her own.

At least with Julia's pregnancy, an end was in sight. That baby couldn't stay in her belly forever. Just enough time to reconnect with her nephew and for Lucy to mend fences with Julia.

A loud whoosh sounded as the breath escaped her lungs. Maybe because she stood on the side of the highway with Brogan, under the hood of her poor baby, as he added coolant. Efficient and sure with his movements, appearing perfect and pristine next to her tired car. Startled by the contrast, Lucy rolled a hank of hair around her finger. She recalled a time when she'd looked pristine and professional next to her shiny, new car. What had happened to that Lucy on the brink of a brilliant future?

"You need help?"

Brogan dropped the hood in place. "I'm good. That should do it, but this car needs work."

So did Lucy. "Sorry you've wasted your Saturday morning. I'll drive over to Grady's and park it in his lot. Hopefully, he'll return before Labor Day."

Brogan brushed off his hands. "You have other transportation?" He carried the empty jug of coolant to his trunk.

"I'll borrow Julia's minivan until she's fixed. Here's money for the coolant." Light feathers danced up her arm as his fingers pushed away the cash in her hand.

"You can keep your money."

"I insist. I need to pay you…or something." A glint sparked to life in his eye, and his crooked smile appeared.

"Or something," he said, closing his trunk, making Lucy jump; whether from the noise or what he implied, she had no idea. "Keys." He held out his hand.

"Huh?" She fished for her keys in the front pocket of her pink paisley shorts.

"I'll drive your poor baby over to Grady's. You can follow in the Jag."

Lucy's head jerked up. "Seriously?" Absolutely not. He'd done enough for one day. He didn't need to sweat in her overheated car that might or might not make it into town.

Brogan plucked the keys from her fingers. "Yeah. Let me make sure she starts."

Lucy trotted behind him, her tan ballet flats crunching in the gravel. "No. I'll drive her. You don't know how she operates. She can be real temperamental."

He shot her an incredulous expression, snorting as he opened the driver's door.

"Typical female. I think I can manage. But maybe you better follow close behind in case I need your help." His condescending tone washed away all the pleasant thoughts she'd been having about him.

"Suit yourself. She's tricky. Likes to sputter and conk off if you don't treat her right. Takes a firm hand." Lucy's car had never acted up until yesterday, but Mr. Cocky didn't need to know that. Tossing his keys in the air, she caught them in her palm.

Brogan laughed. "I've got firm hands. I think she'll like them. Most temperamental women do."

Gnawing her lower lip, she attempted to ignore his sexual innuendo. Slipping behind the wheel of the Jag, Lucy released a sigh of contentment, rubbing her palms over the smooth leather steering wheel. The engine purred to life with zero effort on her part, and thoughts of purring under the ministrations of Brogan's capable hands invaded her mind. *Oh, get over yourself.* He probably had a den of purring cats. He didn't need a lost, mewling kitty to add to his litter. Lucy secretly cheered as her loyal Honda started and then stalled for a few seconds, giving Brogan a hard time. Her poor baby was standing up for her. Lucy would take her victories wherever she could find them. But it didn't take Brogan long to gain control and pull onto the highway heading back to town.

Brogan parked the Honda in the side lot at Grady's, next to a mud-spattered pickup truck. Lucy parked alongside the two old-fashioned gas pumps. Grady didn't believe in technology and had never upgraded his tanks to take credit cards.

"Need to get the rest of my things," she said, preparing to bump the trunk with her hip.

"Wait. Let me try." Brogan depressed the key remote once, twice, and Lucy's Honda, being a typical, traitorous female when it came to hunky men, opened with no problem. "Told you. I've got the touch."

"With cranky, overheated old women…must make you proud."

"Yep." He laughed, reaching for the rest of her bags and totes.

"Hillbilly Bone" played from Lucy's cell, indicating a text. "I'm coming," she mumbled as her fingers typed an answer.

"You crushing on Blake Shelton now?" he teased.

"Nah. Trace Adkins. I love that man's moves." Brogan's interest piqued, evident by his quirked brow.

"Have you heard him in concert?"

"Not really. But I temped concessions at a big country concert in Atlanta, and he was one of the acts." She shrugged. "We could hear snippets but couldn't see anything."

Brogan shook his head as he began loading his trunk with the rest of her bags.

Lucy trotted after him. "Listen, thanks for all your help. If you could drop me at home, I'll grab the keys to Julia's car. I need to make a barbecue run. Apparently, Julia craves anything with vinegar."

Brogan turned after closing his trunk, brows raised in question.

"Look, I've learned not to ask questions. She wants a quart from Hog Wild, and she's paying me to make it happen." Hog Wild BBQ, with its base of vinegar and spices, made the best Eastern-style barbecue in all of North Carolina.

"Hog Wild it is then. Let's go." He opened the passenger door and started to slide in.

"Don't you want to drive?"

"Nope. You're doing fine. You look good in this car." He stretched his left arm out to the back of her headrest.

"Cool! You don't mind if we stop for barbecue?"

"It's on the way. We should get some for Parker too. He's probably devoured every meal in the fridge and has started on his arm by now."

Lucy accelerated out of the parking lot. "Brogan Reese promoting unhealthy pork. When will the madness end?" she teased.

"Everything in moderation, baby."

"Moderation, huh? You don't seem to take your exercise in moderation. You look like you're pretty fanatical." Lucy gave him an offhanded once-over, from the top of his wavy hair to the tips of his Nike tennis shoes, making strategic stops along the way, like his rock-hard chest, narrow hips, and...

Brogan's easy smile went from friendly to sexy as he returned the blatant perusal, giving her a taste of her own medicine. "You like what you see?" His voice held promises of hot, steamy nights under a blanket of stars, with lots of panting.

Lucy grunted. "If you're into athletic-looking, buffed guys…which I'm not."

Boisterous laughter filled the car. "No shit! Tony the dick did you a favor, and don't you ever forget it, Lucy."

It would be a long time before she'd ever forget the deviousness of Anthony and the hurt he'd dumped on her. She parked the sleek Jag at the barbecue shack. Old wooden barrels filled with wildflowers flanked the outdoor seating area at the Hog Wild BBQ. Seasoned smells of smoke and roasted pork filled the hot air. On top of the flat tin roof of the shack, a ginormous, smiling pink pig crossed his humanlike arms over the Hog Wild BBQ sign, looking pleased as punch his kin were being butchered inside.

"Speaking of pigs, Wanda came in the store the other day with Fiona and bought some organic meals."

"She mentioned she was putting Fiona on a diet." Lucy tapped on the closed window at the order counter. "I texted her yesterday. We're getting together tonight." She snapped her fingers. "That reminds me. I need to add rope to my list so I can tie Parker to his bed."

Brogan slipped off his aviator sunglasses and folded them in the vee of his shirt. "Where are you meeting Wanda?" Wary, she gave him a sharp look. His nonchalant stance with shoulder pressed to the wood-beam column did nothing to ease her distrust.

"Hey, Lucy, it's been a long time." Toby Sheldon poked his head out the order window and saved Lucy from answering Mr. Nosy.

"Hey, Toby. How you doing?"

"Can't complain. What can I get ya?"

"Quart of barbecue, coleslaw, and Brunswick stew."

"You want hush puppies with that?"

"Sure, why not?"

"Comin' right up." Toby slid the window closed to the thick air.

Brogan cleared his throat and gave Lucy the censored-dietitian look.

"It's for Parker. You can't eat barbecue without coleslaw, Brunswick stew, or hush puppies. Everyone knows that. It's un-Southern." Lucy pushed her white sunglasses on top of her head. "You've been living up North too long."

"You're avoiding my question. Where're you and Wanda going tonight?" Brogan moved, forcing her to step back until she bumped the water cooler attached to the sidewall. Instead of pulled pork, Lucy smelled mouthwatering Brogan Reese. Her ex-crush and Julia's ex-lover. Erp. That particular thought sobered her every time.

"Why do you want to know? You filing a report or something?"

"Order's up. Here you go, Lucy. Hey, Brogan." Toby slid the bags of food across the counter as Brogan greeted Toby.

Lucy handed over her money. "Thanks. Keep the change."

"Sure thing, Luce." Toby waved the bills in his hand while Brogan grabbed her bags of food.

"Take care, Toby. See ya later." She waggled her fingers at Toby's gapped-tooth grin.

"Good Lord willin' and the creek don't rise," Toby shot back. And didn't that about sum it all up?

Chapter 11

SITTING INSIDE JULIA'S GREEN MINIVAN IN WANDA Pattershaw's driveway, Lucy tapped on the horn. It was nine o'clock Saturday night, and she almost wished she were home in bed. But she'd promised Wanda they'd get together, and she hated to cancel on her best friend. Wanda's white clapboard cottage appeared to be freshly painted, along with the half-brick columns supporting the porch in front. Yellow-and-white-striped pillows sat on the green porch swing, and black shutters framed the windows. Lucy had always liked the old cottages and bungalows that dotted the streets of Harmony better than the two-story Georgian brick she'd grown up in. If she ever lived here again, she'd buy one of these older cottages and fix it up. Lucy gave her head a violent shake. *Gah! Don't even go there.*

The bright-yellow front door flung open, and Wanda lurched onto the porch, yanking on a leash.

"Oh, good Lord almighty," Lucy moaned. She jumped from the car as Wanda tugged on Fiona's collar. "Can't you leave Fiona home?" Sliding open the rear passenger door, Lucy lowered the seat for Fiona to crawl toward the back. Wanda handed her the soft pink blanket she carried.

"Spread it down so she can snuggle on it," Wanda directed. Lucy reached inside and spread the fuzzy blanket. "Come on, baby. Hop on up there…good girl." Wanda petted her snout, and Fiona snorted.

Lucy rolled her eyes. "Isn't it bad enough you have a pink-spotted pig for a pet? Do you have to attach that stupid sunflower to her head and use that gaudy glitter collar?"

"Fiona's depressed, and wearing her favorite collar and flower on her head always makes her happy. Now, quit your whining before I put a glitter collar on you."

Lucy laughed. "I've missed you." She gave Wanda a quick hug. "Let's go. I'm starved, and I need a drink or fifty. It's been a helluva day."

"Did you get everything on Princess Prima Donna's list done?"

"Everything except the most important item…new bras and panties." Fiona gave another snort in the backseat. "Exactly! Even Fiona thinks it's ridiculous. How am I supposed to buy maternity bras and panties? I have no clue where to go. You think I can buy her undies in jumbo packs at Costco?"

Wanda adjusted her sleeveless orange wrap dress that encased her voluptuous curves. Retying the bow at her waist, she gave Lucy a skeptical look. "Costco? If you've stooped that low, it's no wonder Anthony Tiger preferred Shannon…she probably had better underwear."

Lucy chuckled, ignoring the twinge of pain. "I didn't say I buy *my* unmentionables at Costco."

"Praise the Lord." Wanda pushed down on the sleeve of Lucy's white eyelet top, exposing her bra strap and half her cup.

"What the—!"

"I'm checking out the goods. Nice. Like the color.

Where did you get it?" she asked, referring to Lucy's pale-blue lacy bra. "Makes your boobs look real perky." She pushed the sleeve back up and patted Lucy's shoulder.

"That's because they are perky."

"No, they're large, but a good bra can do wonders."

"You should know…Miss Double-D Diva."

Wanda cupped her own huge breasts and lifted. "They are mighty fine, aren't they?"

"Russell always thought so."

Russell Upton had been Wanda's boyfriend since freshman year in college. They'd dated on and off for years, finally tying the knot in a small chapel in Vegas. Wanda wore a short lime-green chiffon cocktail dress with matching veiled pillbox hat, and Fiona wore a lime-green tulle tutu with a sparkly tiara and matching collar. Lucy had flown out to witness the marriage and partied the remainder of the night with Wanda and Fiona by the pool at the Hooters Casino Hotel, while Russell lost all his honeymoon money at the blackjack table. Things kind of went downhill from there. They remained married for about two years before Wanda threw Russell out and dumped his toolbox in the middle of the lake.

"Do not speak that fork-tongued man's name in my presence. I could die happy never laying eyes on him again."

"What are you talking about? I thought you were back together." Lucy stopped at the intersection of Gardenia Avenue and Walnut Street, heading toward the outskirts of town. "You said you went out last night."

"We are most definitely *not* back together. You

know he had the nerve to ask if we could skip dinner to get to the good stuff. He had to be on a job site early this morning."

Russell owned Upton's Construction: No Job 2 Small. "Well, he does work hard. Give the guy credit. What did you do? Push him out the door?"

"No. We had sex, and then I pushed him out the door."

"That's what I thought. Good girl. You sure taught him a lesson." The irony was not lost on Wanda.

"I, unlike some people I know, don't let a little pride get in the way of great sex. And Lord, that man is good in bed," she said in a dreamy voice as if picturing the twenty-one ways they'd gotten it on the night before.

"Spare me the particulars. Unless you tried a new position that I can add to my fantasy life."

"Hmmm, fantasy life. Now that's interesting. Because from what I hear, Brogan 'Fantasy' Reese is no longer only living in your head. Seems he's been sniffing around you like Old Man Cornwaddle's hound dog. Speaking of buff burritos, where is the hot chimichanga tonight?" she added in a bad Spanish accent.

Sniffing around? Craptastic. "I've only been home a day and a half! Where'd you hear that?"

"And just where do you think home is?" Wanda nudged Lucy with her elbow. "Harmony, the gossip capital of the world. Miss Sue Percy said she saw you with him early this morning on the school track. And Jo Ellen Huggins tweeted that you guys were practically doing it over a barrel at the Hog Wild. And—"

Lucy slammed on the brakes, and an indignant Fiona squealed from being jostled. "*What?* That's a bald-faced lie. We weren't *doing* anything except picking up barbecue." Lucy hated being the topic of gossip. She wasn't loco, and she *wasn't* after Brogan Reese.

Wanda bent to adjust the big bow on her gold platform sandal. "Too bad. If I didn't have Russell and his love muscle, I'd be all over Brogan 'Eat My Grits' Reese in a heartbeat."

"Oh brother. I could do without the visuals. Look, Wanda Wonderbust, there's nothing going on between me and Brogan. Have you forgotten that he and Julia have a history? History that keeps repeating itself, if Julia gets her way. And you know"—Lucy arched her eyebrow as she eased off the brake—"Julia always gets her way."

"Maybe. Hard as Julia tries with her successful business and fancy designer duds, she can't completely shed her trailer-park background. The apple doesn't fall far from the tree, my friend."

Lucy shot an outraged glare at her best friend. "Wanda, have you been swinging from power lines again? What the hoot are you talking about?"

"Are you forgetting Babs…your evil stepmother?"

If only. "She's kind of hard to forget."

"Well, Babs isn't the only Brooks woman who sleeps around. Julia may not flaunt her conquests and chase after NASCAR drivers like her mama, but it's no secret Julia shares Babs's proclivity."

Lucy blinked. "*Proclivity*…you back to reading your thesaurus?"

Wanda examined her shiny, painted orange nails. "Everyone knows Julia didn't get pregnant by some sperm bank. Quite a few boots have been found beneath her bed."

"Are you implying Julia's the harlot of Harmony?"

"I'm saying Julia gets plenty of action. She's had more boyfriends than you and I have pairs of shoes. Not all of them are from Harmony." Wanda rolled her eyes. "Around here, she acts all snooty, like getting booty is beneath her."

Julia did have clients in the neighboring cities. Lucy only hoped she practiced discretion for Parker's sake. How could Julia justify all the secrecy? Was she trying to protect Parker? Lucy kept her eyes on the pickup truck in front of her, thinking how her nephew was no dummy.

"Sooo, do you know who the fathers are?" Curiosity and cattiness were a deadly combination, but Lucy couldn't help herself.

"Besides Brogan? Not exactly."

Lucy eased off the service road and parked in front of the Rolling Pin. It was one of the few places that didn't mind pigs as customers.

"Last night, Brogan told Parker he'd take a paternity test to prove he wasn't his dad, so I'm thinking he's not. And I have no clue about the baby Julia's carrying now. She's been very tight-lipped."

"I bet Amanda and Marcia know. Get a few drinks in them, and they'll spill the dirt like an overloaded dump truck." Wanda slid the back door open and reached for Fiona. "I guarantee Julia's dirty little secret won't stay a secret forever. It will come out eventually."

"I'm surprised it hasn't already." Lucy's silver wedge sandals hit the packed, dried red clay. She stopped to adjust her short, ruffled blue skirt, which had twisted around her waist. Bluesy country music reached her ear from the small band that played on the far side of the open-air barn. Wanda cooed to Fiona in her baby-pig voice as they both headed for the restaurant entrance. Lucy had no business judging Julia. She only hoped Julia knew what she was doing, for Parker's sake…and the new baby's.

Lucy made sure the ringer to her cell was turned to high. She had left Parker at home after ordering dinner again from the Dog. She'd served Julia her spinach salad minus the boiled egg with added crumbled bacon, and snuck a double cheeseburger, fries, and large chocolate brownie to Parker, making him swear on his autographed Dan Marino football that he'd stay put tonight and get to bed no later than ten thirty. Lucy had to go on faith that his grunted response meant yes.

A guy wearing a checkered apron over black cargo pants, light-blue Crocs, and backward John Deere cap grabbed two menus and said, "Right this way, ladies. Your party is already here."

"Huh? What's he's talking about?" Lucy said, trying to stop Wanda, who followed him around the old wood tables. "We don't have a party."

"Perfect. I see a cool pitcher of margaritas waiting."

Wanda quickened her pace, and Lucy almost tripped over Fiona. "Doodlebugs. Move it, you fat pig." Fiona snorted, and Lucy could've sworn she'd butted into her leg on purpose. Not that she blamed her. No one liked being called a fat pig…even a pig. When Lucy untangled her feet, she looked up into a pair of twinkling green eyes. Green used to be her favorite eye color, but not anymore. From this moment forward, she was scratching green off her list with a big, fat Sharpie marker. Along with crooked smiles and buffed biceps. Who needed them? She had more important things to daydream about, like the color of her next pedicure or the new season of *The Bachelor*, or when Hostess Twinkies would make a comeback. Not soft, wavy hair that made her fingers itch or strong, large hands that caused her skin to prickle.

Brogan pulled the wooden chair out next to him and reached for her elbow. She tensed at his touch, and he stilled. Their eyes met, and he waited. She felt his visual caress travel her body, even though his gaze never left her face. She didn't understand this game he was playing, but it was time she found out. Relaxing her strained shoulders, she moved toward her seat.

"Hey, Little Lucy. Glad you could join us." The warm caramel of his voice filled in her empty places, making her feel special. And that scared Lucy most of all.

Chapter 12

WITH HESITATION AND ONE SHARP LOOK, LUCY broadcasted her accusations at him: yup, he was toe jam. He sensed the moment the warring inside her head ceased, and she caved. He exhaled, unaware his breath had been trapped. But he instinctively knew, like he knew his granola would become a hit or the New York Giants would beat the New England Patriots in Super Bowl XLVI, that Lucy had appeared in his life for a reason. And that reason was to help him with BetterBites.

"Lucy, Wanda, this is my great friend and business partner, Javier Coloma." Javier stood to pull out Wanda's chair, when his face froze in shock.

"Mmm, Javier." Wanda rolled her *R*s along with her hips, giving Javie her perfected sultry look. "So nice to meet you."

"And this is Fiona. Wanda's pet pig." Brogan pointed to Fiona already curled on her blanket next to Wanda's chair, and the reason for the disbelieving look on Javier's face.

"You have a pet p-pig?" Everyone stared at all 130 pounds of Fiona and her sparkly, girly collar.

"Pigs make wonderful pets…until it's time for butchering, and then…not so much," Wanda said with a flutter of her hand.

All color had leached from Javier's dark, swarthy

complexion, turning him pasty white as he visibly gulped. "You eat your pets?"

"Oh, heavens no! I can't remember the last time I ate my pet, can you, Luce?"

Lucy had already started numbing her mind, if her half-empty margarita was any indication. "I think the last one was Mr. Pigs Feet when you were about nine."

"I think you're right." Wanda nodded as she sipped the drink Brogan served her. "Mr. Pigs Feet had gotten to be *huge*. Three hundred pounds. Daddy promised Mama she'd have all the smoked bacon she'd need for that year," she said in a matter-of-fact tone.

"And you didn't mind"—Javier glanced around the table as if confused—"that your pet was slaughtered for smoked bacon?"

"Oh, I cried for days and days. I don't think I ate pork for two weeks after that." Wanda fiddled with her cocktail napkin. "I made Daddy promise never to kill one of my pigs again." She shifted in her seat, and Brogan and Javie openly enjoyed the wonderful display of exposed cleavage attached to large, jiggling breasts. Hey, any hot-blooded male would've done the same thing. And Wanda Pattershaw had been generously flaunting her assets since seventh grade to the appreciation of all guys near and far.

"Can we stop with the pig and pork conversation? I think Fiona's starting to sweat, and we all know pigs don't sweat," Lucy said, cocking her brow in warning at Wanda.

Wanda smiled and fluffed her big brown curls, batting her eyes at Javier. "Absolutely. Sugar, why don't you tell me all about your fine self? How do you know

Brogan here?" Her long, orange-painted nail pointed in Brogan's direction, but her gaze never left Javie's flustered face.

Javie blinked and then seemed to get comfortable in his chair as he peered at Brogan. "You never told me all the women in this town were beautiful Southern belles," he said, using his heavy-Latin-pick-up-girls accent.

Wanda leaned forward, assuring Javie's gaze stayed glued on her. "That's because not everyone in this town fits that description." Wanda jerked in her seat. "Ow! Stop kicking me." She squinted at Lucy. "What's gotten into you? You've already got one guy…Buffed Brogan here. You don't need Javier too."

Brogan smiled at Wanda. He'd known her since third grade, and she was putting on an act that would make a Broadway director take notice.

"Does the name Russell mean anything to you?" Lucy asked between gritted teeth.

"Not at the moment. Unless you're referring to that hardheaded, no-good, termite-eaten two-by-four."

"You guys know whatcha want for dinner?" The waiter appeared, wearing a black Harley-Davidson T-shirt under cameo bib overalls, with his long hair tied back in a ponytail. He held a beat-up pad and stubby pencil in his beefy hand.

"Ladies first," Javier drawled.

"I'll have the chicken and biscuits, sweet potato fries, and the homemade coleslaw. Oh, and a large plate of scraps for Fiona," Wanda said.

"Me too. Except I'll pass on the plate of scraps," Lucy added.

"Me three," said Javier with a chuckle.

"And you, sir?" The waiter glanced at Brogan.

"He'll have the vegan plate with garbanzo beans, alfalfa sprouts, and tofu. Go heavy on the tofu," Lucy said in a snarky voice as she tipped her margarita to her lips.

Beneath her short skirt, Brogan slid his hand on top of her soft thigh and gave a warning squeeze. Lucy bolted straight in her seat, clamping her legs together, trapping his fingers. Heaven or hell, Brogan only knew his hand had found a home. Clearing his throat, he slipped his fingers free and said, "Ignore that last order and bring me the fried chicken platter with a side salad. Thanks."

Before the waiter left, he refilled their drinks from the pitcher. Javier struck up a conversation with Wanda, and Lucy nudged Brogan with her elbow. "How did you know I'd be showing up here tonight? Is Miss Sue Percy spying for you?" Lucy's citrusy smell made his blood surge, and Brogan wondered if she tasted the same way.

Brogan smiled. "I managed to figure this one out without using Harmony's busybody grapevine. Wasn't too hard. Since there're only a few places in town where Fiona is allowed, and the Daily Grind isn't open for dinner, it had to be the Rolling Pin."

"Oh. Okay." She reached for her drink, and Brogan noticed her hand trembled. "But why this sudden interest in me? And don't tell me it's because you want to look up my skirt, because there're tons of willing girls in town whose skirts you could be chasing. Heck, you've probably been underneath half already."

Nope. Not even close. But this was about helping Lucy help BetterBites. "Here we go," the waiter interrupted as he placed their plates on the table. "Y'all let me know if I can git you anything else, ya hear?" He used his best Gomer Pyle voice, realizing Javier was a new tourist in town. Hot biscuits and crispy fried chicken filled the table.

"This looks divine and smells even better." Wanda sniffed. The waiter bent and set a heaping tray of scraps next to Fiona on the floor, and from the sounds of the snorts, Fiona was as happy as a pig in slop.

"Lucy, have you been by the store?" Javier asked.

Lucy poured honey over her biscuit, ignoring Brogan as he scooted his chair into her territory. "Uh, I've driven by but haven't been inside."

"You should go, Luce," Wanda said. "It's wonderful, and Fiona adores the vegetarian meals. I know Brogan would be delighted to give you a personal tour." She jabbed her knife at Brogan. "Be sure to show her where you store all those yummy muffins." Wanda jumped in her chair. "Ow! Stop kicking me." She scowled at Lucy.

"Brogan tells me you're back in town to help your sister. Do you plan to stay?" Javier asked Lucy.

She stopped chewing. "Uh, no. A nurse is lined up once she comes home with the baby, and Parker will be back in school by then. She won't need me after that."

"I don't know, Luce," Wanda said. "They say postpartum depression can set in and make mothers want to eat their young. And with Julia being perpetually bitchy… you might need to stay until the baby turns eighteen."

Brogan almost choked, his eyes watered, and he grabbed his drink. Javie attempted to cover his laughter with his napkin.

"Wanda, are squirrels juggling knives in your head? Russell needs to hog-tie you and shove an apple in your mouth." Lucy picked up her phone and started texting. "I think I'll tell him to do just that."

"Lucy Doolan, don't you dare." Wanda reached over, snatched the phone, and shoved it down her bra. "There. Now behave. And being hog-tied is not as much fun as it sounds."

The table shook from Brogan and Javier's laughter.

Lucy spoke out of the side of her mouth. "Javier, when you get a minute, reach in there and get my phone back. Believe me, Wanda won't mind."

"She's right. I won't," Wanda purred. Brogan knew Javie wished he could *be* the cell phone nestled between Wanda's breasts.

"Let's dance"—Brogan shoved his chair back, grabbing Lucy's hand—"and give these two some alone time."

"I don't want to dance."

"Sure you do. They're playing Trace Adkins."

Wanda helped by pushing Lucy's chair from the table with her foot. Brogan tugged Lucy around more dining tables to the middle of the sawdust-covered dance floor, where couples swayed to the band's rendition of "Every Light in the House." Slipping his right hand around the small of her back, he pressed her plush curves into his chest. Her smooth hair tickled his chin, and the smell of citrus filled his head. Lucy stood stiff as a telephone pole as he tried maneuvering to the slow beat of the music.

"You gonna dance like a robot all night, or just with me?" He cocked his head and peered into her face, where doubt disappeared and desire took over as her gaze softened. Brogan liked that look as he slightly bent his knees, pulling her closer. "I won't bite unless you want me to," he whispered next to her ear.

"Good to know." She heaved a shaky sigh. "Well, I guess you're better than Clancy Perry over there, looking like he wants to cut in." Looping her left arm around his neck, she rocked her hips to the beat. Brogan swallowed a groan. Right now nothing else mattered. All he cared about was luscious Lucy filling his arms.

"Let's look like we mean it so Clancy or his brother, Clinton, won't get any ideas." He bent as if to kiss her.

"You don't mind if I start singing, do you?" she said, smiling as she moved away from his lips.

Brogan's head jerked back. "Oh, hell no. My ears haven't recovered from this morning."

"I know all the words." Tossing him a saucy look, she started to hum…loudly.

"Shut up and dance." Brogan tucked her back under his chin and shook with laughter.

Chapter 13

LUCY HAD LOTS OF DREAMS. MOSTLY HER DREAMS starred Brogan, always smiling at her with adoration, running the gauntlet of long-legged models and even a teary-eyed Julia without so much as a glance…his entire focus on reaching Lucy at the end of the line. But in all these dreams, they never kissed. Inevitably, they'd get nose to nose…just about to kiss when—poof!—she'd wake up. When that happened, Lucy would bury her head in her pillow and squeeze her eyes shut, willing herself back to sleep to pick up where the glorious dream had left off, but alas, she never got there.

On the dance floor, wrapped in Brogan's arms, Lucy's dreams paled in comparison. She lost her own battle on not melting and nestled against his hard, wonderful chest. Clean soap and sexy Brogan swamped her senses. His yumminess ranked up there with her daily intake of Hershey's milk chocolate nuggets…and that was really saying something.

Comforted by the rapid beat of his thumping heart against her ear, she sighed. The song had changed to a slow country ballad, which matched her dreamy state. When Clancy Perry tapped Brogan's shoulder, Lucy couldn't help but feel a big-ass cranky irritation. Couldn't he see he was disrupting fantasyland?

"Hey, Brogan. You don't mind if I cut in, do ya?" Clancy asked as Brogan stopped swaying but continued to hold Lucy close. *Whatever you do, don't give me up to Clancy.*

"Actually, I do. This is the first chance I've had to dance with Lucy all night. We're kinda on a date…" *Yay! You tell him.* Brogan gave Clancy the don't-bother-me-I'm-trying-to-score look. But Clancy and his older brother, Clinton, weren't the sharpest pencils in the holder, and Clancy pushed up the brim of his ratty straw cowboy hat and stood his ground.

"Yeah, but you've been dancing with her for the last two songs and now it's my turn."

"Uh, we're not taking turns here, Clancy. Lucy is my date." Brogan's annoyance rang loud and clear. He gave Lucy a firm but gentle shove against his side as if to protect her. *You go, Bro-man.*

"You're not on a date. She came in with Wanda and Fiona. I saw her drive up." Clancy splayed his hands against the worn Levi's on his hips.

Clancy had Brogan on a technicality, but Lucy had no intention of siding with either Perry brother…ever. She nodded. "That's true, Clancy, but Brogan's a little rusty on the whole dating thing. He's been living up North and has forgotten how Southern gentlemen behave. Wanda and I are giving him lessons." Clancy blinked and scratched his head beneath his straw hat.

"Yeah. I need all the help I can get." Brogan wrapped his arm back around her waist, just where Lucy liked it, and blocked Clancy with his broad back as he danced her back a few steps. However, everyone in Harmony knew that Clancy and Clinton were short on brains but long on stubborn. Clancy tapped Brogan's shoulder so hard that Lucy felt the reverberation through his thick chest.

"Sorry, Clancy. Not. Going. To. Happen," Brogan said in a low voice.

Clancy snorted. "You think youse some kind of celebrity, with your fancy car and that sissy-ass store, selling high-priced sawdust!"

"He's got you there," Lucy mumbled to Brogan as she gripped his starched, white, delicious-smelling, cotton button-down and tugged. "Don't—"

A sea of Calvin Klein's Obsession and a blur of orange whooshed past Lucy. "Clancy, you devil. I've been waiting all night for you to ask me to dance." Wanda wedged herself between Brogan and Clancy, taking Clancy by surprise as she wriggled against him.

From the left corner of the bar, Dottie Duncan stomped toward Brogan. She wore a pink denim dress with long fringe running down the sides and a determined look on her heavily made-up face. "Come on, Yankee boy. It's about time you asked me to dance, and then you can buy me a drink." Dottie wrapped her sparkly, jeweled left hand around Brogan's neck and nudged his foot with her powder-blue cowboy clog. Brogan looked as if he wanted to argue as his frustrated gaze landed on Lucy over Dottie's bleached-blond beehive hairdo. And just when Lucy thought he'd refuse to take Dottie up on her offer, Javier laced his hand with Lucy's and drew her deeper onto the dance floor.

"One of us had to dance with you…and I lost." Javier laughed at Brogan's scowl as he twirled Lucy around the floor.

─∾─

Brogan tried to focus on Dottie Duncan and her red lips as she talked about the crispy skin on the Rolling Pin's fried chicken and how she wondered if they soaked the chicken in buttermilk, but he could give her only half his attention. The other half stayed riveted on Javier, his best friend and business partner. The one person he trusted more than anyone in the entire world. But at this moment, he trusted him like he trusted used-car salesmen, and he wanted to tear him limb from limb because he was dancing with Lucy…a little too close. No, make that a *lot* too close.

"…you thinking about selling fried chicken at BetterBites?"

Brogan glanced at Dottie's narrowed, piercing blue eyes. "Excuse me…I'm sorry—"

"You can say that again. You're about as sorry as they come. You haven't heard one word because you keep mooning over that Doolan gal. When you going to start thinking with the right head?"

"What? I'm not doing anything—"

"That's right, you're not. Ever since you came back to town five months ago, you've done nothing but mope, acting like a turd on a log, as if the weight of the world rested on your shoulders." She gave his world-weary shoulder a pinch, causing him to flinch. "You listen here, city slicker. I knew your mama. She was one of my best friends, and I miss her like there's no tomorrow."

That made two of them. His throat dried up, and he tried to arrange his face into a neutral expression.

"But she would've been mighty disappointed in watching her only son screw up his life by not getting past the hurt or anger or whatever you got all bottled up inside you. She taught you to grab life by the balls and make the most of it."

"What do you think I'm doing? I happen to know my mother was very proud of my success. She encouraged me to pursue my dreams. I'm not unhappy."

"Horseshit. You don't know what happiness is. But I'll give you a hint…it's not another gourmet food store. And it's not worrying yourself sick over a failed marriage that should've never happened in the first place. And it's certainly not living life half-assed because you can't forgive that deadbeat dad of yours." Brogan had stopped dancing and was staring at Dottie. "Buy me a drink." Dottie turned and marched toward the bar, making the fringe on her dress swing from the boom of her hips.

He followed, wondering how the conversation had skipped the tracks, gone over the cliff, and plunged into the deep sea. What the hell did Dottie know about his happiness? She didn't know anything about his life… or did she?

"Two longneck beers," Dottie ordered from the bartender. "You planning on staying in Harmony and raising a family?"

Raising a family? Living in Harmony? She was talking crazier than a rabid coyote. "Er, Miz Duncan, I really—"

"You can call me Marilyn Monroe, Madonna, or your mama, but don't call me Miz Duncan. Told you… reminds me of my mother-in-law, that nosy, opinionated old battle-ax."

"Right. Sorry about that. Dottie, I'm not sure how this all came about, but I'm only here temporarily, until BetterBites is running smoothly."

Dottie half tsked, half snorted, before tipping the beer to her lips. "You're denser than a box of pet rocks. I guess that fancy school didn't teach you anything after all."

The attitude slapping him in the face was starting to piss Brogan off. He didn't recall ever doing anything to Dottie in the past that would make her mad. He'd always been polite and used his best manners whenever she'd come by the house to visit his mom.

He rolled his stiff neck. "What lesson exactly did I miss at my fancy school?" Not bothering to control the irritation coloring his tone.

"The one on what's really important in life."

"You're right. I don't remember that one being offered in the course catalog."

"Don't get flip with me. I swatted your three-year-old butt with a switch when you fed my cat Lester bananas and he left a trail of vomit from the kitchen to my bedroom door. And I'll swat your butt again." She shifted on the cracked red-vinyl barstool, tapping her long, painted nails on the wood bar. Brogan had forgotten all about the cat incident. He guessed he'd pissed her off after all. "You've been given a second chance to make things right. But you're so busy focusing on what's not important that you're gonna blow it."

He pinned Dottie with a sharp look. "What?" Frustration boiled inside him until he thought he'd crack the beer bottle with his bare hand. "Spit it out. What wrong am I supposed to right? My mom died peacefully. I should know. I was by her side. She never intimated that—"

"I'm not talking about your mama." Dottie's statement made him pause. "I'm talking about your *love life*."

Sheee-it. Here we go again. Brogan took a pull of his icy beer, hoping to cool his hot head. "Miz...er, Dottie, my relationship with Julia is ancient history. We broke up, and I've moved on, and Julia has too. There's nothing—"

"I *know* that. And if you'd get your head out of your ass, you'd know it too."

"Jesus H. Christ. What the hell are you going on about?" he practically bellowed.

Dottie didn't flinch at his outburst. Savoring a taste of beer and grabbing a fistful of nuts, she finally said, "Not Julia, you numbnuts." She swiveled the barstool until she faced the dance floor. "Her sister...Lucy."

Back at the table, Lucy glanced over her shoulder and saw Brogan scowling at Dottie Duncan. *Happy* would not be the word she'd use to describe him at the moment. Lucy checked her cell. Still no text from Parker. She'd been texting him the last half hour to make sure he'd gone to bed on time. He probably had his phone off or something. The "or something" had Lucy worried.

"Wanda, we need to go. I have to check on Parker."

"It's not even eleven yet," Wanda said, reaching for her drink.

Lucy snuck another peek over her shoulder at Brogan still talking with Dottie at the bar and still not looking happy.

"Um, yeah, I know, but he's not answering my texts or calls. And quite frankly, I don't trust him. Not after last night."

"Give the kid a break. What can he possibly do? He

lives in Harmony…with Julia. Don't you think he has suffered enough?"

"Parker's my responsibility now, and I don't want anything happening on my watch. Javier, would you mind giving Wanda a lift home?"

"Not at all," Javier said, his eyes lighting up.

"I want to dance some more." Wanda pressed her hot, glistening flesh into Javier's arm and gazed adoringly into his dark eyes. "Maybe you can teach me to salsa."

"I think I'm going to vomit…inside my mouth," Lucy said.

"I'd appreciate more gratitude coming from you, missy. If I hadn't distracted Clancy with my spectacular cleavage"—she hefted the spectacular cleavage in question with her hands—"your lover boy and the Perry brothers would be knocking heads and busting up the Rolling Pin right about now."

"Lover boy? That's the most ridiculous thing you've said all night. Brogan is not my lover boy!" Just as Lucy yelled that statement, the band stopped playing, and the Rolling Pin had a brief moment of complete quiet. And Brogan Reese stood right behind her. *Gah!* Lucy ducked her head as heat flamed her cheeks.

Brogan dropped into his chair and threw his arm over Lucy's shoulder. "Wanda, I owe you a debt of gratitude." He spoke as if he hadn't heard Lucy's embarrassing declaration. "For distracting Clancy."

Wanda tossed her hair and said, "Finally, someone who appreciates me."

Javier scooted forward. "I appreciate you, *mi cielo… mi amor*," he murmured.

Brogan gathered Lucy close with his arm on her

shoulder and chuckled next to her ear. "Are they for real?"

"I don't know." Lucy pushed her chair back. "But I've got to go and check on Parker before Wanda turns into a bad Spanish soap opera right before my eyes."

Wanda jumped up and stepped over a sleeping Fiona. "Luce, you forgot about Fiona. I'll drive Julia's minivan home with her. Brogan, you can drive Lucy home. Come on, Javier," she ordered. "Teach me the salsa." Wanda left Lucy no choice as she plastered herself to the front of Javier.

"Do you have any idea what's going on?" Brogan asked, confused, watching Wanda and Javier ooze around the dance floor.

"Well…" Lucy tapped her fingers across her lips. "I think they're planning to salsa all night…or something."

"Let's go. I'll take you home," Brogan said.

"No, really. I can wait… Maybe not." Lucy spied a battered straw hat heading her way. Clancy Perry was trolling the dance floor again. Scrambling for her yellow cross-body bag, she said, "Let's pay fast before Clancy works his way over here."

"Leave your keys on the table." Brogan fished for his wallet and threw a bunch of bills down. Standing, he helped Lucy with her chair.

Her heart stammered in her chest. There was nothing sexier than a man with good manners. Lucy slipped the strap to her handbag across her chest, and Brogan pressed his palm to the small of her back as he led her away from the table. Again, her heart somersaulted over his simple touch, warming her insides like homemade chocolate sauce.

Outside next to his Jag, she said, "Hope you're not upset Wanda's hooking up with Javier." Brogan opened her door, and she slid into the buttery, leather bucket seat.

"Javier can take care of himself. They're just blowing off steam and having fun. Wanda isn't gonna do anything foolish to lose Russell." She relaxed for a moment as he rounded the hood of the car. Checking the blank screen on her cell again, she hoped it meant Parker was sound asleep, dreaming about football and video games. Not cruising Main and picking up chicks.

Brogan started the car. "Before we head back, I need to ask you a question."

He sounded serious. Maybe it had something to do with his heated conversation with Dottie Duncan. Or maybe he wanted Lucy's help to get back together with Julia. *Please be option number one.* "Um, sure." She shifted in her seat, tucking her skirt under her leg.

Brogan flashed a naughty grin. "What's this about us being lovers?"

Chapter 14

THE LOOK OF SHOCK ON LUCY'S FACE, AND THE WAY she recoiled from his question, gave Brogan great enjoyment.

"Oooo! So you heard me?"

"The whole restaurant heard you," he said in a calm voice, fiddling with the AC vents.

"Well, you heard incorrectly. I didn't say anything about us being l-lovers." The interior of the car shook as Lucy wiggled around, trying to get comfortable. "I said we were *not*…you know…that." The vague gesture of her hand matched the vagueness of her comment.

Brogan's lips twitched, trying to hide his smile. "Would *that* be so bad…if we were? You make it sound like the possibility is worse than contracting the Ebola virus."

"So, you heard correctly." Her tone was accusing. "Hopefully, everyone at the Rolling Pin realized the same thing. The very idea is not only preposterous, but downright icky."

Okay, now he was pissed. He'd been teasing Lucy because she was fun to tease, and well, he liked her…a lot. But the fact that she thought sex with him was icky was bullshit.

"Are you implying that sex in general is icky or only sex with me is icky?" The outside lights from the Rolling Pin slashed across Lucy's face, and she appeared startled by the question.

"Uh…er, I'm not saying with you"—she used air quotes around *you*—"meaning you. You know, like *you*."

He scowled. "I get the picture."

"What I mean is. Hmm, how do I put this?" She rolled her fingers over her plump lower lip.

"I've got all night." He crossed his arms over his chest and relaxed against his seat.

"I mean, sex with you would be icky because of Julia."

He quirked a brow. What did Julia have to do with this?

"You know…Julia?"

"I know Julia," he said, his patience wearing thin.

"Then you know…" Lucy started to twirl a lock of hair, and he still waited. "…sex would be gross because you slept with my stepsister. Isn't that like incest or something?"

This time it was Brogan's turn to be shocked. "What? Incest! Damn, Lucy, you're fucking nuts."

"I'm nuts? You're the one who dated Julia for two years. That's two years of your life you'll never get back. Think about that." Lucy leaned forward until they almost bumped noses.

"That's right. I dated Julia. *Dated*. I didn't have sex with Julia…*ever*."

"Aha! See. You even admit it. You"—she reared back, and her wide gray eyes met his—"you didn't have sex with her? Ever?"

Satisfaction curled inside him. It was about time she knew the truth. "Nope. Julia and I *never* had sex. We came close a few times, but we never went all the way, and if she's telling you differently…she's a liar."

"Wow." Her body slumped down into the seat. "That blows my mind."

Brogan wished she'd blow something else besides her mind, but he instantly squashed the thought.

"That means Parker really isn't your kid, or this baby either," she stated as if wrestling with the concept.

"That's what I've been trying to tell you and everyone else in town. How did I get this scumbag reputation? I don't remember treating anyone in town like shit." Did he? He stared at Lucy as she bent her short leg on the seat, looking sweet and vulnerable at the same time. His voice hoarse, he asked, "Did I treat you badly, Little Lucy?"

She answered in a quiet voice. "No. You never treated me badly. You always went out of your way to be nice to me. Always tried to make me feel better. I think that's why I had…" She trailed off.

Relief washed over him. He was happy that memories of him were good ones for her. A sigh floated from her soft pink lips. The scent of citrus swirled around his head as she swayed forward. He wanted to taste her mouth. Kissing Lucy was still a really bad idea, but at that moment, he didn't give a shit.

Suddenly bells rang in his ear, and Lucy stopped. "Dammit." He pulled back, digging for the phone in his front pocket. Lucy pressed shaky fingers to her lips as he checked his message. "Sorry. I need to respond to this. It's one of my New York investors." He chuckled. "They aren't kidding when they say that city never sleeps. This guy's still working late in his office on a Saturday night."

As he typed a response about the NYC opening of

BetterBites, reality slapped him into realizing that sticking to his business plan and getting Lucy on board was his top priority. Her marketing skills could be crucial to his bottom line. He hit Send and listened as the email whooshed into cyberspace. He tossed his cell in the phone cubby below the sound system. Checking his rearview mirror, he started backing out of the red clay lot. Lucy had straightened in her seat. Gone was the hungry look directed at him, replaced by the mature business mask she'd perfected. He preferred the other. Maybe another time.

"Listen, I really need to talk to you about something…important. Maybe we could set a meeting at BetterBites?"

Her eyes narrowed. "Still not wearing the naughty maid outfit."

God. If only. "No. What I need won't require the maid outfit, but if you choose to wear one, I won't object."

She gave a censorious clearing of her throat.

"It's about a job. Working for me."

"No."

Okay. Brogan wasn't expecting rejection so quickly. "No? You haven't heard my offer. This is not some temp job, and I'm not Tony using you for your hustling skills. This is a legitimate offer to work for BetterBites in marketing." His eyes focused on the narrow road, but his attention zeroed in on his obstinate passenger, sitting with her arms crossed, her face marred with a stubborn expression. A real offer with a decent salary was about to be laid on the table, and she'd rejected him without even knowing the details.

He stopped at the red light on Gardenia Avenue, and

flicked his left indicator to turn on Walnut Street. "Will you at least hear me out?"

She checked her cell phone and frowned. "Sure. Give it your best shot."

Not exactly brimming with enthusiasm, he thought as he accelerated into the turn. Okay, now or never. "You'd be working on marketing and PR for this location. We need help getting the word out and expanding our customer base. You'd be in the store, of course, but not stocking shelves—although sometimes we all have to pitch in. But we're really in need of your creative marketing skills."

"I thought you did all that."

"No. I have been. But the New York location is where my focus should be now. I oversee the big picture, and Javier takes care of billing and accounting."

"You're the CEO, and Javier's the CFO?"

"Yeah. We're structured a little differently, but that's the idea."

"You won't be hanging around? You need to be in New York soon?"

Brogan got the distinct feeling that would be a plus in his favor. And he didn't like it. "I move around, checking on all our locations. Is that a problem?"

"Is this a permanent position?"

"It can be. There's plenty of room to grow. Depending on how well you do with this store…you could take a look at our other locations." He eased the car around a white Suburban parked on the side of the road.

"I have a responsibility to help Julia. And after she's had the baby, I plan to move back to Atlanta."

"And do what? Take on more lousy temp jobs for

Tony the Tiger?" Anger sliced through him, thinking of Lucy being hung up on that asshole. She deserved better. Brogan was prepared to offer her…*what*? Besides a job, he had no claims on her.

"I have plans. Big plans. I'm not working for anyone else…*ever*." Her tone was resentful and combative.

"Okay, okay. I get that. But maybe while you're here for the next two months, you can help us out and earn some money. I could sure use your expertise."

"What about Julia? She's counting on me to take care of her and Parker."

At the intersection of Walnut and Chestnut, he waited as a group of high school girls crossed the street, talking and texting on their phones.

"You can still do that. Parker will be at football practice starting Monday, and you can check in on Julia throughout the day. It's not like you'll be commuting an hour to and from work. It's a five-minute car ride."

"Hmmm, what's the pay?"

"Thirty bucks an hour."

Lucy paused and then said, "I'll think about it."

Christ. Time was the one thing he didn't have. He needed Lucy on board, and he needed her last month. "How long?"

She shrugged. "A few days."

Brogan swallowed his frustration as he turned into Lucy's driveway and stopped the car. Tomorrow was Sunday. He'd give her two full days. "I'd like an answer by Tuesday morning, no later."

"Okay. Well, um, thanks for the ride…again." She chuckled. "You've been here so many times in the last two days, your car's probably programmed."

He smiled. "Yep. And don't forget...tomorrow morning at six."

"Craptastic." The back of her head thunked against the headrest. "Please tell me his football practices don't start that early in the morning, or I might have to drown myself," she groaned.

Brogan hopped out to open her door. "Nah. They probably won't start before seven, unless the guys are sloppy and undisciplined, and then there's no telling." She swung her silver sandals around and stepped out, shooting him a glare. He caught her citrus scent as she bent to straighten the ruffled blue skirt that had ridden up her thighs, exposing nice smooth skin. Lifting her head slowly, she met his gaze. Heat and desire in her gray eyes mirrored his own before she quickly lowered her lashes.

"I better get inside...have to check on Parker, and—"

"Sure." His feet were rooted to the driveway. After a long, drawn-out pause, he stepped back, creating space between his white button-down shirt and her gold necklace with the pearl drop nestled near her cleavage. Brogan ripped his gaze away from the swell of her heaving breasts and closed the car door. Taking a moment, he squeezed his eyes shut, pulling air into his deprived lungs. Then he turned and ushered her to the house. At the front door, Lucy rested her hand on the doorknob.

He cleared his throat. "Any special requests for tomorrow's treat?"

Large gold hoop earrings danced as she shook her head no. "Surprise me. Thanks again, Brogan. See you tomorrow."

"Yeah, sure. No problem." He rocked back on his heels, watching her disappear inside the dimly lit house. Shoving his hands in his pockets, he headed back to his car, his leather loafers echoing against the cement walkway. "Keep moving and don't look back," he muttered to himself. "Business and pleasure don't mix."

He gripped the cool car door handle, and despite all the warring in his head, looked up. Lucy's silhouette was outlined behind the sheers covering the front window. His hand dropped and formed a tight fist. The sheers fluttered, and the front door light flicked off, casting the house in darkness.

With shaking muscles, Brogan didn't think. He sprinted up the walk and jumped the three front steps. As he raised his hand, the front door flew open, and Lucy stumbled into his chest, slamming the door closed behind her. His arm locked around her waist, and he pushed her against the solid wood door. Her heated gaze focused on his face as he lowered his mouth, trying to take it slow. But the instant his lips touched hers... he wanted it all. He wanted to consume her until they became one. Fire raged through his veins from the scent of her skin, the feel of her curves, and the texture of her lips. He was a goner.

His tongue swept inside her warm, wet mouth, and the kiss turned serious and devouring. The instant her tongue touched his, a shudder ran down his spine. He pressed her against the door, needing to feel the length of her against his body. Her hands moved to his shoulders and gripped his muscles beneath his shirt. She smelled like warm woman and great sex. She brushed her fingers at the top of his collar and spread them through his hair.

A moan escaped her throat, twisting his gut. Brogan spanned his palm over her full breast as he groaned into her greedy mouth. The need rushing through him burned him alive. And he welcomed it. For the first time in a very long time, he allowed the lust to spread its liquid fire. He rocked against her, tilting her head for better access. His thumb brushed her neck and connected with her racing pulse. Their mouths opened and closed as if they couldn't stop feeding each other hungry kisses.

Suddenly he froze. Arms and legs rigid. His head shot up, pulling air into his deprived lungs. "Shit!"

Lucy blinked, her fiery gray eyes in confusion. "What—Omigod!" She pushed at his chest.

Brogan turned, pulling Lucy in front to cover the hard-on pressing against his fly. He blocked his face with his other arm against the glare of the red-and-blue flashing lights.

From the police cruiser idling in the driveway.

Chapter 15

THE KISS SHE'D SHARED WITH BROGAN MUDDLED Lucy's first thought: Was she being arrested for a public display of affection? Wait. That was ridiculous. No law sat on the books stating you couldn't kiss someone by your front door. All right, well, kiss may be putting it too mildly. More like consumed. Devoured. Overwhelmed.

Lucy shook her head and watched in complete horror as Officer Andy Taylor (yes, just like Mayberry…she swore she couldn't have made this up) opened the back door to the cruiser. Parker slunk out with his head down and his arms wrapped around his maroon Harmony High T-shirt. Her knees must've buckled, because Brogan squeezed her upper arms in a tight grip, holding her upright.

"Parker!" she wheezed. "What…where…how…?"

"Brogan…Lucy." Officer Taylor tipped his hat. The passenger door opened as someone else exited the cruiser. He was standing in the dark shadows, and Lucy couldn't make out his features.

"Andy…Vance. What brings you guys out?" Brogan asked as calmly as if they were discussing the next cucumber crop instead of why Parker, her sweet, adorable, no-good, rotten nephew stood looking defiant and defeated at the same time.

Vance Kerner moved around the car in an easy lope, his hands shoved in the front pockets of his worn jeans. His long, dark hair brushed his shoulders, and it didn't look like his face had met a razor in days. "What's up, Brogan? Hey there, Lucy…glad you're back in town," he said in a lazy Southern drawl that contrasted with his hard dark eyes and his sometimes scary rock star/ outlaw appearance.

Lucy's heart rammed against her chest. "Really, people? Pleasantries? What is going on? Officer Taylor, why is Parker with you?" Brogan gave her a gentle shove to the side and a reassuring squeeze with his warm hands.

"Lucy, is Julia home? I need to speak with her about Parker," Andy said in a polite but authoritative tone.

Lucy touched her suddenly dry lips with her tongue that only moments ago had been tangling with Brogan's. "She's asleep." She hoped and prayed. "I'm taking care of Parker while she's on bed rest. You can speak with me."

Andy shot Brogan an uncomfortable look, and Vance moved behind Parker and gave him a nudge. "Maybe you should explain to your aunt what you were doing out so late," Vance said in a rough, raspy drawl.

"Parker, what's it going to be? Either you do it or I will." Andy pierced Parker with a hard lawman stare.

A sudden arctic blast froze Lucy's veins, and she started to shake. She wrapped her arms around her middle. *Please, Lord, don't let it be anything we can't reverse. Please.*

Parker shuffled his scuffed-up Nikes at the loose rocks on the driveway, his head still hanging low. "Um…I snuck out and met up with my friends," he mumbled.

"Were you drinking? Is he drunk?" Her gaze darted from Andy to Vance, trying to keep the panic at bay.

"No! We weren't drinking. I wasn't, anyway."

"He passed the Breathalyzer test. He's clean," Andy added.

"Spill it, Parker. I don't have all night," Vance said in a low, rough voice.

"We, um, well, we were just messing around, and I guess we weren't thinking. 'Cause we got caught egging cars."

Lucy's shoulders slumped in relief or disbelief…she had no idea which. "Okay…" she said slowly, "…like in the school parking lot? Or what?"

"Not exactly."

Not music to her ears.

Andy braced a black boot on the bottom step. "He and his friends were out on State Road 54, throwing eggs at moving cars. And that's considered a felony in the state of North Carolina. Vance here was one of the victims. He called me, and we caught up with the boys hiding out in the Haydens' cornfield."

Brogan's hand rubbed her stiff, cold back. He murmured something close to her ear, but she couldn't hear because of the military aircraft screaming through her head. *Felony.*

"What happens to Parker?" Brogan asked.

"Vance is not going to press charges, and I haven't gotten any calls from the other motorists. I'm willing to let Parker off this time with a severe warning. But the next time"—Andy Taylor gave Parker a don't-screw-with-me stare designed to frightened the most hardened criminals—"I will throw the book at him."

"Um, yeah, that sounds bad," Lucy said, finding her voice.

"Do you understand? A felony is a serious crime. You don't want that on your record," Andy said to Parker.

Parker gave a shaky nod. "Yes, sir," he mumbled.

"I'm not pressing charges," Vance said, "but I want Parker and the other boys to come out to the farm and wash my truck before that egg gets baked on and ruins the finish."

Parker shoved his hands into the front of his board shorts, still avoiding everyone's faces. Like the little weenie that he was becoming. Anger, fear, and love bombarded her all at the same time. She wanted to shake him until his head fell off, and then she wanted to hug and kiss him and tell him everything would be okay. She did neither of those things.

"That sounds fair," Brogan said. "What about the other boys?"

"I've spoken with their parents and told them the exact same thing. They were lucky…so far. If anyone else comes forward and wants to press charges"—Andy shrugged his thick shoulders—"then we may have a bigger problem."

Lucy clutched her throat and gave another shout up to the Lord, praying that no one else pressed charges. "Parker, what do you have to say? To Mr. Kerner and Officer Taylor?" she asked in what she hoped was a stern, adult tone.

"Um, I'm real sorry…Mr. Kerner. I'll be by tomorrow to wash your car." Vance nodded and clapped Parker on the shoulder.

"Parker is working out with me tomorrow at six in the morning. I'll bring him by your place after that," Brogan added.

"Parker?" Lucy prodded, shifting her gaze from him to Andy.

"I won't do it again, Officer Taylor. I promise."

"Make sure you keep that promise. I've got my eyes on you and your friends." Andy tipped his hat to her and rounded the hood to his idling cruiser.

"See you tomorrow, Brogan. Lucy, maybe next time we'll meet under better circumstances." Vance gave a half smile as he opened the passenger door and folded his tall form inside.

Petrified, Lucy watched the taillights of the cruiser exit her driveway. *Holy Mason jar full of moonshine!* What in all of the land of marbles was she going to tell Julia?

"Lucy, do you want me to stay?" Brogan asked in a soothing voice. Stay? God no. She wanted him to take her away. Away from her responsibilities and her troubled nephew. Away from poor Julia about to give birth to another child who would grow up to be a teenager and do horrible teenage things! With sagging shoulders, she released a ragged breath.

"No, but thanks. I appreciate your offer." She pointed to Parker, still shuffling his feet and not making eye contact. "In the house, Parker, *now*. And don't wake up your mom." Parker skipped up the steps, brushing past them both.

After the front door closed, Lucy said, "We're sticking with that six a.m. thing, huh?"

"Sorry. But Parker could use the discipline."

Lucy could just about forgive him, because his fingers toyed with her hoop earring, short-circuiting her brain and turning it into mushy applesauce. Almost. "Krispy Kreme doughnuts. No substitute."

"Try to get some sleep." Brogan brushed her lips with a soft kiss and then moved down the steps toward his car. Lucy struggled to wrap her head around what had just transpired. "Hillbilly Bone" rang from her phone, jolting her back to reality. *Blippity blast.*

Julia.

—◦◦◦—

Lucy found Parker in the kitchen, sitting at the table with a glass of ice water. "Your mom's awake. You going in there with me?"

Parker smeared the condensation on the glass. "I guess so," he said with all the conviction of a crooked politician.

"Oh, okay. Let me bring Julia a fresh glass of water." Could she be any more pathetic? She dreaded Julia's wrath as much as Parker did. Lucy balled her fist to keep from twirling a strand of hair. She and Parker performed dead-men-walking down the hallway as if heading to the electric chair. The glass in Parker's hand shook, and a drop of water splattered on Lucy's shoe.

"Head up. Shoulders back. Take it like a man." Lucy squeezed Parker's arm.

"What in the hell is going on around here?" Lucy had pushed the door open to a glaring, furious Julia, sitting straight up in bed with her bedside lamp on.

"Hey, Julia. Sorry we woke you. Would you like some water?" Lucy spoke in the same voice she would've used while approaching a mad mama mountain lion protecting her cubs. Not that she'd ever do that in a gazillion years, but she thought that might be how she'd sound.

"Parker, why aren't you in bed? And why did I get a call from Miss Sue Percy, saying she saw you in the back of Andy Taylor's police car? Please tell me that woman has lost her ability to spread gossip along with her eyesight," Julia demanded.

"Mom, it's okay. Nothing bad happened," Parker had the nerve to say. "Don't get all cray-cray. Aunt Lucy can explain." Parker sent Lucy a begging look. The weasel.

She narrowed her eyes at him, trying for one of Julia's bitchy glare-downs. When his lips tipped up in a sneaky smile, she knew her glare had failed.

"Will someone please tell me what is going on? I'm losing my patience. Lucy?"

"Sure. What Parker is trying to say is he snuck out tonight and met some friends, and in their infinite wisdom, they decided to hurl raw eggs at moving cars on State Road 54."

Julia's shocked gaze flicked to Parker. "Parker, is this true?" she asked in a surprisingly even tone.

"Yeah, sorta," the weasel had the nerve to say.

"Sorta? Parker, would you mind manning up here. Or do I tell your mom exactly what Officer Taylor will do to you the next time you even spit in the wrong direction?"

"Parker, finish. The truth."

Parker shuffled over to the bed and eased down at the foot. He placed his big hand over the pink blanket covering Julia's calves. "It's not that bad, Mama-bear," he said, using a sweet voice that would one day win over many young girls' hearts. "Connor, Duncan, and I were just hanging out, and we got bored. And then Duncan thought it would be fun to throw eggs at cars. I dunno. It was dumb." He shrugged his skinny shoulders. "But we didn't hurt anyone, and we only hit, like, two cars."

"Oh, Parker." Julia sighed. "What's going on with you? This is not like you."

Uh, not really. Time for a wake-up call. Lucy blurted, "Julia, this boy of yours is gonna turn into a juvie if you…we don't do something about it."

"Lucy, don't be so melodramatic. Parker's just a teenage boy. They do all sorts of stupid stuff. Are you forgetting how you were as a teenager?" A rush of guilt flooded Lucy at Julia's know-it-all stare. "I don't recall any of us turning into juvies. He's learned his lesson and won't do it again, will you, Parker?"

That did it. "Give me a break. I can't believe what I'm hearing. I don't recall any of us committing felonies. Parker, you were wrong and could've gotten in a whole heap of trouble. A felony is nothing to joke about. Not to mention, you could've hurt someone. What if that had been old man Cornwaddle driving down the road, and he swerved into a telephone pole because you scared the crap out of him? And Vance Kerner wasn't too pleased either. You're lucky he's not pressing charges." Parker had the sense to look embarrassed and maybe a little ashamed. "And what about how you lied to me? You swore on your signed Dan Marino football that you would go straight to bed and not sneak—" Lucy stopped at his warning glare. "Er, you promised you would go straight to bed," she finished. She'd forgotten Julia didn't know about the escapade the night before. She wondered why she felt compelled to keep the little sneaker's secret.

"Lucy's right. I'm very disappointed." Julia reached

over and grabbed his hand. "I want you to promise me that you'll behave. You know it's not healthy for me or the baby to get upset." Parker's sullen, bored mask slipped into place. "Do you understand?" He paused and then gave a half nod. "Now, go on up to bed. I need to speak with Lucy."

Parker rose, hesitated before bending down and kissing his mom on the cheek. "Love you, Mama," he whispered.

Julia ruffled his dark wavy hair. "Love you too, my sweet pickle."

As soon as Parker closed the bedroom door, Julia slumped against her pillows and squeezed her eyes closed. "Dammit." Tears leaked from the corners and trickled down her porcelain face.

"Julia, you okay? Can I get you anything?" Fear and anxiety gripped Lucy. This vulnerable, exposed side frightened her more than Julia's bitchy, scary side.

"Have a seat. We need to talk."

Lucy willed her stiff legs to move, and she backed up to the prissy pink chair. "Sure. Go ahead. Talk."

Julia's bright-blue eyes appeared dull and hard. "We need to talk about Parker's dad."

Thunk went Lucy's butt as she hit the seat of the chair. "You mean Parker's dad…like in real dad?"

"Yeah. His real dad." Julia lowered her head and talked to the fringe on the blanket between her fingers. "I've never told anyone the truth. By the time I realized I was pregnant and had decided to keep the baby, we'd already broken up."

Lucy gulped. "He…the father doesn't know? You never told him about Parker?"

Julia eased back until her head rested against the lace pillows, and she stared up at the light-blue ceiling with painted clouds and cherubs, an offensive imitation of the ceiling in the Sistine Chapel. Poor Michelangelo had to be weeping huge tears. "Not exactly. He didn't know at first, and I kept it from him because I was angry and hurt and afraid. But when Parker was three years old, I finally got up the nerve to tell him."

Lucy didn't like the crooked path this story was taking. She didn't feel a happy-smiling-laughing-everyone-cheering ending coming up. "What happened?"

"The usual. He denied it. Called me a whore, along with a few other choice names, and told me never to speak to him again." Lucy winced. "He wanted nothing to do with me or Parker. Can't say I blamed him. He was married by then and had his own family to worry about. He was not about to take on me or Parker, and he certainly didn't want me blabbing to his wife about his illegitimate son."

"Okay. That was really bad. What did you do?" *I don't want to know!* her head screamed.

"What could I do?" She gave Lucy a resigned look. "I was only twenty-two at the time, and he was about twenty-seven. He is…was a popular man with a great career ahead of him, and I was just a nobody. I feared how it would affect Parker. So I kept my mouth shut… spread a bunch of silly rumors to all the right people around town, and went back to work."

Man. Lucy's mind hit a wall over the word *man.* Popular *man.* Who the hoot had Julia gotten mixed up with? This didn't sound like a stupid high school girl having sex with another stupid high school boy down by the lake. This sounded worse…a lot worse.

"I'm only telling you so you'll know why I've kept Parker in the dark. I'm aware it's wrong, and he's old enough to know the truth, but I can't seem to go there with him…yet. And now this pregnancy, which I think Parker resents." Julia pressed her hand against her belly. "I'm at my wits' end. I need help with Parker. I don't want him to hate me because I screwed up. I don't want to raise a worthless juvie who turns into a worthless adult."

Lucy nodded. She understood. But how could she help? How could she correct this? "Okay, tell me. Who's Parker's dad?" she asked above a whisper.

Julia licked her dry lips. "Joe Monahan. He's Parker's father. Was. He's dead now."

Drawing a blank, Lucy asked, "Who? Do I know him?"

"Coach Monahan? Remember the football coach at school?"

Lucy's mouth worked, but no sound came out for several seconds. "*Coach Monahan?* As in Harmony High's winningest coach in the history of Harmony High? That Coach Monahan?"

"The one and only."

"How…where…why…how did it happen? Did he rape you?" Lucy leaned forward and grabbed Julia's hand, squeezing it hard. "Because if he did…I will dig up his sorry flat ass from whatever grave he's buried in right *now* and kill him again with my bare hands."

Julia squeezed her hand back. "No. Stop. It wasn't like that. It was consensual. I knew what I was doing, and believe me, I wanted it." Julia gave a brief, sad smile. "I chased him…he didn't stand a chance."

"But, Julia, you were barely an adult. He should've known better."

"Lucy, he wasn't much older. He started coaching right out of college. I was only eighteen when the affair started and he was twenty-three. How many twenty-three-year-old guys did you know who exercised any common sense?"

Not many. Still didn't. "Did you have a long…fling or whatever?" Lucy couldn't quite put a name to it. Affair sounded too grown-up for what Julia had done back in high school.

"Long enough. Long enough for me to fall head over heels, and for him to get tired of me and move on."

"That slime bucket! He'd better be glad he's dead." Julia chuckled at Lucy's staunch defense of her. "How did he die? I hope it was long and painful."

Julia's expression sobered. "It was. He had stomach cancer. I heard he suffered in the end. He left a wife and two kids."

Now she felt terrible. She didn't wish that kind of pain on anyone. No matter how angry she got. "Three kids. You forgot Parker."

"No. I've never forgotten Parker." Julia's long, dark hair brushed her shoulders as she shook her head. "But I'm going to lose him if I don't get some help. That's why I need you."

Lucy fought the urge to check over her shoulder to see if someone else was in the room. In all the years she'd known her, Julia had never once admitted that she needed Lucy. Of course, she'd asked her to come home because she was bedridden, and Babs couldn't be bothered to leave the NASCAR circuit to help her only daughter. And Lucy had jumped at the chance. Not because she'd been dumped and was out of a job, but because she'd wanted to reconnect with her family and make things up to Julia. But Julia had never said she *needed* Lucy, like tonight, wearing a solemn expression with tears brimming in her eyes.

"I'm here. But what can I do? Short of handcuffing him to my side, I'm at a loss. He's not exactly too happy to have me babysitting as it is."

"I know it's tough, but you won't be doing it alone. First of all, I'll help. Even stuck in this freakin' bed. Make sure he comes in to see me at least twice a day. I want to keep talking to him."

"Okay, that will kill about thirty minutes. What about the remaining twenty-three-and-a-half hours?"

"Football practice will take up a lot of time, but you still can't handle him, I know. That's why you need to join forces."

"With whom? The Harmony Huggers? The Happy Hookers, that group of old ladies who crochet every day at the Daily Grind?"

Julia ignored her. "Parker needs a strong male influence in his life. Not those derelicts he hangs out with."

"Man? What man do I know?" Lucy stopped at the gleam that sparked in Julia's blue eyes. *Please don't say what I think you're going to say.*

"Brogan."

She'd said it.

Chapter 16

MONDAY AFTERNOON, BROGAN WHISTLED AS HE pulled the baking pans from the oven with his fresh batch of hot, crunchy granola. The kitchen smelled of honey, oats, and the bread Margo had baked earlier.

"What's got you so happy, Mr. Wideberth?" Margo asked in her rough voice. "It's not like we got a herd of customers busting down that front door."

"Changes are coming. We will soon have just that… customers busting down our door."

"How? You gonna perform like Magic Mike and strip? I might be offended, but most of the women in this town would eat the granola right off your overly buffed chest."

"Margo, your thoughts must keep you awake at night. Not only am I not stripping…ever. But the thought of having granola eaten off my chest is beyond gross." A vision of Lucy leaning over him, long hair acting as a drape and a smile lighting her face as she licked granola off his bare chest made his cock twitch. Brogan pinched the bridge of his nose. *Stupid, Reese.* Kissing Lucy had been a huge mistake. A huge, awesome, mind-blowing mistake. Because now he knew exactly how she tasted and felt and smelled, and he wanted more. He wanted all of Lucy…heart and soul, and that scared the living crap right out of him.

"Granola, honey, maple syrup…whatever. You need

to stir up something around here. What's Javier working on? Maybe you guys could do a routine together. The Latin Lover and the American Gigolo."

"Two words. Sick. Mind." Brogan shook his head at Margo's flour-spattered face. "You just keep baking and let me worry about sales. Besides, I'm bringing some-one on board to help with that very problem."

Margo peeled off her apron. "Good. Need to check supplies," she said, lifting a clipboard from a peg on the wall. "Hello, there."

Brogan glanced up, and Lucy stood inside the back door with a manila folder pressed to her chest. Relief flooded Brogan, since he'd had no idea if she'd show or not.

"I'm Margo, in charge of baked goods, and you must be what we've all been waiting for."

Lucy gave a questioning look. "Lucy Doolan. Nice to meet you." She extended her hand.

Margo smiled, shaking Lucy's hand. "So you're Lucy…heard a lot about you. Welcome aboard…I hope," she said before disappearing into the stockroom.

Brogan brushed his hands on the apron tied around his waist, then removed it as Lucy's slanted gray eyes pinned him with a long, assessing look.

Clearing his throat, he said, "Glad you could make it." He gestured to the metal door that led to his office. "We can talk in here."

Lucy nodded.

He pushed the door closed, separating them from the kitchen, into a small, cramped room. "Have a seat." He scooped up some loose folders on the guest chair and stacked them neatly on top of the gray metal desk. He dropped into the black leather executive chair. "You have a decision for me?" He rested his hands on top of the desk, trying to strike a pose of complete control when he felt anything but. In the closed-off office, the scent of Lucy's citrus filled the room, making it hard to concentrate on business and not the full bottom lip she gnawed with her teeth. He tried not to stare, but everywhere his gaze traveled felt unsafe. From the nautical-striped blue-and-white silk tank top over a short white skirt, down to the patent-leather orange sandals. Thin gold-and-turquoise bangles jingled on her wrists, and a knotted gold necklace circled her neck. A step up from the Lucy of yesterday morning, walking in hot-pink jogging shorts and a black T-shirt with "I will cut you" across her chest, belting classic Blondie off-key. He and Parker had laughed so hard they could barely finish their run.

"That depends."

He arched a brow. "On what?"

"On whether you accept my terms."

Brogan bit back a smile. He had a few terms of his own, but he didn't think she'd be in the mood to hear them right now. Plastering his business mask on, he nodded. "Whatcha got?"

"Okay. Well, the only way I'll work for you is if you agree to the following." Lucy opened the manila folder in her lap and tipped up the list on top. "I know this job is only part-time, but you're gonna get more than you bargained for. I'll be putting in long hours late at night, especially with scheduling the social media."

Brogan nodded. He understood Facebook, Twitter, Instagram, and other social outlets needed twenty-four-hour surveillance.

"I'll work for forty dollars an hour." Lucy gauged his reaction, but Brogan had won many games of chance. His poker face didn't give anything away.

She glanced at her sheet. "I'll need an expense account. Most of what I'll be doing will be online and not wasting advertising dollars, but I'll also be setting up promotions and meetings, and my expenses will need to be covered for travel, food, and so on." She shifted in her seat. "Which brings up transportation." Brogan leaned forward but remained quiet. This list got better and better. Little Lucy was angling for a car, and he didn't blame her. Her old broken-down clunker probably wasn't worth repairing.

"Um, I'm going to need a car, strictly for business purposes." Her hand fluttered. "For personal use, I'll drive Julia's or mine, if Grady ever returns from his marathon fishing trip." She crossed her legs. "And if this becomes full-time…and I'm not saying that it will, but if it does…I want benefits." She paused and drew a deep breath that did amazing things to her gorgeous chest.

"Is that it?"

She nodded and slid the paper across the desk.

He picked up the list and read over it. "Okay, now I have some terms." Lucy straightened in her seat and nodded, pressing her lips together. "First of all, since you're new to the job and I've never seen your work, you'll start out at thirty-two an hour."

Lucy's head shook, making her dangling gold-and-turquoise earrings dance. "Thirty-five, and that's my final offer."

"Done." Startled, she sat up straighter. He held back a smile.

"Second, as long as you submit an expense report to Javier and he approves, your expenses will be covered. However, if you turn in any receipts from Burger King, McDonald's, or Toot-N-Tell for some garbage you consumed other than an iced tea, it will not be covered." She squirmed in her seat and pretended to study her nails.

"All right, but I draw the line at tree bark and seaweed. Just because I'm marketing this organic, granola-based lifestyle does not mean I have to eat, drink, and sleep it 24-7. You cannot fire me if you catch me eating KFC."

He dipped his head. "As for transportation. Not a problem. Any time you need a car for work, you can drive mine or Javier's. They're both company cars."

"Really? But what will you drive?"

He shrugged. "I'll figure something out. I might buy a truck."

"Cool. I love your car," she said, wearing a look of satisfaction.

"And our benefits package is very comprehensive. Do we have a deal?" He extended his hand across the desk, and she slipped her small, cool palm in his. He wanted to warm it up, along with some other choice body parts, but his fantasy fizzled as she quickly retracted it. "Good. Javier will draw up the papers. Can you start tomorrow?"

"Um, there's one more thing."

"What? New wardrobe? House? Trip to the South of France?"

"Wow. Could I really have those?"

"Shit no."

"Alrighty then. But in order for me to sign those papers, you're going to have to agree to two more things."

Something cold and hard settled in his gut. Something

that felt a lot like dread. The uncomfortable look that came over Lucy didn't make it any better. He braced himself, gripping the top of the desk.

"You need to help mentor Parker, and you can never kiss me again," she said in one fast breath.

Chapter 17

LUCY HAD NEVER TUGGED A LION'S TAIL BEFORE, BUT as soon as the last words tumbled from her mouth, she watched in fascination as Brogan's head snapped back, electrifying his tawny mane, making him look like he wanted to tear her limbs off with his bare teeth.

"No deal," he growled as he shoved back his chair. "Those terms do not belong anywhere on an employer/ employee contract." He paced across the speckled linoleum tile floor, retracing his steps until he faced her, stirring the air with his agitated movements. "What brought this on? Have you been talking to Julia?" Hands splayed on hips, his pose threatening.

Lucy leaned back to escape being burned by fire-breathing Brogan. "Sure. I talked to Julia. She's at her wits' end, and so am I. You seem to be the only one around who can reach him. I don't know anything about raising a fifteen-year-old boy."

"And you think I do?"

Lucy jumped at his bellow. "Lower your voice. You want people to hear?"

Brogan rubbed his forehead. "Jesus." He turned the lock on the office door. Pressing back as if to bar her exit, he faced her. "Look, Lucy, I can't help you with Parker the way you want me to. I know I worked out with him these last two days, but I was only trying to help you."

Exactly. She needed help. He'd be the perfect solution.

He pointed a finger at her. "I know what you're thinking. Forget it. I'm not acting as a mentor or some surrogate dad. No way."

A flash of pain shadowed by regret clouded his strained face. A tense muscle jumped along his jaw. Pictures of the past showed in his murky green eyes. That same look had haunted Lucy the night on the bleachers after his big win. She would've done anything to erase that pained expression. And she almost had…by kissing him. But Julia had expunged that idea from her mind permanently…until recently. Until Saturday night against the front door, when Brogan had kissed all sanity away. Now she couldn't think of anything else.

Lucy moved in front of him and said in a quiet voice, "He needs a strong male figure in his life. It's so obvious he's screaming for attention."

"Look, Lucy…concerning strong male figures, I'm a little screwed up. I didn't have one in my life, and until my sophomore year in college, I'd never even met my dad. I wouldn't count on me as solid mentor material. I've got a business to run. I don't have time to babysit a teenager."

"It won't be all day. If you could spend a couple of hours with him in the late afternoons and evenings, then maybe we can keep the kid out of juvenile detention."

"Lucy, the kid barely likes me. Besides, spending time with him will only give him false hope. Like I'm always going to be there for him." Brogan pushed away from the door and resumed his restless pacing. "I'm not. I'm leaving Harmony. My disappearing will screw him up even more. Believe me, I know." The brief flash of torment returned to his face. The idea of Brogan leaving Harmony for good twisted Lucy's heart into a tight pretzel. "Where's his real father?" he asked.

Dead. Buried. Rotting in hell. Lucy held back the shudder, recalling Julia's account. Not Lucy's story to tell.

She rolled the bracelets on her wrist. "I can't say."

"Can't or won't?"

"Both. Listen, it will only be until Julia's free and moving about. Her baby is due in late September. Once she's back on her feet, she won't need us anymore. Parker goes to school in a few weeks—"

"Exactly! Not enough time for me to get involved." Brogan crossed his arms as if to block any other options.

"Wrong. It's the perfect time. He needs to get his head on straight. Spending time with Harmony's football god will do him a world of good. You can talk football. Y'all can do that guy-bonding thing… spitting, burping…scratching." He rolled his eyes, but that didn't deter Lucy. She had to sell this for Julia and Parker's sake. "And share all the stupid things you used to do as a teenager. He can learn from your dumb mistakes."

"Stupid things? What stupid things?" A hint of a smile appeared. The discomfort and strain in his stance began to seep away.

"I don't know. Tell him how you used to take his mom down by the lake every Friday night to make out." Brogan's brows rose. "On second thought, don't. That might scar the kid for life."

"How'd you know about that?" His determined step forward brought him so close she noticed the rough shadow of his beard growing in and the smooth weave that made up his green cotton polo shirt.

"Everyone knew you took Julia to the lake. Not much stays secret around here. One time Julia lost her bra, and Wanda and I—"

Like a laser, his green eyes fried her. *Ruh-roe. TMI.*

"How'd you know about Julia's bra? I remember that night, and we were the only ones there."

"Julia told me, she—"

"Bullshit. Julia didn't tell you anything. She was mad as hell and didn't want anyone finding out. She made me go back to look for it, and it wasn't there."

Lucy swallowed hard. She remembered like it was yesterday. Wanda and she had hidden in the brush to spy on Brogan, and Wanda had raced toward the edge of the lake and snatched Julia's bra, swinging it in the air like a victory flag.

Brogan snagged her wrist and pulled her into his chest. "You were there, weren't you? You watched us make out, and then you stole her bra."

Mesmerized by the look of hunger he raked over her and the heavy hand pressing on her back, she whispered, "N-no. W-Wanda stole her bra."

"But you watched." His gaze dipped to her mouth. "Did you like what you saw? Did it make you hot?"

Lucy gasped and tried to pull free, but he held her tight. "It wasn't like that. We hadn't planned—"

"Would you like to go down by the lake with me, Little Lucy?" He sounded all smooth and rough, like hot, sizzling, sweaty sex against the wall. He slid his hand up her arm to the back of her neck, pushing his fingers through her hair and holding her head immobile.

"We could make out. All hot and frantic. I could lay you down on my blanket and feel you up," he murmured, his mouth pressed below her ear, sending shivers up her spine.

"This is not smart," she managed to choke out. Her traitorous body disagreed. The simple touch of his breath against her skin lit desire in every fiber she possessed, swamping her resistance.

"But it feels great," he said against her jaw as he nibbled his way toward her mouth. His lips brushed hers, and his tongue teased the corners before sweeping inside. Cold, hard metal hit her butt as Brogan pushed her against the desk and lifted her on top. Lucy squirmed, hating the tight skirt that prevented her legs from wrapping around his lean waist. A moan escaped her throat as his hot palm seared the outside of her thigh, pushing her skirt up and out of the way. Wrapping her legs around his waist, Lucy shivered as he slid his hand around to cup her butt. The weight of her breasts molded to his chest. Her nipples tightened, and heat pooled between her legs. He tasted a little of berries, and a lot of longing and lust. He pushed between her thighs, rubbing his stiff erection against her heat. All rational thought had left the building. He wanted her. She became a puddle of molten goo. It had been a long time since someone had wanted *her*.

It took several raps against the door before reason and regret penetrated Lucy's hunger-starved, muddled head.

She pushed against his chest. "Stop."

"Hey, boss man, we've got customers asking questions. Adjust yourself and get on out here," Margo said through the door.

Brogan straightened, removing his hand slowly from her bottom and the mess he'd made of her hair. "I'll be out in a minute," he called in a husky voice.

"Whatever you say," Margo answered.

Paralyzed, Lucy's brain slowly started to awake, snapping, popping, and zinging. Brogan adjusted himself inside his khakis. "This isn't over. We're not done negotiating," he said as if he had every intention of picking right back up where they left off.

Sweet, merciful MoonPies! Heat prickled her chest and neck. Not sexual heat, but embarrassing heat. Lucy slid from the desktop, tugging down her hiked-up skirt. She inched away from the crush of her life, who held the power to overwhelm her, make her wish for things she'd never have, and then split her heart wide open. "There's nothing else to negotiate. Either you accept my terms, or you don't," she said in a shockingly calm voice.

In agitation, he scrubbed a hand over his mouth. "I'll send Javier in to draw up the papers." He moved toward the door.

"You promise to help with Parker?"

With a hand on the knob, he peered over his shoulder. "Yes, I'll help you with Parker," he said with all the enthusiasm of a man going in for a rectal exam.

"And…the other." She cocked her head.

Desire and the promise of exceptional, wild gorilla sex filled his fiery green eyes. "Just sign the papers."

"But—" The door closed behind him. Legs collapsing, Lucy sat in the chair, wondering how her life had gone from pigeon cuckoo to spider-monkey crazy.

On Thursday night, Brogan stood against the back wall next to the kitchen door, with his arms folded, surveying his crowded store. Lucy had been on the job for only three days, and Brogan watched as the residents of Harmony swilled samples of BetterBites organic beers, ate organic cheeses on homemade bread and crackers, and sampled his granola. Yep. The store was packed. Why? Because this Thursday night was Singles Samplings, followed by Friday night Prepared Meals and Name That Tune with the Harmony Huggers. All courtesy of his new marketing guru…Lucy.

Several single women swarmed Javier by the front counter as he explained the benefits of healthy eating. Brogan watched Arlene Tomlin in leopard hot pants, denim vest, and pink cowboy hat squeeze Javier's bicep as she cooed something in his ear. Brogan's stomach soured at the sight of the Ardbuckle twins, Opal and Emma, in matching bowling outfits with Gutter Gals monogrammed on the back, feeding Clinton and Clancy Percy mango salsa on crackers. He guessed Clancy wasn't opposed to his sissy-ass store after all, when freebies were being handed out. His gaze traveled down the aisles to shoppers examining packages and tossing items in their baskets. That part he liked. And hearing the sweet ring of the cash register bell. But when he sighted Jo Ellen Huggins heading in his direction, wearing a tight Dalmatian-spotted skirt, red ruffled top with sky-high sandals, and the look of a hungry predator, he started to sweat. *Where the hell is Lucy?* He turned to escape when the kitchen door swung open, and Margo shoved a basket of cut-up muffins in his arms.

"Lucy said to put these out next to the hot tea station for people to sample."

"Lucy's in there with you?" He didn't hide the panic laced with relief from his voice.

"Yoo-hoo, Brogan!" Jo Ellen's hand wrapped around his bicep in an amazingly strong grip. Sheee-it.

Margo snickered. "Work it, lover boy." The door closed, cutting him off from salvation. Damn. So close.

"Uh, hey, Jo Ellen. How you been?"

"Why, Brogan Reese, you've been back in town for five months, and not once have you stopped by for a visit. Ooh, are those muffins?" Jo Ellen plucked a muffin piece from the basket in his hand and popped it in her mouth. "These are so-o-o good. Here, try one."

"Nah, I—" Jo Ellen's fingers shoved fresh banana nut muffin in his mouth as she smiled.

"You know, I'm hosting a Mary Kay party at my house next Thursday, and I would love to serve these. What else do you suggest?" she purred. Brogan had a strong feeling Jo Ellen didn't want to hear about healthy food options. She had something more carnal on the menu…with him as the main course.

"Er, I need to put these up front. If you'll excuse—"

"That sounds perfect. A Mary Kay party with lots of women," Lucy piped up, appearing by his side.

"You should come, Lucy. We have so much fun, and I give the best makeovers."

Lucy took the basket from Brogan's hands. "Let me check my schedule. But I know Brogan's free, and he will personally deliver a variety of homemade muffins, along with our chutney-smothered baked Brie, and organic crackers. You'll love it."

Brogan stiffened and fixed her with his steely gaze. She tossed him a cheeky smile. "Lucy, you're mistaken. I'm not free. The Happy Hookers are scheduled for a meeting here next Thursday night." His voice held a threatening edge directed smack-dab at her.

"That shouldn't be a problem, because my party is during the day," Jo Ellen said, clutching his arm in a painful grip.

Lucy tossed her ponytail. "Perfect. Let me write up your take-out order, and you can settle the bill before you leave." Lucy nudged him with her shoulder. "Brogan, introduce Jo Ellen to your new organic frozen bananas dipped in chocolate. I bet she won't be able to eat just one." *Frozen bananas!* Lucy actually had the nerve to waggle her eyebrows, as if Jo Ellen needed any more encouragement.

"Lucy…" He lunged for her, but she'd skipped from his reach and scooted down aisle five. Brogan could've sworn he heard her laughing. As Jo Ellen dragged him toward the frozen-dessert section, Brogan glanced over his shoulder at the blue-and-white tie-dyed dress molded to Lucy's cute butt, swaying down the aisle. He took great pleasure in imagining his palm smacking that butt when he finally got her alone.

"Brogan, you're not paying attention. M-m-m, these are divine." Jo Ellen drew out her last words as she wrapped her painted red lips around a chocolate frozen banana. Brogan hardly refrained from shuddering. Oh, yeah, Lucy may not be able to sit for an entire week.

Before Jo Ellen could drag him over to the champagne and chocolate-covered strawberries station, Dottie Duncan blocked his path with her big hair, fake eyelashes, and ten bejeweled fingers planted on her full hips. "We need to talk," she barked in her demanding voice. "Jo Ellen, I just overheard three gals over by those fancy cucumbers talking about facials. Git on over there and introduce them to Mary Kay." Dottie motioned with her head toward the produce section.

Jo Ellen released the death grip on his arm, smoothing down her skirt and adjusting her top. "Thanks, Dottie. I'm on it." She started to walk off and must've remembered she was dumping him for the possibility of selling more lipstick and blush...*not* that he was complaining. "Thanks, Brogan. See you next Thursday at ten. Don't be late." She blew him a kiss and headed to find girls in need of makeovers.

"You're welcome," Dottie said to the relief written all over his face.

"Uh..."

"Jo Ellen is a sweet girl, and she can flat-out sell some makeup. But ever since she lost Keith Morgan to Bertie Anderson...not that there was any contest," Dottie whispered behind her hand, "she's been desperate for a man."

"Don't look at me. I'm not in the market for a wife."

"Hmmm, not for Jo Ellen, anyhow," Dottie said as she scooped some granola from a nearby bowl into her palm.

"What do you think of my granola? Good, isn't it?" he said, smiling as he tilted his head and dropped some in his mouth.

She grunted. "It beats Grady's hot boiled peanuts. Ever since he stopped making them in a fifty-gallon drum over a fire pit and started cooking them in a crock pot." She shook her head, making her jumbo gold star earrings swing. "Just not the same."

Brogan had forgotten about Grady's Gas & Bait's famous boiled peanuts.

"Somebody needs to offer to make them in the drum again. Grady's getting too old for all that work," Vance Kerner said, clapping Brogan on the shoulder. "Hey, Bro. Hey there, Dottie." He nodded, his dark hair brushing the tops of his shoulders.

"Look what the cat dragged in. Where you been hiding, Vance Kerner? You sure didn't dress up if you're in the market for a wife." Dottie gave Vance a once-over, curling her lip at his ratty torn jeans, beat-up Nikes, and faded black Harley-Davidson T-shirt with "Ride a Hog" over the left breast pocket. Vance gave Dottie a leer as he took a long pull from his beer, looking more like a bad-ass pirate than a best-selling author of two spy war thrillers.

Brogan laughed, reaching for a cold beer in one of the galvanized tubs full of ice set on the table. "You do realize this is Singles Night?"

Dottie humphed. "Of course he does. Nobody needs a wife more than Mr. Bookends. He holes himself up for weeks. Never eats right, and Lord-a-mighty, no telling what that house looks like. Probably hasn't seen a mop in years."

Vance gave her a wicked grin, and Dottie's face flushed to her platinum roots. "Aw, now, that's not true. About the cleaning. Just last week, Ida Hogg came by and went to town. You can see your reflection in my polished wood floors, they're so shiny."

"Who's cooking for you?" Dottie tried to appear

indifferent, but Brogan knew she reveled in the attention Vance paid her.

"That's why I'm here. For some healthy prepared meals." Vance's gaze wandered over the store. "Had no idea you were giving the single women in this town something to get worked up over, Reese. Was this your idea?"

Brogan almost snorted beer through his nose. "Hell no. This was all Lucy's idea. Part of her marketing plan."

"The same Lucy I saw you swapping spit with Saturday night?" Vance asked with raised brows.

"Fuh—" Brogan caught himself before he dropped the f-bomb in front of Dottie. "Screw you, Kerner," he said under his breath. Vance laughed, flashing strong white teeth in direct contrast to his scruffy, dark facial hair.

"Just as I thought." Dottie pointed a long bright-blue nail at Brogan. "I knew you were after Lucy. You better not break her heart, or you'll have me and half this town to answer to," she warned.

"I'm not breaking anybody's heart. Don't get your nose all out of joint." Brogan patted Dottie's shoulder. "Lucy's working for me because we need her expertise." He didn't elaborate on the rest of the bargain.

"We'll see about that. I wanna chat with her about helping me with the Toot-N-Tell." Dottie seemed to be in deep thought as she pursed her lips. But suddenly she cackled. "Look alive, boys. Company is heading your way."

Sure enough, barreling down aisle two on a mission were five women led by Jo Ellen Huggins and Arlene Tomlin, their sights set on Vance and him. *Damn.*

"Thanks for the free beer, Bro. See you around." Vance saluted with his empty bottle and snuck behind the racks of fresh bread to escape the prowling single women.

Yep. Lucy owed him. Big time.

Chapter 18

IT WAS AFTER TEN, AND LUCY WAS EXHAUSTED FROM working the busy singles night at BetterBites. Home at last, she propped her feet up on the pink wicker ottoman, enjoying the cold carbonated fizz of the Cheerwine trickling down her throat. Like Coke except better and made right here in North Carolina. She'd purchased it earlier at the Toot-N-Tell, along with a bag of Cheetos. It had been a long, hard day, and her dogs were killing her. Wiggling her toes with the sparkly turquoise-green polish made her smile. Not having Anthony the pinhead possum eater censor her appearance was a downright emancipation. Ahhh, a little celebration was in order as she swigged her soda.

With Parker in football practice, her mornings started early. She had to have him at the field by seven, packed with lunch and a clean change of clothes. Thank goodness BetterBites made the lunches easy, or she'd be in a real dill pickle. Too bad it didn't offer laundry service. Parker's dirty practice clothes needed to be washed daily, not because he didn't own any extra workout clothes, but because the stench almost gagged her. No way could she allow that stinkiness to pile up in the laundry room.

She slumped back on the soft pink sofa, facing the wall of windows in the sunroom. Lucy enjoyed relaxing in this room. The darkened leaves on the big oaks obscured her view, creating a cocoon of privacy. Julia continued to test her patience as she added to her ridiculous list of errands, and annoyed her with endless text messages all morning, but bringing Parker in to spend time with her gained Lucy a much deserved reprieve. In the past two days, Brogan had stopped by around five to take Parker for some male bonding. Once they shot hoops with guys at the Jaycee Park, and once they washed Brogan's car and cleaned up construction debris around his house.

Parker had seemed okay both times when he'd returned home, but his sullen mask hadn't completely disappeared, and his attitude toward Lucy could have used improving.

She drank her soda after licking neon-orange cheese flakes from her fingers. On the brighter side, she had enjoyed these last few days, working on BetterBites. She'd been busy setting up new Facebook, Twitter, and other social media accounts to better serve this area, customizing the accounts to appeal to the people of Harmony. And then she talked up Singles Samples night to all the right people and *bam*! It had been a huge success. They'd sold more tonight than BetterBites had sold in the last two weeks.

When Lucy had finally cut out around ten, Margo had her arms elbow deep in bread dough, Javier had his fingers on the calculator in front of his laptop, and Brogan had his hands full with four of Harmony's finest single women: Jo Ellen Huggins, Arlene Tomlin, and the Ardbuckle twins. A smile cracked wide-open on Lucy's face as she pictured Brogan nodding and smiling with that deer-in-the-headlights look. If Brogan played his cards right, Harmony's BetterBites would outproduce all his other locations combined.

Lucy sat up and listened. She thought she'd heard the front door open. Parker. If he was sneaking out again, she might have to *cut* him. She jumped up and raced for the door, when she slammed into a cement wall of muscle. "Gah!" She bounced off Brogan's hard chest and almost landed on her butt. "You scared the Twinkies right out of me. What are you doing here?"

"Settling a score."

"Huh?" Lucy brushed the hair from her eyes and raised her gaze to Brogan's hard, furious face. *Ruh-roe.* This did not look like a guy who'd just had his best night since the opening of BetterBites. Why the hoot not? She'd done a good job. He should be smiling and offering a raise. She planted a fist on cocked hip. "What score?" His aggressive step forward made Lucy back up and rethink her stance.

"How about the score where you tried to pimp me out? You know…where you have me bringing food to Jo Ellen's makeup party and serving like I'm a boy toy for hire?" *Bump*, the back of her legs hit the wicker lounge chair angled toward the windows.

"Or the score where you signed me up to provide food at the Clippety Do Dah hair salon to a gaggle of crazy women all intent on picking me apart?" Fingers shoved through his already tousled hair, and he emitted a groan of aggravation. "Or the score where you have me and Javier providing the food and entertainment at Mary Pat's bridal shower? Hell, Lucy, Mary Pat's eighty-four if she's a day. Why is she having a bridal shower…with entertainment? What about those *scores*?" By the time he ended his outburst, Lucy had leaned so far back she fell onto the seat cushion with her legs dangling over the armrest.

Brogan didn't waste any time caging her in with both arms. "Would you care to explain just what the hell you were thinking?" he growled close to her face. Lucy didn't like this Brogan. She missed the smiling Brogan with the clear green eyes and cheerful attitude. The one who had more energy than any bunny she ever knew, with or without batteries.

"I'm marketing. Just like you're paying me to do. In fact, begged me to do." She was doing her job, and she did it very well. She had the numbers to prove it. "You don't like your results? You don't want to sell the food stocked in your freezers or taking up space on your shelves? I must've misunderstood. I could've sworn you wanted to increase traffic and sales. My bad. Must need a refresher course on Marketing 101."

Her impassioned speech would've been more effective if she hadn't felt like an awkward baby goat stuck in a barrel with only her arms and legs dangling out. Brogan grabbed hold of her shoulders and hauled her to her feet, which meant she now stood within inches of his light-blue button-down and his scowling face.

"Marketing, yes. Pimping, no. Where did you get the idea that I was up for sale? I'm not on the menu. Sell granola, sell muffins, sell chocolate-covered frozen bananas, but don't sell me." He shook her shoulders before releasing her.

Note to self: start locking front door. Lucy inched sideways to escape his wrath, along with his exotic smell that always made her want to do something rash, like jump him and suck his neck. "Uh…I understand what you're saying, but you're looking at it all wrong."

Frowning, he folded his arms across his solid chest. "Why don't you enlighten me?"

"Sure. BetterBites is a great, unique place where you can find off-the-wall stuff like that granola crap or those disgusting seaweed thingies next to the spiced ginger." Brogan didn't disguise his exaggerated eye roll. "But it has limited appeal around here." She held up a finger. "Or it's perceived as limited. Harmony is not DC, New York, or Atlanta. I figured the best way to get people to buy into all that organic, healthy stuff you want to unload, we have to sell *you*." She could hear the grinding of his teeth. "I mean, look at you. You've got it going on"—she snapped her fingers in a Z formation— "smokin' hot, buffed, good-looking, and yes…single."

"I swear, Lucy, I'm this close to tanning your hide." An inch of space showed between his thumb and forefinger. "I'm *not* for sale, and I don't perform at eighty-year-old's bachelorette parties."

"You don't have to. Just show up at the parties with platters of food. You and Javier wear those BetterBites green logo shirts, unwrap the platters, be nice, smile a lot"—she shook her finger at his face—"not that growling thing you got going on now. Chat them up a little and then leave. How hard can it be? Just tonight we booked three more parties, and that's not counting the Happy Hookers or the Harmony Huggers already on the schedule." She waited, hoping for his endearing smile to return.

"Lucy, I want to sell a better way of life…a healthier way of eating. *Not* my unmarried status to every single woman three states over."

She reached for her Cheerwine on the wicker end table. "Understood. But there's more than one way to skin a cat. We need to get people to *want* to step in your store…to introduce them to your products. So, we dangle a delectable tidbit that lures them in. Your job is to sell them once we hook them."

"I'm the delectable tidbit?" The edge had disappeared from his voice.

She nodded, sipping her drink. "Sex sells. It's a proven fact."

"Uh-huh. This is how it's going down." He ticked off on his fingers. "For every stupid makeup, hair-curling, knitting, or geriatric sing-along you schedule, you have to book a guys' event too."

"Like a male salon party where guys get haircuts and shaves?"

"Hell no. Like poker night or fantasy football or hoops night. Look for some sports events to sponsor." He gestured in agitation.

"Already working on it. I've put in a call to Keith Morgan. We might be sponsoring one of his tournaments." She placed her drink back on the table.

"Good. Make sure we do."

Somehow his chest filled her vision. Lucy dug her toes into the cotton braids of the rug covering the tile floor. Suddenly she realized she'd been arguing about marketing techniques, wearing only her yellow daisies sleeping boxers and green tank top, braless. How did this happen? She'd been settling down for a night of chillaxing with her favorite junk food and ended up defending the philosophy of "sex sells" in her skimpy PJs.

"Sex sells, huh?" he said as if reading her mind in his

gooey caramel voice, the one that made Lucy's heart beat double-time and her knees shake. He reached for a hank of hair and tugged until she leaned into him. "You buying, Little Lucy?" he whispered, lowering his mouth.

Lucy turned her head in the nick of time, and Brogan's lips brushed her cheek. She pushed on his rock-hard chest. "We had a deal."

"I never agreed to any deal." He stalked her with hungry intent, backing her up as her mind scrambled for something…anything.

"I'm your employee. This isn't proper. Uh…we need to think of Julia." *Bam-o.* He stopped. She mentioned Julia's name, and all the sexy yearning and desire directed at Lucy vanished faster than ribs at a Rotary Club barbecue. The subdued light from the one lamp washed over him but didn't soften any of his features, from his long legs, flat stomach, and wide shoulders to the scowl pulling at his mouth.

"This has nothing to do with Julia."

Didn't it? Everything in Lucy's world had something to do with Julia. Being back in this house with Brogan definitely had to do with Julia.

"The deal was I agreed to work for you, and we don't"—she circled her hand between them—"do this."

"That deal is bullshit. I have a better deal." Goose bumps covered her bare arm as he slid his hand up to the side of her neck, imprisoning her with his hot stare. He pulled until her breasts rested against his chest. "You prove your sex-sells theory to me…right now. Right here."

His lips hovered above her mouth. The unfaithful part of her disregarded Julia and her history with Brogan.

And the stupid side of her ignored Brogan's feelings for Julia and Lucy's fear of ending up hurt.

The instant their lips touched, raw desire ripped straight through to a place so deep, she'd never known its existence until Brogan. His arm tightened around her waist, lifting her on her toes. Brogan drew the very breath from her, making her dizzy. He kissed as if she fed his soul. She felt engulfed. Devoured. Delicious. And she wanted more.

Brogan followed her down on the sofa and growled, "I've pictured you here." His mouth covered hers as she skated her hands up his strong back, loving the feel of his bunched muscles through his shirt.

"Here? On this pink sofa?" she managed to mumble before attacking his lips again.

She felt his smile. "Not exactly. Basically, anywhere with me on top of you." He kissed his way along her jawline until he found her ear, which he nibbled as if tasting a delicacy.

Lucy squirmed and tried squeezing her shoulder up, but his head blocked the way. "That tickles." She sighed, and then giggled. "Stop."

Brogan lifted his head, wearing a pleased smile. Finally. She could live the rest of her life glowing from his lovely smile, and she'd be happy. It had that kind of effect on her.

"Good to know. Now, where was I?" He gripped her waist, shifting her up the sofa cushions, but stopped at the sound of a loud crunch. "What was that?"

"Nothing." Lucy tried pulling his head down so his lips could go back to kissing and not talking. Shifting her again, the crunching sound grew louder. His hand fumbled behind her head. "There's nothing up there. Don't you want to grope a little lower?" She shimmied her hips against him.

He held up an orange Cheeto. "Seriously?"

"I'm off the clock, Dr. Oz. I can eat whatever I want."

Brogan hauled Lucy up and peered down at the smashed bag of Cheetos lying on the cushions. She could feel a lecture on the benefits of healthy eating about to commence. Nothing killed her lust-filled mood more. She wanted to be smooching and touching and feeling and getting all orgasmic. Not listening to the perils of bad nutrition.

She pressed fingers to his mouth. "Don't start." She brushed the bag to the floor, mourning the loss of her favorite snack for only a nanosecond. "I promise never to get caught eating them again if we can get back to what we were doing."

He gave her a carnal grin. "And what was that?"

"The good stuff. My proof on the sex-sells theory." She wrapped her legs around his waist, wanting his heat and hardness where it belonged…between her thighs.

"Still not convinced. I guess you'll have to show me," he murmured before eating his way down her throat the same time his hand slid beneath her top and cupped her bare breast.

"Oh! Um…" She squirmed under his touch. Her nipples grew even harder. Desire and need slammed into her, making her want more. She wanted his mouth everywhere. Brogan's impatient hand shoved her top up, and his hot, wet mouth latched onto her nipple—right there. She spasmed from the shock of it. He sucked, swirling his tongue, creating an ache between her thighs.

Brogan paid her other breast the same fervent attention as his rough palm slid down her waist, over her belly and hips. He slipped his hand under the band of her boxers. Lucy squeezed his shoulders as she moaned. His fingers moved across her slick flesh, and lights danced before her eyes. He lifted his head, and his gaze burned with the fire of dark, smoky sex. Heart pounding inside her chest, she fought to breathe.

"God, you feel great. Wet and hot." His fingers moved across her heat in a teasing dance, and Lucy practically levitated from the sofa. It had been too long since she'd felt overpowering desire pulse beneath her skin, sending her out of control.

"I want to kiss you there," he said, continuing his assault as he blazed a trail down her stomach with his lips and mouth and teeth.

Flames of pleasure singed her flesh as she clutched his shoulders. "Oh…*oh*—"

"Lucy? Is that you?"

Ice froze in Lucy's veins. "Wha—?" She lifted her head and stared into Brogan's stunned face. "Julia," she whispered. She scrambled to sit up, pushing Brogan off as he yanked up her shorts.

"Lucy?" Julia's voice came from the next room.

"C-coming," Lucy croaked, clearing her throat. Brogan jerked her up and pulled her top down from around her neck. Her knees wobbled, and his hands gripped her waist to keep her from collapsing. She attempted to smooth her almost-had-sex-on-the-sofa hair in place. On shaky legs, she managed to move past Brogan toward the front room.

"Lucy, something's wrong…I heard noises—" Julia

met her at the entrance of the sunroom. She took one look at Lucy's disheveled, interrupted sex-capade appearance, and her face registered horror-movie proportions. Julia's eyes went from shocked to scary, bitchy glare-down. And Lucy's still-tingling nipples weren't doing her any favors. "*Lucy*, what…who… Did you just have *sex*? In my *house*? Under my roof? With Parker sleeping upstairs?" Julia came close to screeching.

Lucy knew this was not one of her finer moments. Not because she shouldn't have sex. And not because Parker slept upstairs. *Not* that she had sex…she didn't even have an orgasm (thank you very much, Miss Interloper). This moment hit high on the embarrassing Richter scale because she'd been about to get it on with Brogan Reese. Which was wrong on too many levels to number. But what really infuriated Lucy, aside from the fact that she had no control when it came to Mr. Hotty Beefcake, was Julia declaring this *her* house. When did that real estate transaction take place? Last time Lucy spoke with her dad, he still owned the house, and Julia lived under his roof.

"Look—"

"Julia, you don't look so good…" She and Brogan spoke in tandem.

In a blur, Brogan scooped Julia up in his arms. "Lucy, call the doctor," he barked as he strode toward the living room and lowered Julia in her satin pink bathrobe onto the sofa. "Breathe," he said as Julia groaned and clutched her belly.

Son of a buzzle! The baby? Now? Lucy scrambled for her phone on the end table and knocked it to the floor with her nervous fingers. "Dammit!" She dropped to her knees, her hands shaking as she scrolled contacts and pressed for Julia's doctor. Hurrying to the living room, she stopped next to the sofa.

"Lucy, tell him to meet me at the hospital," Julia said before she rocked forward in pain.

"Hello? Dr. Andrew's service?" she asked the operator. She watched as Brogan brought Julia a glass of water and supported her shoulders as she took a small sip, holding her steady. Lucy explained the situation to the emergency operator. "Just a minute… Julia, she wants to know if you're having contractions, and if yes, then how far apart?"

"I'm having something…a searing pain across my back and middle. They started when I saw you—*arrrgh!*"

Fried frog legs. This wasn't good. How did Lucy explain to the operator that almost having sex with her sister's ex-boyfriend brought on contractions? After relaying Julia's description over the phone, Lucy said, "Uh…okay. I'll bring her in right now." Pressing the phone off, she said, "I need to take her to the emergency room. The doctor will meet us there." Her gaze darted from Brogan's concerned face to Julia's, contorted in pain.

"Go pack her bag and bring it out to the car. I'll drive Julia to the hospital, and you stay here with Parker," Brogan ordered in a no-nonsense voice.

"My bag is already packed. It's in the closet," Julia panted as Brogan lifted her again as if she weighed no more than a puffy cotton ball. Lucy ordered her legs to move, but her mind couldn't get past the picture Brogan and Julia painted—Julia's shiny dark hair falling over Brogan's strong arms, Brogan murmuring soothing words next to Julia's temple as he carried her toward the front door. The perfect, beautiful couple. Lucy's knees knocked together.

"Lucy…now!" She jumped at Brogan's command, and her feet skidded across the Oriental carpet and down the hall to Julia's bedroom.

Brogan was buckling Julia in when Lucy raced down the front walk, carrying Julia's bag. "Here." She handed it to Brogan, he tossed it in the backseat and jogged around the hood.

"I'll call you later with an update," he said, slipping behind the wheel.

"You're going to be fine." But Julia couldn't hear her behind the closed window. "Don't worry about Parker. I'll take care of him," she called anyhow as she watched Brogan's taillights disappear at the end of the driveway.

Chapter 19

DAMMIT. BROGAN GLANCED AT JULIA CLUTCHING HER belly with her eyes squeezed shut. "You doing okay? We're almost there." Julia moaned, and her head rolled from side to side. "Five more minutes." Really ten, but he didn't want to add to her worry. The last time he'd rushed a pregnant woman to the hospital, his wife had been sitting next to him having a miscarriage. His insides burned with the very same searing pain he'd felt years before. No way in hell would he allow it to happen again. Not on his watch.

Brogan gave Julia's hand a reassuring squeeze. "Breathe, Julia. Nice and easy."

Julia released a huge breath. "Whoa. Did you feel that?" she asked, pressing his hand on her rock-hard belly.

"Fuh…was that a kick or contraction?" Brogan gave her a quick glance as he accelerated through another intersection.

"The baby's kicking. All those contractions must've woken him up." She pressed tight to his hand. "There it is again." Baby? More like a bucking bronco. He smiled in wonder over the miracle of life growing inside Julia.

Julia pushed his hand away. "What the frick do you think you're doing with Lucy?" she said in a low voice. The pain etched across Julia's face had morphed into scary anger.

Shee-it. He didn't want to discuss Lucy right now. Especially with Julia. And especially since he had no explanation. He couldn't explain something he didn't understand himself. He'd come over tonight to rip Lucy a new one about pimping him out to the single women in Harmony. He'd wanted to wring her neck… not kiss it.

"Nothing happened. I came by to discuss work—"

"You better not screw with her, Brogan. I mean it. Not under my roof," Julia warned in a flat voice.

Brogan didn't have time to clarify if Julia meant not to screw Lucy ever or only under her roof. He pulled up to the hospital entrance where an orderly met them with a wheelchair and swept Julia away. Brogan knew Julia didn't want him anywhere near Lucy. He understood.

But he had no intentions of obeying.

"Hey, Julia…how you feeling?"

The next morning, Lucy tapped on the door to Julia's hospital room. The antiseptic smell made Lucy's nose twitch. Pale blue washed the walls in the room, and bright sun poured through the vertical blinds. A game show played on the TV mounted on the wall, but the sound had been muted.

The hospital bed propped Julia in the upright position, and meds and fluids dripped through an IV to stop the contractions. The doctor had said Julia suffered from dehydration, which could start premature labor. A surge of remorse swept over Lucy. She'd begrudgingly fetched numerous glasses of water for Julia the last few days, but last night when she'd allowed Brogan to make a meal of her body, hydrating Julia had been the farthest thing from her mind.

"Here, I brought you magazines." She handed Julia three magazines on fashion, home décor, and the latest Hollywood gossip. "There's an article in there about John Stamos and how he has an evil twin bent on destroying the world." John Stamos from *Full House* had been Julia's huge crush back in high school. "Dr. Andrew says you can come home in a few days."

"How's Parker?" Julia placed the magazines on the tray table that held a juice box with a straw and a plastic cup of ice chips.

Lucy plunked her purple handbag on the nightstand next to the humongous bouquet of white and pink roses. Beside the gorgeous flowers sat a card that read *Get well soon. xoxo Brogan.* Alrighty then. Message received. Pinpricks of pain stabbed the backs of her eyes as she blinked away hot tears—from all the tossing, turning, and worrying she did last night, not from the obvious fact staring her in the face that Brogan still loved Julia, and she'd been a world-class fool.

"Parker's worried about you, but I told him the doctor wanted to keep you here for a few days to make sure everything was okay with the baby."

"Good. Thanks. Please bring him by after practice." Julia fiddled with the juice box.

Julia's restrained, cool demeanor unnerved Lucy. Her complicated food orders, ridiculous errands, and self-centered requests would be a warm welcome over this chilly reception. "What else do you want? Dr. Andrew said no work, which means no computer, but maybe I can bring some DVDs or—"

"I want you to stay away from Brogan." Blat. Right there in the open. Julia didn't waste any time. She'd cut right to the chase.

Lucy lifted her chin. "That's going to be kind of hard since I work for him and he's helping with Parker—at your insistence. In case you forgot that one small detail."

Julia's face hardened. "I need to know you're keeping an eye on Parker and not on what's in Brogan's pants."

Low blow. Not backing down, Lucy jammed her fists on her hips. "You've got nothing to worry about. I'm always about my job and my responsibilities. And when I've collected my last paycheck, I'm blowing this Popsicle stand." She snatched up her handbag, causing Brogan's love note to flutter to the floor.

"What do you mean? Where are you going?" Agitation replaced Julia's fury. "You're not leaving me again, are you?"

The nerve. "Uh, yeah, I am." She bent to pick the note off the floor. "Don't worry. I'll run your errands and grow fresh mint for your water, and I'll even buy your underwear until you give birth, but after that…I'm outta here."

"Why would you do that when you have a good job at BetterBites? That's just dumb and irresponsible. This is your home—"

Typical. Julia wanted Lucy gainfully employed but didn't want her to have anything to do with Brogan. Well, it didn't work that way. "Not according to you it isn't. You made it perfectly clear last night that I was trespassing under *your* roof." Fuming, Lucy hefted her handbag over her shoulder.

"That's not what I meant."

Lucy's laugh sounded flat. "Forget it. It never felt like home after you moved in anyhow. You can have it. All that pink nauseates me." She chucked the note onto Julia's lap. "And you can have lover boy too."

Lucy rushed from the room before Julia witnessed scalding tears spilling down her cheeks. Choking back sobs, somehow she made it through the hospital, out to the parking lot, and inside the minivan, where she banged her head on the steering wheel. "Idiot." A sob wracked her chest. How could she have lost her cool like that? She was supposed to remain calm and levelheaded, not cause Julia to go into labor. Lucy reached for left-over napkins in the glove compartment and wiped her wet face. Coming home to Harmony, her expectations had been low. She knew she'd be at Julia's beck and call. But she was willing to do it for her sister and her nephew. She wanted to mend fences. She wanted to be a part of their lives. She wanted a family.

What had changed? Wiping her nose with the napkin, she faced her answer. Her own deluded fantasies about Brogan. *Immature, romantic fantasies... not reality.*

Inhaling deep breaths, she made a solemn promise to change her attitude. From this moment forward, Lucy would be the best stepsister and aunt possible. She'd help Julia have a healthy baby and help Parker adjust to his new sibling. And she'd be the best marketing consultant for BetterBites, increasing their sales beyond their wildest dreams. Because that was *her* specialty. Creating opportunities and desires. And she was damned good at her job.

What she wouldn't be was the "girlfriend stabilizer" while Brogan waited for Julia to rejoin society after her convalescence, picking up where they'd left off. Nope. Lucy and Brogan were never going to happen. Ever.

~~~

"Lucy's avoiding me," Brogan said to Javier, pushing his empty beer mug away. Parker and half his football team whooped it up in the middle of the Dog on Monday night. Six tables had been pushed together to accommodate the kids. Pizzas covered the tabletops, and the boys drank gallons of Coke. The coaching staff and parents sat together within listening range. Not wanting to give anyone the wrong impression about his relationship with Parker, Brogan chose a booth in the corner and had invited Javier to join him.

"Of course she is. I don't blame her. But she's still doing a damn good job." Javier reached for a spicy chicken wing. "She booked a tent with concessions for Morgan's tennis exhibition this coming Saturday. In-store traffic has increased over fifty percent since she started tweeting."

A steady stream of customers flowed through the door of the Dog. The smell of sweet, buttery onions and grilled burgers permeated the air. Country tunes played from the jukebox, and the dance floor held a few swaying couples. Everything Javier said was right. Lucy had performed better than he'd ever dreamed. Her marketing ideas had been effective and right on target. New people dropped by the store every day. And he didn't give a shit.

The other night when he had her half-naked and panting with need played in his head. If Julia hadn't interrupted, he'd like to think he would've put a stop to it before going all the way. He'd like to believe he held a tight rein over the physical urges of his body. He balled his hand into a fist, but these days he wasn't sure of anything.

"Lucy's being careful. You're her boss, and I bet she doesn't want to give this wacky town any more to talk about." Brogan gave a sharp nod. Javier was right. Lucy hated being the subject of Harmony's gossip even more than he did. But having Julia go into premature labor, right after catching them half-naked, had scared Lucy into avoiding him like he was a rabid, horny dog foaming at the mouth.

"You're right. And I don't need the complication right now. New York is breathing down my neck."

"You need a life. Told you we should hire a couple more guys. Ryan Bingham is still interested in hooking up. He's got great New York connections and worked several years with Dean & DeLuca."

"Another round, please," Brogan said to the waitress. He drummed his fingers on the sparkly laminate tabletop. "I know. Ryan's a good guy. But I'm not ready to relinquish that kind of control yet. We're still rocking from the payout I had to make to Kathryn's dad. We need to stay the course and present a united front. I don't want New York questioning who's in charge."

Javier gave an impatient wave of his hand, but the depths of his dark eyes showed concern and pity. Brogan hated that. Because of *his* stupidity and carelessness, he'd almost cost Javier his career.

"Stop blaming yourself. It's over and done with. You did the right thing. You married her," Javier said in a low voice.

"Yeah, and then I divorced her." Brogan remembered how panic had set in and he'd had to get out.

"Not before giving it everything you had. It wasn't meant to be, and BetterBites survived. You think you're the only guy who ever mixed business with pleasure and got screwed in the end? We fixed it, and we're moving forward. New York wouldn't be investing if they didn't believe in us."

Brogan's stomach churned.

"You're pushing yourself too hard. Trying to sell your mom's house, making a success of BetterBites, dealing with New York—" Javier stopped. Brogan knew he wanted to add "chasing the demons of your dad," but Javie never pushed when it came to Brogan's past. "Take a couple days off. I can handle things around here, especially with Lucy's help. And Margo is more than capable in the back of the house."

"I'm fine—"

"Brogan, we're going in the other room to play pinball," Parker said, standing next to his booth.

Didn't spending time with Parker count for taking time off? Not if it gave him a bigger headache than he already had. Brogan checked his watch. He needed to have Parker home around nine. "Sure. We have to leave in an hour. Need any money?" He started to fish for his wallet in his back pocket.

"Nah. Aunt Lucy gave me some earlier." Parker waved to his football buddies. "Let's go."

"Wait." Parker reluctantly turned around. "Where's your Aunt Lucy? I haven't seen her all day."

Parker shrugged. "With my mom. She came home from the hospital today. Aunt Lucy's been doing a lot of stuff from home." Yeah, Lucy had been doing a lot of hiding. Parker shoved his hands in the back pockets of his bright-orange board shorts. "She works for you. Don't you know where she is?" he asked as if Brogan were dumber than bird droppings. Yep. The respect that kid had for him grew and grew.

"Never mind. I'll speak with her tomorrow."

"Whatever." Parker loped off after his friends.

Javier's shoulders shook as he chuckled. Brogan smiled. "I'll shoot you for him…rock, paper, scissors. Loser gets Parker for the next week."

"Not on your life." Javier burst out laughing.

"What's so funny?" Dottie Duncan appeared by their booth with a longneck beer in one hand and a bowl of popcorn in the other. Brogan and Javier both moved to stand. "Don't get up, boys. Move on over, Brogan." She gestured with a tilt of her bleached-blond head. Brogan didn't dare glance at Javie, knowing he'd start laughing again. He slid along the booth as Dottie plopped down and shimmied her black denim-clad butt on the leather seat.

"I was telling Brogan he needed to take some time off. He's been working too hard. What do you think, Dottie?" Javier said with a twinkle in his eye. Brogan didn't disguise his snort. Javier was getting real comfortable with the locals, but two could play this game.

"You both could use some downtime. Haven't heard either of you dating any gals around here." She narrowed her heavily made-up eyes at them.

"Brogan will be delivering food to Jo Ellen's makeup party on Thursday. I'm sure he can wrangle up a date from that group."

"And Javier will be attending the Bible study at Hazel's on Wednesday night, and the Ardbuckle twins are always there." Javie mumbled something like "praise the Lord" under his breath. Brogan smiled at the waitress as she delivered their beers. "Would you like anything?" he offered Dottie.

She shook her lacquered helmet head. "I'm good. Both you boys are full of crap."

Brogan stopped with his beer halfway to his mouth. Oh boy.

"Brogan's not interested in anyone at Jo Ellen's party, unless Lucy's going to be there. And even if she were, he'd probably be too chickenshit to do anything about it." Dottie tilted her head, searching Javier's face. "Maybe you should start dating her."

Javier smiled the smile of a lying, cheating, slimy bastard. "That's a great idea. Not sure Lucy would agree, but I'll certainly give it a good ole college try."

The bottom of Brogan's beer hit the table hard. He hated to kick his best friend's ass, but if he went anywhere near Lucy…he was going down.

Dottie grunted as she grabbed a handful of popcorn. "Lucy's too good for either one of you bums. And I've a good mind to hire her away. I'm sure if I offered more pay, she wouldn't hesitate to work for me."

Javier coughed and Brogan cleared his throat. "Miz Duncan…I mean, Dottie. We value Lucy, and we really need—"

"Who needs Lucy?" Wanda Pattershaw dropped her peacock-feather handbag on the table and slid into the booth next to Javie.

"I need Lucy," Dottie declared loud enough for the entire bar to hear.

"To work for you? But what about BetterBites?"

Wanda's head turned from Javier to Brogan, bouncing her brown curls. "Have you fired Lucy because she won't sleep with you?" Wanda said even louder than Dottie.

"*Wanda!* Jesus. Keep your voice down."

"Can't say I blame her. All you boys think about these days is fornicating. Girls like some romancing. Maybe if you asked her out for a dinner date and dancing, you might get lucky." Did Dottie just say *fornicating* out loud? A hammer started to pound nails inside Brogan's head.

Wanda snapped her fingers. "That's a wonderful idea. I have the perfect guy. He's a carpet cleaner, *and* he plays fiddle in a bluegrass band. Javier, you'd double-date with me and Lucy, wouldn't you?" She batted her big eyes as her pink-painted lips formed a pout.

"*Sí, mi amor*…anything for you. *Shit.*" Javier flinched as Brogan's shoe connected with his shin.

"Who's not dating Lucy because she won't sleep with him?" Clinton Perry shuffled over to their booth, wearing a torn, sleeveless red T-shirt with "Skoal Chewing Tobacco" in black.

His even stupider brother, Clancy, sidled up next to him. "You? You Yankee traitor with a corncob up your ass?" he said, pointing his Bud at Brogan. Great. Brogan didn't have the energy to go another round with shit-for-brains Clancy.

"Is Lucy having trouble sleeping?"

"She needs to see Doc Mayfield for some of those pills."

"Lucy needs a good man."

Holy hell. Harmony at its finest as patrons shouted

out their concern over Lucy. The table shook as Javier started to laugh. And Clancy kept right on talking horseshit.

"…'cuz I've got fifty ways to show Lucy a good time. I'd take her cow-tipping, and I'd sleep with her under the stars by the lake, and…"

"My son Tervis is a good man. He'll sleep with Lucy."

Seething, Brogan ground his teeth as Clancy spoke over the bar chatter, leaning his dirty hand on the table. "I will sleep with Lucy any day of the week and twice on Sunday."

Brogan slammed his fist on the table, making the beer bottles jump. "Lucy is off limits. If anyone sleeps with Lucy, it's gonna be me!" Silence filled the air except for the jukebox playing Tim McGraw's "Real Good Man." Forty-five pairs of eyes stared at him, and forty-five mouths hung open.

Javie broke the thick silence and hooted with laughter.

Wanda purred like a tiger, "*Grrr*… You go, cowboy."

Dottie snickered. "Boy, you're wound up tighter than a Sealy mattress spring."

Brogan looked out and locked gazes with Parker, standing in the middle of the Dog.

"Man, you are such a dweeb." Parker shoved his hands in his pockets, shaking his head, and crossed the room toward the exit.

Yep. That about summed it up. He was a total dweeb.

Chapter 20

"I'VE TOLD YOU, I CAN'T BOWL," LUCY SAID TO THE back of Wanda's ponytail, swinging along with her booty-hugging white shorts. Wanda wore a tight hot-pink bowling T-shirt with "Pin Ups" in black on the back. Lucy crossed the blacktop parking lot to the Ten Pin Alley, tripping after Wanda. Apparently everyone showed up on Tuesday for Rock 'n' Bowl night where classic rock music played along with a cosmic light show.

Wanda turned and yanked on Lucy's hand. "Come on. You're gonna love it."

"Do I have to wear those gross, smelly bowling shoes?" Lucy glanced down at her orange flip-flops slapping against her feet.

"Don't worry. I brought extra socks." Wanda pulled the glass door open and shoved Lucy inside. The sounds of heavy balls rolling and pins crashing filled her ears. "Here." Wanda dug inside her pink-and-white-striped beach tote. "Put this on." She thrust a neon-green T-shirt at Lucy and a pair of white ankle socks.

Lucy shook the shirt out. "Ball Busters." She raised one brow. "How come I can't be a Pin Ups like you?"

"My team's full. The choices were 'Gutter Gals' with the Ardbuckle twins or 'Dry Humpers' with the Perry brothers. I thought 'Ball Busters' was best."

Wanda pushed her into the ladies' room near the

entrance. "This is just for fun. No one is competing. Hurry and put that shirt on." Wanda checked her lipstick in the mirror while Lucy locked herself inside one of the gray stalls.

"I feel bad about leaving Julia." Lucy's voice was muffled as she pulled the green shirt over her head.

"She'll be fine. Tweedle Dum and Tweedle Dummer will entertain her with all the latest gossip."

Lucy gulped as she tugged the shirt down over her boobs. Wanda was referring to Julia's besties, Marcia and Amanda. "That's what I'm afraid of. I kept Julia away from her phone and computer all day so she wouldn't see the gazillion tweets and posts on Facebook." Word of Brogan's outburst last night at the Dog spread like a match to a firecracker tent. She'd been imagining ways of killing Brogan Freakin' Reese. Death by rancid tofu held great appeal.

"Did you see the picture of me?" Wanda asked.

Lucy emerged from the stall. "How could I miss it? Your boobs were like giant bowling balls." She looked in the mirror. "Speaking of boobs…this top is too small. Is this meant for a toddler?" She tugged on the hem, but it barely met the top of her white jean shorts.

"Here, try this." Wanda handed Lucy a tube of lipstick.

"I can't believe I let you talk me into coming out." She outlined her lips with glossy pink. "Everyone is gossiping about Brogan doing the dirty deed with me."

Lucy had managed to avoid running into Brogan all day. She'd answered his texts only when they pertained to work, and ignored all the other attempts at apologies and explanations.

"At least they're not still yakking about Brogan being Parker's dad or wondering if you're gonna glue Julia's eyelids shut." Wanda zipped her makeup bag closed and tossed it in her tote. "They'll move on to the next topic. My prediction: bets will be placed on who Julia's baby daddy is."

Lucy stopped adjusting the elastic that held half her hair up. "Sheesh, I'm not sure I want to know."

Wanda slung her tote over her shoulder. "I do. And I bet after a few or fifteen strong cosmos at the Dog, I can get it out of Tweedle Dee and Tweedle Dumbass."

Lucy followed her out of the bathroom and up to the main floor. "Sweet Home Alabama" blared from the sound system. Lucy spotted the Ardbuckle twins with their "Gutter Gals" team in red and white. Next to their lane, Clinton and Clancy Perry wore black T-shirts with "Dry Humpers" in bright yellow.

"Here." From the check-in counter, Wanda handed Lucy a pair of classic rental bowling shoes with maroon and black sides. "Put these on," she said as she sat in one of the plastic bucket seats and pulled her fun hot-pink-and-white bowling shoes from her bag.

"Awww, those are cute. Why do I have to wear these ugly things?" Lucy said, holding her shoes as if they were contaminated from too many stinky feet, which they were.

"Because you're not a regular bowler. Maybe if you'd stick around longer than two months"—Wanda sat up from lacing her shoes—"you could join our team."

Oh, jelly bellies, no. Pink-and-white bowling shoes would not be strong enough incentive to convince her to stay. Hot dogs, popcorn, and beer smells made

Lucy's stomach growl. She hadn't eaten anything since her strawberry Pop-Tart from breakfast. She'd been too busy waiting on Julia and making sure she stayed hydrated. She'd even hung out and played backgammon with her on the old board Lucy's dad had given them one Christmas. What she didn't do was bring up the past. And she certainly didn't inform Julia of Brogan's asinine public declaration at the Dog last night. She had a sneaky suspicion Julia knew, but neither one of them mentioned it.

"Ready. Where to?" She stood, pulling on the hem of her shirt and glancing around the lanes. Bertie Morgan waved, wearing the same hot-pink shirt as Wanda. No wonder they were named the "Pin Ups"…all of them had bombshell figures. Lucy followed Wanda to the ball rack, and Wanda plopped a marbleized orange one into her hands. "Man, this thing is heavy. You sure I can do this?" She trotted after Wanda. "Where's my group?"

"Next to our lane. With the neon-green shirts."

"Is that Javier?" A guy with thick dark hair and dark complexion had just bowled a strike.

"Where?" Wanda asked, sounding suspiciously innocent.

"That guy wearing the 'Ball Busters' shirt, bowling and high-fiving—" Lucy stopped dead in her tracks, almost dropping the bowling ball on her feet. "*Wanda Wonderbust Pattershaw,* I am going to cut you."

Wanda slid into the mint-green molded seats that housed her team, leaving Lucy standing alone, facing none other than Brogan, wearing her same team shirt and a sheepish grin on his face.

Lucy did an immediate about-face and marched

toward the check-in counter, determined to return her ugly bowling shoes and beat it, even if she had to hoof the seven miles home. She heard Brogan shout her name over Tom Petty's "Free Fallin'" as she dumped her ball back on the rack, but she ignored him. Heat flamed her cheeks, and nasty thoughts filled her mind on all the ways she wanted to torture her *ex*–best friend, Wanda.

A strong hand grabbed her upper arm. "Lucy, wait… please." Lucy cursed her pitter-pattering heart that reacted to his touch and his warm, husky voice. She didn't want to listen to him, and she certainly didn't want to look into her favorite green eyes or be persuaded by his charming, crooked smile. Brogan had other ideas as he turned her to face him with both hands weighing heavily on her shoulders.

"Lucy, please let me apologize… I never meant to say what I said. I never meant to hurt you." To be heard over the loud music and striking of balls hitting pins, he bent his head close…too close. If she'd been in a forgiving mood, she'd only have to lean about two inches, and she'd be pressed against his solid chest and touching his delicious lips. *Ho, no, not this time.* Lucy's head snapped back as if she'd almost kissed a warthog. Brogan's lips curled into a knowing smile that said, *I know where your naughty mind wandered…*

Lucy removed herself from his sexy aura and folded her arms. She fixed him with a stern gaze. "You didn't hurt me. More like embarrassed me to death. Were you drunk?"

The idea of lying must've crossed his mind as she detected numerous excuses pedaling through his brain. But in his favor, he manned up. "No. But I was provoked. When dipshit Clancy wouldn't stop yammering on about fifty ways to get you in bed…well, I guess I kinda lost it."

Lucy gave him points for hanging his head and shoving his hands in the pockets of his cargo shorts. But not many.

"Will you let me make it up to you?" he asked, not looking quite as contrite as she would've preferred. He seemed to be fighting back a big grin.

"Sure. I want a raise. Forty bucks an hour."

"Done."

Too easy. And she didn't want to make anything easy for Brogan "Melt My Heart" Reese. "And I want a new pair of shoes. Michael Kors sandals in black and gunmetal. They have them at Belk's. Size seven."

"You got it."

He didn't even hesitate. "They cost a hundred and fifty bucks."

"Fine. Are we good now?"

No. Lucy's mind scrambled for something to make him quake or cringe. Something that would set him off. Like he'd done to her with his embarrassing public speech about sleeping together. Brogan started to pull her toward the lanes when it hit her. "*And* you have to buy me a huge plate of nachos with that delicious processed yellow cheese, two hot dogs with chili and sauerkraut, fried pickles with ranch dressing, and…you have to eat it with me." That did it. Brogan stopped. Lucy thought he might go ballistic; his eyes bulged and steam whistled from his ears. "Add a hot fudge sundae and Mountain Dew, and then we'll be even."

Brogan's mouth worked, but no sound came out. Lucy

took the time to admire the expanse of his strong shoulders stretching the neon-green T-shirt, and the slight brown stubble covering his square jaw. She appreciated the way his eyes blazed with outrage and then blazed with something even more dangerous, like desire, need, and craving all wrapped together and directed at her. This time he pulled her so close that nothing separated their matching T-shirts. Her breath lodged in her throat as he smashed her against his hard pecs.

"No deal," he growled just above her surprised open mouth. "Unless I'm eating hot fudge off your creamy skin, and dribbling caramel sauce over your pink nip—"

"Stop." She tried wrenching away from his devil lips and the edgy words he breathed into her mouth, but his arm tightened around her waist. "Okay. Forget the hot f-fudge thing, but everything else…I want. And I want it now. I'm starved." She pressed her own lips together in case they went rogue and latched onto his.

Laugh lines crinkled around his eyes as he chuckled. "Everything but that nasty, nuclear nacho shit. I have to draw the line somewhere."

"Replace it with French fries, but no more substitutions."

Brogan dropped a quick kiss on her forehead. "Come on. You can clog your arteries while we bowl."

Brogan wanted to take hot bamboo skewers and stab his eyes out. He knew he'd be seeing Lucy tonight, because he'd promised a year's worth of free scraps for Fiona if Wanda brought her. What he didn't know was that she'd be wearing short jean shorts and a T-shirt that kept inching up, revealing a sliver of smooth skin and his favorite innie belly button.

After buying all that garbage she ordered, he had to sit, without groaning, and watch her lick mustard from the corner of her mouth with the tip of her tongue, which was a practice in pure Chinese torture, but when she fed him fried pickles dipped in ranch and threatened to hold his nose if he didn't chew and swallow, he wanted to throttle her and then gag.

"Oh, quit being such a baby. They're only dill pickles from our local-grown cukes. They're yummy," she said, popping another pickle chip in her mouth. "Now pick that hot dog up and let me see you eat it," she ordered. He'd much rather watch her eat. Hot dog. Banana. Him.

Between his clenched teeth, he said, "Two bites. That's all. My body is a temple. I don't abuse it by eating total crap." He snatched the hot dog from her hand. As he shoved half the dog in his mouth, Lucy drew up her phone and snapped a picture.

"Perfect. Can't wait to post on BetterBites' Facebook page: Owner Brogan Reese enjoying nonorganic hot dog—" Lucy squealed, evading his grasp as he lunged for her phone. She took off running toward the arcade room as he chased her. "No-o-o-o!" she shrieked.

"Go, Lucy!" Wanda yelled.

Brogan enjoyed an evil, maniacal laugh as she boxed herself in between a *Baywatch* pinball machine and Super Bikes Motorcycle Racing. He blocked her escape and wiggled his fingers, hand out. "Give it up." She shook her head and bit her lip, trying not to laugh. She held both arms behind her back, hiding the phone. *"Lucy,"* he said in his best Ricky Ricardo imitation.

"Give me the phone." She yelped as he grabbed her and wrestled the phone from her hand.

"No! Brogan, give it back." She tried climbing him like a ladder to reach the phone he held over his head. Any other time, he'd be taking advantage of her rubbing up against him, but right now, business took precedence. Maneuvering her in a headlock, he tapped Photos on her screen and deleted the one of him.

Lucy struggled with her head pressed into his waist. "You don't fight fair," she muttered into his shirt.

"Of course I don't."

When he released her head, she snatched the phone from his hand. "If I were bigger and stronger, you'd never get away with that."

"But you're not, which is why I can get away with *this*…" Squatting down, he hauled a surprised Lucy over his shoulder in a fireman's carry.

She screeched, "You're gonna pay for this, you butthead." Bertie and Javier clapped as he marched back to the lanes, and Wanda gave a piercing wolf whistle.

"I think I'm gonna barf."

"That's what you get for eating garbage." Brogan dumped Lucy on her feet.

"My, my, sexy Bro-man, you can carry me back to your cave and have your wicked way with me," Wanda cooed, sidling against him and batting her big brown eyes.

Lucy pulled Wanda off him. "Go find your own caveman. Russell's at the bar drinking beer. Hitch your caboose to him."

Wanda sniffed. "Look who's gotten all possessive and doesn't want to share."

"No. You're just greedy," Lucy said to the back of Wanda's twitching hips.

Brogan laughed. "Come on. Let's bowl." He picked up another orange bowling ball and put it in her hands.

Shiny hair flopped around her shoulders as she shook her head. "I can't bowl. The last time I tried, I was ten and had to roll the ball between my legs. It stopped dead in the middle of the lane. The bowling alley guy had to save it. After that, my dad made me sit and watch. I've never been so bored," she added with a huff.

"Amuse me. Give it your best shot. I bet you bowl better than you caterwaul, er…sing."

Lucy narrowed her exotic gray eyes. "You know, you have not shown enough remorse for embarrassing me in front of the whole town. You should be kissing my patootie…not making me angry."

"Don't worry, I plan to kiss your sweet ass and a whole lot more," he rumbled next to her ear, smiling at her flushed baby-doll cheeks. "But first, you need to knock down those pins." The psychedelic strobe lights had been switched on, and the gutters glowed electric blue. Mirrored balls twirled, and "Layla" played through the speakers. Brogan pointed her down the lane. "Just picture my face, and I bet you hit all ten."

"You can do it, Lucy. Show 'em you're a true ball buster," Dottie Duncan hollered above the music. Dottie and Arlene Tomlin had snagged Javier and Brogan to be on their team, along with Lucy.

"Come on, Luce," Bertie yelled from the next lane, doing a boogie step. "Give it your best shot."

Lucy elbowed Brogan in the gut. "Out of my way." She lined up, feet together, with the ball tucked below her chin. Taking three steps, she bent, and his head got dizzy from the expanse of skin her short shorts revealed. Her right arm swung back and then forward, but instead of staying low and releasing the ball, Lucy stood too quickly, and the orange ball went flying through the air.

"Fore!" Brogan shouted before the ball landed in the next lane, where it hit the floor and wobbled to the gutter.

"Whoa. That was spectacular." Javier burst out laughing.

"Duck crap goose. Girl, you need some practice," Dottie said.

"Grr! I told you I can't bowl." Lucy whirled around into Brogan's arms as he shook with laughter. She buried her face in his chest and mumbled something that he couldn't quite catch but sounded a lot like "candy corn niblets and kill me now."

"Hey, that's why you're a ball buster."

"Dang, Lucy...you dented the lane."

"Lucy, I'd be happy to give you private lessons," Dipshit Clancy shouted from two lanes over.

"That won't be necessary. I've got everything under control," Brogan yelled back, hoping hardheaded Clancy picked up on the threat in his voice. Lucy shook, still hiding her face in his T-shirt. Shit. He hadn't meant to embarrass her again. Twice in two days. "Lucy, honey, you okay?" He tilted his head, trying to see her face. "Little Lu-Lu...?" he said softly. The trembling intensified. "Are you crying?" His arms tightened around her, and he rubbed the shirt covering her soft back.

Tears streamed down her cheeks, but before his heart froze, her lips twitched into a huge grin, and she vibrated with laughter. "I told you I sucked." She hiccuped and laughed at the same time.

Brogan reached for some napkins on top of the scoring table. "Well, now, honey, that's one way of putting it." She mopped her wet face with the napkins. "Bowling probably isn't your strong suit. But since tonight's about fun and blowing off steam, I'd have to say, you excelled at that."

She patted his front, trying to smooth the wrinkles. "Sorry I got your shirt all wet."

"It's all good." He never knew anyone who inspired more smiles. "You wanna try again? Maybe if I helped—"

She flopped down on the U-shaped bench seats. A surge of emptiness drained his arms where he no longer held her. He was unable to describe the sensation, but *void* came to mind. What a difference from feeling whole, strong, and vibrant, with Lucy cradled in his arms. He gave his head a shake, warding off the weird notion before it took root.

"Nope." Lucy picked up the pitcher of beer and poured some into a red Solo cup. "Carry on without me. I'm content to watch and sing along to the music."

Brogan visibly winced. Lucy's singing voice could strip paint. As he picked up his bowling ball, "Start Me Up" by the Rolling Stones poured through the speakers, and the sounds only a wounded animal could make reached his ears. Brogan shrugged at Javie's shocked expression as they listened to Lucy singing at the top of her lungs. Brogan started to grin. Suddenly, the bowl in Rock 'n' Bowl night was abandoned. Lucy hopped to her feet and started dancing, along with Dottie, Arlene,

Wanda, and Bertie. Javier threw up his hands in surrender and joined the ladies, gyrating as they danced a circle around him. Brogan caught sight of Keith Morgan winding his way past the check-in counter, wearing tennis gear and a huge smile. Bertie shimmied over to Keith and wrapped her arms around his neck as they swayed to the music together. Russell Upton didn't need an engraved invitation. He hurried from the bar, sloshing beer over his wrist to get to Wanda shaking her ta-tas in his direction.

Content to watch the show, Brogan folded his arms and leaned against the scoring table. Out of the corner of his eye, he caught the Perry brothers weaving their way toward the dancing girls. Brogan moved to block their path when Lucy danced over and grabbed his hand, pulling him into the middle of the group. She slid her hands up his chest and around his neck. Brogan stood confused, searching her face.

"I'm not interested in Clancy Perry's fifty ways of fun. And you still owe me." She tipped her pert nose. "You gonna dance like a robot all night or just with me?" Rocking her hips, she swayed. Brogan needed no further encouragement. Matching his hips to hers, he gathered Lucy close. The void was filled, and his arms no longer felt empty.

Brogan's car sat idling in her driveway. They'd left the bowling alley together over an hour ago, but Lucy still hadn't gone inside. She'd been too busy fogging up the inside of his Jag with lots of lips and tongues and hands and heavy panting. An animalistic sound rumbled in Brogan's chest as his rough hands gripped her butt beneath her shorts. Brogan had released the seat into a horizontal position after he'd kissed her across the console and pulled her on top of him.

Chest heaving, Lucy pushed up into a sitting position, straddling his lap and bumping the steering wheel with her back. "We have to stop."

Lust, hunger, need, and something she couldn't quite name colored his face. With a deep guttural moan, he said, "God no. Not yet." He slid his hands from her bottom to beneath her shirt. Lucy stopped his progress, grabbing his wrists, pressing his palms into her stomach. Her head felt hazy, and she couldn't believe she had the strength to put an end to the best make-out session of her entire life. Brogan took kissing to an entirely new level and then hurled her over into a freefall of dizziness.

She sucked in a breath. "I need to get inside. Julia's probably awake, and she'll..." Julia would not be pleased to hear that Lucy had kissed Brogan like he was the only solid mass in a swaying, upside-down world. He made her limbs weak and sent tremors down her spine, evoking sensations she'd never experienced. Ever. "I...we...can't—"

"Lucy." His sleepy, sexy bedroom eyes traveled up her stomach, over the round swells of her breasts to her swollen lips. "You want to be with me."

With every cell in her body. "We can't. It wouldn't be right. Word will get out, and—"

With a mere crunching of his hard abs, Brogan sat up, shifting her bent leg over his lap and sliding his hands around her waist. "I need you." He nuzzled the side of her neck with his hot mouth. In less than a heartbeat, he made her forget. Head flopping to one side, she bit her lip to keep from moaning.

Hateful reason knocked on her brain's door. "You don't even know me," she managed to say, forcing her hand to push at his broad shoulder.

His head lifted. "What do you mean?"

"We barely know each other. And this…this…craze or lust or madness between us is nuts, because we're practically strangers." He gripped her chin, surveying her expression, and she looked into her favorite green eyes that made rational thought disappear as fast as Nestlé's Toll House cookies at a sorority house.

"What are you talking about? I've known you since you were fifteen—"

His jumping pulse beneath her palm resting on his neck gave her a wake-up call. "You didn't *know* me."

He blinked as her sudden withdrawal became tangible. Her heart plummeted fifty feet down a dark well. In about five minutes, she would curse herself blue for not taking full advantage of his hot body and all the good stuff that went along with it, but she'd never been Fran-the-one-night-stand. When it came to relationships, she moved at a snail's pace. Evident by the eight months she hung on with Anthony the webbed-neck weasel.

"I'm sure you've encountered many girls who have fantasized about you, and yes, I'm guilty of dreaming about you." Only for seventeen short years. "But a summer fling seems risky." And tawdry. "And since neither of us is staying, maybe this isn't such a good idea."

Brogan remained silent but looked as if he wanted to

argue. Lucy started to move off his lap when a band of steel tightened around her hip, stopping her.

"I want to know you." His voice was rough.

"You want to sleep with me."

"That too. But I'm willing to wait." But for how long? She shook her head. "Lucy, this thing between us…you're right, I don't know what it is, but I want to find out. Aren't you the least bit curious? How it would be?" The caramel of his voice poured over her. "How it would feel?" His lips hovered over hers.

Great. Fantastic. Life altering. "I'd feel like a complete moron if I lost my job over it."

His head reared back, and his brow furrowed. "That's ridiculous. That's not going to happen."

"It could. I can't afford—" She glanced down at the console, spying his phone chirping with a text message.

"Dammit." His jaw locked as he read the screen.

"What?"

The warning in his eyes made Lucy nervous. "Look." He turned the phone, and she read: Hey, Bro! don't b late for my party. Bubbly is chillin. xoxo Jo Ellen.

A laugh worked its way up from her belly and shook her shoulders. "Guess she's excited about her Mary Kay party. Wow. Chilled champagne…sounds romantic. Watch out. Jo Ellen might open her door wearing nothing but Saran Wrap and a smile." Lucy howled at his shocked expression.

Brogan threaded his fingers through her hair, holding her head hostage, and smirked. "You're gonna pay for this. Now, *you* owe me."

"Yeah? Says who?" Ruining the tough-act effect with her snickers.

"I do. Thursday night. Me and you. On a date." At his serious suggestion, Lucy's laughter dried up. "And Friday night we're going to the lake."

She scrunched her nose and tried to replicate Julia's bitchy glare-down.

"For Parker's team party. Not…sex." He grinned, wagging his finger in her face. "You've got a dirty mind, Little Lucy."

"No way."

He swooped down for another sizzling kiss. All her feminine parts danced the hootchy-kootchy, but then he removed his lips much too soon. "Come on. I'll walk you to the door."

Laughing on the inside at his predicament, Lucy opened the front door and turned back to Brogan. "Do you own a pair of rip-away pants?"

"What?"

"For the entertainment at Jo Ellen's party. If you need a thong, I have one you can borrow." Slamming the door in Brogan's stunned face didn't silence the string of curse words spilling from his mouth.

Chapter 21

FOR THE NEXT TWO DAYS, LUCY SPORTED A BRAVES baseball cap and dark sunglasses she'd found in her dad's desk drawer as she ran Julia's errands. Pictures of Mr. Neanderthal hauling her over his shoulder and dirty dancing with her at the bowling alley had hit Facebook and every other social media outlet with all sorts of captions like: Harmony's Hottest Couple? Who Better to Bite Lucy than Brogan? Lucy breathed a prayer of thanks that no pictures popped up of the steamy make-out session in Brogan's car afterward.

Focused on her job, Lucy had gotten busy down-loading pictures of Brogan and Javier at the Harmony Huggers' party hosted at the store. Miss Sue Percy led the pack, singing and drinking. And all the women were pictured hanging on the guys. The ones resembling a drunken, geriatric orgy Lucy purposely left off the Facebook page and website. But the tense lines bracket-ing Brogan's mouth couldn't be Photoshopped out. He still didn't embrace being a sex symbol. Lucy wasn't deterred and stuck to her marketing plan. Publicity was publicity. Customers trekked from Raleigh and beyond to check out the store and the Hotties of Harmony: Brogan, Javier, Keith Morgan, and even Vance Kerner, Harmony's famous author.

It was Thursday, and the bucket of cleaning supplies rattling around in the backseat of the minivan reminded

Lucy that Julia must've seen the pictures of her and Brogan online, because today's errand list bordered on insanity. The scent of Clorox permeated Lucy's skin and stank up the car's interior. She hoped she could scrub the smell from her body before her date tonight. She'd just spent the last two hours scouring the kitchen and bathrooms of one of Julia's listings. Julia's assistant was taking another sick day, and the house needed cleaning per Julia's instruction before it could be shown to prospective buyers. The glint of revenge in Julia's eyes gave her away as she delighted in telling Lucy of the task this morning.

Lucy took a swig of her Cheerwine, coating her dry throat. Julia's attempt to ruin her day had backfired, because she was smiling from ear to ear at the idea of a real date with Brogan. It had been a long time for Lucy.

Lucy pulled into the parking lot at the high school, and Parker stood on the sidewalk with his bag and gear at his feet, talking to some of the other players. As she eased to the curb, he grabbed his stuff and threw everything in the back. Sweat, dirt, grass, and stinky boy filled the car the minute Parker plopped in the front seat.

"Hey. How'd it go today?"

"Fine. Coach says I'll get playing time in the scrimmage tonight. Hope Brogan is coming to watch."

Tonight? Doodlebugs. "Uh, what do you mean by scrimmage?" She circled the lot and turned toward home.

Parker threw a you're-too-dumb-to-live look at her. "It's a football game, except we play against each other. For practice," he said as if talking to the mentally challenged. "To prepare for our opponents." Lucy knew what a scrimmage was, but did it have to be tonight?

"Thanks for clarifying…Peyton Manning."

"Is Brogan coming?" he asked again with a tinge of hope in his half-man/half-boy voice.

How did one go about breaking it to her nephew that Brogan had asked her on a date so he could woo the pants off her? "Not sure. We've only talked about work."

"I'll text him." Parker whipped out his phone and tapped his screen with lightning speed. Lucy's heart thudded to a bumpy rhythm as her hopes of dressing up, applying makeup, wearing those kick-ass Michael Kors sandals Brogan had promised her (and had delivered) came to an unsatisfying end.

"I hope he can make it, because I want to show him the sneak play I learned." How could she squelch the excitement Parker tried so hard to hide by insisting Brogan keep this date?

Parker jumped from the car and hauled his smelly equipment out as he clambered to the back door.

Lucy dragged her feet and the bucket of cleaning supplies from the backseat toward the house. Reeking of Clorox no longer presented a problem. She stopped when Toby Keith's "Who's Your Daddy?" sounded from her phone, indicating a call from Brogan. Lucy grinned at her appropriate choice of ringtones.

"Hey," she answered, standing on the back porch, swiping her hand across the sweat on her forehead against another scorching August day.

"Lucy, if I had a dollar for every time someone squeezed my butt or rubbed her perfumed cleavage against my arm, I'd be a millionaire," Brogan groused into the phone. Ah, Jo Ellen's cosmetics' party.

"You must've been a real success. Congratulations. Um, about tonight—"

The sound of a growling tiger hit her ear. "You're not backing out. Not after what I suffered today."

"Didn't you get Parker's text? He wants you to watch his scrimmage."

"The scrimmage starts at five thirty. I'll pick you up at five. Be ready."

"For what? To watch high school football practice?"

"It won't last more than an hour. Plenty of time to make it to dinner. I made reservations at Franklin's, a really nice steak house in Raleigh."

Sounded swanky. Lucy's mind scrambled, cataloging the clothes in her closet. No appropriate outfit came to mind. "Oh. Nice."

"That's right. A nice date, like I promised. I want a good meal, and I want to drink champagne…preferably from your belly button."

The belly in question quivered from his suggestion, and she laughed to cover her nervousness. "Sounds scandalous. Remember, I'm not easy."

"I've taken the cold showers to remind me."

"Not sure I have anything to wear." She smiled, whipping the hot baseball hat off her head.

"A dress would be nice. Panties are optional."

"Thought your idea of a date was getting me *out* of my panties."

"Hoping you'd save me the trouble."

She snorted. "Don't count on it."

"A man can dream," he said around a chuckle. "See you at five. Need to go burn my clothes that smell like grandma's talcum powder. FYI, if you wear fake eyelashes or fill in wrinkles with spackle cream, *please*, don't tell me. Some things should remain a mystery."

"Got it. How do you feel about the smell of Clorox?"

"For bleaching, it's the best. For perfume…not so much. Why?"

"It's a good dinner story. Gotta go, so I can locate my granny girdle from Walmart." Lucy burst out laughing as Brogan dropped the f-bomb before ending the call.

A silly smile played around her lips as she opened the back door and walked into the kitchen, trying not to panic and do cartwheels at the same time. She still had a date. With candlelight, linen napkins, waiters in tuxes, maybe even bananas Foster flambéed at their table.

"What's for lunch?" *Poof!* Her daydream was killed instantly by Parker's incessant question regarding food. Lucy started pulling out containers of organic salads and turkey wraps, courtesy of BetterBites.

"Stop fidgeting." Wanda tugged on the straps of the plunging V-neck dress she'd wrestled Lucy into. Lucy had rushed over to Wanda's for a wardrobe makeover. Not that she was making a huge deal about this date, but okay, yeah, she was making a huge deal. She wanted to be *that* girl…for once. The one that turned guys' heads and made them stumble or lose track of their thoughts. She wanted to be someone Brogan *would* date.

"This looks perfect," Wanda said, stepping back, head tilted to admire her handiwork. "Take a look." She moved away from the full-length mirror in her bedroom.

Lucy's eyes bugged out. She tugged on the hem that barely covered her thighs and slapped her hand to her breasts, threatening to spill from the purple-and-white animal-print dress painted on her body. She looked like a hooker ready for Hollywood Boulevard, not a pretty girl ready for a nice steak restaurant in conservative Raleigh.

"You're kidding, right?" Lucy tried yanking up the neckline. "I'm going on a dinner date…not staking a corner with my pimp. I'm wearing the black-and-silver number over there." Lucy pointed to the dress she'd tried on earlier.

Wanda sniffed. "I thought you were trying to reel in a hot lover, not respectability at the Conways' Bible study," Wanda said, peeling the skintight dress over Lucy's head. "Stop wiggling," she groused.

"The black-and-silver dress is plenty sexy. I'm not trying to start a riot." Or get hauled in for indecent exposure. Wanda's idea of sexy, when it came to appropriate date outfits, could make a stripper blush. Lucy stepped into the more sophisticated black-and-silver dress with a muted swirled pattern, and Wanda zipped up the back. Slipping into her new Michael Kors sandals, Lucy smiled at her image in the mirror. "This is very pretty and dinner appropriate."

"Yes. You look very pretty… But I thought you wanted a *Bro-mance*." Wanda hung the discarded dresses back in her closet. "Your fear of intimacy will dry up your ovaries. You know, I read online that sex on a regular basis can extend your life."

Lucy laughed. "That's rich. Then you should outlive Styrofoam."

Wanda suddenly scooped up her cell phone to read a text. "Hmph. Not on your life, Buck-o," she grumbled as she tapped an answer.

Lucy knew that look. Wanda was probably torturing poor Russell Upton. "What?"

Wanda tossed her phone on the purple velvet chaise. "Nothing. Russell is begging again. Speaking of pigs, I need to feed Fiona, and then I'll help you with your makeup."

Lucy started combing the hot iron through her hair to flatten the frizzies when the doorbell rang.

"Luce, will you get that?" Wanda called from the back of the house.

"Sure." Unplugging the flatiron, she headed for the front door, passing through Wanda's colorful TV room along the way. She pulled the door open to Russell standing on the front porch, wearing worn jeans, blue chambray shirt, work boots, and a sexy smile. He carried a large grocery bag from the Piggly Wiggly in one hand and a bouquet of colorful tiger lilies in the other.

Russell blinked. "Oh. Thought you were Wanda." He lowered his chin and shuffled his feet to hide his discomfort. "Is she here?" His gaze searched past the entry into the sitting room as he stepped over the threshold.

"She's around back, feeding Fiona." Lucy indicated with her hand.

"Come on, Lucy. We need to finish your makeup." Wanda stopped and crossed her arms. "What are you doing here?" she demanded.

Russell's cheeks pinkened under his tanned complexion. "I came to see you, honey-bunny. And I brought fresh scraps for Fiona."

"I thought I told you to go drown yourself in a septic tank." Wanda's lips formed a thin line of displeasure. When she didn't move to take the offerings from his hands, Lucy grabbed them instead and started back-pedaling from the tension-filled foyer.

"Stop," Wanda commanded. "Give me those." She snatched the flowers and bag from Lucy's grasp.

"Tiger lilies...your favorite," Russell said, pointing to the flowers Wanda had shoved under her nose. "Do you think somewhere in your generous heart you can forgive me? I swear, honey-bunny, no one means more to me than you," Russell pleaded.

Ruh-roe. Lucy had no idea what Russell had done this time to ask for forgiveness, and she didn't want to know, but her heart tripped at the pleading in his tone and the sincerity written on his face.

"June-Belle Evans? Really, Russell?"

"That was only once, Wanda. And I wouldn't have gone near June-Belle if I hadn't seen you riding high in that fancy exterminator's truck, looking pleased as pickled turnips. And I saw pictures of you with that new Latin guy." Russell's stance became more aggressive as he splayed his large, work-worn hands on his hips.

"Javier, my new Latin lover," Wanda said with exaggerated flourish, as if she were the latest Hollywood diva.

"Javier is just a friend," Lucy said to an outraged Russell.

"*Wanda*, you and me are gonna have it out. Right here. Right now," Russell gritted out through clenched teeth. "I'm tired of this game, and I want my woman back!" he roared.

Surprise and anger flashed across Wanda's face before a look of satisfaction settled there.

Wanda dumped the flowers and grocery bag on the small red-painted table next to the sitting room. "He's just gonna try and sweet-talk his way into my boudoir without apologizing or even—"

"Horse manure! I've apologized every way imaginable, and even invented a few new ones. And today, I'm gonna confess everything and bare my soul. You can either stomp on it with your fancy gold stilettos or gather it close to your bodacious bosom and never let it go. Your choice."

Russell grabbed Wanda's wrist and hauled her into the sitting room, pushing her down on the red-and-yellow-floral sofa.

Wanda, who tried to hide a silly, pleased smile, shot Lucy a wink.

"Oh. Look at the time," Lucy said, checking her watch. "Gotta go. Good seeing you, Russell. Wanda, I'll text you later." She pivoted on her new sandals and practically ran from the room.

Lucy paced the length of her bedroom. Brogan had said to be ready by five, and it was already ten after. She glanced in the mirror and slicked the rosy gloss on her lips. She adjusted the silver chain around her neck, squeezing the silver heart charm in her palm to keep her fingers from twirling her hair.

"Breathe, Luce. It's just a date. Nothing to get worked up over." She scooped up her silver clutch and headed downstairs.

In the kitchen, Lucy filled a glass with Julia's special water and grabbed a prepared salad from the fridge for her dinner. She'd arranged everything on a tray and walked down the hall to Julia's room when the bedroom door flew open and out stepped Brogan.

"Whoa." He steadied the tray that wobbled in her

hands. "Here, let me." He turned with the tray and disappeared into Julia's room.

Lucy stood paralyzed. What the hoot? How long had he been here, and why was he in Julia's room? Brogan scooted back out, closing the door quietly. "Shhh, she wants to rest. I left the tray on her nightstand," he whispered. He picked up Lucy's cold hand, holding it out to the side as his gaze traveled her body and warmed with approval. "Wow. You look amazing." His head lowered as if to kiss her when Lucy snapped out of her stupor.

"Back up there, Bro," she whispered furiously, yanking her hand away. "What the...where...how long..." Furious, her mind wouldn't allow her mouth to speak coherently.

"Let's go. I'll explain in the car. We don't want to be late for the scrimmage," he said, ushering her down the hall and out of the house.

Fuming, Lucy crossed her arms in the car, hating that Brogan had been in Julia's room. Wild scenarios ran rampant through her mind, all of them ending with Brogan cradling Julia in his arms while they cooed their undying love for each other. Bleh. The beef burrito from Taco Bell she'd eaten for lunch sat like a rock in her stomach.

"You going to talk to me or sit there and pout?" he had the nerve to ask as he drove down her street toward the high school. She shot him one of Julia's bitchy glaredowns (a weak imitation at best).

"Aw, come on, Little Lucy." He unknotted her arms and threaded his fingers through her hand. "Now I can see you better, and I have to say...you're a knockout."

And with that, her heart skipped several beats, and her hand tingled in his.

"You clean up nice too." She admired his pressed lavender-and-white pin-stripe dress shirt tucked into creased navy slacks with tan leather belt. He squeezed her hand, distracting her with his crooked smile. "Why were you in Julia's room just now?" She wanted to sound like the best bodyguard and sister nurse possible, because Julia's welfare was her utmost concern. (Hey, which it was!) But she also couldn't disguise the leaky jealous tone.

He shrugged, pushing his aviator sunglasses up his nose. "I brought some flowers to cheer her up, and we discussed the listing on my house." More flowers… sheesh. Sounded innocent. So why did Lucy feel like a chump?

"What about us? Did you tell her about our… er, date?"

Brogan kept his eyes glued to the road. "Um, no. Didn't want to upset her."

Of course not. Neither had Lucy. But substitute girlfriend still had an unpleasant ring. "Julia knows we're watching Parker's scrimmage, and I told her we were working afterward," he said. *Working. So, that's what we're calling it these days. Hmmm.*

"You ready for some football?" He turned into the high school parking lot.

"Sure." And dinner, along with a side of Brogan. *Think of anything else, like Fiona wearing her stupid purple tutu.*

"We are going out to dinner, aren't we?" Lucy gave the beach towel and small cooler inside Brogan's open trunk a dubious look.

"Absolutely. This is only to tide us over." Holding the cooler, he tucked the towel under his arm and placed his hand on the small of her back. He led her across the parking lot and around the track to the metal bleachers. Brogan held her steady as she climbed halfway up in her new favorite heels. Lucy sat on the towel he'd spread and glanced around at the other parents. Some watched the warm-up, but most of them watched the famous couple with avid curiosity.

"Hey, Lucy and Brogan!"

"Saw your pictures, dancing at Rock 'n' Bowl."

"You two set a date?"

Lucy's cheeks caught fire, and her mouth dried up.

Brogan waved. "No wedding yet. Let's see how our first date goes." He settled next to Lucy, ducking his head.

"Don't you break her heart, Brogan Reese."

Lucy groaned and dug her elbow into Brogan's side as he shook with laughter. "Stop it. You're only making it worse," she hissed under her breath.

"Maybe if we don't make any more eye contact, they'll forget we're here." Brogan opened the cooler and handed her a clear container with cheese, crackers, cut-up fresh fruit, and stuffed olives. He twisted the top off two light raspberry beers. "Cheers. To first dates." His green eyes twinkled as he tapped the neck of her beer.

"Mmm, that's good." A hint of raspberry fizzled on her tongue. "Should we be drinking alcohol on school property?" Lucy whispered from the corner of her mouth, glancing to see if any wacky Harmony residents noticed.

"Probably not. But we're toasting our first date…

they'll cut us some slack. Unless you get falling-down drunk." His grin was wicked. "Not that I'd mind, but Miss Sue's probably lurking, documenting—"

"Takes more than one flavored beer to get me drunk."

"Good. Now we're getting somewhere."

"What do you mean?" She popped a green grape in her mouth.

"Getting to know you. I have a list of questions." He patted the pocket over his left breast.

Lucy's brow furrowed. "Is this like speed dating... you ask ten questions, and then we jump in the sack together?"

"Of course not. Unless you like that idea, and then I'm all for it. Especially the part about jumping in the sack," he whispered close to her ear, frying the remainder of her brain cells.

A loud cheer broke out on the field, catching their attention. "Look, there's Parker." Lucy waved. "Hey, Parks. Have fun!" Parker held his helmet against his hip and seemed surprised to see her. He stood rooted in his tracks until one of his teammates shoved him toward the bench.

Brogan stood and clapped. "Let's go, boys! Hustle!" Players rushed on the field and started to line up. Parker stood with his foot on the bench and his helmet on his knee when a coach motioned him forward. Scrambling, he shoved his helmet on his head, stopped to listen to his coach, and then trotted out to the field.

"All right. Good job." Brogan clapped. Lucy sipped her beer and nibbled on cheese as Brogan stood with his arms crossed. He mumbled as if coaching Parker in his head. Glancing down, he asked, "You doing okay?"

"I'm great." She stood and patted him on the back. "Know what would be awesome?"

"Hmm? That's it! Drop back in the pocket!" he yelled at the field, clapping loudly. "Did you see Parker's pass?" Pride filled his voice, but his eyes never wavered from the game. The connection between Parker and Brogan, from bleachers to field, was almost tangible. Lucy's heart skipped in a happy way. This was exactly what Parker needed. A man helping and cheering him on.

"See those guys down there?" She pointed to a group of young dads hanging outside the low chain-link fence, fixated on the game. "Why don't you join them? I'll be fine," she said to his startled face.

"You sure?"

She nodded. "Go. You can coach better from down there." She'd barely finished speaking when a feather-like peck brushed her lips and Brogan bolted down the bleachers. Bursting with pride, Lucy watched him jog to where the men stood. Brogan shook hands with the group of dads before planting his legs shoulder-width apart and folding his arms, concentrating on the game. If he'd had a team cap, clipboard, and whistle, he could've been on the field, barking orders.

Lucy tipped the beer to her lips and glanced at the container of healthy snacks. What a nice guy. So thoughtful. Sighing, if only he'd packed Little Debbies…she'd be in heaven. Brogan may not know it yet, but he was turning into a darn good surrogate dad.

Chapter 22

AT SEVEN, PARKER FILED OFF THE FIELD, DIRTY, TIRED, but excited that Brogan had shown up. Brogan couldn't stop the grin splitting his face as he congratulated Parker and the other boys. Parker introduced Brogan to his friends, with a ring of pride in his voice, and Brogan's gut clenched in a tight ball. Maybe all those workouts and small talks had actually made a difference. He couldn't be certain, but his pride overflowed watching Parker play during the scrimmage. He'd shown poise under pressure, glancing in Brogan's direction every now and then, checking to see if he was watching. Brogan remembered playing on this exact field, always hoping his own dad would be somewhere in the stands, cheering. After the third game his senior year, Brogan had stopped hoping and never looked for his dad in the crowd again.

"Congratulations, Parker. You were awesome," Lucy said, walking in their direction. *Jesus.* He'd left Lucy the entire game sitting by herself. What a crappy date. He deserved whatever shit she chose to throw at him. Shame burned his face, but Lucy winked and shook her head to indicate she was good.

"Aunt Lucy, can I sleep over at Jason's house? His dad said it was okay."

"Why don't you text your mom and ask her."

"Hey, Lucy, I'm Tom Martin, Jason's dad." Brogan had already met him with the other dads. He'd been two years ahead of Brogan in high school. Lucy shook his hand, and Tom continued to talk. "We'd love to have Parker spend the night, and I'll make sure the boys get to practice in the morning."

"Oh, okay," Lucy said. Brogan almost laughed out loud as her face broadcasted relief at not having to wake up early.

"I texted Mom. She said it was okay." Parker looked up from his cell phone.

"Let Aunt Lucy check your phone, bud." Brogan clapped him on the shoulder. For once, Parker didn't tense and pull on his sullen mask as he handed over his phone.

"Jason, you played some real good defense out there tonight," Brogan said to a stocky Jason Martin, who stood next to his dad.

"Son, Brogan Reese played quarterback for Harmony." Tom pointed at Brogan. "I remember coming home from college to watch him play. He had a strong arm and one of the quickest releases in the state. One time I saw him get sacked behind the line of scrimmage, but he still released the ball and nailed his receiver before hitting the ground. You remember that play, Brogan?"

Brogan chuckled. "Yeah, my ribs are still recovering." Lucy's eyes widened at the embarrassment coloring his face.

"A bunch of the boys and dads are getting together to play touch football tomorrow before the lake party. Can you join us?"

He hesitated. A stack of papers two feet high waited for him on his desk. He should be preparing for New

York. But when a huge grin cracked wide on Parker's dirty face, he hated to disappoint.

"That'd be awesome. Can you? Please?" Parker's blue eyes shone bright with excitement.

Little Lucy gave Brogan a reassuring pat on the back. "If I recall, your schedule's all clear tomorrow. Why don't you take the afternoon off and have some fun?"

"The dads could use a good quarterback," Tom added.

What the hell. Playing mindless touch football might be the ticket. "Sounds great. I'll be here."

"Awww-right!" Parker and Jason jumped and chest-bumped in the air.

"See you tomorrow at five. Looking forward to it." Tom shook Brogan's hand. "Nice to meet you, Lucy. Come on, boys. Let's get you both cleaned and fed." Tom waved as he herded the excited boys toward the parking lot.

"Bye, boys. Parker, I'll pick you up after practice," Lucy called to their backs. Parker nodded and waved.

"Hey, Parker, is that your dad?" They both heard Jason ask.

Jesus. Brogan held back a groan, feeling Lucy tense at his side.

"Nah, he's my uncle," Parker said without missing a beat.

Brogan gathered up the cooler and towel. "Come on. Let's get out of here," he said to a shocked Lucy.

"Did you hear what Parker said?" she whispered as he threw the cooler in the trunk. "Do you think he thinks we…um, we're…the two of us…?"

Brogan opened her door. "Look, the way I see it, anything's an improvement. I'll take uncle over dad any day."

Lucy stopped moving and stared at him. Brogan didn't want to think about Parker and the ramifications of what he'd revealed. He didn't want to think about his deadbeat dad or football or New York. He wanted to *be* with Lucy. More precisely, in bed. But he'd promised her a date, and he'd promised to get to know her, and dammit, he was going to do that or die trying.

"But you'd make such a great dad. Don't you want children?"

No. Yes. He didn't know. Not now. "Not tonight." He pecked Lucy on the lips, because he couldn't resist. "Hop in. I'm starved."

"You and Parker. Always hungry. If I didn't know the truth, I'd think you're related," she mumbled as she slid into her seat.

Brogan started to pull out when both their phones signaled text messages.

Grabbing his phone, he exploded. "What the fuh…" He wanted to bang his head against a brick wall. This couldn't be happening.

"I don't understand," she said, reading her text. "Did you get Margo's text about the problem tonight?"

"Yeah, there's been a mix-up. The Happy Hookers were on the schedule for tonight, but apparently the Bookworms and Historical Society showed up too." Guilt ate at him. He should be helping Margo and Javier, but he'd promised Lucy a date and she'd gone to a lot of trouble. Dressing up. Applying makeup. Looking sexy as all hell.

"I'll call Javier and see what he thinks. Maybe he can rearrange and—"

Lucy grabbed his wrist. "Stop. No one is going home unhappy. Not on my watch. Let's go."

"Where?"

"To BetterBites. This could be your biggest night ever. Let's not lose our momentum." Determination and dedication combined crossed her face as her gray eyes sparked beneath her thick lashes.

"You sure? I promised you a nice dinner."

"You own a grocery store. There's got to be something in there I can eat." Lucy waved her hand. "What are you waiting for? Hit it."

Brogan cupped her flushed cheeks and gave her a hard kiss. "Have I told you that I love you?" he said to her stunned face. He put the car in gear and stepped on the gas.

He loved her. *Stop it. He wasn't serious, you lo mein noodle brain.* He was merely expressing his gratitude with a toe-curling kiss and a meaningless declaration of love. It meant nothing…to him. It meant everything to her.

The minute she walked through the back door, Margo hit her with an apron and handed over a batch of muffins to break up for sampling. Margo sent Brogan to the front of the house, holding a basket of three different types of breads, along with the tapas spreads being featured.

"Work it, big guy. Don't come back until all that bread is gone and your shirt has been ripped to shreds. Them some hungry cougars." Brogan crammed a piece of bread in Margo's mouth and told her to shove it.

An hour later, Lucy finished mixing batter, when Margo handed her a cold beer.

"Sorry about tonight. If I'd known Lover Boy had asked you out, I would've never bothered either of you." She kneaded the dough with her flour-covered knuckles.

Lucy coughed. "Don't be sorry. The success of BetterBites is more important than some silly date."

Margo stopped kneading. "Silly date? He's been nothing but a disaster on two legs these last couple of days. Every time your name comes up, he walks into walls."

"Thanks, but methinks you exaggerate," Lucy said in a funny accent.

Margo snorted. "Think what you want. But that boy has got it bad. I can spot a lovesick dog when I see one."

Love. Not that word. *Lust* maybe or *like*. They were definitely *in like*, but everyone needed to stop dropping the love-bomb. Lucy had witnessed Brogan in love. She'd watched him drool over Julia for two years. Wanting inside Lucy's pants had nothing to do with love and everything to do with libido. Not that she blamed him. *Blippity blip*…she wanted the same thing. They both had this drugging need to do the crazy mattress mambo. Once they'd gotten it out of their systems, the urge would disappear, and they'd move on with their respective careers and lives. Untying her apron, Lucy straightened her dress and gave Margo a quick wave as she pushed through the door to the front of the house, where the party raged at warp speed.

Standing behind the bin of homemade pita chips, she watched Brogan and Javier work the crowd. Lucy covered her mouth in shock as old Miz Cornwaddle patted

Brogan on the butt. He laughed, skirting away from her gnarled hand, and then stopped, his attention riveted on Lucy.

She sucked in a sharp breath. Her straight, ironed hair almost curled at the hot, sizzling look directed at her. A look that had nothing to do with healthy granola, old ladies crocheting doilies, or organic foods, but everything to do with wet, long kisses, heavy panting, and tearing at each other's clothes.

"Get a room, you two," Miz Cornwaddle said with a loud snort. A knowing smile tipped Brogan's lips as he winked at Lucy.

Around ten, the partiers had dwindled, and Brogan gripped Lucy's elbow as she tossed dirty plates and cups in the garbage. "Come on. Stop cleaning. You hungry?"

Lucy's stomach answered with a loud growl. "Maybe a little."

"Yeah, I'm starved too." Brogan brushed a tendril of hair behind her ear. "Let me make it up to you."

Their gazes met, and Lucy's head spun like a pinwheel. Yep. It had to be hunger. How else could she explain the shortness of breath, the hammering heart, and the urge to rip his clothes off with her teeth?

She cleared her throat. "Did you sneak out and buy me a bucket of KFC with mashed potatoes and gravy?"

"I've got something better in mind, my little garbage-eating rat." He draped his arm over her shoulder and squeezed her tight into his side. She breathed in his perfect smell of clean soap and exotic coffee. He'd worked twice as hard as she had and still managed to look crisp and fresh. At some point her makeup had melted from her face. And poor Wanda's dress would need a trip to the dry cleaners, due to a very Happy Hooker spilling a Prosecco cocktail down the back.

"You guys saved the night," Javier said, adding up the register receipts. "This was by far our most successful event to date."

"Great. I knew it," Lucy said. "What are the numbers? I took lots of pictures to post and orders for two more parties."

"Get her out of here," Margo said, handing Brogan a big shopper filled with food. "I'm getting a massive headache."

"Wait…I need to make notes and—"

"Good night, Luce, night, Bro. Thanks again for all your help," Javier called as Brogan tugged her toward the back door.

"Come along, my little marketing maniac. It's been a long night."

Eight minutes later, Brogan pulled into his driveway and killed the engine. "What are we doing here?" Her nerves jumped into hyper mode. The light from the outdoor sconces bathed the porch and front walk. Stacks of lumber sat on his front yard, along with construction ladders and buckets of paint.

"The kitchen is almost finished, and the screened porch has comfortable seating. Since it's not too hot, I thought we'd eat out there."

"Oh. Eating. Right. We're eating food…food from the store."

Brogan lifted the shopper from the back and escorted her to the front door. "For starters. But I could think of other things besides food I'd like to eat right now." His voice held all kinds of sexual promise. *Holy marshmallows between two graham crackers!* So could Lucy, but she'd be wise to squelch the naughty, delectable thoughts marauding her mind, and stick to plain chicken and cornbread on paper plates.

He led her through a maze of boxes in the front entrance, housing new plumbing fixtures. She followed him to the newly renovated great room with its beautiful stacked stone fireplace and old repurposed beams on the pitched ceiling. Lucy's feet skidded to a halt on the freshly stained pine floors to soak it all in.

"This is beautiful." Her gaze wandered from the custom wainscoting on the plastered walls to the floor-to-ceiling windows overlooking the wooded lot. "Was this all your idea?" She turned in a wide circle.

"Some. But really, Bertie had the vision, and she's making it happen. This whole neighborhood is getting a facelift. Lots of new and renovated homes. By making these changes, I can ask a much higher price." His hand pressed the small of her back as he ushered her from the great room to the connecting kitchen.

"Killer. I love the combination of paint and stain." She pointed to the soft gray upper cabinets and stained ebony lower cabinets.

"Still waiting for the soapstone countertops, new appliances, and backsplash. But for now, this makeshift kitchen will do." He placed the shopper on top of plywood acting as a countertop. "The bathroom is down the hall, if you'd like to freshen up."

"Great." Lucy looked down at Wanda's stained dress and sighed. "Could I borrow a T-shirt and some shorts?"

Brogan's throat worked. "Uh, sure. Follow me." He guided her to the updated guest bathroom. "Use this one.

The master is still under construction. Be back in a sec."
Lucy rubbed her palm across the smooth white marble
vanity top as she admired the bronze fixtures and the
large tiled shower with clear glass doors.

"Here you go." He returned with a soft Georgetown
T-shirt and pair of navy nylon jogging shorts. "Make
yourself at home. Towels are clean." He gestured to the
shower. "Soap, shampoo…whatever you need."

She nodded. "Thanks. I'll be fast." She closed the
door on his handsome face, which sported a lopsided
grin, and rested her forehead against the painted wood.
*Stop thinking about pulling him inside this luxurious
bathroom and terrorizing his drop-dead body with soap
lather and hot water.*

Shee-it. Brogan tried not to picture Lucy naked in his
shower, using his soap and his shampoo, but the longer
the water ran, the wilder his thoughts ran. He uncorked a
bottle of Pinot Noir with more force than necessary. He
wondered what she'd do if he just happened to open the
bathroom door, peel off his clothes, and join her inside
the steamy shower. The same shower with swiveling
showerheads and adjustable body sprays. *Dammit. Get
a grip.* Lucy didn't need bucking Brogan tapping on her
door or anything else right now. He'd promised her a
good meal, conversation, and to get to know her. Not
hot, slippery, up-against-the-wall shower sex with a wet,
soapy Lucy. Sweat beaded his forehead. He tore off a
paper towel and swiped his brow, and got busy plating
their food: creamy mac and cheese, a healthy, organic
version; fresh salad with raspberry vinaigrette; and pork

tenderloin with balsamic glaze. Not the Angus beef he'd been craving, but still tasty. He carried their plates to the screened-in back porch and set them on the table. He lit three candles and picked up the bottle of wine.

Brogan's thoughts tumbled around in his head, all centered on Lucy. He knew her better than she gave him credit for. She was hardworking, smart, and funny. She constantly brainstormed, but instead of dumping her ideas on someone else to execute, she took the initiative and put the ideas in motion. And beneath the snark beat a heart of gold that wanted to reconcile with her stepsister, even though Julia had stomped on Lucy's heart more times than she could count. And despite his teenage attitude and disrespect, Lucy showered Parker with love and patience. Lucy offered more in one day than most people did in a lifetime. He truly believed that, but he didn't think Lucy did. Her insecurities from her past kept her from believing and trusting in herself. Spending this time with her, Brogan hoped to change that before he shoved off to New York.

As he picked up a wineglass, the sound of Lucy padding toward him, fresh from her shower, lifted his head. His hand wobbled, spilling wine on the table. She wore his large T-shirt that hit midthigh, and wet hair knotted on top of her head. Loose strands were already starting to curl around her face. Curls he remembered from back in high school. This side of Lucy was soft and lush and edible. His mouth watered, and he lost all interest in the food cooling on their plates.

"Hope you don't mind, but I used your shampoo." She glanced down at her slim bare legs and small pink feet. "Sorry, I don't look very nice for our date, but I couldn't wear that stained dress a minute longer." She looked incredible. Brogan had trouble swallowing what felt like a ball of steel wool. Pulling out her wicker chair, he tried hiding the painful erection straining the back of his zipper.

"Mmm, this looks yummy." She slipped into her seat and picked up the paper napkin with delicate fingers. Brogan gave his head a vicious shake. *Be a gentleman.*

"Wow. You went to a lot of trouble. Little votives and clear plastic plates. I must be special," she teased as she sipped the wine he managed to finish pouring without spilling another drop.

"Only the best for my guest." He grinned at her rosy cheeks and spiky eyelashes.

"It's delicious, and really perfect," she said after tasting the pork. "I mean this piece of property." She gestured to the back of his wooded lot. "Can you see the lake from here?"

"Yeah, in the winter when the trees are bare."

"Too bad you're selling. I'd be tempted to stay after all these beautiful renovations."

He'd be tempted to stay too, if—*keep your eye on the ball, dumbass. You have a job to do in New York... not Harmony.* "You could buy it. I'd give you a real good deal."

Lucy scrunched her pert nose. "If Julia's handling the sale, believe me, I'll be raked over the coals. Anyway, I'm leaving Harmony, just like you." She spooned mac and cheese in her mouth and groaned, licking her lips. "I'm officially your slave for life."

He gulped more wine. He'd never survive watching Lucy get orgasmic over mac and cheese. Burning the retinas in his eyes held great appeal. Anything would be less painful than watching Lucy make love to a plate of noodles.

Unaware of his sexual frustration, Lucy asked, "When you finally get married, where *do* you plan to settle down?"

And *that* worked. Brogan would rather eat expired sushi from a gas station vending machine than think about marriage.

"I've been married and have zero plans to repeat the performance." Lucy choked, almost spewing wine. Brogan gave her clap on the back. "You okay?"

She reached for her napkin and blotted her mouth. "You were married? I had no idea. When? How long?"

He shrugged, trying to dislodge the stones burying his heart. "Several years ago. It didn't last long. We separated after a few months." Lucy drilled him with her undivided attention. He sighed and settled back in his seat. This was old news, and really, he'd made no secrets about his life. "During our separation, we tried working it out for about three years. But after the miscarriage, there didn't seem to be much holding us together."

Concern softened her expression, and she whispered, "A baby. I'm so sorry. I had no idea." She covered his cold hand and squeezed. "You must've been devastated. Is that why you don't want to be a dad? Because you lost your baby?"

No. Yes. Maybe. Hell, he didn't know. "Look, I won't lie...having a baby scared the crap out of me. I would've stood by my child, but I wasn't looking forward to fatherhood. I didn't have a great role model." His laugh sounded raw. "I had *no* role model, and from what little I know of my dad, I'm sorry his blood runs through my veins."

Surprising him, Lucy jumped up and planted her palms on the table. Her damp hair had fallen from the loose knot and tumbled around her shoulders in glorious curls. She looked soft and sweet and mad as hell. "Brogan Freakin' Reese! You listen to me. You are not your dad, and you never will be. When have you ever shirked your responsibilities or run from a challenge? Take Parker"—she gave a huge eye roll—"*please*, take him. Because of you, he's walking taller and actually working hard toward something."

"That's the football. Has nothing to do with me."

"Moose muffins! You've made a difference, whether you see it or not. And you'd make a wonderful dad." Lucy leaned forward and poked his chest with her finger. "You know, dipweed, your mom was a great woman. She didn't raise a dummy or a coward. I think she raised a pretty darn good man."

Brogan pulled her onto his lap, wrapping his arms around her hips. "Did you just call me Brogan *Freakin'* Reese?" Lucy wiggled her butt to get comfortable and made his ever-present hard-on ache. He clamped down on his back teeth.

"Is that all you got from my impassioned speech? I call you that when I'm angry…in my head."

Clean soap and warm Lucy, a phenomenal combination. His gaze dropped to her vulnerable neck, where he wanted to plant his mouth. "Is that all you call me?" he murmured as he inched closer.

"Mostly. I can think of a few other choice names. Want to hear them?"

He cupped her smooth bottom, making her jump. "You're not wearing my shorts."

She shrugged as she worked the buttons loose on his shirt. "Too big. They kept falling down. Figured you wouldn't mind." Storm-cloud gray darkened her eyes as he slid his hands up her waist and along her sides.

"Are we going to do this, Little Lucy?" His face lowered to the curve of her exposed neck, and he opened his mouth against her hot skin. Her pulse leapt against his tongue, and her hands curled into the fabric of his open shirt.

She nodded, making her curls bounce on her shoulder. "Yep. No strings attached. I'm not interested in being your girlfriend. And I don't want the Harmony busybodies chirping and cheeping and picking it apart, morsel by morsel." What she left unsaid, he still heard. She didn't want Julia to know. He didn't either. He didn't want to be the cause of any more frantic emergency room runs, and he didn't want to create more friction between Lucy and her sister.

Small puffs of air escaped her pink lips as he brushed the sides of her breasts covered in lace. "No strings attached. You got it. Let's make the most of our short stay in town." Tunneling his fingers through the damp curls at the base of her neck, he slammed his mouth against hers.

⌁

Crazy thoughts careened through Lucy's head as Brogan kissed her like she was his last lifeline and he was dying. No-strings-attached sex? Where had that come from? How was she going to pretend he meant nothing to her after making love? Impossible. She'd already fallen halfway in love.

"I can feel you thinking," he murmured against her lips. "Having second thoughts?"

"No," she breathed. She cupped his face and swirled her tongue in his hot mouth. No more thoughts. Loco Lucy Doolan was going to have her man…if only for this one perfect night.

"It's not too late. We can talk some more or play Parcheesi." He rained kisses around her jaw and down her neck. Lucy's head fell back to give him better access.

"Do you know how to play Parcheesi?" she panted.

"Heck no. I don't even own the game." He lifted his face, eyes glazed with lust. "Please tell me you'd rather have sex than play some stupid board game."

Her hands slid to his shoulders, and she nibbled kisses across his strong chin and over his bottom lip. "I want you. Now. Tonight."

Brogan suddenly stood with her in his arms. "I've been dreaming about this moment since the first day I spotted you."

He gave her a little toss in the air, and she squealed, clutching his neck. "What are you doing?" He strode through the dark great room and down the even darker hall.

"Having fun. That okay?" He grinned.

"Only if you don't drop me."

He pushed open the door with his shoulder to a shadowy bedroom. The open draperies allowed the moon's glow to illuminate the lone chair, sitting next to a small chest beside the large unmade bed. "At some point, I'll have to drop you." He covered the carpeted floor in three strides and then tossed her high in the air.

"Squeee!" she screamed before landing on his bed with a bounce. "If this is your idea of foreplay, you need some work." She laughed.

Brogan crawled on top of her, pushing the T-shirt up and over her head before she could stop bouncing. His hands moved to her shoulders, and he slid the straps to her silver bra down her arms.

"Damn, you're pretty." His fingers skated across the lacy cups, pebbling her nipples and then flicking open the front clasp. Pushing the cups aside, he sat back on his knees and stared. A sudden shyness came over her. Brogan must've sensed Lucy's discomfort, because he snagged her wrists, pinning her arms by her sides. "Don't hide anything." His voice was rough. He lowered his mouth to hers, and the kiss grew wild and hypnotic.

Lucy struggled to stay afloat. She was sinking and drowning in a harsh sea of physical and consuming need. His deep-throated groan matched hers. She pushed him back, panting. "Brogan." The longing in his dark green eyes made her feel desired and wanted. Something she'd never felt. She loved his nice, caring side, and she loved this side, the sexy, tantalizing, tough guy all concentrated on one thing…her.

She stroked the stubble on his jaw. "You need to lose some clothes. I want to see you." Bouncing from the bed as if spring-loaded, he undressed so fast that Lucy started to chuckle. "You're so easy. I can't believe the Happy Hookers didn't have you stripping tonight."

He pulled her on her side to face him, stroking her back with his warm fingers. "Don't bring up Happy

Hookers, Harmony Huggers, or Jo Ellen Huggins unless you want my dick to shrivel up like a raisin. Nothing could get me out of the mood faster than those people."

Shriveled would not be the word she'd use to describe the hard erection pressing against her stomach. "No. We don't want that, do we?" she whispered, flattening her palm against his chest and rubbing her fingers through the light dusting of hair. She worked her hand down his spectacular, washboard abs and over his lean hip. Brogan gave a vicious groan and moved her hand to his shoulder. His green eyes burned bright, locking on hers.

"Not so fast." He pushed her back on the mattress and followed. "I want to make this last." He lowered his head and gave her another blistering kiss, claiming her mouth like he owned it. Liquid heat pooled between her legs. She clung to him, begging for more, urging him on with her legs wrapped around his hips. He dragged his hot mouth down her throat, licking her skin, telling her she tasted like juicy fruit, and how she made him hard. He moved lower until the tip of his tongue swirled her nipple before sucking it inside his wet mouth.

She jolted from the sizzling heat, gripping his shoulder and running her fingers through his soft hair. Her breath grew choppy, and her skin caught fire. "No...no more. Please." He looked up through sexy, heavy lids, wearing a wicked, carnal smile that promised more. A lot more. Lucy threw her head back and groaned. "I'm not kidding, Brogan. I can't take it," she gritted out through her teeth.

"I'm just getting warmed up." He trailed kisses down her sternum, around her belly, tickling her navel with his moist tongue. Her head thrashed as she gripped the sheet with her fists. "Do you like that?" His fiery breath heated her oversensitive skin. She swallowed hard, nodding. "Good, because it only gets better."

"Oh God," she moaned and dropped her head. He trailed a row of kisses right above the narrow elastic of her silver panties. He nipped at her hip and his breath grew labored. "What are you doing?" she panted, watching him slip his fingers underneath the elastic.

"Getting ready for dessert." Lucy's eyes crossed, and she bit her lip. He peeled her panties off and knelt between her legs, leaving her exposed. "I've waited forever." His voice held almost a reverent quality. He lifted her bottom with his big, capable hands as Lucy's legs shook. Chuckling, he bit the inside of her thigh. And then he brought his mouth down and feasted.

Lucy screamed his name, jackknifing off the bed. Brogan showed no mercy as he relentlessly teased and sucked until she finally came apart.

"Oh-h-h! Brogan," she cried, as a violent orgasm tore through her insides, and a fountain of sparklers blasted from the top of her head. He kept taunting her until she stopped shuddering and collapsed in a puddling heap against his sheets. He kissed his way up her thighs and around her belly. Lucy couldn't move because she'd melted. "Oh my *gosh*. What was that?" she whispered.

"The best orgasm I've ever seen," he answered in a husky voice. She cracked one eye open. Brogan hovered over her, leaning on his side, wearing a cocky smile.

Lucy tried to flutter her hand. "It's been a really long time, and I was inspired." A desire to explore his body, his texture, his scent overpowered her exhaustion. She wanted to know all of him, the way she wanted to own his heart. But since his heart would never be hers, she'd settle for this one night. Her gaze slid down to his impressive cock, and suddenly she felt alive and ready for more. Rolling, she pulled him on top, raining kisses on his solid chest and shoulder. Brogan held her head still, kissing her with a desperation that had been absent before. Desire and greed sizzled Lucy's nerve endings as her kisses told the same story. Desperate to be one with him, Lucy broke away on a gasp. "Condom. Now. *Hurry.*"

Brogan smiled. She tightened her fists on his shoulders and shook him, breaking his close examination of her. "Don't make me hurt you."

"Wouldn't dream of it." He pressed into her, loving the feel of her nipples stabbing his chest as he reached over her head and fished inside his bedside drawer. "One condom, coming up."

"Give it to me." She snatched the black shiny packet and pushed him off with amazing strength for someone so small.

"Yes, ma'am. You're in charge now." He stretched out, folding his arms behind his head, fascinated by the jiggle of her breasts as she tore the packet with her teeth.

"No. I'm desperate. Ready?" A sensuous smile curved her lips as she straddled his legs and rolled the condom down his cock.

His breath hissed through his teeth and his hands slid up her thighs, encircling her waist. He lifted, positioning her over him, and watched in painful pleasure as she took her sweet time sliding down his shaft until she was completely seated. Slowly she rose, rolling her hips. Her head dropped back. Unable to endure the torture, he gripped her waist, moving her up and down as his own hips bucked. Sweat trickled down his temples.

With half-closed eyes, he watched Lucy ride him, and his cock grew harder.

"God, you're so tight," he said between clenched teeth.

"More," she urged and tried to control the rhythm. "Please…don't stop." Her panting grew labored. *No way.* He lifted and rolled her on her back. Her breasts bounced as he pushed inside her, and her eyes closed as moans purled from her throat. She dug her heels into his back and clutched his shoulders.

Hard and deep, he drove into her again and again. Clinging to him, she matched each thrust of his pumping hips. He tensed, and her inner muscles tightened around him. "Come for me again," he growled. "You can do it, love." Lucy was so close. She shook; her breathing grew choppier. "That's it," he urged. The first wave rolled over her and crashed into him, and she screamed his name. With one last powerful thrust, he held himself deep, groaning her name until he shattered. Brogan collapsed on top of Lucy, their bodies slick with sweat.

After a solid minute of trying to catch his breath, he asked in a rough voice, "You okay? Did I hurt you?"

"No. But you are now. I can't breathe." She shoved against him, and he rolled on his side, his arm still heavy around her waist.

"I think you tried to kill me," he said, struggling to draw air into his lungs. "I've never come that hard in my life."

"Then I'd get to say you died with a smile on your face."

"With you, I just might." Brogan kissed her damp forehead. A rumble from her stomach vibrated his arm. "You still hungry? I have dessert…chocolate mousse."

Lucy shot straight up with an amazing burst of energy, as if they hadn't just had mind-blowing, head-banging, wild-monkey sex. "Chocolate mousse!" She glared, lips swollen from his kisses, body glowing from their lovemaking, and curls sticking up in disarray.

A beautiful sight. Afraid the roaring noise in Brogan's ears was the sound of him losing himself to her, a tremor of unease snaked up his spine. Fortunately, the no-strings-attached ultimatum knocked some sense back into his head, and he relaxed.

"Why didn't you tell me earlier? We could've been eating chocolate mousse instead of having sex."

"You'd prefer chocolate mousse over sex?" he asked, sounding incredulous. "If your answer is yes, then I must not have done my job right."

"Well…before tonight, the answer would've definitely been yes. Hmmm, now it's a toss-up." She tapped her lip. "Too bad we can't have both."

Brogan yanked her on top of him and gave her a wicked grin. "Who says we can't?"

Chapter 23

LUCY RUMMAGED THROUGH THE WHITE TISSUE OF HER shopping bag and pulled out the new yellow bikini with the peek-a-boo cutouts. She'd hit a few boutiques in Raleigh on a personal shopping spree. It was Friday afternoon, and the oppressive heat hadn't let up, not that she expected cool temperatures in the middle of August. At least swimming in the lake this afternoon would be a nice change.

Swimming. With Brogan.

Her lover.

Goose bumps prickled her skin. To distract herself, she checked her phone. Crickets. She'd been trying to reach Wanda all day with no luck. Lucy hoped everything was okay between Wanda and Russell. Normally, Wanda would've been psycho-texting, calling, or even throwing rocks at Lucy's window to get the dirt on her night with Brogan. Not that Lucy would've disclosed every steamy detail. Like that amazing thing Brogan did with his tongue and cold chocolate mousse and her belly…uh, yeah, she wouldn't be sharing that. Or the new trick he taught her with his swiveling showerhead. Phew, hot flashes. Must be this heat.

Guzzling her cold Cheerwine, she accidently spilled half down her shirt. Steamy, hot thoughts of Brogan had kept flustering her all day, and her work had suffered. She'd almost posted pictures of Dottie Duncan and Sweet Tea, posing in front of the Toot-N-Tell on the Keith Morgan Tennis Academy's website. And this afternoon, she mistakenly handed Julia her new naughty panties, made from a scrappy piece of blue lace, instead of the stretchy maternity undies she'd requested.

Lucy peeled off her wet, stained shirt and blotted her flushed cheeks, remembering Julia's bitchy glare-down, followed by the embarrassing lecture. With a straight face, Julia had mentioned she hoped Lucy wasn't doing anything to embarrass the family. *What? Uh, hello? Kettle, it's me, pot.* Tempted to point out the obvious, Lucy had refrained, not wanting to start another argument with Julia over Brogan. Trying to build that bridge of sisterly bonds, one plank at a time, was like trying to build a bridge with toothpicks in a hurricane. But Lucy had no intentions of throwing in the hammer.

And yet Julia still wanted Lucy to work with Brogan (just not in the buff) and have him help with Parker. Lucy had thrown her hands up in frustration and left Julia to her freshly minted water and her bipolar personality. Besides, Lucy had her own agenda. She would keep seeing and working for Brogan until…well, she didn't exactly know, but she planned to live in the present and enjoy every delicious, heart-throbbing, head-swirling, toe-tingling moment. All those elusive feelings and emotions associated with love and sex coursed through her, giving Lucy an unbalanced sensation so foreign, and yet so right.

She shimmied into the skimpy bathing suit and turned in front of her mirror. Erp. Risque bikini…oh my. Lucy gulped. Wanda would be so proud. But Lucy had been doing lots of things out of her comfort zone lately. Like telling Brogan she wanted a no-strings-attached relationship. As if the sex meant nothing and she wasn't the slightest bit affected by his steadfastness, kindness, intelligence, or humor. As if he didn't treat her…like she was important and made a difference.

Lucy's successful marketing for BetterBites had led to even more work. Keith Morgan wanted her to promote the tennis academy and reorganize its entire social media platform. He even arranged for Lucy to meet with a couple of hottie, ranked ATP players, helping them set up their accounts and giving pointers on promoting themselves. Funny, how Loco Lucy, who had left town with her head bowed in shame, was now highly desirable and branding herself as an effective marketer for businesses big and small.

Everything had changed. Lucy pulled on a pair of white shorts and a silk aqua camp shirt that she knotted over her bikini. She shoved her white cover-up, towel, and yellow flip-flops in her beach bag. She'd changed. Yeah, her reasons for not wanting to come home still existed, but they didn't choke her air passage like before. Having confidence in one's own ability was a huge ego booster. Oh, and having sex worked wonders too. She almost tripped, wiggling her feet into orange Toms, remembering the good-bye kiss Brogan had laid on her that very morning. Out in the open. Against the front door. With her legs wrapped around his waist. Who knew being bad could be so good.

Checking her face in the mirror, she adjusted her sleek ponytail and scooped up her beach bag. She flew down the stairs and into the kitchen to fix Julia's dinner before heading out with Brogan. Her first date…down by the lake. It only took seventeen years to get there.

—⁓—

Brogan twisted the rope bracelet around his wrist. He could think of a hundred other things he'd rather be doing than sitting in Julia's creepy pink bedroom. Like skydiving without a parachute or swimming with water moccasins. But he'd put this conversation off too long, and it needed addressing. He could hear Lucy rattling around in the kitchen, preparing Julia's dinner. He glanced at his watch; he needed to be at the football field in thirty minutes, ready to play ball. What he really wanted was to be back at his place with Lucy in his bed, licking chocolate mousse off her cute belly.

"Is this about Parker or Lucy?" Julia's troubled voice snapped him back to the reason he was staring down at his athletic socks. No way would he discuss Lucy with Julia or anyone right now. They were two consenting adults, and their "relationship" didn't need dissecting by the local committee of busybodies.

He hesitated, taking a moment to decide what to say next. "It's about Parker. It's about his dad." Julia's blue eyes dimmed with worry as she twisted the pink blanket between her fingers. "I'm sorry if this is painful, but you've got to understand. I've been put in an awkward situation with all the gossip in town. And, Julia, it's time Parker knew the truth. He's been disturbed by it too." He watched her throat work as she swallowed. Brogan continued. "Take it from me…you *don't* want to do this to your son. Not knowing is way worse than knowing the truth…no matter how bad it is."

"I'm s-sorry. I know I haven't been fair, and I never meant to hurt you with everyone speculating about you being Parker's dad." Her forced laugh held a bitter tone. "I also didn't expect you to return."

Funny. Neither did he. "Why all the secrecy? And what about this baby's father? Please, Julia, I'm begging you. Don't do the same thing to this child."

Julia cleared her throat. Brogan extended her water glass, placing it in her trembling hand. "It's not something I'm proud of," she said after a few sips. "Both were accidents, but with Parker's father, I…uh, really thought I was in love." Her head hit the pillow and her eyes closed. "Remember Coach Monahan?"

Brogan shook off the dark thoughts swamping his head. "Joe Monahan? Sure. He was a great offensive coach. Attended his funeral when he died about five years ago. Why?" Suddenly, he was afraid of the answer.

Tears leaked down Julia's face. She swiped at her cheeks. "He's…he was Parker's dad."

Silence filled the room. Brogan had no idea if he and Julia still breathed. Finally, he swayed, hitting the back of the chair with a solid thud. "Damn. I had no idea."

"Yeah, you and everyone else in town. Lucy knows, because I just told her. I was young, stupid, in love, and handled things very badly. I guess I haven't changed."

"Did Coach know?" Joe Monahan had been young and cocky and a helluva good coach, pushing the team further than they'd ever dreamed of going.

"Eventually"—her hand fluttered—"water under the bridge."

"Okay. I don't need details." Nor did he want them; he refused the picture of Julia and Coach Monahan to form in his mind. "But Parker still has a right to know. It's not fair to keep him in the dark. He's old enough.

He's a good kid and has talent, and with the right influences, he's going to be okay."

Brogan handed Julia a Kleenex. "What about this baby's daddy? Does he know? Is he in any position to be part of your lives?"

"Yes, but it's complicated."

Brogan narrowed his gaze at Julia, willing her to face reality and do the right thing. "What's it going to be? You better not be waiting another fifteen years."

Her shiny dark hair caressed her shoulders as she shook her head. "I'm going to settle things in the next few weeks. I won't keep this baby's father a mystery. Not this time." Brogan's expression must've appeared doubtful, because she continued, "I promise. Harper Doolan's already threatened to take this house away if I don't come clean." She snickered. "Not really. But he's concerned. He only wants me and my kids to be happy."

"What about your mom?" Mother of the Year didn't jump to mind when Brogan conjured up Babs Doolan. He remembered her being self-centered and slightly distracted.

"Oh, she's already bought a tiny NASCAR jumpsuit for the baby. She plans to visit with her latest boyfriend, the new tire specialist with the Richard Petty Motorsports team."

Brogan chuckled, picturing Babs with her boy toy, wearing an electric-blue-and-black fire-retardant suit. Okay…they were making progress. Maybe Julia would do right by her kids. "Sounds good. You've got a lot to look forward to." He started to rise.

"What about Lucy?" He stopped, and Julia's blue eyes seared him in his seat. "What's going to happen to her when you finally leave Harmony?" Brogan clenched his fists. He still had no intentions of discussing Lucy, especially with Julia.

"I want Lucy to stay, and I don't want you breaking her heart. You know, she's been in love with you since high school." Accusation hung heavy in the air. "It's going to be tough for Lucy to regroup when you leave for good."

"Look, Lucy knows the score. Hell, she's the one who set the boundaries. I have no intention of breaking her or anyone's heart when I leave Harmony."

Julia's lips thinned. "Do you plan to keep her at BetterBites? Maybe if she knew she had a permanent position, she'd think twice about leaving."

"Lucy can keep her job as long as she wants. We plan to offer her a promotion, which would include marketing for all our locations." Julia's face brightened. "But Lucy may have different ideas. I can't force her to stay."

Julia smirked. "You have strong powers of persuasion. If anyone can get Lucy to stay, it's you."

"I'm not making any promises."

Chapter 24

"YOU AND JULIA SURE TALKED FOR A LONG TIME."
Lucy threw her beach bag in the backseat of Brogan's
car. "What about?"

"My house. She's ordering an appraisal." Brogan
didn't meet Lucy's eyes as he buckled up and turned the
key in the ignition.

"Ah. Well, if anyone knows about pricing and selling
houses, it's Julia. You're smart to be using her."

Brogan grunted as he turned toward the high school.
Hmmm. Not too talkative, about Julia anyway. Okay.
Change of subject. "You ready to play some football?
Parker is beyond excited. You've been elevated to hero
status." Another grunt. Brogan kept his focus on the
empty stretch of road ahead of them. A bad vibe came
over Lucy. In her mind, she pictured a sheepish look on
her lover's face as he avoided eye contact right before
breaking up with her. Lucy's stomach rumbled, not from
hunger, but from panic. "Everything okay? If you want
to be with the guys tonight, I totally understand." Don't
dump me...*please*. "I've got plenty of work to catch
up—" Brogan swerved into the empty parking lot at the
First Baptist Church right outside her neighborhood and
slammed the Jag in park. *"What the—?"*

"Come here," he growled and pulled her across
the leather console until his lips locked with hers in a
demanding kiss. In less than two heartbeats, he made

her forget who she was. Stunned, she didn't participate until Brogan slanted her head for better access, caging her head between his hands. She groaned and circled his neck with her arms. This was more like it.

"I don't want to be with the guys tonight. I want to be with you," he whispered against her lips. His heavy breathing echoed inside the quiet car, and he rested his forehead against hers. "If I hadn't promised—"

"Shhh. It's all good." She cupped his face, memorizing his every feature. "I'm looking forward to watching you *old* men try to relive your glory days. I can't wait to be head cheerleader. You know tradition states that head cheerleader always dates the quarterback."

Brogan blanched. "Your cheerleading doesn't involve singing, does it?"

Lucy shifted back to her seat. "Maybe."

"Just be sure to sing when the opposing team has the ball. It's sure to break their concentration."

"Absolutely. I'm not above playing dirty." They both laughed and squeezed each other's hands.

—◦◦◦—

After the touch football game, Lucy, Parker, and Parker's friend Jason piled in Brogan's car. They headed for the lake for swimming and grilling hot dogs, burgers, and s'mores. Brogan had supplied some appetizers from BetterBites and a few cases of his specialty beers. The boys ran screaming toward the lake, jumping and splashing and being, well, boys. Lucy helped some of the other moms set up the condiments and paper products on the picnic tables while the men fired up the grills.

Brogan tapped Lucy on the shoulder with a cold beer in his hand. "So, what'd you think?"

"About what?" She finished straightening the red plastic tablecloth.

"My spectacular playing out there. Did you see that pass I managed to make with three boys pulling on my jersey?" A cocky smile spread across his handsome face.

"Uh, was that the one where you passed the ball and then landed flat on your butt in the mud? Or the one where you threw an interception, and they ran it down and scored?"

"Neither, smart-ass." He hooked his arm around her neck. "As head cheerleader, you're supposed to do more fawning and gushing over my amazing arm and bulging muscles."

"That was your last cheerleader girlfriend. Don't confuse us again, *Bro*." Lucy couldn't keep the snark from her voice. Brogan questioned her with a strange look. "What? I'm just saying—*ooh!* Put me down!" she squealed as he hauled her over his shoulder and trotted over the sand toward the lake. "*N-o-o-o!* Not in my clothes!"

Brogan dropped her in the middle of the long dock. At the end, the boys were jumping into the water, showing off with cannonballs and jackknives. "Lose the clothes. You've got two seconds." He kicked off his leather thongs and peeled his T-shirt over his head. Wolf whistles pierced the air from the shore.

"Woo-hoo! Now we're talking."

"Flex those muscles, Buns of Steel."

"Lordy, I feel a faint comin' on."

Lucy glanced over her shoulder at the other women

drinking beers, making catcalls, and laughing. Brogan paid them no attention, too focused on what Lucy hid beneath her clothes.

"Now, Lucy," he gritted as he started to untie her knotted camp shirt.

She toed off her Toms, brushing his hands away to finish the job. "Payback's a bitch, dude. Remember that." She shimmied out of her short white shorts.

Brogan whistled through his teeth. "Nice." He fingered the silver circle holding the skimpy triangles of yellow fabric together. Passion and desire lit his eyes, making Lucy wonder how long the suit would remain on her body.

"Aunt Lucy, you coming in or not?" Parker called from the middle of the lake.

"She's coming. *Right now*." Scooping Lucy up in his arms, Brogan marched to the end of the dock.

"I'm perfectly capable of walking on my own, Mr. Atlas."

"Hope you can swim."

Before Lucy could respond with a biting comeback, she was flying through the air. Then she landed with a big splash in the warm lake water. As she surfaced, pushing hair from her eyes, Brogan popped up right next to her, shaking the water from his hair like a dog.

"You lose your bikini?" Hope laced his voice as he reached for her. Lucy ducked, adjusting her suit under the water, resurfacing a few feet away.

"You wish," she said, treading water. With a predator's gleam in his eyes, Brogan stroked toward her. Lucy squealed, splashing him in the face before kicking as hard as she could to escape. "Parker. Boys. Attack

Brogan. Now," she yelled and laughed at the same time. "Hurry!"

"Here, Aunt Lucy." A neon-pink noodle glided over the water in her direction. Lucy straddled the noodle to stay afloat. The boys jumped and horsed around, wrestling with Brogan. More dads joined the fray, and boys were lifted and tossed in the air with much whooping and hollering.

"Might as well enjoy the show." Some of the moms had drifted out on rafts and noodles, and one handed Lucy a cold beer.

"Thank you. And what a show it's turning out to be." Lucy laughed, enjoying the beer cooling her throat.

"I hope they don't drown each other," Jason's mom, Sally, said, shifting on her raft.

"The scenery is migh-tay fine," said one of the young moms who'd been howling from shore. The women all nodded in agreement and toasted with their beers. And by scenery, they weren't referring to the pine trees clustered on the shoreline or the low sunset creating a pink glow. No. They meant Brogan and his sleek, wet, powerful body as he simultaneously dunked two boys by the head. "Oh, baby," someone murmured. "You don't mind if we ogle your delicious boyfriend, do you?"

Boyfriend? Okay. Lucy resisted the urge to enlighten everyone that she and Brogan were merely sleeping buddies. It might make her sound a little slutty or sleazy or horny. Or all of the above, which she was.

"Certainly. Ogle away."

"Sweet mother…that man could eat popcorn and drip greasy pizza cheese on my satin sheets any day of the week."

Lucy nodded. She couldn't agree more.

—∿∿—

Only a few parents remained as Brogan and Lucy helped clean up around the bonfire. It was close to ten o'clock. All of Margo's homemade brownies had been consumed, as well as the remaining beers and bottles of chilled white wine by the adults. Brogan helped load the last of the supplies in the back of Tom and Sally Martin's car. Parker, Jason, and two other boys had left to spend the night out together, which meant he had Lucy to himself for one more night.

"That's the last of it," he said, closing the hatch to the Martins' car.

Tom shook his hand. "The boys had a great time. Nice seeing you back on the football field." Brogan grinned. It had felt good too. The Martins waved their good-byes as they drove away on the dirt road.

Turning slowly back to the lake, Brogan watched as Lucy tossed a few leftover dirty cups in the garbage and dusted off her hands. One bonfire still burned, illuminating the dark shoreline. The smell of burgers and smoke lingered in the air. A silver path created by the half-moon sparkled over the still water. Lifting her head, Lucy caught him staring.

"What? Why the big goofy grin?"

Brogan crossed the sandy grass in four strides and reached her. "Finally, alone." He pulled one of her loose curls. Lucy followed, leaning into his chest where he'd wanted her all day. "Time to start that second date." He pressed his fingers into her waist over the white cover-up, tilted his head, going for her luscious mouth.

"Start?" Lucy looped her arms around his neck,

touching her lips to his and kissing all the lucid thoughts from his head. He wrapped his arms around her and squeezed, lifting her off her toes.

"We're going to get all hot and bothered, making out, groping each other under the moonlight, and then I'm going to whisk you home and back into my bed," he said in between nibbles and kisses on her mouth and down her throat. He grabbed her hand and dragged her over to where the blanket was already spread over the rough ground. The trees rustled in the slight breeze, and the loud sound of chirping crickets filled the night air. Guiding Lucy to her knees, he joined her on the blanket and quickly stripped off her cover-up, leaving her in that perfect, skimpy, teeny-weeny bikini. His hands had drifted to her barely covered breasts when she stopped him with her palms pressed against his chest.

"Wait. Are you sure we should be doing this, here… now?" Her eyes were feverish with excitement. "What if someone sees us?"

Shee-it. At this point, he didn't care if all of Harmony sold ringside seats.

"We're perfectly safe." Pushing her down, he hovered over her, bracing his weight on his arms to keep from smashing her into a sand pie.

"Brogan?" she asked, blinking, sounding confused.

"Yes, it's me. How nice of you to remember."

Lucy appeared dazed. "Just checking. Not sure if this is real or fantasy," she whispered as he lowered himself and nibbled on her neck, tasting a little sunscreen and a lot Lucy.

"The only fantasy here is the one coming true inside my head. The one where I'm in this exact spot, making out with the prettiest girl in town." Her sigh filled his ears. And like each time before when he'd started kissing Lucy, their kisses grew more frantic and needy.

Moments later he lifted his head. "Having trouble seeing in the dark. You don't mind if I do a more thorough examination?" She bit into her lower lip, trying to suppress a moan as his hand cupped her breast over her bikini top. Brogan worked his other hand behind her neck and quickly loosened the bow holding up the top. Pushing the triangles of fabric aside, his palms made contact with her taut nipples. He shot her a heated look and then gave his full attention to the perfect mounds heaving before him.

His mouth closed over one tight peak. Lucy bucked beneath him as she gripped his shoulders, stinging his flesh with her nails. Her eyes mirrored his passion as he sucked and kissed his way around her breasts. An overpowering need slammed into him. The need to taste her all over. To lick her satin skin from the top of her creamy breasts to the bottom of her ticklish toes. The need to possess her tonight...now.

"Mine," he murmured as he licked a path from her ribs down to her curvy belly. Lucy moaned, panting his name and writhing beneath him, but Brogan, intent on his task, held her down as he nipped at her waist and lower. Her flesh quivered and contracted everywhere he touched, making him bolder in his purpose. He started to peel down her bikini bottoms when she gasped.

"Uh, Brogan"—*pant, pant.*

He needed to taste her, breathe in her essence, and then he needed to claim her...own her...bind her to him. He pushed off her bottoms. He slid his palm up the

smooth length of her thigh. "I want to give you this." He
gently worked his fingers between her clenched thighs.
"Open for me." Lucy hesitated for only a half second.
Her legs spread wide, she shuddered as he ran his fingers across her slick flesh.

"Oh *my*," she groaned.

He cupped her behind, lifting her hips for the access
he craved. Breathing her scent, a thought struck him like
a thunderbolt of lightning.

He needed her.

For more than her marketing abilities. He needed
her on a daily basis. His heart probably knew this fact
way before his head had climbed on board. But Brogan
chased the thought away, refusing to give it power and
refusing to admit that she controlled him. He focused
on giving her pleasure…putting her first. He rubbed
his stubble along her sensitive inner thighs, loving the
sound of her labored breathing as he kissed a hot trail
toward the core of her silky flesh.

"You're so slick…for me." He kissed her inner thighs
before sliding his tongue inside her heat.

"B-Brogan," she moaned, arching her back and
thrusting her hips up with a physical demand for more.

"Mmm, my favorite dessert." His tongue danced
around her swollen flesh as he teased with bold strokes.
Her head thrashed from side to side; moaning, she
clutched the blanket with her balled fists.

"Like that?"

"Sweet, merciful coconut muffins! Don't toy with
me," Lucy yelled.

Laughing, he swirled his tongue at the center of
her core. She grabbed his head and pulled him tighter,

sighing her pleasure. He held her hips with a firm grip and twirled his tongue around her silken folds, sucking until she arched her back and breathed his name.

Desire singed his insides, pouring through his veins. Her pleasure left him hungry and wanting, aching with need to plunge deep inside her. Lucy panted and quivered from the aftereffects of her orgasm. Suddenly, she pulled him down on top of her.

"I want you...*now*," she groaned and then gave him a kiss that made him mindless, stroking her hand across his chest and lower, working it inside the band of his swimsuit. He pushed his trunks down to release his throbbing cock. He had no defenses against the melting look in her liquid gray eyes. He became dizzy in the head, and his lust overwhelmed him. Locking her legs around his waist, she rocked her hips and he willingly answered her body's request and plunged inside her wet, sweet heat. He deepened his thrust, her hips arched, matching his rhythm, and her eyelids fluttered closed.

"Open your eyes," he said, his voice hoarse. "I want to see your face when you come." *As I make you mine, all mine.*

Her eyes widened, and she panted, "Yes." Sinking deeper, he became part of her. An animal-like noise penetrated the sultry night air, except it was really Lucy, thrashing beneath him.

"Ah, there's the spot," he said on a throaty moan. He hit her sweet spot and felt electrified. They were both *so* close.

Her legs gripped his thighs, and he bent his head for another kiss. She cried soft little moans, urging him to move faster and deeper. He dropped his head against her neck, gasping for air, fighting his own orgasm, wanting her to come first. Her hands slid down his slick back and grabbed his behind. She stiffened and finally screamed his name on her release.

Brogan's head snapped back; a gargled sound slipped from his throat. He pumped his hips, gripping her tightly. With a roar, he exploded and came inside her. At that precise moment, Lucy became his salvation. The light to his dark. He sank into the surrendered feeling and the raw passion of their lovemaking. His orgasm wracked every cell in his body until he collapsed on top of her.

She lay limp beneath him, breathing heavily.

"I think you tried to kill me again," he said between gulps of air.

"So this is what I've been missing all this time down by the lake." Pant, pant. "We started at R and went barreling into triple X," she said in a husky, sex-satisfied voice.

He slowly pulled out of her and rolled to his side. "Nah, maybe X, but certainly not triple X. I'd need a whip and restraints, and you'd need a naughty nurse outfit."

Lucy gave a low chuckle, sighing. "In your dreams."

Brogan's head hit the blanket with a thud. "Shit! What a fucking idiot." Stars swirled before his eyes, blinding him.

"What?" Alarmed, Lucy sat up, covering her breasts. "Did someone see us?" Her head whipped around as she scanned the patch of dark woods.

If only. That would be one hundred times better than what they did. "Do you realize we had sex without a condom?"

"Oh. Uh, yeah…that's bad. Let me think how bad." She started to count on her fingers. Brogan held his breath, praying. After a beat, she said, "I think we're safe…maybe."

"Fuck," Brogan groaned, squeezing his eyes shut. "I haven't been this stupid since I got drunk and had sex with Kathryn. And we all know how that ended," he said, refusing to keep the frustration from his voice. He reached for his swim trunks and yanked them up his legs. "When do you expect your next period?" Panic was starting to claw its way up his spine and circle his throat.

Lucy pulled up her bikini bottoms and started to retie her top. "In a few weeks. Don't worry. You'll be the first to know." Anger tinged her voice.

The peaceful calm and rightness of the night just moments ago vanished like a puff of smoke. The wind had picked up, blowing grass and leaves in their path. Brogan felt his whole life being hauled up and tossed around like the dead leaves on the ground. How could something that felt so right…perfect, be so wrong? He shook out the blanket; sand and grass went flying. Horrible scenarios crowded his mind, all ending with another baby not living. *Stop. That's not going to happen.* He got busy putting out the low-burning embers of the bonfire. Lucy was slipping on her shoes and stuffing things back in her beach bag. Her agitated movements indicated her level of anger.

"Let me help you." He reached for the bag.

Snatching it away, she said in watery voice, "I can do it."

Brogan froze. Lucy continued to ignore him. He

peered closer at her lowered face. His heart stuttered and stopped pumping blood in absolute fear. "Are you crying?" She swiped a hand across her face. He felt like crying too.

"No. Leave me alone." She tried to push past him, but he couldn't let her go. He tugged on her hand and folded his arms around her.

"Please don't cry." He brushed the tracks of her tears with his thumb. "I'm sorry. I didn't mean to hurt you. It's just when I'm with you, my head stops functioning, and all the blood rushes to my stupid dick."

"That's not all that's stupid," she grumbled, snuggling against his chest as he rocked her in his arms.

"I know. It's just…for some reason." His mouth had suddenly dried up. How did he say this without baring his soul? Which would be the second stupidest thing he'd done tonight. "It's just…you mean…a lot to me, and I end up breaking all my self-imposed rules." Like making love without protection and needing her like needing oxygen.

Lucy looked up with flushed cheeks and spiky, wet eyelashes. "I'm sorry, Brogan. I should've stopped you, but…my brain wasn't working either." He pressed his lips to her eyes, kissing away the remaining tears.

"I think we'll be fine. I really shouldn't be ovulating this early." Yeah, but he had Olympic swimmers. They'd probably tread water until the time was ripe. Crap.

"Come on." He smoothed back her tangled hair. "Let's go back to my place. We both need showers, and I have a drawer full of condoms," he said, trying to lighten the mood. Nothing he could do now except sweat and wait.

The unease crawling along Lucy's skin after realizing she'd stupidly had unprotected sex had almost dissipated. A few more rounds with Brogan, starting with inventive foreplay in the shower, rocking the wall in the dark hallway, and finally ending in bed kept her mentally and physically exhausted and happily sated.

Brogan stretched beneath her, making her cheek rub against his hard chest. The smell of rich coffee and expensive soap filled her head. The best smell ever.

"You doing okay?" he asked, his hand twirling one of her curls around his finger.

Lucy tilted her head up and smiled. "Could be better. Got any chocolate mousse?"

"Yeah, but I'm saving it for later." His grin was wicked. Lucy rubbed his arm until she reached his thick wrist, and played with the interesting bracelet he always wore. The blue-and-green nautical rope felt soft from many years of wear and tear.

"Why do you always wear this bracelet?" Brogan stiffened beneath her, and Lucy watched as his smile vanished and his lovely green eyes clouded. "Tell me," she whispered, stroking the stubble covering his strong jaw. For a moment, she didn't think he would speak, and then he heaved a heavy sigh.

"Back in college, my mom's uncle contacted me and told me he'd located my dad." Alarmed by the seriousness of his tone, she wrapped the top sheet around her and sat cross-legged in the middle of the bed. "So I decided to drive to South Carolina, where he was living, and meet him." He shifted, resting against the headboard.

"Was this the first time you'd ever met him?"

He nodded. "Yeah. Didn't know much about him, except the few stories my uncle had shared."

Lucy's heart started to crack in tiny pieces. "What happened?" She feared the answer would not be good.

"He owned a small hardware store in Gaffney." Brogan fiddled with the bracelet that held all the secrets. "I was a nervous wreck. I sat, sweating in my beat-up Jeep Wrangler," he added in a subdued tone.

Lucy gave his hard thigh a soft pat, not sure how to comfort him, and hurting all the same. "How long did you sit in your Jeep?"

"Who knows, but it felt like hours. I watched customers coming and going, hoping to maybe catch a glimpse of my dad, even though I wasn't sure I'd recognize him. Finally I manned up and went inside."

She locked fingers with his and squeezed. "Once inside, I spotted him right away. He was behind the counter, ringing someone up—"

"How'd you know it was him?"

"Looked just like me. Same hair, eyes, height. We could've been brothers."

"Wow."

"Yeah, wow. He came from around the counter and said, *Hey, I'm Don Reese. Can I help you?*"

Lucy lifted her head, eyes wide. "What did you do?"

"First I froze, and then, I finally shook his hand and said, *I'm Brogan.*" He stopped talking, and Lucy held her breath. With a sigh, he finished. "That was the longest minute of my life. My dad stood there in shock, not speaking. And then he broke down and bawled."

She gulped, trying to keep from bawling herself.

Brogan cupped her face and gave her a soft, poignant kiss, filled with sadness.

"I'm sorry. I know this is painful for you," she whispered around the tears clogging her throat.

"Yeah, but sharing it with you somehow makes it better." She kissed him again with heat and heart. "Luce, remember that day back in high school when you waited for me on the bleachers after that big win?"

Flushed, Lucy tried hiding her face in Brogan's sweet, delicious neck. "Yeah. I remember," she murmured against his hot skin. She just wished he didn't remember. Her first failed attempt at seducing her sister's boyfriend. Lucy preferred to keep that jewel buried under six feet of granite.

"Sometimes even after a huge win, I'd get depressed because the entire game I'd be hunting and watching and looking out for my dad, thinking he'd show up…just once to see me play." He tangled his fingers in her hair. "And when I saw you that night…somehow you made it all better. Knowing you were always there waiting for me." He shrugged his big shoulders. "I just remembered that and wanted you to know I appreciated it."

Lucy cupped his face with her palms and spoke to his somber eyes. "I'm glad I was there too. I never knew what made you so sad, but I'm glad I was a friend to you."

"You were always a good friend." His sad eyes crinkled into a smile. "Want me to finish the story?" he murmured around nibbles on her lips. Not to be distracted by his kisses, she urged him to continue.

"Please finish."

He angled his arm behind his head and sighed.

"Anyway, I had no expectations of a relationship. I just wanted to meet him. He finally stopped sobbing and led me to his office. For the first hour, we chatted about business, the Super Bowl…just small talk. The second hour, we talked about me and my life. He asked questions about college and my football career."

"Did he know you played in high school and at Georgetown?"

"He knew some. I think he kept tabs on me." Lucy squeezed him tight, hoping to give him strength. "The third hour, we talked about his life, but I could tell he was growing uncomfortable and didn't want to answer my questions. He'd remarried, but didn't divulge much else." His chuckle lacked humor. "When he basically clammed up, I knew it was time to leave. I had a long drive back. My dad promised he'd stay in touch and told me to call him anytime. We man-hugged, and all I wanted was to get out of there fast before I started crying like a baby." Brogan stopped; his chest heaved with heavy breaths. "When I reached my Jeep, he came running out of the store, holding a brown bag, and said, *Son, I want you to have this*. In the bag was this bracelet." He turned the bracelet on his wrist.

"What'd you say?"

"Just, *thanks, Dad*." Brogan swiped at his eyes. A lump in Lucy's throat kept her from speaking. "That was the last time I ever saw him. And the only thing he ever gave me was this bracelet."

Chapter 25

LUCY WAS IN LOVE WITH BROGAN REESE, AND HE loved her back. Finally. The gods were smiling down upon her instead of snarling and shaking their fists. She knew this without a doubt, because Saturday morning, Lucy woke early, wrapped around Brogan like a tortilla around a bean burrito. He still slept, breathing evenly, allowing Lucy the glory of studying his peaceful face.

After the heartbreaking story about his dad, he'd proceeded to make love to her as if she were the most precious person in the world and he never wanted to let her go. Thinking of his love made her toes curl. He didn't exactly shout, *I love you* as he climaxed. Those words never passed from his lips. But he didn't have to say it, because Lucy could read the look in his beautiful green eyes. And he touched her as if she were a fragile Fabergé egg worthy of his utmost care and protection. So, yeah, that had to be love. And Lucy shared those exact overwhelming, heart-swelling, head-flying feelings that made her want to dance and sing down Main Street.

"What are you smiling about?" he rumbled in a rusty morning voice.

"How comfy my human pillow is."

Undulating, Brogan gave a huge stretch; then he heaved and rolled over, pinning her beneath all his scrumptious muscle.

"Know what I want?" he asked. She had no idea, too busy luxuriating in the nibbles and ticklish kisses he scattered down her neck and along her heaving chest, but she hoped he wanted her. "A huge breakfast with all the fixins'. I'm starved. You wanna go to the Dog?"

"Huh?" Lucy was having trouble focusing, because her throbbing down-under parts were warming up for another round of mattress gymnastics.

"Come on." He smacked her hip. "I've got the morning off." He planted another kiss on her mouth and slid from the bed.

Lucy flopped against the headboard. "Ugh. You may have the morning off, but my boss is a real hard-ass, and I have to work. I need to get ready for Keith's tournament today. That food isn't going to sell itself, you know."

He pulled a pair of gray Georgetown athletic shorts over his spectacular walnut butt, blocking her view. Lucy sulked, thinking of the unfairness of life.

"Tell your boss to go screw himself," he called from the hallway as he padded to the kitchen by way of the bathroom.

Lucy sat up in the middle of the messy bed that showed damning evidence of the sexy sport they'd played the night before. What she'd really like was to tell her boss not to screw himself, but to screw her... now! The scent of delicious coffee being freshly brewed wafted to her nose, and Lucy scrambled from the bed. Searching for her panties, she ducked under the bed with her bare tush waving in the cool morning air when she spied an old baseball bat. She reached for it, wondering when Brogan had time for a baseball league. Snatching a T-shirt and pair of shorts from his chest of drawers, she dressed, scooped up the bat, and followed her nose to the kitchen.

"Come to mama," she purred as she spied hot coffee and banana nut muffins from BetterBites sitting on his makeshift countertop. Brogan had started to blend another one of his noxious smoothies. "Hey, Zeus, god of the Olympics…found your baseball bat. It was hiding under your bed. You playing Harmony league ball now?" He shut off the blender and gave her a questioning stare as she gripped his old wood bat.

"Nope. I always sleep with that bat under my bed wherever I am." He plopped on the industrial metal barstool next to her with his smoothie in one hand and pulled the bat from her grasp with the other.

Curious, Lucy reached for a muffin. "Why?"

A blanket of sadness darkened his eyes as he peered at the bat. Sorry for bringing it up, she went back to eating her muffin and drinking her coffee, except now they'd lost their delightful flavors, tasting instead like dry tree bark. Brogan drank his smoothie in contemplative silence.

"When I was little, I used to lie awake at night and worry about my mom, about not having much family."

Lucy slid off her stool and moved between his knees. "What about your mom's brother?"

He nodded, slipping his arm around her hip and pulling her close. "He was rarely around. And when you're a frightened kid, logic doesn't usually reign supreme. I always felt the urge to be protective, so I slept with this bat under my bed, you know…to protect us." He shrugged his big shoulders, placing the bat on top of the counter. "Been doing it ever since. Old habit."

"Oh, Brogan." She sighed, crying on the inside for the frightened little boy he'd been. Lucy rained kisses on his lips, nose, and eyelids. "Childhood sucks."

His eyes blazed with heated desire and something more…need…love. "Come here." He claimed her mouth and soul-kissed her silly. Much too soon, he unlatched his lips from hers with a satisfied pop. "Damn, woman. You're dangerous." He patted her bottom. "Gather your things, and I'll take you home before the hard-ass fires you." He sent her a lusty wink.

She gathered her lake clothes and shoved everything in her beach bag while he pulled on a T-shirt and shoved his feet in some old tan Top-Siders. He picked up her bag and his car keys, and she scooped up her coffee and half-eaten muffin, following him to the car.

"Brogan, is your uncle still living?" Lucy asked once settled inside the car.

"Yeah, but now he's my aunt."

"What?"

He grinned. "It's true. He decided to become a woman."

Lucy said under her breath, "Sheesh. And I thought my family was complicated."

—◦◦◦—

Lucy fanned herself underneath the food tent at the tennis academy where fans gathered to watch the Pro-Am tournament. She'd been selling healthy boxed lunches from BetterBites and Margo's special desserts, along with Brogan's healthy granola. Bailey and another girl from the store showed up with more turkey wraps and sandwiches in time to relieve her for an hour.

Brogan had dropped her home that morning, leaving her dazed from his thorough kiss good-bye, and left to run a marathon or climb Mount Everest backward or something. Lucy still hadn't heard anything from Wanda and was beginning to worry. If Wanda didn't return her calls today, Lucy was not above breaking and entering her house to check for dead bodies... mainly Russell's.

Fortunately, she wouldn't have to break the law. She watched Bertie and Wanda strolling toward her booth. Bertie wore stylish white walking shorts and a halter-top twisted from an orange-and-yellow silk scarf. Very classy. Wanda...oh, Lord. Lucy had to blink to take it all in. Wanda flaunted her cleavage in a fuchsia ruffled top with plunging neckline. She wore very skinny navy-blue capris and navy-and-white striped pumps with five-inch neon-yellow heels...not exactly tennis tournament-approved apparel. They both had on floppy straw hats and Jackie O sunglasses.

"Hey, Luce, you ready to take a break?" asked Bertie.

Lucy ignored Bertie and glared at Wanda. "Where the hoot have you been? I've been worried sick."

"Sick? I highly doubt it, since you were spotted leaving Beefcake Brogan's house *two* mornings in a row and locking lips with him by your front door." Wanda flashed a shrewd smile. Lucy glanced over her shoulder, afraid the paparazzi were present, or worse, Miss Sue Percy. How did this keep happening? God, she prayed no one had witnessed the X-rated sex down by the lake.

"Who told you that?" she whispered as she moved away from the booth. "What are you, a slimy reporter for the *National Enquirer*?"

"Let's get to the box before I melt in this broiling heat," Bertie interjected, herding both Lucy and Wanda to one of the sponsor's luxurious boxes. They all helped themselves to the free beer, and Lucy snagged a cup of M&M's. Bertie excused herself to check on Keith, and as soon as she exited, Lucy blasted Wanda with both barrels.

"What's going on with you? You don't call, email, or text. What did you do to Russell? Did you hit him over the head with an iron skillet and barbecue him like in *Fried Green Tomatoes*? Don't tell me he's swimming with the fishes at the bottom of the lake."

Wanda waved her hand. "Calm down, CSI. Russell lives. Although it was touch and go there." Wanda flopped down on the white leather love seat. Her smile faded as she played with the cocktail napkin shaped like a yellow tennis ball.

"You okay? Anything I can do to help?" Lucy inched closer to Wanda, not liking her subdued personality. "You know you can tell me anything."

"Have a seat, Luce. There is something you should know."

Lucy's knees wobbled. She *really* didn't like this serious side of Wanda. Sitting down hard on the edge of the Carrera marble coffee table, she said, "Tell me. Is it Fiona?"

"Fiona's fine, enjoying some of Brogan's healthy scraps." Wanda drank her beer and gave Lucy a steady stare. "What do you know about Julia's baby daddies?"

Thrown for a loop, Lucy stammered, "W-what? What do you mean?"

"Do you know who they are?"

"I know for a fact it's not Brogan, if that's what you're getting at. Please don't believe all that baloney gossip." Lucy didn't feel free to reveal the identity of Parker's dad. That was Julia's announcement. But for a town that seemed to know how many times Lucy blinked a day, she couldn't figure how Julia's secret was never leaked. Julia had talent for sure.

Wanda continued in a low voice. "Well, that may be true." She removed her hat and fluffed her brown curls. "Believe it or not, I know who *this* baby's father is." Lucy's jaw dropped open. "You have to give me your solemn promise you won't breathe a word until I say it's okay. You swear? Not. One. Word."

Lucy gulped and nodded. "I swear," she whispered, crossing her heart with her finger.

Wanda's gaze darted around the interior of the sponsor box, checking for nosy Harmony residents. Her dark brown eyes landed back on Lucy, frying her to the spot.

"It's Russell."

Stunned, it took a moment for her brain to register. "Did you say Russell? As in *your* Russell?"

"That's right. Russell, the good ole love muscle." Wanda eased back and struck a casual pose and proceeded to tell Lucy a fascinating tale about how Julia would call Russell regarding construction work on her sale properties. All normal, until Julia started calling him to see about personal repairs on her house. And one weekend, when Parker was out of town visiting his grandmother, Julia invited Russell over for some grilled burgers. And asked him to check out her plumbing...but not the pipes under her sink.

That panicky feeling started to creep its way up from

Lucy's gut, curling its clammy claws around her heart and squeezing. "I just can't believe it. What were they thinking? Hello? Can we say birth control?" *Snap!* Lucy's mouth closed on those last two words. Who was she to preach? She and Brogan had been just as careless, caught in their own uncontrollable, smoggy-headed lust. Maybe lust was too harsh. More like unbridled, uncontained, bursting with love. Yeah, yeah, yeah, *she* loved, but Brogan…not so sure.

"The condom broke." Lucy refocused on Wanda's story. "I've been trying to tell you for years…Russell's love muscle is a mighty powerful thing." Humor lit the back of Wanda's eyes before they quickly sobered.

"Aw, Wanda, what are you going to do?" Lucy slid next to her on the love seat, draping her arm around her best friend's shoulder. "Did you give Russell the final heave-ho?" Lucy couldn't remember a time when Wanda and Russell weren't either jumping each other's bones or arguing like two flea-bitten alley cats.

Wanda absently smoothed Lucy's white-and-coral cotton skirt and gave her knee a reassuring pat. "No. Actually, Russell and I are going to give it another shot." Lucy's head reared back. "Yeah…I've forgiven him." Wanda cocked one brow. "It's not like I've been a lily-white saint, you know."

"What about the b-baby? What's Russell going to do?"

"Be part of his or her life. We both are. I'm not letting Julia take that away from Russell. She's not going to keep this a mystery for fifteen years and have Russell's baby grow up without a father. With my guidance, he'll make a super dad," Wanda added smugly.

"Good for you. You'll both be great. What does that make you? My ex-sister-in-law? Parker's stepaunt? My evil stepsister? Oh, sorry, that's Julia." Lucy snickered.

"None of the above. We'll be Russell, the baby's daddy, and Wanda, his kick-ass lady wife!"

Lucy jumped in excitement. "You mean it? You and Russell are getting married again?"

"Yep. After I pin Julia like a squirming insect under a microscope. She's gonna come clean if she doesn't want Wanda Wonderbust making her life miserable."

If anyone could scare the truth out of Julia, it would be Wanda.

Lucy threw her arms around Wanda's neck. "I'm so happy for you. You will make the best parents. The best."

"I agree." Wanda returned Lucy's hug. "Now I want to hear about you and Brogan," she said, rolling her *R*. "I need all the dirty, naughty, sexy details. I'm looking for size and style techniques."

Buttered popcorn balls! Lucy didn't have a choice but to spill like an undercover spy being grilled by the KGB *because* Wanda's wonderbust was locked and loaded and had Lucy in its sights.

The next two weeks passed in a love-filled, hot-air-balloon-floating, fairy-tale kind of blur for Lucy. Parker managed to make friends on the football team, and his hero worship mounted as Brogan continued to watch his practices and give him man-to-man advice. And Lucy's heart soared over the newfound love she had for Brogan. And he demonstrated the same…okay, not with words, but action. Because whenever she came within two feet of him, he'd reach out and touch her or kiss her or drag her behind his office door, causing her face to bloom hot pink when she'd emerge, straightening her clothes and smoothing her sex-tangled hair. Yep. Life tasted better than a batter-drenched, deep-fried Snickers bar.

One night Brogan surprised her with tickets to the Trace Adkins concert, and even bought a pair for Parker and a friend. In her excitement, Lucy jumped him and almost knocked him on his butt in a bucket full of wet paint.

The only stumbling block keeping her from complete euphoria was Julia. The disapproving looks, snarky comments, and extra load of useless errands flashed like a warning sign. Seemed Julia had lost everyone's undivided attention and didn't like it. Things would only get worse when Wanda got around to confronting her. Lucy hoped like hell she'd be running one of Julia's stupid errands when the poop hit the turbo fan. The only other niggling worry—more like an epic worry—had to be that Lucy's period hadn't come. Yet. She still remained positive and kept reassuring Brogan.

Lucy dusted her hands and read the recipe next to her on the kitchen counter for the third time. Tonight, she was surprising Brogan with a homemade, healthy, organic dinner, personally delivered to his house in celebration of their two-week anniversary. Lucy even swallowed her mortification (along with a few M&M's) and shopped at Wanda's favorite store, Scanty Panties, on the outskirts of town. She purchased a sexy red lace thong and matching push-up bra, and planned to wear it under her zippered, black lace dress. Brogan had no idea of her surprise, but she'd instructed him to be home by seven, with an appetite.

Parker would be spending the night out for one last summer fling before school started on Monday.

With a glass of water in hand, Lucy pushed the door to the bedroom with her shoulder, and Julia, wearing a frilly pink robe and a pinched expression, looked up from reading a fashion magazine.

"Here you go. Freshly minted water. I'm making a really healthy meal for dinner: beef stir-fry with avocado salad."

Julia reached for the glass. "Interesting how you've decided to learn to cook all of a sudden. It wouldn't have anything to do with all the sex you're having with Brogan, hmmm?"

These days, Julia didn't hesitate to lash out with her razor-sharp tongue. Lucy bit the inside of her cheek to keep from responding.

"It's all everyone is gossiping about. Miss Sue practically ran a front-page article in the *Harmony Herald*. You might as well acknowledge the relationship."

"Why? You never did. I'm just taking a page from your book."

Julia visibly bristled. "Well, take this page while you're at it…he's going to break your heart like he did mine, and he's going to leave Harmony and return to his real life in New York. The same way he did all those years ago. He's not interested in Harmony, marriage, or kids. Remember that."

Lucy flinched as if Julia had thrown sand in her face. "You broke his heart, not the other way around. I don't plan to do the same thing." Lucy flashed a smug expression, trying to cover the fear coursing through her veins. Unconsciously, she pressed her hand to her belly, knowing Julia's scenario was dead-on if Lucy turned up pregnant. *Sweet caramel apples on a stick. No!* There was no pregnancy, because Lucy willed it to be so. Shaking the ugly thoughts from her head, she marched back to the kitchen to cook a delicious meal for her Bro-man.

Julia was wrong. Dead wrong.

—⁓—

Brogan strolled through the back door of BetterBites, whistling a nameless tune. He stopped at the counter where Margo worked and grabbed a handful of granola.

"What's got you dancing in your loafers? Forget it. I already know. Where is your Lucy-love?" Pushing through some dough with a French rolling pin, she smirked at him.

"Gave her the day off. She's been working too hard."

"Yeah, keeping you happy in bed."

Brogan flashed a cocky grin. "I think the happiness is spread all around. Haven't heard any complaints."

"Probably because you're howling like a coyote."

Brogan laughed hard. "That's for sure."

"Don't you have to be in New York in three weeks? What's going to happen to Lucy?" Margo scowled at him as if he were a bottom-feeder drug dealer with no scruples. The New York deadline loomed over his head, but he'd been toying with the idea of convincing Lucy to meet him there after Julia had her baby. She could jump on board with some marketing ideas. Shit. Who was he fooling...he wanted her with him, by his side.

Everything about Lucy seeped between his ribs and lodged in his chest, taking up permanent residence. In the past, his relationships lasted only a few weeks. He didn't want that anymore. And he'd already survived a bad marriage. He sure as hell didn't want that. But he *did* want Lucy. A really good friend. Someone he more than cared about.

Brogan snatched another handful of granola and tossed it in his mouth. He grabbed water from the cooler and flipped through the orders on a clipboard hanging on the wall. He struggled to focus on the notes as his mind wandered to the past week. Grinning, he remembered Lucy's excitement when he'd presented her with the Trace Adkins tickets. You would've thought he'd handed her the crown jewels. After jumping him and appropriately thanking him by rocking his world, she'd rushed home to get ready. At the concert, Brogan had enjoyed watching Lucy sing more than Trace. In typical Lucy fashion, she'd danced in the aisle and sung at the top of her lungs, croaking like a bullfrog in heat, not caring that she embarrassed Parker and his friend, sitting one row in front of them. At the end of the concert, her gray eyes had burned bright, her cheeks had glowed a pretty pink, and she'd said, "That was awesome. Thank you so much. I'll never forget this night." Pleasure filled his chest. He'd never known a woman like Lucy…full of life, sass, courage, and a heart of pure gold. His friend.

"Mr. Reese? You have someone who wants to see you in the front." Bailey stood inside the swinging door that separated the back of the store from the front and interrupted his happy Lucy memories.

"Thank you, Bailey. Do you know who it is?" She

shrugged her shoulders, popping her gum. "Okay. I'll be right there." He took another swig of water and brushed off his hands.

As he crossed the store, he'd reached the bins that held the packaged granola when he stopped cold. A wave of shock, followed by panic and confusion, blasted him like a stick of dynamite to the chest. Brogan stared at a man's profile. He was standing near the front window, examining the assortment of green teas.

His father.

How many years since that long, nerve-wracking drive from Georgetown to Gaffney? At least fifteen. He'd never seen or spoken to his dad since. Oh, he'd tried. But every time he'd called, his dad hadn't answered. A few times his dad's wife would pick up, but she'd acted pissy and brushed him off with some lame excuse. After several years, he stopped trying.

Brogan didn't move. Didn't breathe. But somehow his father sensed his presence and looked up. A slow smile curled his weathered lips.

"Hello, Son." His dad dropped the tea bags on the table with a shaky hand. Brogan knew his dad was close to seventy-five in age, but his complexion was drawn, and his color didn't look good. What little was left of his tawny-colored hair had grayed. And his short-sleeved shirt hung loose from his now-skinny frame. He looked closer to ninety-five.

"Do you have a minute to talk?" Don Reese asked in a raspy voice.

Brogan snapped out of his stupor. "Sure. Would you like to step in my office?" He was surprised by how normal his voice sounded.

"That'd be fine. Real fine." Don shuffled, stopped, wheezed, and then started to shuffle again. Brogan hesitated, unsure whether to help him or leave him to his own devices. He chose the latter and led the way to his office in the back. Margo looked up from shoving pans of bread in the oven; concern etched her scowling face.

"Please make sure I'm not disturbed," Brogan said in her direction as he held the office door for Don. Closing the door, he watched his father hover over the guest chair, holding the back as if he might fall.

"Have a seat, Don. What can I do for you?" Brogan asked as he sat behind the desk and clasped his hands together to hide his nerves. Sweat, cold and sickly, trickled from his hairline down his spine.

Don managed to bend his knees enough to sit. He fiddled with a worn nautical bracelet around his shriveled wrist, similar to the one Brogan wore. Brogan instinctively fingered his as he cleared his dry throat. Refusing to start the conversation with a bunch of inane prattle, he remained silent. He hadn't called this meeting.

"Uh, Son…it's good to see you. What's it been? Five years?"

"Yeah, five years times three, but who's counting?" The hurt he'd kept bottled up leaked from his voice.

"Fifteen years? That long, huh? I had no idea. You've got a real nice store here. Quality product. I can tell. Kind of ironic we both landed in the small-town retail business." His dad gave a rusty laugh.

Shit. That sobering thought made Brogan itch to post a For Sale sign, don a three-piece suit, and hit Wall Street…yesterday. Reigning in his shaking fury, he said, "So, here we are. What can I do for you? You need money?" His old man's head snapped back, and his watery eyes sparked. Must've hit a nerve. Too bad.

"Keep your money. I came here to talk to you about your family."

"What family? I don't have any family." Except for Uncle Ray, who now went by Raylene, but he'd be damned if he would bring his mother's brother into this.

"Your stepmother, my precious Louise, died a few years back…" Stepmother. Precious? That bitch who never let him speak to his dad? Oh no, *he* didn't. Brogan was not about to acknowledge that woman as his step-mother when he'd never even had a dad.

"…sold the hardware store because I got a little sick and couldn't keep it running," Don kept talking. "Doc says I'm doing fine, just need to take it easy, and I'll live for another fifty years." A wracking cough overtook him, shaking his frail frame as he pulled a red bandana from his pocket and covered his mouth. Bullshit. Death had come a'knocking. The sickly-sweet smell, mixed with nasty drugs, hung in the air. Brogan recognized the death smell from sitting by his mother's bedside. His heart constricted painfully over an absentee father who never cared about him, because now it was too late. The opportunity to know his dad had already slipped through his fingers.

"Why now? What made you come see me after all these years, Don?"

Don's eyes flickered over the use of his given name. But Brogan had stopped thinking of him as Dad years ago.

"I need to tell you about your family."

"*Jesus!* I told you I don't have any—"

"Yes…yes, you do. You have a half brother and sister."

The bomb that went off inside Brogan's head caused temporary hearing loss. A brother and sister he'd never met and didn't even know existed. Not possible. Brogan growled low. "What are you saying, old man?"

Don leveled his watery gaze at him without flinching. "Your sister, Ashley, is thirty-five and your brother, Neal, is now…er, he's thirty-one or thirty-two. Can't keep it all straight in my head."

Thirty-five? Brogan had a sister one year older than him? How? Don hadn't left his mother until Brogan was two years old.

That sick panic feeling swelled and morphed as Brogan realized this nightmare wasn't close to being over. "I don't understand. You were having an affair before you met and married my mom?"

Don shifted in his seat; color seeped over his pasty, gray face. "Not exactly. I was married to Louise *before* I met your mother."

"Excuse me?" He was clearly confused. "Okay, you divorced Louise and then married my mom?"

The color seeped from his drawn complexion, turning it even grayer, and his eyes filled with tears. "No, Son. I was still married to Louise when I married your mom."

It took a moment to register, but as the news hit him, Brogan gripped the edge of his desk to keep from reeling back. "You were married to both women…at the same time?" His chest heaved. "You were a *bigamist*?"

Don slowly nodded, and his thin lips drooped in a frown. Brogan's blood boiled as it all became crystal clear. The secrets, the lies, his mom *never* speaking about his dad. His dad and Louise never wanting anything to do with him. He was the living proof of his dad's crime. If they never acknowledged him, no one would be the wiser. The dirty little secret everyone wanted to keep hidden.

Brogan gave his chair a violent push as he stood. "You committed a felony, and that's why you never wanted anything to do with me. You lying, cheating sack of shit!" He barely tamped down the urge to wrap his hands around his father's scrawny neck. "Did my mother know?"

With unsteady limbs, Don stood, grasping the front of the metal desk for support. "No, no. Your mother found out once the divorce was final. I felt I owed her at least that." Don's thin shoulders straightened, and he skewered Brogan with a hard stare. "Everything you know about me is right. I was a liar, cheater, and spineless bigamist. Sorry ain't gonna fix anything at this stage of the game. But for what it's worth, I *am* sorry. Your mama was a good woman, and she raised you real good. Don't hold no grudges against your mama. You keep all that blame on me, where it belongs."

Damn straight. Brogan not only blamed him—he felt nothing but rage. Not an ounce of pity for his dying sperm donor. It was almost a relief having everything Brogan resented about his father confirmed by his own pathetic story. At least he finally knew the truth. If Don expected absolution for showing up today to confess and ease his conscience, he was going to be sadly disappointed. Brogan had no intention of absolving him. He'd leave that up to his Maker.

Don wheezed as his thin shoulders shook, overcome

by his rattling cough. A tap at the door snapped Brogan out of his trance. He opened it, and Margo thrust water at him. Brogan thanked her with a nod and handed the water to his dad.

"Here."

"Thank you, Son. You're a fine man." He drank unsteadily, dribbling some water down the front of his shirt.

After Don had taken a few sips, Brogan, unable to stop himself, asked around a lump in his throat, "W-why did you abandon me? Why did you leave and never look back? Were Mom and I that bad?"

Don shook his wobbly head. "I thought I could handle both. Back then I was in sales and traveled a lot, which is why your mama never knew the truth. Your mama was a fine woman and wouldn't continue to see me unless I married her." He hung his head. "I'm not proud of abandoning you, but I knew Louise would never accept you, nor would polite Southern society. It ain't like it is today. Louise would've been shunned, and her children shunned. So, I cut bait, thinking it was best for everyone." He met Brogan's injured gaze. "If it makes you feel any better…I wasn't much of a father to your half sister and brother either."

Oh yeah, he felt marvelous now. His dad had treated all his kids like shit.

"I continued to travel until about twenty years ago. Louise made me settle down, and that's when I bought the hardware store."

"That's quite a story. Anymore illegal marriages and abandoned children roaming around?" Despite his sarcasm, Brogan shook in fear of the answer.

"N-no. Not that I'm aware of."

Jesus. His dad was a regular gigolo. Love-'em-and-leave-'em Donny Reese. And to think he carried the man's DNA. No wonder Brogan was always on the move. Perfect example of the apple not falling far from the tree…they both wandered, afraid of commitment. Afraid of settling down. Brogan felt sick to his stomach.

"Well, I need to be shoving off. I've taken up enough of your time." His dad extended a trembling hand. Brogan hesitated but finally slipped his hand around his dad's, giving it a gentle shake, feeling nothing but flesh and bones.

"You have a way home?" Another lump clogged his throat.

"Oh, sure. Your sister, Ashley, is waiting out front. She drove me here."

Half sister. Brogan tried clearing any sympathetic feelings muddying up his head as he escorted his dad to the front door. He stopped by a barrel of Granny Smith apples and shoved two in a bag. "Here, D-Dad. For the road."

"Thank you, Son." His dad reached for the bag and gave Brogan a sad smile. "Ashley will appreciate it."

Brogan gripped the door handle and nodded. He didn't want to think about his sister, sitting out in a car on Main Street, or his brother…who knew where. He held the door open and watched as his dad shuffled over the threshold into the August heat.

"See you around," Brogan said in a hoarse voice.

His dad stopped as if he'd forgotten something, but then gave a wobbly nod and said, "Have a good life, Son."

Brogan watched as his dad dragged himself down the sidewalk. Complete numbness settled over him, freezing him in the heat. He released the door, and it slid closed. He should have been feeling release…liberation, freedom from all his pent-up anger and resentment. The truth shall set you free, and all that bullshit. So now he knew. His dad was a runner, going from woman to woman, not taking responsibility for his actions. A bigamist, deserting Brogan and avoiding the law. More afraid of being shunned by polite Southern society than doing the right thing and accepting his son in his life.

Brogan reached for one of the green apples, rolling it around in his hand, noticing a few bruises, just like his heart… He was always the kid who never got over being abandoned by his father. Always waiting…hoping his dad would show up and embrace the son he never knew. And then he became the man who never sustained a relationship with a woman. He'd been dogged by his dad's stigma his whole life, living with the phobia of becoming just like him. That constant anxiety destroyed his marriage, because Brogan couldn't overcome that drowning sensation. And the same would happen with Lucy, his *good* friend. He didn't want to hurt Lucy. Pain stabbed the inside of his forehead, and Brogan squeezed the bridge of his nose. Everything centered on the compulsion not to repeat tainted Reese history. Better not to get involved than to destroy lives along the way. He could think of only one solution. Always the same one: cut his ties and move on.

A low growl set fire to his throat. Hurling the apple across the store, he nailed a display of stacked bottles of flavored vinegars before storming out.

Chapter 26

LUCY CLIMBED THE PORCH STEPS TO BROGAN'S HOUSE and pushed her way through the front door, carrying two shoppers loaded with her homemade beef stir-fry, fresh bread from BetterBites, crisp spinach salad, and a nice bottle of champagne. And for dessert: yummy flourless brownies that Margo had taught her how to make. She glanced at her silver watch…right on time.

"Hey, Brogan? I'm here with your surprise," she called as she dumped the bags on the newly installed soapstone countertops that gave his kitchen a warm, old-world glow. Lucy stopped to adjust her scanty panties from creeping up into uncomfortable land. She unloaded the food and pulled out plates, glasses, and utensils. She lit a kitchen candle that smelled of rosemary she'd discovered in one of the upper cabinets.

"I hope you're hungry. And this time I'm talking about food," she called out with a chuckle.

Satisfied with her bounteous display, she smoothed the front of her black dress, unzipping the top enough to give Brogan a tantalizing view of her lacy red bra. Wanda had insisted Lucy take a page from her book on how to lure men. Feeling ridiculous because Brogan was a sure thing, she acknowledged that it still never hurt to spice things up a bit. Reaching for the champagne, she popped it open. Time to start this anniversary party. She filled two flutes and sauntered down the dark hallway, wearing what she hoped was a sexy, come-and-get-it smile.

"You ready for your surprise?" she said, entering his room. Lucy halted as her smile slowly faded. Something was wrong, starting with no sign of Brogan and the empty bedroom that looked as if it had been swept clean. Her gaze traveled around the room. The bed linens had been stripped, and the top of Brogan's dresser no longer held his multiple sport watches and loose change he kept on a small tray. Lucy inched toward the cracked closet door, peering inside. No shoes, no shirts…nothing except empty hangers and some old shoeboxes. Lucy gripped the stems of the flutes to stop them from shaking.

"What the…?"

Silence filled the room, heavy and ominous. Lucy took a fortifying gulp of champagne, allowing the bubbly liquid to burn the back of her throat, as her mind raced through the numerous scenarios. None of them good. What happened? Where was he?

"Brogan?" She tried to keep the alarm from her voice as she checked the adjoining bathroom. Spotless. No shaving cream or toothbrushes. The countertop had been wiped clean. Lucy worked her way back down the hall, peeking her head in the other two bedrooms and baths. No sign of life. From the great room, she could see he wasn't out on the screened porch. And when she opened the door to the garage, his car was gone. Okay. There must have been an emergency. Lucy sent up a silent prayer, hoping no one was sick or injured. With unsteady hands, she placed both flutes on the kitchen island and reached for her handbag to retrieve her cell, when she stopped. There, propped next to the blender

Brogan used to make his morning smoothies, was an envelope with Lucy's name scrawled on the front. Somehow she'd missed it while preparing their meal.

"Good. This is all good. He left me a note that will explain the emergency." Tamping down the panic that threatened to ricochet through her now alarmingly cold body, she reached for the envelope.

Lucy paused, trying to slow her breathing as she fumbled with the envelope flap. Pulling out the note, she unfolded the paper. Her eyes widened as she read:

Lucy:

Can't put off NYC any longer. Been hanging around Harmony too long, and NYC is my priority now. You've been a great friend and big help to BetterBites. But we both knew from the beginning that this thing between us was a fling. No strings attached, right? And it was never my intention to come home permanently. Hope we can go back to the way things were and remain friends. You still have a job with BetterBites as long as you want it. It was nice reconnecting with you. Take care.

Brogan
PS: If you're pregnant, please let me know, as I'd like to help with child support.

Lucy read and reread the short, impersonal note before it slipped through her stiff fingers and fluttered to the floor. She blinked uncontrollably, trying to see past the red burning her eyes. *Friends? Fling?* Was she missing something? They'd been more than just friends these past two weeks. Lucy knew it, and Brogan knew it. And now Brogan was denying it. But why? *What?* Lucy picked up her champagne glass and knocked it back in one huge gulp. Then she did the same with Brogan's before dropping onto a barstool with her head in her hands. He'd cut and run without saying good-bye and without telling Lucy the real reason. Something or someone had gotten to him. Because only a few hours ago he'd been looking forward to this date. Lucy's mind raced, trying to piece the mystery together. She moved to pick the note up off the floor and read his postscript again as the acid in her stomach churned. *Let him know if she was pregnant because he'd like to contribute to the cause*, as if she were some freaking charity. He was running scared from her and the possibility of a baby. As if she would trap him like that. Okay…yeah, she wanted him. And if she was pregnant, she wanted him in her and her baby's life permanently. But she'd never trap him or force his hand. Would she?

She scrambled for her cell phone, hoping beyond hope he'd left a message or a text. There had to be another explanation that made sense and didn't crack and crumble her heart into a million pieces. With sweaty fingers she tapped the screen of her phone, only to see she had no missed calls or texts. Without thinking, she called Brogan's cell. After three rings, it went straight to voice mail. Lucy asked him to call her in what she hoped was a calm voice. Then she texted him the same message.

Numb, Lucy sat for the next hour, holding her silent phone. With dry eyes, she watched the sun go down over the lake…along with her hopes of hearing from Brogan go down with it.

—–∿∿∿–—

It was Monday morning, two days after Brogan had dumped her via impersonal note, and Lucy had already dropped off a very sullen Parker for his first day at school. He wasn't taking the news well that Brogan had skipped town. Neither was she. And for once, she didn't have a pithy explanation to ease Parker's pain. Lucy feared he'd revert back to his old pranks and old friends, and she didn't know if she had the strength to deal with it. Everything was barreling straight to hell in a handbasket on high-speed Rollerblades.

Lucy sat in Wanda's sunny kitchen, drinking another cup of weak tea to calm her raging stomach. Wanda kept repeating the same thing over and over again.

"Luce, something happened. Something or someone got to him in a big, bad way. Because I know Brogan would never leave like this."

"Fried baloney. I showed you the note and his lame texts from yesterday, saying we both need to get back to our real lives. End of fairy tale. Mind you, there's been no conversation, because he's too chicken." Afraid Lucy would break down and beg him to take her back. Which she would…if he'd only give her another chance. Pathetic. Lucy swiped an errant tear from her cheek.

"Oh, Luce. There has to be a real explanation. This is not like Brogan." Wanda bent and gave Fiona a distracted pat on the head.

"You got any more of those Hostess CupCakes?"

"Sure." Wanda plopped the Hostess box on the table,

along with the bag of half-eaten Cheetos. "Knock your-self out."

Lucy reached for a cupcake but then pulled back her hand. "Maybe I shouldn't. My stomach is still rumbling."

"You think? What'd you expect, four cupcakes and a pound of Cheetos later?"

"I'm upset. I always eat junk in large quantities when I'm upset," Lucy grumbled, holding her tummy. "I don't know, Wanda. It's like he's beyond my reach. He refuses to speak with me. He has shut down and shut me out. For good. I seriously don't think he's ever coming back."

"Well, maybe Javier can shed some light on it. I invited him over." Distressed, Lucy gripped the table's edge. "Calm down. He's not the enemy. Here he is now." Wanda watched a car pull in her driveway. "I'll let him in."

Lucy dropped her head in her hands and groaned. She didn't want to face Javier, Brogan's best friend. They'd probably shared a good laugh over Lucy's delusion about love, relationships, and marriage. And how Lucy never learned from her past mistakes. Was it her destiny to fall for the wrong guy every time?

"Talk to her before she goes into a diabetic coma," Wanda said as they entered the kitchen. Lucy stared at Javier, followed by Margo and Wanda. Margo carried a container of scraps for Fiona.

"What the hoot? Who's manning the store?"

"*Hola,* Lucy. *Cómo estás?*" Javier pulled out the chair next to Lucy and indicated for Margo to sit. Margo handed the scrap container to Wanda.

"Hey, Lucy. The store's covered," Margo said, worry creasing her face.

"About Brogan—" Javier started.

"*Don't.* Don't justify his actions to me." At Javier's confused expression, she added, "I know I'm a delusional idiot and thought we had…something good… great." Lucy's voice trailed off.

"Listen to me." Margo shook Lucy's shoulders, gaining her attention. "Brogan had an unexpected visitor on Saturday. His dad. And it wasn't good. They argued in his office. I heard the whole thing."

Lucy blinked, taking a minute to gauge Margo's serious expression and Javier's sympathetic one. "How did you hear everything?" Lucy would rather focus on the mundane than face the implications of what the meeting meant.

"I eavesdropped," Margo said indignantly. "I wouldn't be a proud member of the Harmony Busybody Grapevine if I hadn't."

Everyone around the table stared at Lucy with a mixture of pity and love. Lucy swallowed more tea just to give her hands something to do other than twirling her hair into corkscrews. Grateful to be surrounded by friends, she nodded for Margo to continue.

Margo regaled them with a tale that made Lucy shiver and the hairs on the back of her neck stand on end. Beginning with Brogan learning he had half siblings, to his dad being a bigamist, and ending with Brogan's fit of rage as he took down an expensive display of vinegars with an apple.

"There's nothing wrong with his throwing arm, I'll tell you that." Margo's lips thinned. "Place still stinks all to be damned like vinegar."

"Lucy, I probably know more about Brogan and his

personal demons than anyone. It seems this time he confronted them literally and figuratively. I think meeting his dad on Saturday was some sort of breaking point. He finally got answers to questions that have plagued him his entire life." Javier gave Lucy's hand a squeeze.

"Okay…I get the whole horrible dad issue, and I even get running to hide and lick his wounds, but leaving a Dear Jane and then refusing to talk this out… How am I supposed to combat that? He says he wants to move on with his life, which doesn't include me or Harmony." Her shoulders slumped. "I really believe he's never coming back." Lucy met their concerned faces. "Ever."

Silence hung over them like a large, ominous black cloud. Wanda boomed, scattering the cloud and the air. "That's ridiculous. First of all, he still has to sell his house, and secondly, he needs to be here for BetterBites, but most importantly"—she paused for dramatic effect—"he's going to come home for *you*." She pointed a manicured nail at Lucy. Everyone nodded in solemn agreement, but Lucy wasn't convinced. They hadn't been rejected by an empty house, a pathetic note, and a silent cell phone.

"How do you propose we get him back?" Margo asked the group.

Javier fiddled with the plastic floral placemat on Wanda's table. "We need to give him some time. He has to work this out on his own. I've seen him shut down for a few days, or a few months, depending on his state of mind. I think this hit him real hard."

Months? She didn't know if she could last that long without hunting him down and throwing herself at his feet, begging him to love her.

"Ha, my bootie patootie! I know a way to get him back," Wanda responded to Lucy's stricken expression.

"Uh, Wanda, this is one time your wonderbust won't get the job done. Don't get me wrong, Brogan would enjoy the show, but…I don't know."

"I do." Wanda stood and adjusted the silver belt over her tight blue sundress. "I've got other weapons in my arsenal besides my fabulous bust." Pride rang clear in her voice.

"You care to share it with the rest of us?" Lucy asked, clearly afraid of what Wanda might be plotting.

"Nope. You're just going to have to trust me."

And the next two weeks went downhill from there.

By Friday, Lucy didn't know if she had the flu, or if she couldn't get out of bed because of her broken heart. Thirteen days had passed since she or anyone else had last seen or spoken with Brogan. Lucy managed to fix Parker's breakfast and see that he caught the bus before she rushed to the bathroom to hurl her cookies. And yes, literally cookies…two boxes of Oreos she'd consumed the night before. Wanda arrived in time to hustle Lucy back to bed, promising that she'd take care of feeding Julia and pick Parker up from football practice. She left Lucy with a little ginger ale and some saltine crackers, and cleared the room of all her social media devices, including her cell phone, laptop, and iPad.

"You need your rest. Don't worry. I'll alert Dottie and Keith and your other accounts that you're taking a sick day," Wanda said as she tucked covers around Lucy.

"B-but what if he calls?" Wanda knew exactly who *he* was.

"You'll be the first to know. Now get some sleep. You look like death warmed over."

"Lovely," Lucy mumbled before closing her tired eyes.

~~~

Wanda Pattershaw stood in the threshold of Lucy's bedroom and watched her friend fall into a restless sleep. Wanda was no doctor, but she didn't need an MD to diagnose what really ailed Lucy. And it wasn't a broken heart, although that may be causing Lucy's depression. Nope. Wanda knew like she knew her own bust size: Lucy was carrying a little Brogan bun in her oven. Wanda had never been pregnant, but she'd witnessed enough friends go through the ordeal and recognized the signs. Smiling, she thought of how happy Lucy and Brogan would finally be. She quietly closed the bedroom door and worked her way downstairs. Yes in-deedy. She couldn't wait to be maid of honor. With Wanda in charge…she'd see that everything went according to plan…her plan.

Reapplying her devil-red lipstick in the foyer mirror, Wanda arranged her brown curls and gave the mirror a cocky smile. Time to take on Julia and give her something to really think about, like how *not* to lie to your friends and family.

Wanda tapped on the bedroom door before letting herself in. Julia looked up from her laptop, and surprise registered on her face before she masked it.

"Hey, Wanda. What brings you here?" Her voice was pleasant, but the wariness in her eyes gave her away.

Wanda's gaze roamed the Pepto-Bismol pink room and the cherub mural on the ceiling. Maybe she'd find out who painted it, thinking she'd like one painted in her own bedroom, with a naked David strategically posed over her bed. Settling in the guest chair, she said, "Thought we could have ourselves a little chat.".

"Oh? About what?" Julia's wariness remained as she closed her laptop and slid it to the side.

"I've got a long list, and you have nothing but time. Might as well get comfortable, because I'm not leaving until we've settled a few things."

"What the hell are you talking about?" Julia sounded nervous.

Oh, I bet you have a good idea. Wanda wore a pleasant smile and asked, "You okay with water and liquids here? Wouldn't want you to get dehydrated or anything."

Julia picked up her tumbler of water and swallowed a huge gulp. "I'm good. What's on your mind?"

Wanda crossed her legs and adopted a casual pose. "For starters...Russell. I know everything." She addressed the fear skating across Julia's face. "Russell has confessed and is mending his wicked, wicked ways."

Julia sputtered, "I don't know what you've heard, b-but—"

"I've heard it all, sister. The where, the how, the why. When my man confesses, he comes completely clean. In case we're not on the same page, let me spell it out for you." Wanda skewered Julia with her fiercest stare. "I know Russell is the father of this baby, and I know you will never, *ever* get your hooks into him again." Julia squirmed beneath her covers. "Yes, I understand the love muscle's potency, but Russell's officially off the market. I'm the only recipient of his powerful love from now on."

"Wanda, *please*!" Crimson bloomed on Julia's cheeks.

"Drink some more water, because I'm just getting started."

Shooting Wanda the bitchy glare-down, Julia crossed her arms in a huff.

"Here's how this is going to play out: first, Russell will be a part of this baby's life. No more secrecy. No more lying. Russell wants to know his child and wants to help with support. Russell has rights too. Agreed?" Wanda mirrored Julia's bitchy glare-down. After several tense moments, she said between clenched teeth, "I'm waiting…"

"All right. Russell can be a part of the baby's life," Julia said grudgingly. "We'll work out every other weekend or whatever."

"You're damn right. He's going to be a big part. Russell will make a great father, and I'm going to be a kick-ass stepmother." Wanda rubbed her hands together in glee, loving the thought of helping with Julia and Russell's kid.

Julia rolled her eyes, groaning. "Oh Lord. Are you done torturing me yet?"

"Not even close. Second, you are going to sit down with Parker *this* afternoon, and you're going to tell him the truth about all of it."

"No. The time is not right. He's upset about Brogan leaving, and I don't want to hurt—"

"Cut the pig shit. No more excuses. The kid's almost sixteen, and he has a right to know. I'm marching him in here, and I'll be standing right outside that door, listening. And if you don't tell him all the facts…I will."

"Do you know? Did Lucy tell you? I'm going to kill her," Julia snarled.

"Lucy's lips are sealed, but not for long, make no mistake about it. So warm up your vocals and start singing like Carrie Underwood, unless you want your son to hate you for the rest of his life." Big tears filled Julia's eyes. "Don't start blubbering now. I'm not done." Wanda handed Julia a tissue, along with more water. "Finally, and this will be your kindest act since you've graced this earth." Sarcasm laced Wanda's tone. "You're going to help Lucy by getting Brogan to come back home."

"As if I have control over Brogan." Julia sniffed.

"No, but he'll listen to you about Lucy."

"What makes you say that?" Julia asked with heavy suspicion.

"Because he loves Lucy, and she loves him."

"*What?* You're crazy. There's a difference between lust and love. I should know." She gave a self-deprecating laugh.

"Yeah, you've lived in denial for years, and how's that working out? I know Lucy and Brogan's affair was a whirlwind, but they've both been hit hard. They're in love, and as an expression of that love"—she paused, gaining Julia's riveted attention—"you're going to be Aunty Julia in about eight months."

"*W-what?*" A coughing fit hit Julia as her shock went down the wrong pipe. "No way."

"Way. However, Lucy has no clue. She thinks she's suffering from the flu, so this is going to surprise her as much as it has you."

"Dammit. I told her not to do this. I can't believe she's this dum—" Julia stopped at the incredulous expression lighting Wanda's face.

"You are *seriously* not going there, right?" Julia had the good grace to appear sheepish. "That's what I thought. Look, Julia, do us all a favor and redeem yourself. I'm not asking for an apology from you for sleeping with my man. As far as I'm concerned, it's over and will never be repeated. Ever. But I am asking you to do the right thing by Lucy. You have an opportunity to do something good for your sister. Lucy deserves her own happiness. And so do you." Hope followed by doubt skittered across Julia's perfect features. "Imagine how great it will make you feel to help your sister. You'll look and feel ten years younger." On that last word, Julia's ears perked up. "Let's work on spreading wonderful news and not vicious gossip. You owe it to Lucy and Brogan." Julia's lips thinned, and then she finally conceded and gave a slow nod.

Wanda stood, ready to leave. "Good girl. Now, let's recap. One. Russell Upton is this baby's father, and you will acknowledge that fact wearing a smile." Wanda ticked items off on her fingers. "Two. This afternoon you have a come-to-the-Jordan cleansing talk with Parker. *And* last but certainly not least, I expect Brogan home within the next two weeks. That should give him plenty of time to wrap up his affairs in New York."

"How are we going to break the news to Lucy?" Julia whispered fiercely.

"I'm already on it. You will make an appointment with your OB-GYN, and when you get there, be sure Lucy gets the test." Wanda picked up Julia's cell phone and handed it to her, wearing her don't-mess-with-the-Wonderbust expression. "Are we clear?"

"Crystal."

"You won't regret it. Now, what would you like for lunch?" Wanda asked.

"Can I trust you not to put laxatives in my food?"

Wanda nodded. "No problem. But arsenic…um, not so sure."

Chapter 27

"AUNT LUCY, DO YOU THINK BROGAN IS COMING back?" Parker asked in a low voice as he ate a healthy after-school snack at the kitchen table. Lucy continued to stare at the contents of her handbag, trying to wrap her head around her unexpected news.

"Aunt Lucy?"

"Oh, uh…yeah, he'll definitely be back." *Just not for me.* "He has BetterBites to check on." Parker ducked his head, looking defeated. "And of course, he wants to see you and, er, your mom and the new baby." Having no idea if any of that was true, Lucy sat next to Parker, hating the slump he'd fallen into since Brogan had left two and a half weeks ago. If she could have wrung Brogan's neck, she would have, and then she'd kiss him and never let him go.

"Mom told me, um…about my dad," Parker mumbled into his snack plate. "Do you know who my real dad is?" He watched Lucy, making sure he didn't miss a thing.

"Yeah, I do. And I'm happy you know too. You inherited Joe Monahan's great athletic ability," she said, trying to coax a smile from him.

He shrugged his half-boy/half-man shoulders beneath his football T-shirt. "I guess. But you wanna know something, Aunt Lucy?" He pierced her with his gorgeous, sad blue eyes. "Deep down, I wished my dad was Brogan."

Lucy's heart thumped right up into her throat. "Oh,

Parks." She wrapped him in a bear hug. "Don't you worry, everything will turn out fine. I promise." Lucy shot prayers up, hoping she spoke the truth. Pulling back, she said to his worried face, "Get your homework done, and I'll take you to practice later."

He nodded and started to finish his snack but stopped. "Aunt Lucy, are you leaving too?"

Startled, she gave her handbag a nervous glance. Maybe. Probably. "I'll be here until your mom has her baby in a few weeks. And then…we'll see. Okay?"

Parker swallowed hard. "I don't blame you if you leave. I haven't made things real easy for you."

"No, you've made things bearable for me." She squeezed his shoulders. "I love you, Parker…more than ever. Don't you forget it. You hear?"

He smiled his adorable smile and gobbled the remainder of his snack.

———

Lucy stood in her bathroom, staring at her pale, tired face. She pulled the bottle of doctor-prescribed prenatal vitamins from her handbag.

Knocked up.

Pregnant.

Life changing…forever.

She tossed a vitamin in her mouth and chased it down with some water. She and Julia didn't share the same genes, but they sure shared the proclivity for pregnancy and single motherhood. Yep. Single. Because a herd of wild buffaloes couldn't get her to trap Brogan in an unwanted, loveless marriage…*again*. Lucy recalled Brogan's first marriage and how it had traumatized him.

She knew he didn't want a repeat performance. His disappearing act had made that abundantly clear.

Marveling at the idea that life was growing inside her, Lucy started rubbing her stomach. A thrill of excitement coursed through her, along with its counterpart, a stab of ice-cold anxiety. At four and a half weeks, the little poppy seed growing inside her had already done a tap dance on her hormones, making her tired and queasy most of the day, but she loved him/her with a ferocity she couldn't explain. Of course, she was scared spitless. Doubt, the fire-breathing dragon, would keep rearing its menacing head, making her nervous and unsure, but the same could be said for any major life change. And if Brogan chose to lock himself away from ever experiencing true love and the tiny life that grew within her, then he had serious, *serious* problems. And Lucy wasn't equipped to deal with them. She straightened her spine, because along with raging hormones and indigestion, Lucy had a plan. For once in her thirty-two years, she'd be putting herself first.

Pregnant.

Knocked up…again.

Brogan slumped back in his hotel chair with the phone to his ear, not hearing Julia's story on the other end. His mind had zeroed in on the word: *pregnant*. It was late Saturday night, and he'd been gone from Harmony for three weeks, working long hours on the new flagship store, trying to forget his life back home and trying to banish Lucy from his mind. Nothing had worked, including massive amounts of Advil or the collection of empty beer cans littering his room. Julia had explained that she and Lucy had visited the doctor this past week, and yes indeed, Lucy was pregnant. It had come down to this: Lucy would eventually get around to telling him, and he'd feel guilty and trapped. He'd do his best, but it'd all go down the toilet before long. Just like before.

"...and I think she's planning to leave." The urgency in Julia's voice brought Brogan out of his self-pity stupor, along with the word *leave*.

"Wait. What? Who's leaving?" He pinched the bridge of his nose.

"Have you been listening to a word I've said? Wake up! I'm trying to tell you Lucy's pregnant and leaving Harmony as soon as I have my baby."

Brogan sat up on high alert. His head suddenly clear as glass. "Leaving where? Where is she going? Who's going to take care of her? Did she say when?" His hand tightened in a death grip on his cell phone. "She's not going back to that dickhead Tony Tiger, is she?" The baffled, beaten feeling he'd been experiencing minutes before magically disappeared, along with the heavy guilt. Every thought centered on Lucy leaving.

His Lucy leaving with *his* baby.

Not if he had anything to say about it.

Gone was the suffocating feeling, suddenly replaced by an overwhelming surge of freedom, sweeping from his head to his feet, breathing new life.

Woozy, Brogan lowered his head into his hand. In the past, he'd kept his emotions locked away, always at a safe distance, but this time, his heart ruled and decided on a different course.

He'd fallen in love with Lucy. Love. Off the chain,

over the moon, can't say her name, in love. And it scared the living crap out of him.

Confronting his dad and running off to New York hadn't solved a damn thing until this very moment. No longer would he allow his past to control his life. His pathetic dad, the screwed-up bigamist, had to live with the ramifications of his poor decisions. Brogan was not a screwup and had managed to keep the messy aspects of his life to a minimum. Yes, his career meant a lot to him, but he didn't need it as a crutch to prove his worth. He needed Lucy. In just two short months, she'd become an intrinsic part of his life. He loved her and missed her… and he wanted his baby. He wanted it all.

"…I don't know the details. She hasn't exactly shared her plans, but you need to hurry back. If Lucy means anything to you, come home and work something out." Brogan refocused on Julia's urgent message.

"Lucy means everything to me. *Everything.*" Rearranging his work schedule in his mind, he said, "It's gonna take me a few days to finish here, but I'm coming home. I'm coming home to Lucy. And, Julia, please don't say a word to her." Lucy had stopped trying to contact him three days after he'd left. He didn't blame her. He'd treated her like shit. "I need to make this right. I don't want to spook her. I'm sure there's a voodoo doll with pins sticking in it, wearing my face."

"Provided by Wanda, no doubt. By the way, I think an offer is coming in on your house."

"That was fast." Brogan shrugged off his dress shirt but couldn't shrug off the feeling that selling his house was a bad idea. "Stall them. I need time to think."

"You do realize I'm having a baby in two weeks."

"Yeah, hold off on that too."

"My legs are crossed, but I'm telling you…this baby wants out."

Brogan massaged the back of his neck, thinking of how Julia had changed for the better. "Thanks, Julia. You did good."

"I did, didn't I?" He heard the smile in her voice. "Now get back here, and don't blow it. And, Brogan… you better not break my sister's heart again, or I'm gonna have you run through town buck naked and barefooted."

She'd do it too. "I won't give you any cause. I swear on my life."

"Good. Don't make me regret being nice."

Brogan cracked a smile for the first time since confronting his dad at BetterBites. "I'll text when I hit the road. Remember, not a word to Lucy."

———

Lucy ended her call and typed a few notes on her iPad, pleased with the way her plan was falling into place. She'd already set meetings for presenting her marketing/social media package to three businesses in Blowing Rock, North Carolina: The Mountain Club Community Center, Speckled Rock Restaurant, and Hounds Tooth Lodge. All three sounded very interested in what she had to offer and looked forward to their meeting. Lucy planned to leave Harmony after Julia had her baby. Her due date was at the end of September, less than two weeks away. Once the baby was born, and everyone, including the baby nurse, was comfortably situated back home, Lucy would hit the road. Prepared for the next phase of her life.

After a long conversation with her dad, Lucy had sold him on her business plan, and he agreed for her to live for the next eight months in his mountain home, working and growing her baby. Lucy looked forward to increasing her clients in the quaint, touristy mountain town. She'd be only a few hours from Harmony—close enough to stay in touch, but far away from Brogan…*if* he ever returned.

Lucy scheduled an appointment with a nice hair salon in Raleigh for a fresh look and then called Grady to make sure her poor car was safe enough to drive to the nearest used car dealership, where she planned to dump it and buy something more reliable.

Shutting down her laptop, she left her phone untouched on her desk. She had stopped waiting for a call that never came, and by leaving her phone, she was less tempted to check every thirty seconds or so. Somehow, Brogan would have to become a distant memory in order for her to survive the next five to fifty years. Of course, they'd have to share custody, but she hoped to be secure in her new life and over his harsh rejection before that day arrived.

Clearing the depressing thoughts from her head, she went downstairs to prepare Julia's dinner. Julia had surprisingly stopped with the useless lists of errands, and had even been sweet in sharing some of her pregnancy stories. If you can call vomiting four times a day, stretch marks, and weird cravings like salmon-covered ice cream sweet stories. Lucy wasn't so sure. More likely, Julia was trying to scare her into never having sex again for as long as she breathed. Solid tactic, because it was working.

Lucy put her fear of babies and single motherhood on the back burner as she prepared Julia's meal of kale salad with grilled organic chicken. On the other hand, Julia had nagged, argued, and even pleaded for Lucy not to leave Harmony. Her idea of a big happy family included Lucy living here, where they could both raise their kids together. Seeing herself as Julia's permanent maid and gofer made Lucy shudder. However, having friends and family around to help deal with the day-to-day of parenthood did hold some appeal. And she would miss Parker something awful, and even Julia. In their weird, stilted way, they'd formed a bond that was growing stronger every day. And Lucy was most proud of that. But the urge to conquer this chapter in her life on her terms compelled her even more. She could do this. She wanted her career by her rules. And by all that was holy…she was no longer *loco*!

At the sound of a loud knock, Lucy headed for the front. As the door opened, Wanda and Russell stepped into the foyer. "Hey, what's up?" she asked, surprised at seeing them both.

Color infused Russell's cheeks, and he shuffled his loafer-clad feet.

"We're here to visit Julia," Wanda said, dropping her handbag on the bench.

"Sure. Go on back. I'm fixing her dinner. You guys hungry?"

"Nah, Russell's taking me to the Dog later. You wanna come?"

Lucy shook her head. "Got a big day tomorrow."

Displeasure pinched Wanda's features. She had sided with Julia (a first!) in wanting Lucy to stay in Harmony and not move away. "Russell, head on back. I'll help Lucy with dinner." Wanda had no intentions of helping…more like lecturing and browbeating.

"Okay, honey-bunny. Don't be too long." A look of pure terror dashed across Russell's face before he moved toward the hallway. Lucy knew the feeling and felt sorry for him.

"Aren't you afraid of leaving them alone together?" Lucy whispered in a worried tone.

Wanda grabbed her by the elbow and pulled her along to the kitchen. "Nope. He has repented for the error of his ways. Besides, after me, he has no energy left for anyone else." She grinned like someone who enjoyed sex…a lot. "Now, what the hell do you have to do tomorrow that's so pressing? You better not be sneaking out of town without telling anyone."

Tossing the salad, Lucy glared at Wanda. "No, oh bossy one. I'm getting my hair done, and I'm trading in my car. Need something more reliable. I'm becoming a mother, you know."

"All the more reason you should stay here, so I can check on you and lend a hand." Wanda sat, plopping her elbow on the table with her head in her palm, looking unhappy and upset.

Dropping the salad tongs, Lucy sat in the chair next to her. "Don't you see? I have to do this on my own. I'm not moving very far, I promise. You can always come for a visit and stay with me. I'd miss you if you didn't."

"How far?" Wanda narrowed her eyes. "Where're you moving?"

Lucy shifted in her seat. She'd hoped to keep her

destination secret until she'd left and gotten settled. She didn't want uninvited guests showing up unexpectedly, or the Harmony nosy bodies announcing her every move and wanting updates on her pregnancy.

Lucy hedged. "It's not completely decided yet, but—"

"The truth." Wanda crossed her arms.

"As soon as it's final, you'll be the first to know." Lucy held her breath, waiting for Wanda's explosion.

"Hmmm, and if you don't, I'll hunt you down and snatch you bald." She pushed back her chair and stood. "Better go check on Julia and Russell before I have to turn the garden hose on them."

"Thought Russell had mended his ways."

"He has. It's Julia I don't trust."

—⁓—

Brogan slammed his car door in Julia's driveway and moved up the walkway to the front door. Wanda and Julia had promised Lucy would not be home and they'd help him formulate a plan, since he'd screwed up royally. He wouldn't blame Lucy if she spit in his eye and told him to go screw himself. He deserved worse.

The door opened before he reached it, and Wanda stood there, wearing jeans, a red tunic with a plunging V-neck, and an impatient look on her face. "It's about time. Get in here. We've got to fix this mess you made."

"Good to see you too."

"We don't have time for pleasantries." Raking her gaze over him, she said, "You're gorgeous as always, but you already know that."

Brogan chuckled as Wanda pulled him down the hallway and then pushed him down into the nauseating pink chair next to Julia's bed. Brogan greeted Julia with a weak smile.

"Okay, let's map out our plan." Wanda handed him a pink pad and pen from Julia's nightstand. "Take copious notes."

"Are we planning another D-Day invasion?" He shot them both incredulous looks.

"We can't rely on you not to screw this up," Julia said, clearly exasperated with him.

Brogan shifted uncomfortably. "Okay. What should I do to reach Lucy without her running? I need help in setting that up."

"You're gonna need more than that," Wanda mumbled under her breath.

"What?" Brogan couldn't afford any more surprises; becoming a father was all the surprise he could handle at the moment.

Wanda shrugged and sat on the edge of Julia's bed. "How you doing there, Little Mama? You don't look so good." She rubbed her leg.

Julia shifted with a slight groan. "I'm fine. Just tired of feeling like a water buffalo."

"This won't take long, and then you can rest," Wanda said.

Brogan handed Julia her water. "I appreciate all your help, Julia." His voice was low.

She squeezed his hand and smiled. "As long as you do right by Lucy, we won't have any problems." Brogan could read the threatening glint in her eyes, which said, *Don't screw up, dumbass*. He nodded in agreement.

"So, Lucy plans to move away after the baby is born. Your job is to stop her and convince her to stay here."

Paying attention, and suddenly starting to sweat, he asked, "Where is she moving?"

"She won't say," Julia said, sounding hurt.

"Let's not dwell on that right now. It's unimportant," Wanda said.

Tapping down his panic at the thought of Lucy leaving town, Brogan swallowed. "All right. Tell me how to stay one step ahead of her. That's what I need to know."

"Write this down, Mr. Too Gorgeous to Live." Wanda jabbed her finger at him. "You have a ring?"

"Ring? No. Why?" He held the pen poised as he questioned Wanda.

Both Wanda and Julia groaned together. "Because the only way you're going to convince Lucy to stay is by giving her exactly what she wants. And for some strange reason, she wants *you*." They both rolled their eyes at his wary expression. "Trust me. Do exactly as we say, and you'll thank us later."

He couldn't control the smile spreading his lips. He was being shanghaied by the best in the business. Brogan got busy writing. "Number one: do exactly as manipulating, vicious meddlers direct. Number two..." He looked up, pen poised.

"Buy a ring!" they both chorused together.

"And not from Walmart or Cheap Diamonds by the Dozen. You march your tight butt into Bailey's or Tiffany's and buy the prettiest ring they have to offer."

He smiled as he wrote. "Got it. What else?"

"Call the hospital," Julia said.

"What does that have to do—*shit!*" Brogan jumped up. "Wanda, call the hospital and tell them we're on our way, and bring some bath towels." Shocked, Wanda darted her gaze from Julia to Brogan. "Julia's water just broke."

"I'm on it!" Wanda reached for the phone as she raced to the linen closet.

Brogan rummaged through a dresser drawer, pulling out a dry nightgown. He removed Julia's covers and handed her the gown. "You want me to turn my back or something?" He was clueless on what to do next.

Julia grabbed her belly. "Get this wet thing off me, and let's *go-o-o*," she groaned in pain.

Shee-it.

"Wanda, hurry up and get in here. I need your help." Full-blown panic had set in.

"Huh?" Lucy reread the urgent text from Wanda. "Oh, oh!" She gave the guy processing her car papers a look of panic. "Those better be ready in one minute, because my sister is having a baby, and I need to get to the hospital." Five minutes later, Lucy was racing out of the dealership parking lot in a nice used black VW Tiguan. No more compacts, because she needed room for her baby. *Baby! Please Lord, let me get there in time for Julia.* But first, she had to grab Parker from practice. Wanda had already texted him and told him to be ready.

Both she and Parker raced through the automatic doors of the hospital and took the elevator up to the maternity ward.

Lucy squeezed Parker's cold hand. "Don't worry, Parks. Your mom's an old pro at this. She and the baby are going to be great," she said, trying to convince both of them.

Parker swiped his arm across his sweaty brow. "It's not even her due date. She had another week."

"No worries. Sometimes babies come early. They'll both be fine," Lucy said, hoping she sounded confident, even though she shook like a baby bird on the inside.

They raced to the nurses' station to inquire if Julia was in labor. The harried nurse behind the counter looked up at a dry-erase board and shook her head. "Not yet. She's in room 3102."

Lucy sucked in a deep breath as Parker tapped on Julia's door. Wanda swung the door open. "About time." She pulled them into the cramped room, where Julia was hooked up to monitors with an IV taped to her hand. The smell of baby lotion hit Lucy's nose, and she noticed soft pink walls with bunny wallpaper border in green and white. Wanda handed a panting Julia some ice chips, Russell wiped her brow with a damp cloth, and Brogan held her hand, murmuring something low— *Brogan!* The room started to pitch, and the bunny border swirled dizzily around her head.

"Aunt Lucy? You okay?" sweet Parker, the only one to notice, asked.

She patted his arm, trying not to grip it for dear life. "Yeah. Just need some air. I'm gonna step out for a sec. Go kiss your mom, okay?"

Lucy stumbled from the room and sat in one of the metal chairs lining the hallway, with her head between her legs. "Miss? Are you okay?" a nurse asked, pressing her cool hand to Lucy's shoulder.

Lucy nodded between her legs. "Just feeling a little faint—"

"Up." The nurse grabbed her under the arm. "Lie down

here." She helped Lucy onto a gurney in the hallway and shoved a pillow under her feet. "How's that?" she asked.

"Better, much better," Lucy said with her eyes half-closed.

"Are you pregnant?"

Both eyes flew open. "Um, yeah." *I'm carrying that toe jam, pond scum's baby in there, holding another woman's hand.*

The nurse nodded. "It's not uncommon, but if it persists, you need to see your doctor."

"Sure. Will do." Lucy started to feel better as anger fired up her blood.

Wanda came bursting through the door. "Lucy. This is no time for a nap. Julia's about to give birth. Come on."

Lucy rose slowly, checking for dizziness. At the sound of a loud, psycho scream, she slid off the gurney in complete fear. A doctor in scrubs blew past her, followed by the nice nurse, and disappeared into Julia's room. Lucy froze, and her legs threatened to buckle. She couldn't do this. She jumped at another roof-lifting screech.

"Lucy, *now!*" Wanda waved from the door.

Lucy picked up her cement blocks disguised as feet and moved toward the room. Once inside, she couldn't see anything except the back of the doctor, sitting between Julia's legs in stirrups, Wanda hugging a terrified Parker in the corner, Russell holding Julia's hand, wearing a pained expression on his face, and...and Brogan, supporting Julia's shoulders. At the doctor's command to push, Brogan loaned Julia his strength as she screamed in agony and pushed.

"That's it. One more big one. Come on, you can do it," the doctor said. Lucy's eyes stayed glued to Brogan, admiring his strength and resolve, and then moved to her sister, who showed the greatest courage of all as she pushed a human from her body. Only moments later, Lucy jumped at the sound of a small cry. She craned her neck, trying to see around the doctor and nurse.

"Congratulations. You and your husband have a beautiful baby girl." Lucy jerked at the word *husband* at the same time her heart spasmed for joy over the baby. She watched as everyone congratulated Julia, and Brogan wiped her sweaty brow. Tears leaked from Lucy's eyes. She'd witnessed the miracle of life, along with Julia's tired smile, glowing face, and Brogan's proud grin. Lucy slipped from the room and from their lives unnoticed. It was vital she get moving. She raced down the hall, swallowing her sobs. She missed hearing Julia call her name.

———

Lucy had left. More like bolted. For several days she'd outmaneuvered everyone and managed to avoid Brogan between getting Julia and the baby settled and instructing the baby nurse. It was entirely his fault, and all of Harmony was not about to let him forget it.

Not that he was helping his cause. Brogan couldn't eat or sleep and barely had a civil word for anyone in town. At the rate he was chewing people up, he'd killed all the goodwill Lucy had created with BetterBites. But he couldn't help himself. He was going crazy. Lucy refused to answer his calls or his texts. Yeah, he deserved that. She still hadn't given Julia her whereabouts, even though Lucy had reassured her she wasn't moving very far.

But Brogan could read between the lines: Lucy couldn't bear to face him and had run. Ten days had already passed since the frantic trip to the hospital. Julia and her baby girl were settled and flourishing. But Julia worried about Lucy almost more than he did, and it was starting to sour her milk.

"Brogan. Open up." Wanda pounded on his front door. It was early Monday morning, and he was still nursing his first cup of coffee.

Brogan shuffled to the door, wearing only boxers, a three-day beard, and sleep-deprived eyes. "What?" he grumbled, pulling the door open.

"Whoa. Lookin' mighty fine, Bro-man," Wanda purred as her gaze made a slow trail up his body. "My heart's all aflutter."

Brogan scratched his bare chest. "Whatever." Turning back to the kitchen, he left Wanda to her own devices.

Wanda poured herself a cup of coffee and leaned against the kitchen cabinets, surveying him as if he'd just been released from the psych ward. "Don't you want to know why I'm here?"

"Unless you have news of Lucy, not particularly." Wanda slapped a slip of paper on the island countertop. "What's that?"

"Lucy's address. She's staying in her dad's house in Blowing Rock." Brogan snatched up the paper and stared at it, not believing his eyes. "She has appointments today and then visits her doctor this afternoon at four. His address is on there too." Brogan gaped at Wanda, wondering if he was dreaming. "I suggest you get your fine butt in your car and head for the hills, er, mountains."

Brogan had leaped up before she'd finished speaking and raced to his hall closet. Yanking the door open, he pulled out a pink and blue baby bag, covered in marching yellow ducks, stuffed to the brim. And then he opened his pantry and pulled out a shopper from the Toot-N-Tell crammed with Lucy's favorite junk foods, including Cheerwine and Cheetos.

He'd grabbed his keys off the hook and shoved his feet inside loafers as he opened the door to the garage when Wanda said, "Hey, you might want to get dressed first."

Huh? Brogan looked up and then down at his bare chest and legs. "Dammit. I don't have time for this." He shoved the bags at Wanda. "Put these in the backseat while I get dressed."

He threw on a pair of jeans with a pink-and-white-striped dress shirt, splashed water on his face, brushed his teeth, and was pulling his car out of his garage in less than four minutes. Wanda stood with her hands on her hips, shaking her head. "Thanks, Wanda, you're the best," he said from the open window. "You mind locking up?"

"Sure. Don't you dare come back here without her."

His thoughts exactly. He would refuse to take no for an answer, and he wasn't leaving the mountains without Lucy by his side.

"Wait!" Wanda yelled. Brogan stopped as she trotted up to his car. "You have the ring?"

Panic slammed into him like a twenty-foot wave until he remembered. "Yep. It's tucked inside the baby bag."

"Ooh, can I see it?"

"Hell no. Now, get out of my way before I run over your toes."

―〜〜―

Grinning like a clown, Lucy stared at her six-week-old blob on the sonogram photo. That was her little gray blob with its beating heart. She rested her hand over her belly on her navy knit skirt. No bulge yet. She placed the photo gently inside her brown leather handbag and shrugged into her navy-and-cream bouclé jacket. It was almost five o'clock, and she was dead on her feet. The doctor said the fatigue would ease up in the second trimester, but for now, she should grab those naps when she could.

Pushing open the glass office door, she stepped outside into the crisp, clean mountain air, which worked wonders in reviving her. Resting her plum-colored sunglasses on her nose, she smiled over her productive week. She'd already signed two new clients and had enough work to keep her busy for a while. A huge difference from where she'd stood a week ago. When she'd discovered Brogan had come home for Julia, she'd been devastated. All the time he'd been away, ignoring her calls and texts, *dumping* her…he'd been in contact with *Julia*, and even made it back in time for her delivery.

After that emotional realization, Lucy shed the Dunce Cap of Fools for good. She deserved better. She deserved someone to love her. Complete package without hesitation or doubts. No more lying, cheating sacks of lizard dung, and no more ex-crushes who broke hearts like hickory nuts and ran back to ex–prom queen girlfriends for another round. She'd find what she needed, and she'd accept nothing less.

Lucy adjusted the handbag strap over her shoulder as her foot hit the first brick step, and then came to an abrupt halt. Wobble went her knees as she almost fell out of her brown patent heels. Chest tight. Heart constricted. Could she be hallucinating? Lucy slid her sunglasses back to the top of her head and squinted. There at the bottom of the steps, holding an overflowing Toot-N-Tell bag with a drooping, pitiful bouquet of daisies, stood Brogan Freakin' Reese.

Lucy struggled to breathe as all her feelings for Brogan came crashing back. Just like that. Her firm resolve disappeared into thin air. As much as she'd cursed him for breaking her heart, she'd never stopped loving him.

"Lucy, don't move," Brogan said in a rough voice. "I need to speak with you. I have so much to say…please."

Rooted to the ground, Lucy's feet wouldn't budge as Brogan inched closer, his fierce gaze never leaving her face. "How'd you know…?" Duh. That damn Wanda, who never could keep her piehole shut. Brogan stood in front of her on the lower step, leveling their heights. Lucy stared directly into his tired, anxious green eyes.

"Don't blame Wanda. Everybody's concerned about you. The baby won't drink Julia's milk because she's curdling it with worry. Parker mopes around, snarling at anyone who comes near him…especially me. And Margo beats the bread dough as if it's my face."

"Did Julia order you to bring me home?" She folded her arms as if to protect the precious blob growing inside her.

"No. But I was given strict orders not to blow it." Lucy inched back on shaky legs. But the desperate look in Brogan's eyes kept her from running. "Listen. I know I've been an ass. A complete moron…" He could say that again. "But these last few weeks, I've taken a good, hard look at my life. And the only thing I liked about it was you."

Lucy's heart doing the butterfly went for a flip turn. Brogan dropped his head and stared at the ground. "For years, I've been paralyzed from taking chances and living my life." He lifted his head and pierced Lucy with his earnest expression. "But then I run into you on the side of the road, and it was as if I'd been hit by lightning with your pretty eyes, sultry smile, and snarky comebacks. *You* hold the ticket to my freedom. I was just too dumb and stubborn to realize it. I want it all, Lucy. I want you."

Yeah, but for how long? Lucy slicked her suddenly dry lips, thrilled but confused by his confession.

One side of Brogan's mouth tipped up in a half smile, and his eyes glimmered with doubt and hope. He reached for one of her curls. "Your hair…it's all curly again…I like it."

"Yeah, well, I needed a change. Besides, it's easier than all that ironing." She sniffed, running a hand over the back of her spongy curls. "Listen, I appreciate…you know, the effort, but I'm doing great here. I'm not ready to come home yet."

A cloud of sadness hung over Brogan at her words. "Lucy, I know I've hurt you. And I know it's me you're running from. But you left without saying good-bye. You didn't even leave me a note. Why?"

Because he'd broken her heart in a million pieces, and she couldn't bear witnessing his reunion with Julia.

"You were there for J-Julia…I didn't want to get in the way." Her voice wavered.

Brogan grabbed her elbow. "You're wrong. I was there for you. I came home for *you*." He loosened his hold, and Lucy shifted back.

"Look, Brogan, you're forgetting something. Something real important. I'm having a baby." She pulled the sonogram photo from her handbag. A spark of happiness flitted across his face as he held the picture of her grainy, adorable blob. "I know you don't want this pregnancy. I understand completely, and I'm willing to do this on my own. I refuse for me or my baby to be anybody's mistake or lifelong regret."

"Lucy—"

"Let me finish." She raised her hand. "Contrary to what you believe, I had no intentions of falling in love, and certainly didn't plan for a baby, but I *did* fall in love, and a baby's on the way. You suffered a miscarriage, a bad marriage, and a troubled relationship with your dad. I get that. It's something you'll have to work through." Lucy spoke to her feet. "I'm happy with my decision. I answer only to myself and my b-baby," she said above a whisper.

"*Our* baby." She raised her eyes in surprise. "I want *you* and our baby. Not for the short term, not out of guilt, not because I feel trapped, but forever." Brogan rubbed his hand across his mouth. "I'm sorry for running out on you, for leaving a shitty note. I'm sorry for not talking to you…with you. I didn't mean any of it. It's no excuse, but I was lashing out at the one person close to me…the one person I love." He moved nearer. "Look at me…I'm holding a huge bag of junk food, all your favorites." Brogan handed her the wilted daisies as he shifted another bag from his shoulder. "And this baby bag is jammed with things we're going to need… diapers, bottles, rattles, booties, and there's even a baby football in there."

Brogan dropped the junk food bag on the step, and Lucy bit her lip to keep from smiling. Curious people exited the building and stopped to watch. "I haven't slept in days, I can't think straight, and I even ate an entire package of Oreos because that's how much I've missed you. That's how much I love you."

Tears welled in Lucy's eyes. She lowered her head, trying to blink them away. She'd waited a lifetime to hear those words from him. (Well, not about the cookies exactly, but you know…) Was it too late? Was this just for show? Floating before her watery eyes, she spied a small white feather. She glanced up, following more white feathers as they floated off Brogan's shoulder. She caught one with her fingers. "Uh, Brogan, are you molting?" He shook his head, and more feathers soared up. A giggle slipped from her lips. "What is going on here?" She plucked feathers from his shirtsleeve, noticing for the first time his disheveled, unkempt appearance. "Brogan Reese, your shirt's all wrinkled, you haven't shaved in forever, your hair needs a trim, and your eyes look swollen."

Brogan dug inside the baby bag, releasing more feathers. "That's because I rode in a cargo truck hauling a million squawking chickens."

Shock widened her eyes. "But why—"

"My Jag broke down somewhere outside of Yadkinville, and I hitched a ride."

Reverse déjà vu. She wished she'd been a witness,

cruising in her new SUV. He'd battled live chickens to get to her. The ice surrounding her heart had melted at the first chicken feather, and now it bloomed, ready to burst from her chest.

Cupping his scruffy face with her palm, she said in a soft voice, "Brogan, tell me why you rode halfway across the state in a chicken truck, carrying wilted flowers, bags of junk food, and baby diapers." She smiled into the beautiful, rugged, tired face that she loved and would love forever.

"Don't you know?" He shifted his head to kiss the inside of her palm, making Lucy's toes tingle, along with her more important female parts.

"To get to you, so I could give you this."

There in his large palm sat an open black velvet box with an engagement ring of white diamonds surrounding the most gorgeous canary diamond Lucy had ever seen. In awe, she touched the face of the yellow gem with the tip of her finger. "Is this for me?" she whispered.

"On one condition." Lucy jerked her head up and stared into his sparkling green eyes. "I come with the ring. It's a package deal." Lucy's smile grew broader. Brogan dropped the baby bag next to the shopper and moved up the step. He dropped to one knee, in front of everyone spilling from the office building and watching. "Lucy Doolan, will you marry me?" The crowd, including two pregnant women, all quieted down, waiting.

Lucy tapped her finger against her lips. "Hmm, I don't know. You're a bad influence on the baby, bringing all that junk food. My body is a temple…only healthy, organic food from now on." Brogan threw his head back and laughed.

"Come on, lady, give the guy a break."

"How romantic."

"She's got three seconds before I knock her out of the way and take her place."

Lucy's hands trembled as she stared at the crush of her life…her *only* crush.

"Lucy, my love, keeper of my heart, how long are you gonna make me suffer?" Brogan pleaded, still kneeling, holding the gorgeous ring.

"You really want me? Remember, I can be loco."

"Never. You're lovely and perfect for me. I love that you can't carry a tune in a bucket. I love that you hate to exercise but do it anyway. I love your courage and your strength. And I love your big heart that you try to hide with humor and snark." Brogan's eyes and voice softened. "I used to believe that never repeating my mistakes and running from my past was the only way to live. I'd stopped living long ago…until I met you. You brought joy and love back in my life."

"I'll marry him!" someone sniffling yelled out.

Lucy, kind of liking this begging side of Brogan, prolonged his agony a bit more. "Gosh, I was really looking forward to being a single mom and—"

Brogan pushed to his feet and shoved the ring on her finger. "But most of all, I love that you never give an inch," he said before wrapping her in his arms and kissing the chicken feathers right out of her. The crowd clapped and cheered, and Lucy started to laugh against Brogan's firm, delectable lips. "Is that a yes?" he murmured.

"Yep. You've got me. No backing out, now or later."

"Don't want to," he said, nibbling her lower lip.

"How about we celebrate back at my place?" She rained kisses along his jaw and chin.

Brogan held her within the circle of his arms. "I thought you'd never ask."

Epilogue

PROPPED ON THE PINK WICKER OTTOMAN IN JULIA'S sun porch, Lucy stared at her swollen feet and ankles. She felt like a bloated, beached whale ready to pop. "Arrrgh! Someone put me out of my misery." She leaned her head back on Brogan's strong shoulder. "Nine months is way too long for anything to grow inside you."

Brogan kissed the top of her head. "Only two more weeks, babe. You can do it." Lucy snuggled against her wonderful, kind, sexy, hunky husband. The only thing more wonderful was their soon-to-be-born baby daughter. Thrilled to be having a girl, they planned to name her Charlotte Elise after both their mothers.

It was early May in Harmony, and Lucy's due date was looming. She and Brogan had tied the knot back in late October, down by the lake, with everyone from Harmony and for miles around showing up. A proud Harper Doolan had given Lucy away, while Wanda, Julia, and Bertie had stood in attendance, wearing deep-purple dresses and carrying orange-and-pink bouquets. Javier and Vance Kerner had been groomsmen, and Brogan had asked Parker to be his best man. Brogan had even invited his half brother and sister to the wedding, whom he'd been making an effort to get to know. Brogan's dad had died a month after his last visit and had left Brogan a considerable sum from his will, along with the worn nautical bracelet from his wrist. Brogan put half the money away in a trust for the baby, and the other half in a money market account for Parker. He truly treated Parker not as a nephew, but as a son.

Everyone had danced, drank, and feasted on food provided by BetterBites, Hog Wild, and the Dog. A round candy table had been set up and included clear bowls and apothecary jars of M&M's, Mallo Cups, Hershey's Kisses, Red Hots, MoonPies, and Cheetos, all provided by Dottie Duncan and the Toot-N-Tell. When Lucy hadn't been dancing with her gorgeous husband, she had been rocking her seven-week-old niece in her arms. Baby Lucy, her namesake. Lucy hadn't cared if baby spittle messed the scalloped lace neckline on her empire-waist wedding gown; she was gaga, head over heels in love with her perfect baby niece and couldn't wait for her own baby to join the world so they'd be inseparable playmates. Brogan had kept his newly renovated house and had given it to Lucy as a wedding present, along with hiring Bertie to help decorate the nursery. Brogan spent the majority of his time working in Harmony. He and Javier had hired three capable guys to help manage their other locations.

Lucy shifted to get more comfortable, and Brogan supported her shoulders. "Where's baby Lucy, my precious angel? I haven't seen her all day." Russell Upton entered the room, carrying a squirming, eight-month-old cherub, wearing a pale-green sundress with bright-pink bloomers, and orange gunk stuck in her dark, fuzzy hair. "Here." He plopped her in Brogan's lap, because he still had one. "She just spit up all her peas and carrots, and was trying to eat one of Julia's furry pink socks."

"Well, pink is your favorite color, isn't it, my angel?"

Lucy cooed in a baby voice as she kissed her niece's grubby hand.

"Pookie Bear, could you bring me some ginger ale? I'm feeling meh." Wanda lounged on the other wicker chair, holding her five-months-pregnant belly. Russell gave Wanda a kiss and hurried from the room. "Luce, all I can say, if I get as fat as you, I might have to shoot myself." She and Russell had gotten married for the second time last November...*inside* the Methodist church. And they'd honeymooned at Harper Doolan's mountain house in Blowing Rock.

Brogan patted Lucy's stomach. "Lucy's not fat... she's just—"

"Watch it. Or you may never play with your favorite toy again," Lucy warned.

Brogan's eyes twinkled. "I think that's *your* favorite toy, and I wouldn't dream of depriving you," he whispered, nibbling on her ear.

"Please, not in front of the baby...or me. I'm about to vomit over here," Wanda grumbled.

Baby Lucy pounded Lucy's fat belly with her fist, making silly, gurgling noises. "Don't you pay any attention to your stepmama. She's just mad because she can no longer wear her skintight, leopard-spotted hooker dress, and she's afraid her boobs might explode," Lucy said in another baby voice to her niece, but grinned at Wanda.

At the sound of yelling voices, everyone lifted their heads. Suddenly, Parker burst into the room, followed by Russell and Julia. "Uncle Brogan, my mom says I can't go to football camp this summer, because she has me signed up for some nerdy science fair. Tell her no, please," Parker begged.

Julia shoved a water glass with fresh mint at Lucy. "Here, drink this." She pointed her finger at Parker. "I said no such thing. The camps don't conflict with each other, but if you don't clean up that pigsty you call a room, you're staying home all summer, babysitting and running errands for me." Julia's voice had escalated in warning.

Lucy sipped her water. "Trust me, Parker, you don't want to run your mom's errands." Julia shot Lucy her bitchy glare-down and then blew her a kiss with a wink.

Parker hunched his shoulders and struck the sullen teenage pose. "That's so unfair, Mom. Tell her, Uncle Brogan. She'll listen to you—"

Baby Lucy's face turned redder and redder as her family's voices grew louder, and she started to cry in that horrible, high-pitched baby scream that could pierce ears and break glass. "Aww, come here, my little angel." Lucy picked her up from Brogan's lap and rocked her. "You want Aunt Lucy to sing you a lullaby?"

"No!" everyone chorused together.

Startled, Lucy looked up and then laughed at the anguished expressions staring back at her. "My singing is *not* that bad."

Julia grunted, reaching for the baby. Parker rolled his eyes, Wanda gave a loud snort, and Brogan wrapped his arms as best he could around Lucy's expanded middle.

"Uh, babe, yeah, it is. I'm afraid you're banned from singing to anyone's baby…including ours," he said in his warm, caramel voice before kissing the song right out of her head. Lucy's heart soared with love, and the baby kicked inside her for joy.

Acknowledgments

If I could personally thank each wonderful person I've encountered during this exciting journey, I would, but alas, I must keep this brief…

My gratitude to all the hardworking people at Sourcebooks, especially editors Deb Werksman and Cat Clyne, and publicist Amelia Narigon. You guys make it look so easy.

Thank you to my sisters for your endless support and keeping my spirits up, especially during my unforeseen illness. Your prayers continue to work miracles.

To all my tennis peeps…thank you for the delicious meals you provided for my family, your prayers, and for holding my spot on the team. I hope to be back on the courts real soon.

To Paige, Sharon, and Jennifer, for your upbeat encouragement, spreading the word to everyone you know, and for being so gracious in hosting me in your lovely homes while visiting my favorite place—Miami. (I'm coming back!)

To my agent, Nicole Resciniti, your advice is always invaluable.

And finally, to my amazing son and daughter. You give my life meaning and I'm thankful every day for the blessings that are you. Without you, none of the rest matters.

About the Author

Michele Summers writes romance designed to make you laugh with spunky heroines, witty heroes, and wacky characters, along with a satisfying happily ever after. Michele started her fiction writing career after Hurricane Wilma hit Miami and she was without power for over a week. Bored to tears, she scrounged for a legal pad and pen and, with the help of a trusty flashlight, started writing. Thrilled to have found another creative outlet, she's been writing ever since, when she's not working as an interior designer or personal chef, playing tennis, or raising her two wonderful kids. Presently, she resides in North Carolina where she grew up, but she still misses sunny South Florida, swaying palm trees, and wearing open-toed shoes…every day! Michele's work has won recognition from the Dixie First Chapter, Golden Palm, Fool For Love, Rebecca, and Fabulous Five contests. She is an active member of the Heart of Carolina and Florida Romance Writers chapters of RWA. You can contact Michele at her website, www.michelesummers.com, where you will also locate her other social media buttons.

Find My Way Home

Harmony Homecomings
by Michele Summers

—⁓—

She's just the kind of drama

Interior designer Bertie Anderson has big dreams for her career, and they don't include being stuck in her hometown of Harmony, North Carolina. After one last client, Bertie is packing up her high heels and heading for her dream job in Atlanta. But her plans are derailed by the gorgeous new owner of that big old Victorian she's always wanted to renovate...

He's vowed to avoid

For retired tennis pro Keith Morgan, Harmony is a far cry from fast-paced Miami—which is exactly the point. Keith is starting a new life for himself and his daughter Maddie, and he's left the bright lights and hot women far behind. Bertie's exactly the kind of curvaceous temptation he doesn't need, and Keith refuses to let their sizzling attraction distract him from his goals. Keith and Bertie both have to learn that there's more than one kind of escape, and it takes more than wallpaper to turn a house into a home.

—⁓—

For more Michele Summers, visit:

www.sourcebooks.com

Return to You

A Montgomery Brothers Novel
by Samantha Chase

New York Times and *USA Today* bestselling author

She will never forget their past...

He can't stop thinking about their future...

James Montgomery has achieved everything he'd hoped for in life...except marrying the girl of his dreams. After a terrible accident, Selena Ainsley left ten years ago. She took his heart with her, and she's never coming back. But it's becoming harder and harder for him to forget their precious time together, and James can't help but wonder what he would do if they could ever meet again.

What readers are saying about Samantha Chase:

"Samantha Chase really knows how to tell a story."

"Perfect romance! Love it, love it, love it!"

For more Samantha Chase, visit:

www.sourcebooks.com